PRAISE FOR THE NOVELS OF *NEW YORK TIMES* BESTSELLING AUTHOR KRISTY WOODSON HARVEY

The Summer of Songbirds

"A warm, hopeful story of friendship, love, and second chances. Put this in your beach bag immediately."

—Emily Henry, #1 *New York Times* bestselling author of *Book Lovers*

"Harvey reminds us that sisterhood can take many forms . . . With a strong dose of nostalgia, the book will appeal to Mary Kay Andrews and Katherine Center fans, who will revel in the support the women demonstrate for one another."

—*Booklist*

"Equal parts moving and nostalgic."

—*Southern Living*

"Beautiful, heartwarming . . . [an] ode to female friendship and the places that shape us into who we are."

—*Good Morning America*

"Filled with heartfelt emotion and endearing characters . . . A celebration of summer and sisterhood."

—*Woman's World*

"An engaging story of friendships that last a lifetime, with all the drama, love, and painful truths that entails. Truly wonderful. Brace yourself—you're going to want to be a Songbird, too!"

—Susan Mallery, #1 *New York Times* bestselling author of *The Sister Effect*

"Your big summer read has arrived! A beautiful, bubbly celebration of everything we love about summer. A story to savor . . . and share with a friend."

—Susan Wiggs, #1 *New York Times* bestselling author of *Sugar and Salt*

"A champagne toast to friendship, love, and the joys of summer. Read the brilliant first sentence and you'll never want to leave."

—Nancy Thayer, *New York Times* bestselling author of *All the Days of Summer*

"Bright and sweet. Filled with strong women with real struggles, a community that supports one another, and love stories that will warm your heart, this is a tight healing hug of a novel."

—Sonali Dev, bestselling author of *The Vibrant Years*

"For anyone who ever went to and loved a sleepaway camp, Southern bestselling sensation Kristy Woodson Harvey's latest novel is the one for you."

—Katie Couric Media

The Wedding Veil

"Masterfully woven . . . a literary homerun."

—*New York Journal of Books*

"A perfect blend of historical fiction and modern love. I didn't want it to end."

—Fiona Davis, *New York Times* bestselling author of *The Magnolia Palace*

Under the Southern Sky

"A heart-wrenching tale of love and loss . . . Fans of women's fiction will devour this."

—*Publishers Weekly* (starred review)

"Harvey delivers a fresh and unforgettable portrait of modern parenthood and the thoroughly traditional ways that love continues to conquer all."

—*Booktrib*

Feels Like Falling

"This is more than a novel about friendship; it is also a story for friendship: you will find yourself sharing it with everyone you love. Dive in; the storytelling is delicious!"

—Patti Callahan Henry, *New York Times* bestselling author of *The Secret Life of Flora Lee*

"Fans of Mary Kay Andrews and Mary Alice Monroe should add this to their beach read lists."

—*Booklist*

PRAISE FOR THE PEACHTREE BLUFF SERIES

Christmas in Peachtree Bluff

"As sweet as a candy cane, heartwarming as a cup of cocoa, and as endearing as the familiar sights and sounds of a small-town Christmas. It's the kind of gift readers will unwrap with glee."

—Mary Kay Andrews, *New York Times* bestselling author of *The Homewreckers*

"Consider this the book equivalent of a warm and fuzzy pair of socks."

—E! Online

The Southern Side of Paradise

"Kristy Woodson Harvey's very best. This novel had me laughing, crying, and wanting to hop on a plane and head south. I loved every page."

—Camille Pagán, bestselling author of *I'm Fine and Neither Are You*

"Woodson Harvey has been called a major voice in Southern fiction, and her latest novel delivers a healthy dose of her signature wit, charm, and heart."

—*Woman's World*

The Secret to Southern Charm

"The characters will leap off the page and into your heart, and you'll find yourself rooting for them so fervently, you'll forget they're not actually real. Another masterpiece."

—Kristin Harmel, *New York Times* bestselling author of *The Paris Daughter*

"Harvey's growing fan base will find another great beach read in this second novel in her Peachtree Bluff trilogy. Harvey is an up-and-coming Southern writer with staying power."

—*Booklist*

Slightly South of Simple

"My prediction is that writers come and writers go, but Kristy Woodson Harvey is here to stay."

—*HuffPost*

"Heartfelt . . . I look forward to getting to know this cast of strong Southern women even better."

—*Deep South Magazine*

ALSO FROM KRISTY WOODSON HARVEY AND GALLERY BOOKS

The Wedding Veil

Under the Southern Sky

Feels Like Falling

THE PEACHTREE BLUFF SERIES

Christmas in Peachtree Bluff

The Southern Side of Paradise

The Secret to Southern Charm

Slightly South of Simple

The Summer of Songbirds

A NOVEL

KRISTY WOODSON HARVEY

G

GALLERY BOOKS

New York London Toronto Sydney New Delhi

G

Gallery Books
An Imprint of Simon & Schuster, LLC
1230 Avenue of the Americas
New York, NY 10020

First Gallery Books trade paperback edition March 2024

GALLERY BOOKS and colophon are registered trademarks of Simon & Schuster, LLC

Simon & Schuster: Celebrating 100 Years of Publishing in 2024

For information about special discounts for bulk purchases, please contact Simon & Schuster Special Sales at 1-866-506-1949 or business@simonandschuster.com.

The Simon & Schuster Speakers Bureau can bring authors to your live event. For more information or to book an event, contact the Simon & Schuster Speakers Bureau at 1-866-248-3049 or visit our website at www.simonspeakers.com.

Interior design by Kathryn A. Kenney-Peterson

Manufactured in the United States of America

10 9 8 7 6 5 4 3 2 1

Library of Congress Cataloging-in-Publication Data
Names: Harvey, Kristy Woodson, author.
Title: The summer of songbirds : a novel / Kristy Woodson Harvey.
Description: First Gallery Books hardcover edition. | New York : Gallery Books, 2023. | Summary: "Four women come together to save the summer camp that changed their lives and rediscover themselves in the process"—Provided by publisher.
Identifiers: LCCN 2022049527 (print) | LCCN 2022049528 (ebook) | ISBN 9781668010822 (hardcover) | ISBN 9781668010839 (trade paperback) | ISBN 9781668010846 (ebook)
Classification: LCC PS3623.O6785 S86 2023 (print) | LCC PS3623.O6785 (ebook) | DDC 813/.6—dc23
LC record available at https://lccn.loc.gov/2022049527
LC ebook record available at https://lccn.loc.gov/2022049528

ISBN 978-1-6680-1082-2
ISBN 978-1-6680-1083-9 (pbk)
ISBN 978-1-6680-1084-6 (ebook)

To my fabulous friend Millie Warren,
who took me back to camp and helped me find this story
(while we may or may not have been stranded at sea)

PROLOGUE

CAMP HOLLY SPRINGS

June 14, 1998

THE FIRST DAY OF CAMP HOLLY SPRINGS IS LIKE SHAKING A BOTTLE of soda and taking off the cap: an overflowing, effervescent explosion of sweet, delicious chaos. Girls and their parents, counselors, and staff members fizz over in every direction, campers squealing with joy at being reunited, first-years sobbing with fear, counselors and staff trying to comfort or celebrate, and parents seeking someone with whom to discuss their *very specific list of concerns.*

But six-year-old Daphne Miller isn't fizzing or sobbing. She is simply studying, taking in the green travel trunks being unloaded from back seats, the brothers and sisters—who likely spend most of their time at home bickering—promising to write, the mothers slathering layers of zinc on their daughters' noses as if they can make it last for two weeks.

Daphne's aunt, June, owns Camp Holly Springs, and her mother, Melanie, didn't come to camp drop-off. She is busy relocating them from the only home Daphne has ever known in sleepy Cape Carolina to Manhattan so they can live with her brand-new husband, Vincent. In fact, Melanie was so preoccupied by the move that she allowed young Daphne to fly here alone, a fact that horrified her aunt June. A six-year-old girl should not, in June's opinion, be an unaccompanied minor. But, then again, June is not in charge. Melanie is.

Last night, Daphne shared June's double bed in her small director's cabin, where June lives all year. "I know it's hard to be away from your mom, but we are going to have the best summer. This is just the beginning for you, Daphne," June said. "I came to camp for the first time when I was your age. So did your mommy. So did Grandma Laura. You are a legacy." That made Daphne's heart swell with pride. Her aunt, mother, and grandmother were camp-raised by this same snaking blue-green stretch of river next to June's tiny home. Daphne has been spoon-fed stories of campouts in the woods, talent show disasters, and sneaking cookie dough from the camp kitchen her entire life. She has been preparing for this moment for as long as she can remember, when she would leave her mother to spend a summer making memories and—she's heard—best friends.

But right now, looking around at the soggy, sniveling group of babies being dropped off at the Songbird Cabin, where the youngest campers stay, Daphne feels like she's been sold a bill of goods. She can't imagine making friendship bracelets in the arts and crafts hut with any of these girls, who are acting more like preschoolers than rising first graders.

Then June approaches their cabin. June, the director, is royalty here. Everyone fights for her attention, her respect. Because she is the one who makes dreams come to life.

Today, June feels proud and happy because opening day of camp is what she and her team work for all year long. It is as if Holly Springs knows this. The grass looks greener, the river sparkles brighter, and the sails on the boats point higher toward the sky on the first day. Even the fifty-year-old raw wood cabins, with their screened doors and windows, seem less rustic and more charming.

Even while June's time is divided among campers, parents, and staff, her thoughts are always with her niece. She worries because, unbeknownst to Daphne, her sister—Daphne's mother—isn't only moving. After being clean and sober for seven years, she is back on drugs, the demon she has fought relentlessly. The only change is Melanie's new husband and his pie-in-the-sky promises. June doesn't trust him.

Upon seeing her niece, June kneels down and wraps Daphne in a hug. She hopes no one else can see the tears that fill her eyes. Today is a huge day for June, but she is scared for her sister, for her niece.

Over June's shoulder, Daphne spots Lanier, a girl she knows vaguely, who was in the other kindergarten class at her school. Then she spots Mary Stuart, who looks shy but sweet. Daphne loves the stack of woven ankle bracelets she is wearing and needs to know how to make them. Lanier and Mary Stuart smile tentatively at Daphne. She smiles back shyly.

As Lanier and Mary Stuart approach, June can tell, in the way only a camp director who has been at this a very long time can, that these three have a special connection, a spark. June gathers Mary Stuart and Lanier in her hug with Daphne. It is a magic hug that, somehow, gives them a glimpse into what they have to look forward to this summer. Their lives are about to change.

"It's here," June says. "Your first summer." She pulls back to look at Daphne, Mary Stuart, and Lanier in their matching Camp Holly Springs uniforms. She takes a deep breath. "The summer of songbirds," she says. "Girls, I can promise you one thing: This will be the best summer of your lives."

Daphne, cheered by her aunt's words, wordlessly reaches out to take Lanier's and Mary Stuart's hands. They are songbirds. Songbirds help each other, right? She will make them feel at home here. She knows she can. So she puts on her brightest face, the one she sometimes has to fake when her mom is sick. Only, this time, it's real. "Come on!" she yells.

"Fair winds and following seas!" June calls behind them, the traditional camp *See you later* filling her heart with pride. She watches as the three little girls run off through the seemingly endless expanse of green under a perfect blue sky. She doesn't know where they are going, but that is part of the Camp Holly Springs magic. Little girls can be free here. They will find a place. Of that, she is one hundred percent sure.

You belong here, she wants to call after the three little girls. *Because at Camp Holly Springs, we all do.*

Daphne

HARD THINGS

Subject: Hard Things

To: daphne@millerlaw.com; lanier@bookmasters.com

Dearest Songbirds,

I AM GETTING MARRIED TOMORROW!! CAN YOU EVEN BELIEVE IT? (That is me screaming at you.) This is going to be the best day of my life, obviously, especially because you two are here to do my hard things!

Daphne—Could you please call the town of Figure Eight about extending our noise permit tonight? They're telling

Ted's mom we can't have music after 10 p.m. for the rehearsal dinner dance, and she's freaking out.

Lanier—Could you please email Ted's mother (from my account, obvs) and politely tell her that, yes, I will be offended if she wears white to my wedding? I mean, *seriously*?

Love you to the ends of the earth and cannot wait to see you rocking those bridesmaids' dresses!

Fair winds and following seas,
Mary Stuart

I cross my legs underneath my desk in my office and look out the third-floor window of what always has been my favorite building in the charming downtown of Cape Carolina. My desk is positioned so I have an expansive view across the tree-lined street of the ice cream shop, the Old-Fashioned Candy Shop, and, conveniently, the dentist's office in between. If I lean over, I can just make out the Intracoastal Waterway between the buildings.

I smile, about to form my voice reply, when I see that Lanier's weekly "Hard Things" email has come through as well. This is nothing new. We've been sending these emails since we graduated college. And we've been doing each other's hard things since we were eight-year-olds at Camp Holly Springs, when each of us had something we didn't want to face that didn't bother another one of us in the least. We tackled each other's hard things and found the strategy so effective we never stopped.

Subject: Re: Hard Things

To: daphne@millerlaw.com; marystuart@harrispr.com

Dear Songbirds, Blond Division:

Mary Stuart, I will certainly respond to your vapid soon-to-be mother-in-law with an email that makes you seem both charming and witty. As for my list:

MS: I am hosting book club next month, and I just cannot with the menu. Can you plan it, pretty please?

Daphne: One of my vendors is refusing to give me a refund on forty cases of a single title they shipped because they're saying I placed a non-returnable order. I ordered four cases for the bookstore. *Four*. Not forty. Help!

FWAFS,
Lanier

"Finn!" I call to my amazing paralegal, who sparkles in so quickly I can only assume he has been standing there waiting.

"Are you ready for your smoothie, my golden goddess?"

Finn just came on board to help me. Had I partly hired him because he was a six-foot-four package of muscle who loved Andy Cohen as much as I do? Perhaps. But he was also a rock star employee.

"What flavor are you having?" I ask. One of my favorite parts of our office remodel is the gorgeous break room, complete with sleek refrigerator/freezer drawers and a Vitamix that I had hemmed and hawed over as if I was purchasing a new Rolls-Royce. Verdict? Worth. Every. Penny. I walk toward the smoothie station, and he follows me.

Finn peers into the freezer drawer at the choices delivered this week. "I think I'd like that new mint chocolate chip flavor," he says definitively.

I nod. "I need a little pick-me-up. How about a cocoa cold brew?"

Finn shoots me his Colgate commercial smile. "I'll get the conference room ready for your nine o'clock. Do you need anything before then?"

As I am about to say no, I have an idea. "Actually, yes. Want to play tough lawyer with the town of Figure Eight and fix a problem for Mary Stuart's wedding?"

Finn looks puzzled. "I always want to play tough lawyer. But why?"

How to keep this simple . . . "Mary Stuart, Lanier, and I do each other's hard things. Mary Stuart finds arguing with a town about a noise permit hard. Me? Not so scared of the confrontation."

"You? Confrontational? No." Finn winks at me. "I'm on it. I'm always here for your hard things."

Finn presses a button on the blender, and it springs to life as I open the refrigerator drawer and retrieve one of the refillable glass water bottles with stainless steel screw tops that have replaced plastic in our office. They are so beautiful they give me goose bumps. And all thanks to Mary Stuart, who procured them for me at a shop in her town about an hour away. In exchange I helped her fine-tune a pitch for a PR client she was trying to snag.

I point toward my office, deciding to email my friends back before my meeting. "I'll be ready in five."

Finn nods.

I sit back down, hit the Siri button on my keyboard, and say:

Subject: Re: Hard Things

To: lanier@bookmasters.com; marystuart@harrispr.com

Songbirds,

I am giving you the day off. My day is blissfully devoid of hard things. Off to sever heads for both of you.

Sending love and cannot wait to see you at Mary Stuart's WEDDING!

Fair winds and following seas,
Daphne

As I type the word *wedding*, my stomach rolls. It makes me think of Huff, my ex and, incidentally, Lanier's brother. Huff and I haven't seen each other much since our breakup seven years ago, but since he moved back to the area from Baltimore last month, we keep running into each other. And those run-ins keep getting longer . . . And I know all the reasons we cannot be together and yet, I cannot. Stop. Thinking. About. Him. I am dying to know if he is going to Mary Stuart's wedding. I could just ask Mary Stuart if she invited him, but I haven't told her Huff and I are back in touch. I'm not sure how Lanier will feel about it, and it doesn't seem fair to tell Mary Stuart and not Lanier.

I pick up my phone. Then I put it back down. Then I pick it back up. I'm being dumb. So I text:

Going to MS's wedding tomorrow?

He must have his phone in his hand because three bubbles appear immediately and a few seconds later he replies: Why? Hoping my killer dance moves might rub off on you?

I laugh. Huff is a truly terrible dancer. *I think you meant to ask, "Am I afraid your dance moves might kill me?"*

No bubbles. Was I too mean?

But then a ridiculous dancing dog GIF appears followed by *Unfortunately, I'm on call tomorrow night. So I'll have to give you dance lessons some other time.*

Huff is a surgeon, so of course his work comes first. But my heart is simultaneously falling that he won't be there and pounding at the idea of "some other time." Finn walks back into my office. "Hey," he says, "Smoking-hot baby daddy is on line one." I smile at the embarrassment of quality men today and roll my eyes at Finn.

Finn can't quite understand why I can't make things work with Henry's dad, Steven, and takes every opportunity to remind me how hot he is. As if I didn't know. Five years ago, I decided to take surf lessons to celebrate two years of sobriety. Steven was the charming, hilarious instructor I randomly chose on Google. By the second lesson, he had taken me to dinner, by the fourth we were practically inseparable, and then, well, Henry happened. Steven was only twenty-three when I got pregnant, two years younger than I was, and we weren't at a place to consider marriage or a real, true future. But I considered the pregnancy a huge—albeit slightly scary—gift. While I wouldn't say I'd been worried about my sobriety sticking before that, every now and then I missed relaxing with a glass (okay, bottle) of rosé or the focus (and sleep!) the pills I abused had given me. Henry washed all those urges away. I would read years later that all trauma is a result of separation and that healing is sometimes found in connection. I know that doesn't help everyone, my own mother included. But I credit my son, my ultimate attachment, with truly healing me.

As a bonus, Steven, whom I had expected absolutely nothing from, turned out to be a fabulous co-parent. He spent his weekends with

Henry at my house in Cape Carolina so I wouldn't have to miss my son, and he, a free spirit who had never held a baby, wouldn't be fully responsible on his own. It was a great system. Growing up with a totally absent father—even the almost three years I lived with him I barely saw the man—I think I just expected Steven to want an out. He decidedly did not. Sometimes I wanted to squeeze Henry's face and say, *You have no idea how lucky you are to have a father who loves you this much!* I mean, I didn't, obviously. He was only four, and that would be weird.

I pick up the receiver. "Happy Friday, baby daddy," I say. "Excited for the wedding?"

"I sure am. In fact, I have a flight to Cape Carolina this morning, and I wanted to see if I could fly you and Henry to Figure Eight tonight. I can drop you back off on Sunday."

Steven is not only a former professional surfer who now teaches lessons, but when the waves aren't great, he's also a private pilot. He sometimes mentions continuing his training and getting his commercial pilot's license, but I can't fathom that shaggy-haired, savagely tan beach bum having any sort of corporate gig. And that is fine. His laid-back vibe is a balm to my soul. I am saying, "Oh, man, that would be awesome!" as Finn peeks his head in and, eyebrows raised, whispers, "Wendy Carlson is here to see you."

"Hey, Steven, I've got to run. Just text me where to meet you and what time."

As we exchange goodbyes, I look up at the clock above the door. My meeting with Bryce, Lanier's fiancé and the contractor who made modern magic out of my tiny office space, is in just ten minutes.

But Wendy Carlson is one of my best clients. She owns a lighting and flooring company that I'm helping her expand to four major markets in North Carolina. To be honest, she was kind of a mean girl when we were in high school together. But she was one of my first clients when I moved back to town and started my solo business-law practice—as was Bryce's mother, who connected me with her son when she heard I was looking to upgrade my office.

I still contend that I got busy so fast because Mary Stuart launched a ridiculously huge PR campaign when I came back home and hung my shingle. The fact that I graduated first in my class from law school and was filling a niche in a town with too few attorneys probably didn't hurt either. But Mary Stuart made sure I was in the local paper and magazine and landed me interviews on radio and TV stations. She had even orchestrated an entire "Best of" campaign that included dozens of business categories so that I could be voted "Best Attorney." All that self-promotion made my skin crawl, but she loved it. Again, hard things made easy.

"Wendy and I don't have an appointment," I say, which is dumb because Finn obviously knows this, and that is why he looks so stressed out.

"I know. But she's in the conference room and says it's urgent. She's out almost a hundred thousand dollars from a client who hasn't paid her for multiple jobs."

I scrunch my nose as I stand and walk out of my office. Cape Carolina's population hovers in the low five digits. I know almost all the contractors here, and I can't imagine any of them getting behind on their bills and not paying people like Wendy—especially in today's market where everyone has more business than he or she can handle. I sigh. "Okay. I'll give her a few minutes now, and if we can't squeeze her in later, give her my lunch hour."

Finn shakes his head. He hates when I give people my lunch hour. He always says, *You are a single mother, and that is your one hour off the whole day.* On the flip side, working through lunch is one more billable hour toward giving my son the future he deserves.

My hand is on the stainless handle of the glass door leading into the glass box that is my conference room, nervousness rising in my stomach for a reason I can't quite name. Wendy Carlson, who I can see through the glass, is texting and looking downtrodden—not at all like her usual confident (and yes, still a *little* annoying) self. I open the door. "Wendy, what's—"

She interrupts. "That Bryce Jenkins is the most deceitful, manipulative son of a bitch I've ever met."

My breath catches as my best friend Lanier's left hand, with its sparkly sapphire engagement ring, flashes through my mind. Bryce Jenkins. The son of one of my best clients. The contractor who made my office en suite bath dreams come true. Lanier's fiancé. Who *I* introduced her to.

Finn, studying me, gasps. "Oh my God." He puts his hand to his chiseled jaw.

"Oh my God," I repeat.

And, just like that, I realize my entire day has changed. I do, indeed, have one very hard thing. And I would trade it with absolutely anyone.

June

BACK IN TIME

MY MOTHER USED TO SAY CAMP HOLLY SPRINGS WAS WHERE SHE felt closest to God. She would lie in bed with my sister, Melanie, and me, stroking our hair, regaling us with tales of her summers spent by the river, beneath the live oaks. I always had trouble reconciling the mother in the shirtwaist dresses who never let Melanie and me wear bell-bottoms or crop tops with the little girl who loved waterslides and campfires, sleeping in a bunk with no air-conditioning and singing songs in the dining hall.

We grew up counting the six summers until we got to go to Camp Holly Springs, and I cried and cried when my parents filled my mother's old green trunk to the brim with white starched shorts and green-trimmed, collared shirts that made up the Holly Springs uniform for my sister. That Melanie, who was two years older, got to go without me not once but *twice* seemed like a cruel joke.

I couldn't remember Melanie coming home from camp last year. But, this year, when it was time to pick Melanie up two weeks later, I got to ride in the back of my mom's brand-new Ford Country Squire wagon. Dad had gotten it for Mom while Melanie was at camp, and I couldn't wait to show it to her. The back window was rolled down, and I was sprawled out drinking an ice-cold Pepsi from a glass bottle, throwing salted peanuts in the top and taking sips, the mixture of sweet, salt, and bubbles exploding in my mouth. It was the taste of childhood. Of summertime.

When I saw Melanie, she was covered in spots. I thought she had chicken pox. We had both had it the year before, and I could still smell the calamine lotion if I concentrated. But Mom laughed when she saw them. "Looks like the Holly Springs mosquitos are just as vicious now as they were when I was at camp."

My sister hugged me hard. She smelled different, earthier, not like her usual pretty pink soap. I thought she must have hated camp, covered in all those bug bites, but the first thing she said was, "Mom! I want to stay the whole summer next year!" Then she looked down at me. "Actually, I only want to stay the whole summer when Junie is there too."

I wanted to cry, but I didn't know why. I didn't feel sad. I was so happy. My sister only wanted to go to camp for the whole summer if I could go with her. I adored my sister, wanted to be her.

And I couldn't wait to go to camp.

That night, in our shared room, Melanie got up and opened the window. "I can't sleep in all this still air," she said. Camp had changed Melanie.

"What about intruders?" I asked.

My parents were always talking about intruders, although, to my knowledge, Cape Carolina didn't have any.

"There aren't intruders at camp," Melanie said. "It's so far out in the woods that most people don't even know it's there. And, June, you wouldn't believe the waterslide. And we learned how to kayak. I can shoot a bow and arrow now! Did I tell you that?"

I wanted to listen to my sister talk forever. But, well, I was only five years old. I felt myself start to drift off, the cadence of her voice carrying me away. The last thing I heard was, "Next year will be your Songbird Summer, Junie. You'll get to be a Songbird, just like Mom and I were."

I fell asleep that night dreaming of flying in the sky with my sister, out of town, over the river. I woke the next morning to the sun streaming through the open window, a little bird sitting on the windowsill. This must be what it felt like to sleep with the windows open. I stretched, somewhere between sleeping and waking, still half in my dream. And I knew one thing for sure: It was going to be nice to be a Songbird.

That five-year-old girl had no idea that one day she would be without the three people she loved most: that sister and those parents. And she never could have imagined that she would one day own that camp whose stories captured her imagination from toddlerhood. But here I was, now fifty years old, sitting at the desk that had been in this same camp office since my mother's Songbird Summer.

I always thought about my niece, Daphne, in moments like this, when I was trying to find ways to stretch the dwindling money in the camp account, the ledger I still kept by hand open in front of me. I thought about her when I had calls from developers offering me obscene amounts of money to level the fifty-two waterfront cabins, mess hall, offices, dance building, craft center, and sailing hut that had been my life's work. But I especially thought of her when Jillian, my perky assistant and a former camper, burst through the door, a thick printout in her hand.

"Final roster!" she practically sang.

I couldn't help but smile. With the opening session of Camp Holly Springs's four two-week summer sessions beginning in three months (some girls, like Melanie and I, stayed all four!), there would still be a bit of movement in this list. A few girls would get cold feet, strep throat, a broken arm—but, by and large, this list contained the names that would fill our slice of paradise with their sweet smiles and big voices all summer. I tried to ignore what Jillian and I had discussed ad nauseam over the past few weeks: the list was smaller than we needed it to be. Instead, I focused on the good. The front page was filled with campers attending their first summer here. "This is so exciting!" I exclaimed. And despite my financial woes, I meant it. This was why I did this job. I loved to watch these girls develop the sea legs and self-confidence that weeks of independence gave them. As Jillian handed me a cup of coffee, I sank into my happiness.

"It's worth fighting for, June. I know we need to get creative about how to keep camp open, but we can do this."

I nodded, but my eyes flipped to the business card that was clipped to my ledger. *Price Development.* A number was written, in Sharpie: $5,000,000. Their starting offer had been $3,500,000 for the three hundred fifty acres of pristine, unobstructed water view. When I said I wasn't interested in selling, most developers went away. David Price kept raising his offer. I would lie in bed at night here, alone, listening to the cicadas chirping, the frogs conversing, the moonlight streaming through the windows, and reason that I had bought this summer camp more than twenty-five years ago—the first time it was failing—and had a good run. Now it was time to let it go. Not for the money. But because, after the pandemic shut our doors for a whole summer, I couldn't, even with the moderately successful next year we had, keep it open.

But then morning would come, and I would have a change of heart, not wanting to take away the place where little girls like Daphne—girls who didn't have stable families and home lives—came to be made strong and brave. Then I would inevitably find myself behind this aging, chipped laminate desk with my ledger, a line of tape pouring out of my giant adding machine, to see if I could make the math work. It never did.

Jillian sat down across from me and sipped her coffee. "What time are you leaving for Daphne's?"

I was so lost in my thoughts that, for a moment, I forgot why I was going to Daphne's. "Oh! Mary Stuart's wedding!"

Jillian laughed. "You need a break, June."

Mary Stuart was another one of my Holly Springs lifers who came to camp when she was six and stayed until she was a twenty-one-year-old counselor. She was one of Daphne's best friends, along with Lanier, who was also due to walk down the aisle soon.

Jillian leaned over the desk, looked at my ledger, and sighed. "Have you told them how much trouble we're in?" Jillian asked. "Maybe Mary Stuart can work some of her PR magic. Or maybe Daphne can help us get a loan somehow."

The thought made my throat feel tight. If only I had been more aggressive in asking for the Covid funding the government provided, we might not be in this mess. But the funding window had long closed. "I can't tell them. Not yet."

"Well, it will work out. We'll save it. You'll see."

I didn't have the heart to tell her she was wrong. I had put every penny I had received after my parents died into this camp. I had sacrificed everything for it. And now . . . Wanting to change the subject, I said, "Do you think Daphne will ever get married?"

Jillian laughed. "Well, if she didn't marry Steven . . ."

Steven had tried to make things work with Daphne when, after a few months of dating, she discovered she was pregnant. She adored him but thought he was too young, too unstable. But she was really the one who could never quite commit. She had sworn up and down from the time her mother died that she would never get married, never have children. Everyone who'd ever loved her had left her. I wanted to argue with her, but what leg did I have to stand on? I'd never done those things either. Henry was a welcome surprise to all of us, but my niece seemed set on the not getting married part.

"Actually," Jillian amended, "I take that back. If Daphne didn't marry *Huff*, then she was never going to get married."

Huff and Daphne had been madly in love in their twenties and, when things went south between them, her relationship with Lanier—who was practically her sister—almost didn't recover.

"Oh my. We're really going back in history now, aren't we?" I joked.

Jillian tapped her finger on my open ledger. "That's what I want you to do. I want you to go back in history to when things at camp were great and you didn't have to worry about any of this. Have fun at the wedding. Visit with the girls you love most. Dance with a man." She waggled her eyebrows at me. True, it wasn't terribly easy to meet age-appropriate men when you lived at an all-girls camp year-round. Of course, if I took my off-seasons to have a life like everyone hounded me about constantly . . . But no. Camp was my bubble. I was safe here. And, as I'd learned quickly, being a camp director was a year-round gig. It wasn't just getting ready for the summer or being there to supervise. There were fundraising campaigns to launch, camp nights to host, books to balance, and a million other things I'd never thought of before I became a director myself. I didn't have time for anything else.

My phone beeped and I looked down at a text from Daphne.

June, I have a problem.

I sighed, looking back at the ledger open in front of me. *Don't we all, Daphne. Don't we all.*

Daphne

YOU JUMP, I JUMP

I AM STANDING STOCK-STILL IN THE GLASS CONFERENCE ROOM I usually find so calming, my heart racing out of my chest. *What in the world has Bryce done?*

Wendy Carlson doesn't have time to elaborate before the door to our office chimes and Bryce himself flies through the door yelling, "Daphne!" He is in his usual jeans and polo shirt, his cute black glasses giving him this Clark Kent air that I find totally adorable—for Lanier, anyway. He is my height, five eight, much taller than my super petite friend who lies and says she is five two. The first time I met him at a meeting with his mom almost two years ago, I just knew Lanier would be into him. I set them up on their first date a few weeks later, right about the time Bryce and I had our first meeting about my office remodel. They were both attractive, successful, fun, and, let's be real—single people our age in Cape Carolina were hard to come by. Before Bryce, I'd worried Lanier would leave our hometown—and me—because she couldn't find her person here. Fortunately, she fell in love with Bryce, and I looked forward to meetings about flooring options over cocktails with my favorite couple.

I shake my head, hoping he won't say what I think he's about to say. I have been Bryce's attorney for more than a year now, but I've been his family's business attorney since I passed the bar four years ago. Bryce's mom is one of the queens of McCann Media, a national corporation that houses several of its most popular publications in Cape Carolina. God love her, she took a chance on me because, as she said, people had done the same for her when she was young. Attorney-client privilege will probably prevail here no matter what, but if I just don't have to hear whatever leaves Bryce's lips then *maybe* I can still tell my friend about this accusation. Maybe.

"I'm finishing up a meeting, Br—"

"I can't believe you would show your face here!" Wendy yells.

Instantly, Bryce transforms into the Bryce I know. Cool. Calm. A little *too* charming. It's like a switch has flipped. "Wendy, how long have we been friends? I'm telling you. I'm good for the money. One of my jobs is behind on paying me, but—"

Wendy puts her hand up. "I'm in danger of not making payroll this month. I've been bankrolling you for months. I'm done." She pauses. "And I'm not your friend. Not anymore."

I look at Finn, who jumps into action. "Ms. Carlson, I have you down at noon to meet with Ms. Miller. I'm very sorry, but she has an appointment with another client now."

To my surprise, she gets up from the end of the conference room table. She puts her finger in the center of Bryce's chest, and I feel my breath catch. You can tell by looking at Bryce that he's not one for physical confrontation. But Wendy? Wendy got suspended once for pulling out a girl's extensions so . . . "You're going to pay for this." She turns to me. "I presume you'd never represent this *scum*, so I will see you at noon." She walks out in a huff. Representing either of them would be a conflict of interest, so whether she comes back is of little consequence.

This is one of the seedier scenes to have played out in my pristine office. Business law in a small town is usually more contracts and less showdowns over money. My initial reaction, as I sit Bryce down and take the seat across from him, is to be on his side. After all, we are friends. I should be Team Bryce. This has to be a misunderstanding.

Then I remember the brand-new truck he just bought, the huge house he is building to live in with my best friend. Mary Stuart and I have questioned how he is doing all that he is doing. But Bryce's mother is a McCann with the family money and business savvy to prove it, so we assumed he had some sort of trust that had come through. My head throbs.

"This isn't what it seems like," Bryce says. "But I'm here because I'm in trouble."

I nod, caught between sympathy and anger. "I can see that."

He puts his head in his hands. "I don't want to file bankruptcy."

My eyes widen. Bankruptcy? This is serious. "So how bad is it?"

"Four major projects are in jeopardy." He sighs. "I'm taking responsibility for it. I have another builder who's going to finish them, but in the meantime, I need to figure out how to keep people like Wendy from suing the homeowners. I don't want them to find out what happened."

I laugh incredulously. "Bryce, what is going on? You aren't paying your vendors or subcontractors?" Now my head is *really* hurting. Not only is Bryce in trouble; the homeowners and business owners he's working for might be, too. If he isn't paying for the work that's been done on their houses, they could ultimately be responsible for the bills he took their money for—the bills he never paid.

He looks sheepish. "Well, I mean, I had it under control. I got a little overextended, so I was using money from one project to pay for a previous one. It was all going to be fine, but then—"

"But then it wasn't," I fill in. What he is doing is highly illegal. "Why did you need the money? Are you in trouble?" I lean closer to him, peering at his face. "Are you on drugs?" I know what on drugs looks like. I dealt with a mother on and off drugs for much of my young life. I can even spot the hard-to-spot, super common ones like too much Valium, off-prescription use of Adderall, and mixing antidepressants with alcohol.

"Daphne, calm down. I'm not on drugs." He looks down at his hands. "It was all going so well, but then I got overzealous with my purchasing . . . and, well, I need you to help me."

There is more to ask, but I have to know one thing first: "Please tell me you've told my best friend."

He grimaces and leans back in his chair. "I haven't told her. And if I can keep the homeowners from finding out, she won't have to know. No one has to know."

I scoff. "How will they not know? How many people do you owe besides Wendy? And how much?" He clears his throat but says nothing, and my heart starts to race. I am way too emotionally involved in this to be impartial. "How much, Bryce?"

"Close to a million." He cracks his knuckles. "But I swear, I've got this, Daphne. It's handled."

I shake my head. "I can't take this case, Bryce. Wendy is my client—who knows who else." I run through my mental Rolodex. I gasp. "Did you do this same thing on Amelia and Parker's pool house?"

He nods slowly and I feel my blood run cold, thinking of the adorable Cape Carolina couple with the cutest twins, who also happen to be my clients—and McCann Media employees. They live in this old family house way out on the end of the peninsula that is too great for words. I recommended Bryce to them. And now, I know, if they didn't have paperwork signed guaranteeing that Bryce had paid the vendors and subcontractors—paperwork that would be very unusual for a residential build—they would be on the hook for all the money he has stolen. I feel a little guilty over the relief that swamps me knowing I did have that paperwork signed. And I make a mental note to always protect my clients in this way in the future.

"Bryce, this is serious. You might have ruined people's lives. You could be in huge legal trouble."

He shakes his head. "No, it's going to be fine. I'll fix it." He sighs and shakes his head. "But how am I going to tell my mother?"

Bryce, unlike most people, does at least have a safety net. He *can* right this wrong. Even still, I feel my anger rising. How could he put Lanier in this situation? For better or worse, her reputation is tied to his now. "Well, good, great. You fix this. I can't help you, but I wish you well." In this moment, I very much do *not* wish him well. I feel my blood pressure rising as he stands up, and I can't help but add: "Lanier has a right to know. You're marrying her. And I'm sure whatever it is, she'll understand. She loves you."

I don't know if she will understand. I don't, but he isn't giving me much to work with.

"Daph, I don't know that she will. Lanier is the greatest thing that ever happened to me, and I can't lose her. I can't take the chance that she won't forgive me."

I roll my eyes, but, I mean, of course she's the greatest thing that's ever happened to him. She's amazing. "I assume you know you have put me in an impossible situation." I feel my face reddening. Over the past few years, I've become practically expert at remaining cool under pressure. But now I can't stay calm.

Bryce shakes his head again. "I'm sorry, Daphne. I really am. But I'm not going to tell Lanier, and you can't either. Because if you do, well . . . You understand the repercussions."

As Bryce walks away, I realize he might have been dumb enough to get himself into this mess, but he was smart enough to trap me in it with him. I can't tell Lanier what's going on without breaking the attorney-client privilege oath I take seriously. But Lanier is my best friend, my sister. And the only thing that has ever come between us is the secrets we have kept. I won't let that happen again.

• • •

This is pretty much the worst-case scenario, I am realizing as I sit in the carpool line at my son's school. The whole scene seems like it must have been a dream. A nightmare. I pinch myself. Nope. I'm definitely awake. Which means my lunch meeting with a furious Wendy was real too. Bryce's actions are about to cause a lot of collateral damage, I'm afraid.

I tap my fingers on the steering wheel, wondering why June hasn't called me back. It isn't like it's summer, when she's busy helping girls into kayaks or over homesickness. I can't tell her what's going on, but I need to hear her voice. She is my safe place.

My stomach is in absolute knots. In fact, I'm not sure I really understood that phrase until today. I glance up at the empty school playground. No kids have come out yet. I have at least ten more minutes of waiting in the line and *why isn't June calling me back?*

My phone rings and I jump. But it's only Finn. Although maybe that is better. I can actually talk to him about this. "Hey."

Finn starts rambling. "You won't have to break attorney-client privilege or tell Lanier. It won't be a problem. People will find out when one of the subcontractors or homeowners talks and when they do it will be all over the news and—"

"Finn!" I interrupt. "Think. I'm *McCann Media's* attorney."

I lean my head on the steering wheel.

"Oh . . . right. It won't be anywhere. Because they own all the newspapers, radio, and TV stations."

"Yup. And even if they didn't, I can't really see this making the news. I mean, a contractor not paying his bills isn't exactly exciting." *Until he gets arrested*, I add in my head.

The fifth graders in their matching khakis and red polos file out onto the playground, which means Henry, who is in preschool, will be out after the older children get into their parents' cars. Seeing them, I can't help but remember all the days Lanier and I played on this very playground, skipping rope side by side, saying we'd marry brothers so we could be sisters for real. I have to tell her what I know.

Finn is back at it with the chattering, and I love him for the distraction. "Well, it isn't *that* bad, right?" he says.

"Finn! He literally stole almost a million dollars from people! And the shitty thing is, worst case, he'll probably file bankruptcy and walk away scot-free. Those people he's stolen from will get totally screwed, maybe even lose houses or businesses. And he'll just get away with it."

The only real, true punishment for Bryce would be losing Lanier. Which he will because I will tell her. *And then Bryce will turn me in to the bar. And I will get disbarred for breaking attorney-client privilege.* Which, well, I probably should. I took an oath to protect my clients' secrets. If I break that oath, my career is over.

Then I think of Lanier again, of her family. This would affect all of them. I remember how close Lanier's mom, Paula, and my mom became when they met at camp pickup for the first time. Paula loved my mom in spite of her periodic relapses and stints in rehab; she took care of both of us. I spent so many school nights at Lanier's house because my mom was strung out. Paula—who always waited to make sure Mom showed up—would take me to their house and feed me a snack, make sure I showered, fix my hair, help with my homework. She let me move in with them when, after my mom died, living with my dad became unbearable. She got little more than my undying love and devotion in return, which dictated that I should tell. For Lanier's sake, yes, but for hers too. Even though it would mean losing my job. Even though it would mean putting my child's future in jeopardy.

But wouldn't that break the oath I had made to myself when I found out I was pregnant? That I would give Henry a stable future at all costs? It's why I had ended my relationship with Steven. If we ever broke up, Henry's life would be uprooted; if we were happily coparenting, he would always have two parents who got along. He would never have to feel untethered like I had. If I told Lanier, I would save her future, but put his in jeopardy. It was an impossible choice.

"I can tell her," Finn says, breaking me out of my thoughts. "I'll tell her and then you don't lose your job. I'll lose mine."

What a love he was. "If only it worked like that, sweetie."

"Is this an I jump, you jump situation?"

"I'm afraid so." I sigh. "We just need to take a deep breath." And we both do, audibly.

"Well, my golden goddess," Finn says a few seconds later, "you have months before she walks down that aisle. *Months*. We'll figure something out. We will."

Among the throngs of children, I spot Betts, a little girl in Henry's class, filing out the front door. I make it a personal policy to never be on the phone when I pick Henry up.

"I have to go," I say. "Thanks for everything. Thanks for staying so

I could get Henry. And please have a good weekend. This is my problem, not yours."

"Well . . . You jump, I jump, Jack."

I laugh. His words make me feel slightly better. But not nearly as good as when I get out of my car and my tow-headed bundle of Paw-Patrol-backpack-wearing joy tears down the sidewalk and into my arms. He has my green eyes, Steven's olive skin, and precious, tousled curls all his own. "Mommy! It's time for the bookstore!"

Henry and I go to Lanier's bookstore every Friday afternoon. It is our routine, a routine that, I hope, Henry will look back on and remember fondly as part of a safe, stable childhood.

I hug him tight, breathing in the scent of the Johnson's Baby Shampoo I still use on his four-year-old hair. My baby. The one I have sworn to protect. "Of course we're going to the bookstore!"

And I know then, without question, that I cannot ruin my child's life. I cannot lose my job. My home. My stability. Even if that means lying to the sister I never had. Even if that means losing my very best friend.

Lanier

CAMPFIRE SECRET

"HOW DID YOU GET OVER HERE?" I ASKED A COPY OF JANE AUSTEN'S *Emma,* which was inexplicably mixed in among the books in the Harry Potter section.

Seeing the books made me think of Annalee, the previous store owner, and how she used to swear she survived off "Harry Potter days," when a new book in the series would come out and there would be a line of people around the block at midnight waiting to get it. She would do an entire week's worth of sales in a few hours. Now, thanks to a combination of increased tourism, an emphasis on shopping local, and a general post-pandemic uptick in reading, we had a "Harry Potter Day" at least once a week. Business was great.

I climbed the wooden ladder with its brass fittings and track that always made me feel like Belle from *Beauty and the Beast* and reshelved *Emma* in the appropriate spot with the rest of the Austens in the Classics section. As I did, the front door tinkled. "Welcome to Bookmasters!" I turned to see my best customer: my mom.

Mom was dressed in head-to-toe Lululemon, not a hair out of place. I'd never quite understood how she could spend an hour on a Pilates reformer and not break a sweat, but thirty-plus years of experience had proven that it was possible. She was holding something to her chest like a secret she couldn't wait to share.

"It's here!" Mom chirped. "The proof for the wedding invitations is here!"

I gasped, taking the cream rectangular piece of paper from her. We both studied it briefly, my eyes filling with tears as I ran my finger around my name and Bryce's in perfect calligraphy. My best friend Daphne walked through the open door, holding her son Henry's hand. "Guess who's here?" she called in a singsong voice.

"Why, my best buddy Henry, that's who!" I scooped him up. "There's something special in the Henry spot. You must go see!" Behind my desk, on the bottom shelf, I always kept a treat for Henry. A new book, a piece of candy, a cute freebie from a publisher.

Daphne smiled at her son and then at me. "Daph, the invitation!" Mom exclaimed, and as she handed her the paper, I could have sworn Daphne's face fell. But she recovered quickly, and I realized I must have been wrong. No one—not even my mother—was as excited about this wedding as Daphne. She said it was because she was never getting married, so this was basically her wedding too. Which is why I had perhaps spent longer picking out her maid of honor dress than I had my own gown. It was my day, but I wanted it to be perfect for her, too.

"Wow! Is it invitation time already?" Daphne asked Mom.

"Almost! Just think, I'd been worried Lanier would never meet a man in Cape Carolina. And then you introduced her to Bryce, and it's like the stars aligned."

Mom wasn't wrong. Bryce was so right for me. He was literally building things all day, every day. He was stable and steady—a direct contrast to me, who would always rather have her nose in a book, her head in the clouds. I mean, he wasn't perfect. But who was?

Daphne bit her lip. "Oh, well, I wouldn't say that I had a huge hand . . ."

"Don't be modest," I chimed in. "I owe my eternal happiness to you."

She laughed, but it seemed forced. I pushed my tortoiseshell frames up my nose.

Henry tore around the corner, striking a Superman pose and holding a book high in the air. He put it nearer to his face. "P-r-e-s-s H-e-r-e," he sounded out.

"Whoa! Buddy, that reading is off the charts!" I put my hand up for a high five and he smacked it.

"Lanier, would you read it to me please?" he asked, smiling with dimples that were destined to break a million hearts.

"Buddy, go play with the trains for just a minute," Daphne said. "Mommy needs to talk to Aunt Lanier."

"Okay!" He ran off to the children's section at the back of the store, which featured the same BRIO train sets Huff and I had played with here as kids.

"So, what do you think?" Mom asked Daphne.

She grinned broadly. "Oh, it's just gorgeous. Absolutely gorgeous." Daphne paused and reached her hand out for the invitation again. "The engraving is perfect, the crest is beautiful . . . And I cannot believe that John agreed to pay for them." My dad was known for his thriftiness. She raised one eyebrow, a talent I'd been jealous of my entire life.

I knew what Mom was going to say before she said it. "He didn't, exactly. But, girls, that will be our little secret." She winked. That had been Mom's line for as long as I could remember. Bought an extra pair of shoes? Our little secret. Got Botox and didn't want Dad to know? Our little secret. Snuck chocolate after school when Dad had made us all give it up for Lent? Our little secret. But, as I'd come to find out, not all of Mom's "little secrets" were actually that little . . .

"And when do these go out again?" Daphne asked.

"Eight weeks!" Mom practically sang.

"Eight weeks," Daphne said. She bit her lip again.

"Hey, what's with you today?"

She smiled almost automatically. "Nothing! I'm just so excited!" Maybe I was reading too much into it. Daphne's plate was really full.

"Sweetie," Mom said, "before I go, ring me up for whatever new hardback you think your father might like."

I smiled and walked over to the New Releases shelf, grabbing a new crime novel Dad would love. Mom and Dad must have hundreds of unread books for as many as they bought from me each week. Not only did they help keep me in business, but they were also the reason I had this store in the first place. I had gotten a full scholarship to Duke—my father's alma mater—and my parents had promised I could put what they saved for my tuition toward a down payment on a house. (It wasn't enough for Duke, but it was a nice nest egg.) But I didn't need a house; I needed this store. My parents' scrimping and saving set me up with the down payment for my dream career.

I rang Mom up, giving her my ten percent book club discount. Yes, owning this store meant a lot of long hours, late nights at author events, and online book sales, which, quite frankly, I despised. But the reward of spending a life surrounded by books, the joy of receiving advance copies and the smell of all those fresh pages . . . It was a dream come true.

Daphne walked over to the counter as I handed Mom the book and she handed me her credit card. "You know," Daphne said, "this wedding is coming so fast, and with Mary Stuart champing at the bit to get pregnant, I was thinking maybe we should move your bachelorette party up." Mom sighed, taking her credit card back and putting it in her wallet. "Oh, you girls. On that note, I'm going to leave and let you plan your weekend of debauchery." She shouted, "Love you, Henry! And love you, too, sweetie." She kissed Daphne on the cheek. Ever since Mom met Daphne and Melanie, she had been a second mom to Daphne and a support system for her mother. Melanie's death was a battle Mom clearly felt she had lost. But, after all they'd been through together—and the two years she lived with us—Daphne was practically her daughter. Every now and then, it pained me to remember that, in all likelihood, she once believed she would be her daughter-in-law one day too.

"Bye, Paula. Let me know how I can help. You know I'll do anything at all!" Daphne said, waving as Mom walked out the door.

My phone beeped in my hand. I looked down at the screen.

Huff: *Mom has sent me thirty-seven pictures of the wedding invitation. Can you imagine when you have a kid?*

I hid my smile, not wanting Daphne to ask what it was about. Huff was the one thing we didn't discuss. So maybe that's why I asked, "How are things going with Walt?" Walt was a guy Daphne had met a few weeks ago and been on four or five dates with. She said she liked him, and I took that as a good sign. I think, secretly, I always hoped Daphne would find "the one" despite her proclamations she'd never marry, and then I would be off the hook for ruining her chance at happiness with my brother.

Daphne shrugged. "He's a nice guy. I like him. But I'm not going to see him anymore."

"Daphne!" I scolded. "You literally always do this." *Except with Huff.* I felt a pang of guilt. "Why would you break up with him?"

"Because I know he ultimately wants to get married, and I'm not going to marry him, so what's the point? It wouldn't be fair."

I rolled my eyes. "Daphne, you have to date someone before you can decide if you want to marry them. That's the whole point."

"No, the whole point is that I already know I'm not going to. Besides, it's hard enough to have the 'Hey, by the way, I'm sober' conversation on the first or second date when they inevitably want to order drinks. How do you think it feels to have the 'Oh, by the way, my mother died of an overdose and my dad and I literally haven't spoken in years' conversation?"

"Yeah, but that isn't your fault," I interjected.

"Maybe not. But it also doesn't exactly scream, 'Yay! Perfect to bring home to Mom!' "

My heart broke for Daphne. I never even considered this might be an insecurity of hers. "Daph, they'd be lucky to take you home to their mom. You just don't ever give them the opportunity."

"Maybe not. But, unless I'm really into them, it's easier to just move on than to have the hard conversations." She shrugged, and I realized she was finished talking about this for the day.

"Okay. Bachelorette," I said, changing the subject. "Look, I don't want something big." After her history with her mother—and a scare of her own seven years ago—Daphne didn't drink, so I didn't want her to feel pressured to plan a big, splashy weekend. "Let's just do a girls' night here."

Daphne shook her head. "I have another idea. What if we went back—just you, me, and Mary Stuart—and spent a long weekend at camp?"

I gasped, clasping my hands together. My favorite memories were from Camp Holly Springs, but I hadn't been back in almost ten years. Gosh. It was hard to believe we were *thirty*.

I had been a counselor there for the last time the summer before my junior year of college. I'd planned to work there for two more summers, like Daphne and Mary Stuart had, but I'd begged off, saying I'd been offered an internship I couldn't refuse. In reality, I couldn't face Rich, my crush-turned-boyfriend, who I had let down in the worst possible way. He was the current director of Camp Rock Springs, the all-boys camp adjacent to Holly Springs. I'd pushed thoughts of him aside for years, even though I knew, logically, that the chances I'd end up with someone I met at camp were negligible.

"Oh, Daph! What a great, great idea! I haven't been back since . . ."

She winced. "Ugh. I know. But you'll be okay going back now, right?"

The full-time staff would just be moving back and, as the properties for Camp Holly Springs and Rock Springs literally touched—and several employees worked for both camps—there was a chance we would see everyone who was returning for the summer. I was surprised to find that the thought of running into Rich filled me with equal parts dread and euphoria. Daphne searched my face. "Do you want to see him?" she whispered.

Did I want to see him? And, if so, what did that mean? "I don't know. I mean, maybe. I guess I want him to see that I've grown up now, that I'm not that same girl who made all those stupid mistakes and nearly ruined his life all those years ago." I laughed, but it was forced.

"I doubt you ruined his life. I think he forgave you. I think he would have completely forgiven you if you'd—"

"Okay!" I shrugged, not wanting to think about that terrible time. "Well, let's hope I don't see him. Then I don't have to unpack how I feel about it. But, in the meantime, I think a bachelorette at camp is a wonderful idea!"

She smiled brightly. "I'll talk to Mary Stuart and get some dates. And I'll make sure June is all ready to help us reenact our glory days. The blob, the zip line, sailing—"

"Campfire!"

"Campfire!"

"La-nier!" Henry called, saying my name as if it was two separate words.

I turned toward him. "I'm coming, buddy!"

When I looked back, Daphne was staring out the window distractedly. "Hey." I put my hand on her forearm. "Are you okay?"

She nodded. "Lanier, you should know . . ." She paused, then pinned on that fake smile again. "You're getting married in four months!" she practically squealed.

I sensed something there besides excitement. I assumed she was worried about how our relationship would shift after I was married. We saw each other at least a few times a week right now.

"Nothing will change," I said. "I promise."

She smiled, maybe a little sadly. "Of course things will change. But that's okay. I only want you to be happy. I want you to have everything you've ever dreamed of."

I still felt like there was something she wasn't saying. But Daphne had never been one to spill everything that was going on in her life. And, well, because of attorney-client privilege, there was so much she couldn't talk about anyway. And that was just as well because, of all the girls at camp, no one—and I do mean no one—could keep a campfire secret quite like Daphne. It was one of her best qualities and made her an incredibly loyal friend.

As I walked back to her son, that bright little light that had surprised and delighted us all, I hoped against hope that he would love his summers at camp as much as we did. And, even more, I hoped that one day he would find a best friend as wonderful as Daphne.

Daphne

SONGBIRDS AND THE SKY

THE EXPANSIVE FOYER OF MARY STUART'S PARENTS' HOUSE IN FIGURE Eight is how I imagine the interior of a beehive. Wedding planners are rushing around, calling out orders, florists are shuffling flowers in and out, a random waiter or two is darting about. In the midst of it all, a massive number of bridesmaids and groomsmen are standing around, waiting for photographs.

Being in a wedding in your thirties is generally kind of awkward, especially when they're like this one and the bride and groom—who have collected an inordinate number of friends over the decades—decide to have them *all* in their wedding party. And since Mary Stuart and Ted have known each other only eighteen months, none of her friends really know any of his friends, so twelve random men and twelve random women have to negotiate taking photos together and walking down the aisle arm in arm while someone's slightly irritated spouse looks on. It's annoying and a little uncomfortable in the best of worlds.

Everyone else has had enough to drink while getting ready that they probably don't notice the discomfort. But I, the sober one, feel it. This makes me partly grateful that Huff isn't here, even though I'd hoped he would be. But that was just as well. We shouldn't be in such close proximity. And I shouldn't be thinking about him this much, especially when my mind should be occupied with how to get through this wedding and handle the Bryce situation, preferably without losing my law license and/or breaking Lanier's heart. That was going to be tricky.

I walk over to a long table lined with beautiful bouquets. The ceremony is about to begin, and I realize as I am choosing my bouquet, shaking it gently so as not to get water on my pale blue bridesmaid's dress, that this day is taking a turn for the better. Because I hear a voice I know very, very well say, "Fancy seeing you here." In the instant before I turn around, my heart races.

I gather myself. "Huff." I can't help but grin, and I instantly look around to make sure Lanier can't see this innocent interaction and get the wrong idea. But as my pulse pounds and I look up into those shocking blue eyes—Lanier's eyes—that can still render me speechless, everything inside me feels like Jell-O. And as Huff wraps me in a hug, I realize that maybe this isn't the wrong idea at all. In fact, if I had any sense, I'd beg him to run away with me right now. Instead, I pull away and say, "What's fancy is how I didn't run into you for years and lately it's all the time." I raise my eyebrows and he smiles. "And I thought you were on call."

"I couldn't miss Mary Stuart's wedding. She's practically a sister to me."

"Is she?"

Mary Stuart grew up an hour away from Lanier and me, so while we arranged the occasional get-together growing up, she was our camp friend, plain and simple. Huff barely knew her.

"Would I have traded being on call tonight for Christmas Eve if I didn't really, *really* want to come to Mary Stuart's wedding?"

Paula is going to kill him when she finds out he is on call Christmas Eve, which is the biggest night of the year in their family. I laugh and study his face. "Okay, okay. Tell me the truth: Did you really just 'run into' me at the grocery store two weeks ago?"

He grins at me in that way that makes me melt. "Hand to God, the grocery store was a coincidence." He pauses. "Now, did I 'run into you' in the Coffee Cove, where I happen to know you go get a pick-me-up at two every afternoon? Maybe not."

I laugh, marveling at this spark that is still between us, even seven years after we broke up. I have also marveled at it, my heart racing a mile a minute, in the frozen foods section at the Piggly Wiggly and during a "quick" catch-up-over-coffee that lasted three hours.

"Well, if I'm being completely honest, I didn't just happen to be in Little Washington last week at the boat ramp either. I may or may not have overheard that you were trout fishing."

Huff gasps as if in shock. He is not in shock at all. I obviously had no business being an hour and a half from home at a boat ramp on a Saturday while Steven had Henry at a baseball game. But four hours later, we were still riding around the river, totally lost in each other, and Huff hadn't so much as baited a hook, making me think that was the only place I had any business being after all.

I take in his imperfectly tied bow tie and, as if by impulse, untie it. I begin to tie it back, neater, and Huff asks, "How's Henry? I stalk you relentlessly on Instagram, so, I mean, I saw him in his new police uniform. I know he's here to protect and serve. But in general."

I laugh, pulling the ends of the tie tight. "He's cute, isn't he?"

He nods. "He looks shockingly like you."

"Well, when you meet Steven, you might change your mind."

His face falls, and I realize mentioning Steven is a misstep. I let my fingers linger on his tie, so close to that face I loved for so long. So I add, "But he does look like me. And thank goodness. Let's face it: I'm the one who did all the hard work to get him here."

"I can't wait to finally meet him," Huff says. "He is all Lanier talks about."

Shit. Lanier. I smile a little uncomfortably, reminding myself to breathe, reminding myself of all the reasons we cannot, should not, will not be together. But trying to convince myself of all that when Huff is in a tux just isn't fair.

"Huff!" Mary Stuart calls from somewhere behind the swirling mass of bridesmaids and groomsmen and assorted family members waiting for their turn in front of the lens. I have forgotten any of them are there. For a solid minute or so, it was just Huff and me. I will myself to *stop it* as Mary Stuart hugs Huff.

"So excited for you, Mar," Huff says. "And don't let Ted forget we have a big game next week." He walks toward the door. Mary Stuart sidles as close to me as she can get in her giant gown. "Big game?" I ask her.

"Yeah. Ted and Huff play on a physician's pickup basketball league." I want to ask more questions, but she gives me a knowing look. "It has been years. You've changed. We're all older. I think Lanier would understand."

But Mary Stuart wasn't there. She didn't live through the time my best friend, my *sister*, and I weren't speaking. She didn't see how, even after I was finally the one to break the silence, we never talked it out. We built a massive bridge over a dumpster of trash that we hoped would disintegrate. And, well, largely, it had. It seemed our baggage was compostable, thank goodness.

"Bridesmaids and groomsmen, line up!" I hear the photographer call.

Lanier pops up between Mary Stuart and me, making me jump. "After this, champagne!" I smile, even though I know I won't drink it, as we file out onto the front steps, staggering bridesmaids and groomsmen. Even during times of extreme stress, ever since I got pregnant with Henry, I don't really want to drink. I work hard on my sobriety. Every day involves journaling and meditation, yoga and mantras. And I still go to therapy, although not as often as I used to. But I remember so clearly how scared I was then, how bad I felt all the time, how my life revolved around my next pill, my next drink. I never want to go back to that. That said, I just celebrated seven years of sobriety and, while that's exciting, it's also the year my mother relapsed. I'm not *worried* necessarily. More like hypervigilant.

Mary Stuart is waiting patiently at the bottom of the steps for Ted, who is talking to Huff. It breaks my heart a little that I've never seen them play in what I'm sure is a ridiculous grown-man basketball league. Lanier is on the other end of the line from me and I lean out a little, blowing her a kiss, feeling ever so slightly guilty about the innermost thoughts about her brother I'm having trouble controlling.

The photographer is busy lining us up by height and calling out orders. Huff and Ted each have one of Mary Stuart's arms and are helping her climb the steep steps where we are all standing so that the bride and groom can take their place at the center of this calamity. I don't want to catch Huff's eye, but I can't help it. After getting Mary Stuart situated, he walks a few steps over to me and sweeps a piece of hair off my face. "Picture-perfect," he says, holding my gaze for a minute too long. Then he walks away.

It is only a moment, a millisecond. His skin hasn't even touched mine, but, still, it makes my heart stop. I think that I am the only one to notice this electricity, but Adam, the tuxedoed groomsman beside me, asks, "What the hell was that?"

The bridesmaid standing next to him, Gray—who I know of vaguely thanks to all the gossip about her scandalous marriage to a much younger tennis pro—waggles her eyebrows at him. "They used to . . . you know."

I glare at her because I don't want Lanier to somehow hear this.

"Ohhhh," Adam replies. "You know, I felt that tension. I really did."

I roll my eyes and hiss, "Stop it."

"That's not all," Gray, who I have liked very much until this moment, says. "She was his lobster."

"Seriously," I say through gritted teeth. "This is not Lanier's favorite topic."

Gray waves her hand. "She knows he's still in love with you. Hell, I'm his sister's friend's cousin and *I* know."

Another bridesmaid whose name I cannot remember chimes in. "Oh yeah. It's such a sad story. We all thought you would eventually find your way back to each other."

The groomsman beside her, one of Ted's friends from home, adds, "Yeah. Total heartbreaker."

I can't tell if he's joking, but I can't disagree.

Annie, the photographer, says, "Excuse me! Bridesmaids! Could you please look at me?"

I turn to Adam and say, "Thanks a lot."

"What?"

"Now I'm the problem bridesmaid, and she's going to make sure I look like shit in every picture."

He gives me a once-over. "We both know that isn't possible."

And I start to like him just a little more.

• • •

Many, many photos taken and bottles of champagne drunk by everyone but me later, we have made it to showtime. We are lined up. The groom is in his place. The groomsmen are standing at attention beside him. Mary Stuart and Ted are getting married outside, under a tent at her parents' gracious home, and I wonder if perhaps the five-inch stilettos she chose for us to wear might not be the most appropriate footwear for making our way through soggy earth. As the music swells and I walk down the aisle, I feel Huff's eyes on me. The five-inch heels immediately feel like ten.

I turn just in time to see my darling four-year-old boy walking hand in hand with Mary Stuart's precious goddaughter. He hates every inch of the white linen shorts, white knee socks, and matching jacket he has been forced to wear. But he looks so cute as he marches down the aisle holding the rings, seriously instructing the flower girl every time she is to throw a petal, that a murmur of laughter circulates.

He stands beside Ted and, looking back for me, grins. I give him a big thumbs-up. *Whew.* Now if he can only stand still and behave for the nine minutes this ceremony will take, we are golden. Steven, who's sitting beside June, is watching him like a hawk from the audience. He has promised to retrieve him the instant the ceremony ends and be in charge until the babysitter arrives because being a bridesmaid is a lot of work. Even when we were dating, he was always thoughtful like that. I should have fallen in love with him.

I spot Huff sitting in the sixth row, the only person not looking at the bride as the music changes. His eyes are on me. Mine lock with his, and I look away nervously at first, but then I glance over a second time, then a third. He still hasn't looked away. And what I've avoided all this time is clear: I could never fall in love with Steven because I still loved Huff.

Huff is looking at me like it should have been him waiting at the end of the aisle, me walking down it. But then I remember my mother wailing over her breakup with her short-lived husband. *Never marry a man you love this much*. Her word was gospel, and even all these years later, I can't forget.

I clear my throat, focusing as Ted vows to be all Mary Stuart's forever. He looks like he can't believe it. I turn to catch Lanier's eye, and I think of all the nights we laid in our bunk beds at Camp Holly Springs and dreamed of this very moment, of how we would get to be each other's bridesmaids. I spot Bryce, who is looking at Lanier. And, for a moment, I hate him less because he looks so in love. He makes an apologetic face when he sees me.

As the priest says, "Should anyone present know of any reason that this couple should not be joined in holy matrimony, speak now or forever hold your peace," I imagine myself at Lanier and Bryce's wedding, being the maid of honor who dramatically shouts, "I object!" I have a feeling that moment would have a less cinematic ending in real life than a movie.

Then the ceremony is over. I walk back down the aisle, glancing briefly at Huff. All the questions that can never have answers flood my mind. What if, after our breakup, I had seen him one rainy night in a restaurant, and we'd been able to start over? What if we had shown up at the same Christmas party when he was home for the holidays? What if I had met up with him for spring break his last year of med school like he'd asked? But there was no what if. There was only now.

Feeling flushed and a little light-headed, I walk upstairs alone as the guests make their way from the tented ceremony area to the beautiful patio where appetizers are being served and everyone is flocking to the bride and groom. Standing in Mary Stuart's old bedroom, I retrieve my lip gloss from my bag and start fluffing my hair. When the door opens, I expect to see another bridesmaid.

But it is Huff. He strides through the room and sits casually on the small sofa at the end of Mary Stuart's old bed, and I vow that I won't sit down too. In fact, I pretend to ignore him, applying my lip gloss and putting it back in my bag. We have spent hours talking these past few weeks, but we have both danced around the question Huff asks me now as I rustle around in my purse: "Daph, what are we doing?"

I can't explain what makes him so irresistible, what makes me sit down beside him. Well, no. Maybe I can. It isn't how he looks, although he does have this certain ungodly tall, muscular thing happening in an all-American football player meets Ralph Lauren model kind of way. But beyond that, what draws me to him is that he sees this part of me, this way-deep-down part that I have managed to hide from *everyone.* Everyone except him. Huff knows the raw, ruinous part that tried to take me down. Huff would have gone down with that part of me without a second thought. And so I have to think that maybe leaving him was the only selfless gesture of my life. By leaving him, I saved him. From me.

I sigh. "Huff, we're not doing anything. We've been down this road, you know? Lanier doesn't want us dating, and I know why. I get it."

"But we're different now," he says. "You're different, Daphne." He pauses. "If you can tell me that these last few weeks you haven't felt what I feel, that you haven't imagined our next run-in the second we walk away, then I'll go home and I won't bother you again." He grins. "I might send you hate mail on Christmas Eve when I'm working. But that will be the end of it."

I know he's right, but I don't know how to repair what is broken between us. I don't know how to go back in time and be different. So I just say, "We should go." I stand up.

He stands too. He takes a step closer. I want to tell him to stop, only I can't.

"But if you *do* feel what I feel," he continues, "then I think we should try this again. It has been years, Daphne, and I still think about you all the time. I want to text you when something happens that you would think is funny. I want to ask your advice when I've had a hard day." He pauses again. I bite my lip, but I don't tell him that I also think about these things. When the thread of your life is sewn so tightly into someone else's, creating a new fabric doesn't mean the old one—durable and strong—disintegrates.

"Have you ever had this, what we have, with anyone else?" he asks.

It's brave, the way he says it.

"Does it matter, Huff? I mean, honestly, does it?"

He starts to open his mouth but closes it. He doesn't have to say anything. I know his question: *Why didn't you stay?*

Seven years ago, it seemed like such an easy answer, one my mom would have been proud of. *Love never leads anywhere good.* But as I stand in front of him now, this boy that made me safe, that made me feel loved, I wonder if maybe I was wrong all this time. Maybe love is all there is. And maybe, I'm seeing clearly now, I let it slip through my fingers.

Lanier

PLAYING WITH FIRE

THE WEDDING CEREMONY WAS OVER; THE BRIDESMAID RESPONSIBILities were finished. It was time to cut loose, relax, dance at the reception, and, obviously, obsessively critique everything down to the tiniest detail so Bryce and I would know what to do at our own wedding.

Music filled the night air and shoes were piled all around the pool deck so people could dance with an abandon I assumed was caused by the signature martinis that were being handed out like water. When you got right down to it, people having fun was the only thing that mattered.

Only, I wasn't quite having fun yet because I couldn't find Bryce. Where *was* he? It seemed like I was always looking for him lately. As I walked toward the house, I noticed my brother among the throngs of people and made my way toward him. He was too busy staring at something across the pool to notice me. I followed his gaze to see what he was so fixated on: Daphne.

She was laughing, holding Henry. She was something to see. But Huff had been down this road with her before, and it had ended horribly. Surely he wasn't thinking about that again? The idea made my stomach turn. He wasn't going to come to the wedding. And then he did. Was it to see her?

Huff turned as I reached him and almost jumped, as if I had woken him from a dream. "Hey, sis. Great party, huh?"

I nodded. "It's beautiful."

"You'll be doing this in just a few months." He paused, studying my face. "Hey, are you okay? You've been weird all night."

"I could ask you the same thing." I looked across the pool at Daphne, who was kissing Henry goodbye, Steven kissing him on the other cheek, as Henry held the hand of the sitter who was taking him home. I had to admit: When Daphne told Steven that she was pregnant and breaking up with him on the same day, I expected disastrous results. I thought her stepping back from their relationship to give Henry a stable life was ridiculous. It had all worked out beautifully, but at the time, I had questioned: If she'd gotten pregnant by Huff instead of Steven, would she have done the same thing? Or would they be a family now?

He shrugged. "I don't know what you mean."

"You do know, Huff. You're playing with fire. I love her, but she will burn you. Every time."

Huff sighed. "You don't know that, Lanier. Things change. She was in a bad place back then. Can you imagine the stress of going to school and holding down a job to pay for it all and managing everything in your life without any help from your parents? It brought out the worst in her, sure. But she isn't that girl anymore."

"Things change," I said. "People don't." I paused. "And, yes, she's in a different place in her life, and no one is prouder of her sobriety than I am. But she still doesn't want what you want." I looked over at her and Steven. I had an idea. "Plus . . . I mean, look at that happy little family. No one could come between them."

Huff studied my face. "I thought they were broken up."

"What gave you that idea?"

"Well, for one thing, they live in different towns."

Damn it. How did he know that? I laughed it off. "You know Daph. She needs her space."

I looked back over at Daphne, who was dancing with my dad. She had him laughing so hard that it made me smile. What's more, I didn't want her to change. I loved her. And I loved Huff. And their being together couldn't do anything but ruin that.

"I guess you're right," Huff said.

I pointed to the house. "I'm going to see if I can find Bryce."

Huff looked puzzled. "Want me to help?" He glanced back at Daphne.

I patted his arm. I knew what it was like to be at a wedding with an ex, to have all those old feelings rise to the surface. Thinking of that made me wonder if I would run into Rich McNabb during my bachelorette party weekend, and if those old feelings would flood back if I did. But that was so far in the past it didn't matter.

I walked into the house, where a few people were milling around, and spotted Bryce whispering into his phone in a corner on a leather bench by the door. It seemed like every time I looked for Bryce lately, I found him on his phone. I watched him for a moment, noticing how he seemed agitated—a little red, even. When he looked up and saw me, he ended the call quickly and rushed toward me.

I crossed my arms. "Bryce. What is going on?"

He shook his head. "It's just a work thing, babe."

"On a Saturday night? I'm sorry, but no one on your crew is working on a Saturday night." I thought for a second, then gasped. "Are you having an affair?"

He rolled his eyes with a smile. "Yes, Lanier. The secret's out. I'm having an affair with my mom's seventy-nine-year-old secretary." He held up the phone so I could see JENNY OWENS on the screen.

I did a gut check. I didn't actually think he was having an affair, but something had seemed off the last couple of weeks. All the champagne I'd had finally made me feel brave enough to say, "It's just that every time I turn around, you're on the phone, hiding somewhere."

He took a deep breath and smoothed his tuxedo jacket. "Honey, I'm sorry. I promise I'm dealing with something work-related. I also promise I'm not having an affair. Why would I mess this up when I have the greatest girl in the world?"

He leaned over, and I accepted his kiss halfheartedly. I furrowed my brow. He was a contractor, not a CIA agent. He didn't need to be so secretive. I knew Bryce—and everyone in his industry really—was having a hard time keeping up with demand, that workers were almost as scarce as materials, and everything was costing way more than quoted. But he could open up to me about this stuff. He just never did.

Bryce took my hand and twirled me around, putting his party face back on. "All I know is that it's Saturday night, it's gorgeous out, I have the most beautiful date here, and I want to show her off on that dance floor. Would you do me the honor?"

There he was. My Bryce was back. As he wrapped his arm around me, holding me close as we walked slowly back out to the pool, I wished I could help him fix whatever was going on at work. As we stood at the top of the steps, bathed in moonlight, watching the dancers crowding the floor, he said, "Babe, the stress of my job lately has me thinking."

"Thinking?"

"Yeah. I mean, instead of arguing with subs and apologizing to homeowners for supply chain issues I have no control over, I want to spend more time with you, help plan the wedding."

Bryce had stayed as far away from wedding planning as humanly possible, so this felt out of left field.

He cleared his throat. "What would you think about my working with my mother?"

I pulled away from him. "But, honey, you've worked so hard to build your business!"

He shrugged. "I know, but this has always been the plan. It's a family company, and I'm supposed to take it over. It's kind of why I was born."

Now I was really confused. I mean, yes, sure, Bryce had gone to business school before he got his contractor's license for that reason. But he loved what he did. "But you always said you'd never work for the family business."

"I know, but that wasn't reality. And I would be continuing the family legacy. With my wife."

"Your wife," I repeated. Even though I loved the way it sounded, something about this didn't sit quite right with me. "What am I missing? I'm confused here. You've spent years building your relationships with clients and doing beautiful work you're proud of. I mean, our house . . ." I put my hand over my heart. Our future house was a thing of beauty, and Bryce had built it almost all on his own.

He crossed his arms, his face darkening. "You have no idea the pressure I'm under, Lanier."

I looked around. Okay. So maybe that was true because he *wouldn't tell me.* But, even still, I couldn't very well hash all this out in the middle of a wedding without causing a scene.

"I need you to get on board, please, because I've already started wrapping up projects I can and handing over things I'm in the middle of," he said. His tone was so light, I almost missed what he was saying.

I gasped. "You can't quit in the middle of a project! You did this without even consulting me?"

"Lower your voice." Bryce looked around. "Without *consulting* you? I'm sorry. I didn't know I had to ask your permission for every move I make."

I crossed my arms. I was fuming. "Every move you make? Bryce, you didn't pick out new running shoes. You quit your job. That's one of the single biggest decisions a person could make, and you didn't even think to ask me about it. That's a problem. A big, huge problem." I paused, a realization washing over me. "So when were you going to tell me? Because it obviously wasn't now."

"Tomorrow," he said. I could tell he was trying to regain his composure. "I was going to tell you after the wedding."

I was dubious at best. "And all those phone calls? If they weren't about work, what were they about?"

He was sheepish. "Well, they were for work. Just my new work."

I laughed ironically. "Which is exactly why you didn't want to work for your mother in the first place. Remember? Long nights? No weekends? Zero work-life balance? You wanted time for us. You wanted time for our family."

"Well, Lanier, sure. That's all true. But we aren't even married yet. We don't actually have a family."

I glared at him. "You are absolutely right. We do not."

I walked down the steps into the throngs of people dancing and talking around the glittering swimming pool. This was supposed to be a happy night where I was solely focused on celebrating one of my best friends. I had pictured how Bryce and I would dance, how everyone would be dazzled by our love. I tried to calm myself down, but I couldn't help but think: If he could keep a secret this big, what else was he not telling me?

When I looked back, hoping to find my fiancé following me, he was laughing instead, eating a cocktail shrimp with one of the groomsmen. And I started to feel like maybe I didn't know him at all.

Daphne

GRAVITY

THE SUMMER OF 1998, THE SUMMER IT ALL BEGAN FOR MARY STUART, Lanier, and me, was the summer I realized I didn't have a normal family. The three of us were lying around in the Songbird Cabin on a rainy afternoon where we had just learned that if we put our legs up high enough, we could use our feet to pop the mattress on the top bunks up in the air. We'd been so busy at camp, I hadn't had time to feel homesick. But now, on this rainy day with no outdoor activities, it hit me: I missed my mom. Mary Stuart and Lanier missed theirs, too.

If my mom had taught me anything, it was that songs made people happy. So I decided to teach Mary Stuart and Lanier the lyrics to my favorite song my mom had taught me, Madonna's "I'll Remember," to brighten our spirits.

I was popping Lanier up in the top bunk when she hung her head over the side and said, "Hey, how do you know all the words to this song anyway?"

"Madonna is my mom's favorite singer, and the rule is when one of us cranks up her CD on the stereo, we have to jump on the bed and sing."

They looked at me like I had two heads.

"Your mom knows Madonna songs?" Lanier asked incredulously as Mary Stuart asked, "You mom lets you jump on the bed?"

"Your moms don't?"

They both shook their heads.

It came out through games of truth or dare and little nothing anecdotes throughout the week that Lanier's and Mary Stuart's moms never fed them cereal for dinner and McDonald's was a rare treat, not a three-times-a-week staple. And I got the distinct impression that their mothers would never leave them at home on a Saturday night with the TV as a babysitter while they had a date. Mostly because they were married, but also because, I was discovering, other moms didn't leave six-year-olds home alone. I wasn't concerned about those things. Just interested. You only know your reality until you're introduced to another one.

Twenty-four years later, I still remember those realizations, how each layer we peeled back drew my friends and me closer, made us a real family. And twenty-four years later, I'm realizing as I dance my heart out with all the other bridesmaids, trying not to think about Huff being in my general vicinity, my two best friends and I still remember our parts to the song I taught them that rainy Tuesday. I belt out the first line and Mary Stuart chimes in with the second. Lanier shouts her line into the crowd of dancers. Then we all bring it home, together, "I'll remember!"

Our singing has not improved. But our love, I'd venture to say, has grown even deeper. "Have you heard Henry sing this?" Lanier shouts to June, laughing.

She nods. "How do you think I know the lyrics?"

My mom was not perfect. But she taught me Madonna songs and bed-jumping freedom.

June; Lanier's parents, Paula and John; and Mary Stuart's parents join our little circle, and I'm reminded that while my mom might have been the fun one back then, there was another reason my life was noticeably different from my friends'. There still is. Mary Stuart and Lanier have amazing, doting fathers who took them for ice cream and to father-daughter dances and to Build-A-Bear when they were growing up. They have fathers who walk them down the aisle and show off their goofy dance moves. I never had that.

Maybe June notices something in my face because she slides closer, takes my hand, and squeezes it. When the music slows, we trail off to the side of the dance floor and Paula and John follow. Mary Stuart turns to her dad for a dance. John puts his arm around me. "When you get married, do I get to walk you down the aisle?"

I lean my head against his shoulder. He truly is the closest thing I've ever had to a father. "John, you know I'm not getting married."

"Well, if you change your mind, I'm available." He does a little cha-cha step and says, "And don't forget our dance."

We all laugh. He walks away to get us some cake, and Paula asks, "Is it hard, Daph? Nights like these?"

Paula never avoids the hard stuff. She never has. Even when my mom was still around, it was often Paula who mothered me. She gave a horrified and aghast Lanier and me "the talk." She always knew the right thing to say when we had broken hearts or drama with friends. Not with each other. No. Lanier and I never fought—except the one time.

I shook my head. "I don't even know my father, Paula. Even those three years I had to live with Ray, we were like Craigslist roommates with different schedules."

After my mom died and I moved in with my dad—who'd left when I was eighteen months old and only showed up a handful of times in the eleven years that followed—I was pretty much on my own. Sure, sometimes we watched a TV show together and sometimes he took me to the batting cages. There was even one time he took me to his new girlfriend's trailer at the lake for the weekend. But, in retrospect, that was more to appear like a loving father to her; it had nothing to do with me. Most of the time I lived with him we simply coexisted, passing each other silently in the hallways.

"Even still . . ." Paula trailed off.

"I always think about it," June said. "I'm fifty years old and every wedding is a reminder of the parents I lost."

I nod. "Well, every wedding is a reminder of the parent I lost. But Ray I never had."

That was true. When I moved in with Ray, a part of me had been hopeful that we would find a way to connect. That was a pipe dream.

Bryce approaches and nods for me to come over to him, and I wonder what sort of father he'll be. "I'm going to grab some water," I call, but everyone is having so much fun they barely notice.

"What do you want?" I ask, quietly, coldly, once I'm off in the corner of the pool deck with him.

"I handed off all my jobs," he says. "I'm going to go work for my mother."

I raise an eyebrow at him. "O-kayyyy . . . Why?"

"Because those were her conditions. She helps me dig my way out of this mess, I come work for the family business."

I shake my head.

"What?"

"I just don't get it, Bryce. You have the world at your fingertips. You have the money and the family and the fiancée and everything. What else did you need?"

He looks out at the dance floor at Lanier, then back at me. "I grew up in this perfect family of these uber-successful people and I didn't want to be handed everything. Do you have any idea the pressure I have been under my entire life to make it big on my own?"

I cross my arms. "Bryce, for most of my life I didn't have anyone who cared whether I ate dinner, let alone became successful in business, so you aren't going to out–sob story me."

"Okay, fine. But do you know how utterly humiliating it was to have to run to my mother, to have to beg her to save me because it was all smoke and mirrors? Because I lost it all?"

I do feel the tiniest bit bad for him. "Do you know who will understand the need for personal success bringing out your worst colors?" He rolls his eyes. "Your fiancée. Because wanting to prove herself made her do some dumb things when she was younger. But you owe it to her to tell her. And even if you don't think she deserves the truth, Cape Carolina is tiny. She will find out."

He shakes his head. "I don't think so."

"Why in the hell not?"

"Everyone has to sign an NDA before they get their first payment. And who wouldn't want their money?"

That was, I suspected, Bryce's latest in a long line of incorrect thoughts. I was certain there was *someone* who would rather make him—or his family—pay. Local media made a lot of enemies. "Have they all signed?"

He bit his lip. "No. But I'm hopeful they will."

So there were still a million reasons Bryce wasn't in the clear. He had to know that all the vendors and subs were pretty tight in Cape Carolina; they would all be talking about this. "She deserves to know," I say. "This is far from an airtight plan, and, trust me, she will find out. It will be a lot better coming from you than a stranger."

"Daphne, you're being unreasonable. I'm not a bad guy. I got in over my head and got behind on some payments. It's not that big a deal."

I nod. "Great. Then if it's not that big a deal, tell her."

He shakes his head again.

"You stole hundreds of thousands of dollars from people, Bryce. How can you sugarcoat that, even to yourself?"

He put up his finger. "Not stole. Got behind on paying. This is basically in the past. Everyone has a past, Daphne. Even you, if you'll recall."

It was kind of a low blow. It was also true. But my past *was* in the past. Bryce's situation was unfolding in real time. "I want to be really clear," I said. "If you don't tell her, I will."

"You know you can't do that," he says.

"And why not?" I know why not, but I wonder if he's callous enough to actually say it to my face.

"If you tell, I'll turn you in to the bar, Daphne. I'm sorry. But I have to protect my family."

I want to slap him. His *family*? Protect his *family*? "*I* am Lanier's family." I pause. "Bryce, I am fully aware that telling her means breaking an oath, one I take seriously. If I tell her, I will absolutely turn myself in." I start to leave, but I can't resist one last jab. "Because I, unlike you, have principles."

I walk away, seething. Needing a minute, I walk inside the house. I can't bear the thought of going into Mary Stuart's parents' giant bathroom, which I'm sure is full of a dozen chatty, drunk women in evening gowns, so I head for the unmarked powder room in the back corner of the long hallway. I need to clear my head.

I open the powder room door and feel it hit someone. "Oh my gosh!" I say. "I'm so sorry!" But then my eyes adjust to the light. In one smooth motion, Huff pulls me into the room, reaches above my head, and slams the door shut as I hit the lock. "I'm not," he whispers, his nose grazing mine.

"You're here," I say, touching his face.

"I've always been here," he says.

It's like muscle memory takes over and no time has passed at all. Before I know what's happening, Lanier and Bryce and the most impossible choice I've ever had to make fly out of my mind. All that's left is Huff. My mouth is on his and my arms are around his neck, and he's lifting me up and I realize that this is what is missing in my life. He is what is missing.

And that memory, I think, the way it feels so normal and urgent, is what allows me to kiss him with my legs wrapped around his waist, the chiffon of my dress trapped tightly and uncomfortably around my legs. We kiss until we cannot breathe and he, panting, lowers me onto the sink. In my mind, for a moment, this is just another party with loud music and me undoing his leather belt, worn smooth with use, with a practiced hand that is used to freeing him from his pants as quickly and efficiently as possible.

He hikes my dress up and sweeps my thong to the side and is inside me with such perfectly practiced tenderness that he puts his hand over my mouth to cover the noise I make a millisecond before I make it. Our mouths are intertwined, and he is pulling me closer and closer like maybe this time he can make me stay, like maybe this time our story can have a different ending. And I realize that this entire day has been leading to this moment.

The past few weeks we've avoided the talks about "us," but, even still, we've grown closer and, at times, it feels like we haven't skipped a beat. While I want this to be a stupid wedding fling, I know that it is more than that. I know that I have carried Huff in my heart all these years; I have never let him go.

As if we've been practicing it every day for the past seven years we've been apart, our breaths quicken and fall at the exact same pace, a crescendo in a melody that we had, at one time in our lives, practiced until perfect. He kisses me one last time, rests his forehead on mine, and I marvel at how perfectly in sync we still are.

I smile, but Huff doesn't. He steps away, and I can see the reality of this moment hitting him. We are not teenagers. We are thirty and thirty-two years old, and we should *not* have done this.

A look of terror crosses his face. "I can't."

Sadness and guilt flood through me all at once. "I know," I say quickly. "I'm sorry. We shouldn't—"

He interrupts me. "No. I can't be apart from you again. I need you, Daphne. Seeing you these last few weeks has reminded me that what I have with you, I don't have with anyone else. Not *this*," he points from himself to me, and I know he means our chemistry, our physical connection. "But the way we see eye to eye, the way we challenge each other. Leave Steven. We should be together."

Now I am panicking, and I try to make a joke. "You are ruining our cool, nostalgic, super-hot wedding sex."

It sort of works. He flashes me a small smile, and I absolutely melt.

"Besides, I'm not with Steven," I say. "I haven't been with Steven for years. I thought you knew that."

"But Lanier said . . ." His face registers his sister's lie, and he bangs the heel of his hand on the wall. "Damn it, Lanier."

I am, I have to admit, upset now too. She told him I was with

Steven? The tiniest part of me has hoped she would approve of this relationship now, if there ever was one. But Lanier apparently still doesn't trust me.

"Daph, forget Lanier. Let's do this. Finally."

I consider his offer briefly because, well, it's what I *want* to do. But I shake my head. "If we get together right now, Lanier will know it's because we met up at the wedding and she'll blame me. She'll be furious."

Huff sighs and rolls his eyes. "Damn, Daph. Why do you care so much? What happened back then was a long time ago. She has to realize that."

He is partially right. But our big breakup, when we were twenty-three and twenty-five, had less to do with her and more with what I'd thought was the right thing. But it was easier to blame her than to blame myself. Seven years ago, I still had my mother's voice in my head—and her addictive nature in my body. I was afraid then that love would drown me, just like it had my mother. Lanier pleaded with me not to take Huff down with me. I loved him too much to do that.

The irony that I later found myself sober, pregnant, and starting a family with a man I didn't love as much wasn't lost on me.

But instead of saying that, I say, "Huff, you have this big, magical, amazing family. I have Lanier. So losing her would be like losing everything and everyone."

He wraps me in a hug. "You have me, Daphne," he whispers. "You always have." He pulls back and kisses me. "You are all I care about. I'm not going to lose you again."

I look up into his sad eyes, and I start to feel that same thing I have always felt for him. And I realize: As much as I'm trying to deny it, I've already made my decision. "We'll wait to tell Lanier?" I whisper.

He nods. "As long as you want."

He kisses me, and despite how things ended last time, I know—have always known—that we belong to each other. Like sand and the ocean. Like flowers and the soil. Like songbirds and the sky.

• • •

Huff and I stagger our times leaving the bathroom. After he leaves, I fix my hair in the mirror, reapply gloss to my swollen lips. All the while, I'm smiling. I can't wipe the huge, Huff-imposed grin off my face. When I pass Bryce walking through the front hallway, I can't even be ruffled because I am so filled with this wonderful feeling.

I glide outside to the patio to stand next to June. Do I look different? Can everyone see how finding where I'm supposed to be—and who I'm supposed to be with—has changed me?

The beautiful, and, well, a little sweaty bride throws her arms around June and me. I can tell she is tipsy. As we watch people start to clear out, she focuses her attention on Bryce, who is schmoozing some cute waitress a few steps down on the pool deck. I want to throw my glass at him.

"I just don't think he's right for her," Mary Stuart says abruptly, gaze slightly unfocused. Then she gasps, as if realizing she didn't mean to say that out loud.

Sometimes I underestimate Mary Stuart. She is tall with this long blond hair that always falls perfectly into place and these adorable bangs that perfectly frame her face. This glittering life force—half Zen master, half golden retriever—surrounds her. She is one of those people who just makes everything better. She is the go-to publicist for local celebs: authors, up-and-coming bands, famous chefs. And, I'm seeing now, she's a better judge of character than I am.

"Really?" June asks. "Why?"

Mary Stuart shakes her head. "I shouldn't say this, but I just worry.

I've always felt like he's distracting her or something. Whisking her away on all those fancy trips and building her that amazing house and I don't know . . ."

"Yes, what a jerk," June says, rolling her eyes at me.

I shrug, but I soften toward him then. Because while, yes, I do think Bryce is trying to make Lanier happy, I also think he's underestimated his fiancée. Lanier's happiest moments are in her tiny condo with her book and her tea. For him to think he has to impress her with big displays makes me realize he doesn't know her as well as he should—you know, embezzlement aside.

"I don't totally disagree," I admit.

June gasps. "I thought you loved him. For a little while, you talked about him so much I was afraid you had a secret crush that was going to end very poorly."

I laugh. "*Loved.* Past tense. And I did love him, but never for me. Only for Lanier." Then I pause. "Am I a horrible matchmaker?"

Mary Stuart smiles. "Nah. You picked me, didn't you? And we're a perfect match." She winks.

I did. I picked her. And Lanier. And Huff, who is nowhere to be seen. I picked Steven, who is motioning for June to come dance with him. She laughs and joins him on the dance floor. But the fact that Bryce snowed me so completely shakes me. Maybe he isn't a bad guy; maybe he just made a bad choice. Maybe I should let it go. But whether Lanier lets it go is a choice she has the right to make.

"Think we could break them up?" Mary Stuart asks suddenly.

Everything inside me lights up. Why haven't I thought of this? I don't have to tell the truth. I don't have to get disbarred or choose between my best friend and my family's stability. The answer is so clear, and it was right there all along. "Yes!" I say. "Yes! We just make her see what we see, and she'll call off the wedding." This gives me an idea. "Hey, could you do Lanier's bachelorette at camp weekend after next?"

Mary Stuart nods. "For sure. Can Lanier?"

I'm going to say that Lanier has only two weekends she can't make work, but I can see Mary Stuart's mind has floated somewhere else, her eyes glassy. I follow her gaze across the pool to Ted. She sucks her breath. She looks at me, her face scrunching in horror.

"I just became a Hoffenmeyer."

I smile. Ted and Mary Stuart are kind of a mismatch. Ted is plain, a little chubby, and exactly Mary Stuart's height when she isn't wearing heels. She didn't accept his offer of a first date for weeks after they met at a magazine launch party Mary Stuart was coordinating and Ted was attending. But Ted chased her relentlessly and, once he finally caught her, he worshipped her. She seemed genuinely happy, and that was what mattered.

"But you love that Hoffenmeyer over there with all your heart," I remind her.

She smiles, and we watch as Huff joins Ted, clapping him on the back. Mary Stuart looks at me seriously. "I know you're never getting married and blah, blah, blah, but I swear, Daph, if you find someone you love as much as I love Ted, I think you'll change your mind."

I don't answer, but as Huff catches my eye, smiling at me from across the way, a tingling knowledge washes over me: I already have.

June

HAPPY PLACE

THE GLOW OF THE WEDDING HAD WORN OFF, AND I WAS BACK IN MY happy place—my camp—knowing that it might not be my happy place for much longer. I walked to the end of the long dock and sat down, feet swinging, like my sister and I used to do when we were little girls. I hadn't been able to save my sister. And now, I might not be able to save Holly Springs.

I took a deep breath, listening to the rustle of the light breeze through the trees on the riverbank. The wooden swim platform bobbed effortlessly in the river twenty-five yards in the distance. I could still remember the first time I swam all the way out to it alone, how I felt like I could take on the world, I could do anything, be anyone. Where had that little girl gone?

She was tired. Tired of fighting a battle every day. And, while I thought the fight was worth it, registration was down, donations were down, and we'd even lost a few grants for scholarship campers. I needed to be out provisioning for Lanier's bachelorette party this weekend, but I had a phone call to make first. It was one I didn't want to make, but at this point, it was inevitable.

I sighed and got up, walking back down the dock, taking in the sight of the sailing hut, the scattered cabins, and the basketball court as I made my way toward my office. I remembered the day I made the command decision, twenty-six years ago, to buy an ailing, aging girls' summer camp. It was impulsive at best, insane at worst, but I was twenty-four years old and feeling a type of pain I didn't know was possible.

After my parents died in a terrible car accident—and left both me and Melanie a sizable amount of money in their will—I wanted to go where I felt safest, happiest. Only one place came to mind.

When I got to camp the day after their funeral, it looked eerie, desolate, lonely. I was used to this place being filled with excited girls and young women holding painted welcome signs, hugging, cheering, waving. But now, all of that was gone. A chain hung at the camp entrance with two removable placards attached: NO TRESPASSING. FOR SALE.

I knew instantly I would use the money my parents had left me to buy Camp Holly Springs.

I unfastened the clasp holding the chain to an eye hook, ignoring the NO TRESPASSING sign. That didn't apply to me. I drove to the director's hut, and when I opened the door, Karen Stevenson, the camp's owner, had her head down on the office desk. She startled when I entered.

"June!" She stood to hug me.

"Hi, Karen." I burst into tears, the story of my parents' death pouring out.

It was only when I finished that I realized she was crying too. "I'm so sorry, June. Doubly so. I'm sorry about your parents, and I'm sorry to say that I've lost the camp," she said. "I can't afford to keep it open anymore, this magical place that so many little girls have come to love."

I nodded. "I want to buy it."

She laughed, wiping her eyes. "No, June. It isn't profitable anymore. I can't let you. I'll probably sell it for the land. Trust me, this is no investment."

"What do you want for it?"

It was a little bit more than my inheritance, after taxes. I told her what I could pay, and Karen sent me away. "Sleep on it, June. If you still want it in a month, I'll agree. I won't sell it to anyone else."

One month later, we signed the papers. Karen agreed to stay on in a volunteer capacity through my first summer. We visited colleges and sororities, offered nights off, flexible weeks, and community service hours for counselors. It took three years to get Holly Springs back in the black, but we survived. And for twenty-three years after that, we thrived. I still couldn't understand how my wonderful camp didn't qualify for so many of the federal funds that businesses received during the pandemic to keep them afloat. But every application was rejected; every answer was no.

And so, now, there was only one thing left to do.

I sat down at my desk in the director's office, picked up the heavy black phone that had been on this desk—remarkably—since the camp opened in the late 1940s, and dialed Rock Springs, our brother all-boys camp just down the river. Our finances weren't tied together, but our fates were. Brothers and sisters and friends attended these two camps. We had events together all summer long. I didn't expect Rich to answer, but I recognized his voice right away when he did. "Rich, it's June."

"Oh, hi," he said. I could hear him brighten, and I wanted to yell, *This isn't a happy call!*

I sighed. "This isn't a call I wanted to make, Rich, but I have to tell you something—in confidence, of course."

"Oh, okay." I could hear the nerves in his voice.

"I've tried, Rich. I swear I have. I need you to know that. But I can't keep the camp going anymore. After losing an entire season to the pandemic . . . Well, now, we aren't even making ends meet. I know we made a pact not to sell out, but, Rich, I don't have a choice. I have an enthusiastic investor, and I think I have to let the property go."

There was silence on the other end of the line. We had sworn that we would hold fast to our camps, not sell out because of the money being waved in our faces. But I wasn't being swayed by the money. My back was against the wall. I could no longer bail out the ship that was sinking me. "When are you going to tell the developers?" Rich finally asked. "I want to be prepared because once you say yes, I'm going to be bombarded again." He paused, as if deciding whether to remind me. "Plus, there's the staffing issue . . ."

"I know, Rich. I know. And I really am sorry." Rock Springs and Holly Springs shared several executive-level employees. Not only would I lose the camp, but at least two of them would lose their jobs.

I wrapped the phone cord around my finger. How would I reacclimate to a world that had moved past corded phones, to a world where decent cell service was always a thing? The developers offered to leave me two acres to build my dream house. But I couldn't stay, looking out over the water at this place that had stolen my heart and watch it change irreparably, go from rustic cabins to condos or whatever other travesty they'd build here. "Daphne is hosting a bachelorette party here this weekend. I'll tell the girls then and the developers after that."

"You must be devastated, June. I wish I could help." Rich cleared his throat. "But I hope the party lifts your spirits. Who's, um, Daphne having down?" Rich was trying to sound casual, but anyone who knew him would know who he was asking about.

I laughed. "Mary Stuart . . . *Lanier* . . ." I paused. "It's actually Lanier's bachelorette party," I said gently.

"Oh," he sputtered. "I had no idea." He paused. "Well, then, I'm happy for her."

"You sound it."

We both laughed, and the normalcy of the conversation was a balm for my heart, which felt so very battered this morning.

"I'm sorry, June. I really am. The relationship between our camps for all these years has been really special, and I hate to lose it."

"Yes," I said, trying to lighten the mood. "But can you imagine if this had gone the other way? If the girls' camp couldn't have dances with the boys' camp anymore, it would have ruined us! The boys will be relieved for another night of no girls allowed."

Rich laughed. "I think the boys will be sorrier than they let on. Some special matches were made at those dances."

As we said our goodbyes, it hit me that he might have been talking about himself and Lanier. And everything inside me ached for him. Rich had dated in the years after he and Lanier broke up, of course. But I had a feeling that his crazy schedule made it impossible for him to really get to know anyone on a deeper level. Even still, he seemed happy. I knew what it was to choose camp over a traditional family. Rich had made the same choice. For almost three decades I had believed it was the right one. But now, staring down the barrel of being alone, my life's purpose taken from me at fifty years old, I wasn't so sure.

I had imagined growing old here, handing the camp over to a new executive director but staying on to dry the tears of homesick campers, continuing to mother hundreds of girls every summer since I had never had children of my own. I had made a sacrifice. And it was only now, as I gathered my bag to head back to my cabin, that I wondered whether I had made the right choice after all.

Daphne

CROSSES

"NO, YOU HANG UP FIRST," I SAY, EMITTING A SOUND THAT CAN ONLY be described as a giggle as I drive past the Camp Holly Springs sign.

"You know that's impossible," Huff says. "I will reschedule my next surgery to avoid hanging up first."

After a few more rounds of this, I finally bite the bullet and hang up. I am going to *have to* wipe this Huff-induced, thousand-watt grin off my face if I want to hide what is going on from my best friends. Ever since the wedding, Huff and I have been talking and texting nonstop and, on Steven's weekend with Henry, I snuck away to Huff's house for dinner. It isn't just that being back with him gives me these delicious butterflies; it's easy. It's right. And I am living for the next time we'll be together. I've never been happier. So I will just have to channel my glee into *Bachelorette Party! Woo-hoo!*

The arm of the front gate at Holly Springs is up, and the gatehouse is empty. When campers arrive, it will be manned to make sure no one comes in who shouldn't—and no one goes out. But any good counselor can find the path through the woods from Holly Springs to Rock Springs . . .

I pull down the road, which is lined with huge oak and pine trees. It's as if it has been cut through the forest while maintaining as much of the foliage as possible. I'm surprised that I get warm tingles all over. The first time I came here is never far from my mind, and, for just a moment, I am six again, thrilled to spend the entire summer with my aunt.

Now, as I drive past the swim lake with its brightly colored blob, twisty slide, and my personal favorite, the slip-and-slide that is positioned perfectly on the hillside so it drops directly into the lake, I think of all the good times I had with my best friends here. And I focus on the task at hand. If Mary Stuart and I are able to convince Lanier that Bryce isn't a great guy, maybe I won't have to choose between my law license and my best friend. Maybe I can have everything I want. Is that even possible?

I pull into the parking space in front of the doctor's quarters, a wood cabin with three separate rooms where the doctors who volunteer their time during the summer live. That way, they're available to see patients in the infirmary in case of emergencies, or, more likely, the "rumpy rash" girls get from too much time in wet bathing suits. A thud on my car window makes me scream with delight.

I leap out and practically tackle Mary Stuart. "How are you, old married lady?"

She laughs. "I'm great. Super great!"

"Well, I'm thrilled, but maybe let's not be the poster child for marriage this weekend?"

She laughs. "Nope. No poster child here. But we can't be obvious. Subtle sabotage is the way to go."

"Speaking of subtle . . ." I reach onto my front seat and pull out the Tupperware full of penis-shaped Jell-O shots Finn has made for this blessed occasion.

Mary Stuart nods seriously. "Class all the way."

I hand them to her. "Your hard thing this week, my friend."

She shakes her head. "I couldn't bring myself to make them." She pauses. "Hey, I'll help you unload, but let's decorate and then go sit by the river before Lanier gets here."

I nod. Twenty minutes later, the doctor's quarters are laced with streamers and a raunchy take on pin the tail on the donkey that features a super-cringy man in a thong. Mary Stuart and I are sitting in a pair of chairs by the sparkling river, waiting for Lanier and June. "Be honest," I say. "How is it being married? I mean, I know it's new, but how do you feel?"

She looks over at me sleepily and smiles. I take comfort in the smattering of freckles across the bridge of her nose that has never changed. "I feel safe. I feel like I crossed some sort of finish line."

"That sounds . . . nice? Although maybe I'll get there sooner rather than later." I immediately regret my words. Keeping this secret's going to be tougher than I thought.

She sits up, at attention. "Oh my gosh! Are you dating someone? Like seriously?" Then she gasps. "You and Huff seemed pretty flirty at the wedding . . ."

I can't straight-up lie to her. I just can't. So I make a face like she's being ridiculous. Fortunately, it works.

She snaps her fingers. "Are you finally getting together with hunky surfer god?"

I shake my head, and she sighs. Mary Stuart and Lanier cannot understand why Steven and I aren't together. For years, it was obvious that he was too young, too immature for the commitment of a child *and* me. But now it is abundantly clear to me what my reservations were: Huff. My reservations were Huff. "I love Steven. I always will. But I'm not *in love* with him, and what we have just works, you know? We coparent like a dream, and Henry's world is stable. I'll do anything to keep it that way."

"Any man that will stay at your house on his weekends with your child is kind of the dream coparent. But Daph, be honest: Do you think having Steven so much a part of your life holds you back from finding your person?"

I shrug, but I know the answer. It doesn't hold me back at all. Because I have already found my person. And now I just have to hope I am brave enough to let him love me the way he wants to, that I can overcome that little voice in my head telling me I am my mother, that love will ruin everything, that letting another man in my life will ruin Henry's.

"Okay. So there's no steamy love affair. But how was it seeing Huff at the wedding?" It's almost like Mary Stuart knows what I'm thinking.

I know I can hash this out with her. I know she will be on my side, squeal about our hot bathroom sex. But I can't risk Lanier finding out. Not yet, anyway.

So I just say, "Oh, you know. Kind of nostalgic. A little weird." I pause, but before I can continue bluffing, I hear June trill, "My girls! You are here!"

I turn and stand to see my tiny aunt, with her short, cropped hair and green Camp Holly Springs T-shirt, running toward us. Sometimes, when I see her, I get a flash of my mother. They couldn't be more different. My mother had long hair, perfectly applied makeup, and was as glamorous as all get out. June could not be fresher-faced. But they have the same lips, the same cheekbones, and the same forehead, which sometimes breaks my heart just a little. We envelop each other in a group hug that feels so familiar that, in the next breath, I'm happy I have a reminder of my mother and the good times.

June pulls away. "Well, I broke the news to Rich that Lanier is getting married."

Mary Stuart makes a horrified face, but, in an instant, it changes to inquisitive. "Wait. Do you think he's still pining for her?"

We share a glance, and June is too quick, too attuned to the ways of women—and most especially the three of us—to miss it.

"Do not meddle, girls. I'm telling you. You never come out on top." She pauses. "But yes, I will say there was something a little like longing in that poor man's voice."

"Longing," Mary Stuart says. "I can work with that."

"Girls . . . What are you up to?"

June raises her eyebrows because, without relaying any details, I have intimated that something shady is going on with Bryce. Even before this debacle, she had a lot of questions about him. But I wrote her suspicions off as a general distrust of men. I wonder if that is why she is still alone, or if it has more to do with being so scarred from losing everyone she has ever loved. Everyone except for me, that is. I long to pull her into her tiny cabin, curl up in her chair, and get her advice about Huff and Lanier and Bryce and everything going wrong in my life. But I can't. I'm a grown-up now, and these secrets are my crosses to bear. She has her own crosses, and, not for the first time, I wonder if I will ever truly know what they are.

Lanier

GOOD TASTE

I HAD NOT BEEN MY BEST SELF SINCE THE WEDDING, TO PUT IT mildly. Bryce and I had bickered about everything except the fact that he had quit his job and started working for his mother. Every time I asked him why he had done this total one-eighty on his career, he changed the subject or said something cutting. I knew I needed to delve deeper, but there was something holding me back. The only thing that had kept me going was looking forward to my bachelorette party. Well, that, and this bright, shining moment.

The door to Bookmasters opened with the happy tinkle of a bell that always meant good news. A book-loving customer, a child wanting to learn something new, or, best of all, the mailman! The UPS woman! The FedEx guy! Today's visitor was Judy the mailwoman, with a stack of manila envelopes. That meant early copies of the books I'd been waiting for had just arrived. "I left a couple boxes around back, too," Judy said.

I scanned through the envelopes, tucking a few under my arm, and pointed to the counter. "I left some books for you," I said.

She put her hand to her heart. "Have I ever told you that of everyone I deliver to, you're my favorite?"

I looked at her skeptically. "I know Mr. Adams at the deli tips you twenty bucks like every day. There's no way that's true." I paused. "For the record, if I could afford it, I would too."

"What you lack in cash, you make up for in good taste."

I laughed. It was true that I gave books to Judy quite often. Not every day, but at least a few times a month.

She grabbed the books as I opened a bill from a distributor. "Let me know what you think!" I said. "I still need your 'Judy Pick' for next month." Our mail lady was nothing short of a local celeb. Obviously, she got a staff pick.

She squeezed the books to her chest. "Best day ever!"

A text from Mary Stuart came through on our group chain saying the exact same thing.

I texted her back furiously.

I'm out of here as soon as my replacement walks through the door. My bags are packed. My car is gassed up. I cannot wait.

It was immediately followed by a text from Huff.

Call me if you need bail money this weekend.

I sent him back an eye roll emoji.

There's only so much trouble we can get into at camp . . .

Uh-huh. You have a short memory.

The bell tinkled again, and when I looked up, I didn't feel happy, which terrified me. Because one should feel happy when her fiancé walks through the door with roses.

"I'm here to bring a peace offering," Bryce said, approaching the counter.

The flowers *were* beautiful.

"Bryce, I don't want a peace offering. I want a partner. If we're going to be married, we need to be a team. We can't keep secrets. Which is what I've been saying."

He set the roses down and sighed. "That's not reality, Lanier."

Something washed over me. Anger? Fear, maybe? "I'm sorry, what? *That's not reality?*"

"Look, no one can know everything about someone. These couples who are like, 'Oh, we're totally honest with each other?' They're lying. She's DMing her old boyfriend and he's keeping private tabs for his porn."

I was flabbergasted. "So, is that what you're doing?"

"No. I'm just saying that this idealized version of coupledom doesn't exist. I love you. I want to be with you. Isn't that enough?"

I felt like we had diverged quite far from the main issue, which was his quitting his job without telling me. But maybe there was a bigger issue. A fundamental issue. For the second time in far too short a period, I wasn't sure I knew this man at all.

"I literally don't know what to say to you right now. I'm getting ready to leave for my bachelorette party weekend, and I'm not sure I want to celebrate being legally bound to a man who doesn't believe the truth is important." I paused. "Is this what you're bringing to your new journalism career? Gloss over the facts and tell whatever story you want?"

Bryce rolled his eyes. "I'm there for the business end, not the stories. And I think you're being really immature."

"Okay. Well, thanks. I think that's the note you leave on."

He took a deep breath. "Lanier, we're in our thirties. There's no way I know everything about you."

"Of course you do!" I knew that wasn't *exactly* true. But, still, it didn't sit right with me. The only thing I'd ever kept from Bryce was something that didn't affect our relationship; it was in the past. But his job—and his inability to tell me the truth about it—*did* very much affect our present.

"Okay, fine. Whatever," Bryce said. "I'm just saying not knowing every bit of someone isn't the worst thing. And, look, even when we're married, some decisions are still going to be personal. For each of us. This was one of those."

Before I could respond, the bell tinkled and my most bookish employee, Kimberly—a woman in her midsixties with streaks of pink in her gray hair—entered. I pinned on a smile. "I'm so glad you're here! Thank you so much for taking over so I can leave this weekend."

As she approached the counter, I said, "I've left the story time volunteer's number out in case you want to call to remind him, and Judy just brought a delivery that needs to be shelved. I've left a spreadsheet of preorders that should be arriving in the next couple of days, and—"

"Lanier, I've got this. I've worked here for years."

"Yes. Okay. I know."

"Go have fun. Don't worry about a thing."

"I won't! Thank you!" I walked out the door, purse in hand, with Bryce following me. I deliberately left the roses.

He opened my car door, closing it behind me. I didn't want to leave angry, so I rolled down the window. I was all ready to smooth this over, make up, and kiss goodbye until he said, "So, back there. You were honest with Kimberly? You weren't worried at all about leaving for the weekend? That happy face you put on—that was real?"

"Of course it wasn't real!" I snapped. "But I don't want to marry Kimberly!"

I started the car and drove away before I could say what I wanted to, the thing I couldn't take back: *And, right now, I don't want to marry you either.*

• • •

It is more than a little difficult to pretend to be in happy, bachelorette party spirits when you have left things in such colossal disarray with the man you are supposed to marry. But I was trying my absolute best to seem like the glowing, blushing bride-to-be because Daphne, who I knew was insanely busy, and Mary Stuart, who had left her husband in that can't-breathe-without-you phase of newlywedness, and June, who was probably a little over bachelorette parties, had put so much time and energy into making this the perfect weekend.

"Do we need our life jackets?" Mary Stuart asked as Daphne readied one of Camp Holly Springs's many Flying Scots for our sunset cruise down the river. She was, without a doubt, the best sailor I had ever known. She had gotten us out of a lot of scrapes. And, yeah, maybe she'd gotten us into a few too . . . But that's why we loved her. She made everything more fun. And now, she was so excited for me, she couldn't keep the grin off her face. That was a good friend.

"I mean, we're at camp," she said. "Let's play by camp rules, right?" She tossed us each a life jacket.

"Do you have a radio?" I joked. There was no one in the tower so there wasn't anyone to radio to anyway.

"I'd leave your phones," Daphne said. "It's gusting pretty hard out here, and I don't want anything to get wet."

She had her blond hair in a long braid, and her face was clean and makeup-free. My best friend had a lot of great versions. Mommy Daphne. Lawyer Daphne. But Camp Daphne? I loved her best of all.

We stepped into the boat, and like old times, Daphne handed us each a jib line while she took control of the main sail and the tiller. "Remember when we had to take the sailing test without these?" she asked.

"Yeah, I remember. I failed the first two times."

She put her hand to her mouth. "Sorry. I forgot that part. But you eventually passed!"

I waved it away. "I did—and at least I *tried*," I said, looking pointedly at Mary Stuart.

She shrugged. "I'm sorry, okay. I'm good at horses. I'm great at lacrosse. Not everyone can be a star sailor."

The wind caught the sail, and we were off on our sunset cruise, in the direction of Camp Rock Springs. It was a little loop we knew well, one that would have us back at Holly Springs in an hour or so.

"Man, we had some fun nights with those guys when we were counselors, didn't we?" Daphne asked, as if reading my mind.

"Some of us more than others," Mary Stuart said.

I rolled my eyes, pretending I didn't immediately think of Rich McNabb, about those nights I thought our love would last forever. "Guys, this is my bachelorette party. We're supposed to be talking about my deep, forever love with Bryce, not dancing around a failed relationship from years ago."

"Nonsense!" Mary Stuart protested. "Your bachelorette party is where you wax poetic about what might have been. It's when you get everyone out of your system before you're legally bound to one man forever."

That was an interesting theory. I looked at Daphne. She nodded. "She's totally right. Plus, I mean, it's a bachelorette party. There aren't supposed to be rules."

On that note, Mary Stuart popped the top on a tiny bottle of champagne and handed it to me. I loved the sound of the wind on the mainsail and jib sheet, the feeling of being so close to the water. And it was all the better when Daphne was captaining. I had sailed a handful of times since camp, and I loved that I could still do it well. But today, it was even better not to have to do it at all. Bryce hated sailing, so it probably wasn't something I would do a lot of in the future.

"This is the best bachelorette party I could have ever imagined," I said. "My two favorite friends, my favorite place, low-key perfection."

"Wait until the stripper gets here on his sailboat." Mary Stuart wriggled her eyebrows.

I picked at the label on the champagne bottle and looked up at Daphne. "Since we're in the middle of nothingness, I feel like I need to unburden myself. But I can't have you holding this over my head once we get back to shore."

Daphne raised her eyebrow, but it was Mary Stuart who chimed in. "You know you can tell us anything. Camp rules."

"When we get back to shore it never happened," Daphne reminded us, as if I could ever forget what "camp rules" meant.

Mary Stuart motioned that her lips were zipped.

"You guys, Bryce quit his job and went to work for his mother and didn't even tell me. And, I mean, it isn't an easy job to quit. He literally just, like, passed his in-progress builds off to another builder. He keeps saying it's a 'personal decision,' but I have to think there's something he's not telling me."

Mary Stuart nodded sympathetically, while Daphne, who had been taking a sip of water, started to choke. She put her hand up, signifying that she was okay.

Mary Stuart glared at Daphne. "That couldn't feel great," she said.

I peered at Daphne, who pretended to be concentrating really hard on the mast but was actually concentrating really hard on avoiding eye contact with me. “Daph? Did you know Bryce had quit his job?”

She bit her lip. I was such an idiot. That’s why Daphne was acting weird. Of course she knew something was going on.

“Don’t consider what you’re going to say. Did you or did you not know about this?” As his attorney, this was something she would have needed to have been involved in on some level. Right? There were contracts he’d have to break.

“I didn’t actually find out until the wedding.”

My eyes widened. “How could he just walk away from in-progress builds without any legal counsel? And why wouldn’t you have told me after you found out? Is there something else going on?”

She took a deep breath. “Lanier, you know this is hard. There’s so much I can’t say.”

I crossed my arms. I knew I was deflecting. I should have been directing my anger at Bryce. But instead, it came spewing out at the one person who always had my back.

“I know you know something. You’re supposed to be my best friend!”

I expected her to apologize. Instead, she came back at me. “Do you think it’s easy for me? Do you think it’s fun knowing that I have to hide stuff from you? But I do!” She raised her voice. “I have a four-year-old who depends on me for *everything*! I can’t risk my life and livelihood because you can’t have an adult conversation with the ass-hole you aren’t even sure you want to marry!”

I turned to Mary Stuart for sympathy, but she was looking at Daphne in shock. Daphne was frank and she said what she thought. But she was usually steady. She wasn’t steady now.

“Y’all, don’t fight,” Mary Stuart said. “This is a hard situation for both of you.”

"She acts so high and mighty," I said. "It's not like she has some epic love story."

"You know what, let's drop all this and focus on having fun," Mary Stuart said, trying to make her tone light. But we were in too deep now. There was no turning back.

That was when my stomach began to roll. "I never said I didn't want to marry him." I looked down at my hands. "I've maybe *thought* it, just a teeny bit. But what I said was he didn't tell me about quitting his job. You think I shouldn't marry him because of that?" That's when I definitely knew Daphne was keeping something from me. And it was big enough that my best friend thought I shouldn't marry my fiancé.

"I just want you to be happy. I don't want you to have any misgivings going into your marriage. And, well, I've worried that I pushed Bryce on you, that you were still pining for Rich and—"

"You didn't just say that." I was furious now.

"You could just apologize, you know," Mary Stuart said. "Rich would forgive you. I know he would."

"What is wrong with you two? Rich? I wasn't even twenty-one! That was ages ago!"

"Not *ages*, Lanier," Daphne said. "No matter how long it has been, I want the best for you. Sue me."

Mary Stuart laughed, and I glared at her. "I'm sorry. It was a funny lawyer joke. I couldn't help it."

"So I suppose you're on her team, too?" I asked.

"I plead the Fifth," Mary Stuart said.

Mary Stuart and Daphne were in stitches, but I was still fuming. This was why it was hard to be three best friends. Someone was always a little left out.

"Turn the boat around," I huffed. "I want to go back to the dock.

Right now." Suddenly, with no warning, the boat came to almost a complete stop.

"Daphne, this isn't funny."

"Lanier, I'm flattered, but even I can't control the wind."

I looked around. There really was no wind. So, like a child, I turned my back to both my friends, looking out over the wide river. We were half an hour away from camp. In fact, we were considerably closer to Rock Springs than we were to Holly Springs. I could see the riverbank, but there wasn't anything on it. We were really, truly in the middle of nowhere. But surely a boat would come along sometime, right?

"Daph, are we stuck?" Mary Stuart asked.

"Well, until the wind picks back up, I'm afraid to say that we are."

"Oh my God!" Mary Stuart was definitely the panicker of the group, and I could tell that Daphne wasn't in a soothing mood. So, even though I was mad, I turned back around and said, "Mary Stuart, it's fine. The wind will pick up soon. This has happened a million times before."

"But those other million times we could radio to base camp, and someone would come tow us!" she said shrilly. "Those other million times the sun wasn't starting to set!"

She wasn't wrong. But the number one lesson when on the water—one that we had learned the hard way a time or two—was don't panic. Daphne was totally relaxed. I was mad but not worried. So I decided to distract Mary Stuart the best way I knew how: by talking about my relationship. "I think I just felt like there would be a sign," I said.

"For what?" Mary Stuart asked, cocking her head.

"Rich."

Mary Stuart and Daphne shared a knowing grin.

"You don't have to be so smug. I guess I figured that if I was supposed to be with him we would run into each other, or he would reach out to me or something."

"Lanier," Daphne said calmly, "do not bite my head off. I am not criticizing you. But why in God's holy name would he reach out to you? The man would have to be a masochist!"

I hated when she was right. But she was.

"She doesn't love putting herself out there," Mary Stuart said.

"Thank you, therapist one and two, for the analysis." I sighed. "No, I shouldn't be saying any of this. Things with Bryce have just been kind of rocky, and I think it's giving me jitters. But I love him."

"And it's also so convenient that you found him in Cape Carolina," Mary Stuart said.

I couldn't tell if she meant it as a slight. "I'm not marrying him just because we both happen to be in Cape Carolina." *But would we be engaged right now if that weren't the case?*

"No one meant that," Daphne said.

I had more I wanted to talk to them about, but the wind still wasn't picking up, and I was starting to get nervous. Not a single boat had passed us on the river, and the sun was beginning to dip below the horizon. "Guys," I finally said after a few minutes, "what the hell are we going to do?"

"Well, I've been thinking about it," Daphne said. "I have no idea what time it is, but June will be back at camp by seven at the latest. When we aren't there—and neither is the boat—she'll put two and two together. She'll come get us." She seemed incredibly confident.

"Or she'll think we're grown women and we went somewhere, and she won't look for us."

Daphne shook her head. "She's a camp director, Lanier. Lost children, even when they're thirty, aren't acceptable. She'll find us."

I wished I felt that sure. I looked down and realized there was a paddle. "Should we try to paddle back?"

Daphne shook her head. "Not yet. It's pretty far, and I think we need to conserve our energy."

"What if we rowed to Rock Springs?" Mary Stuart asked. "It's closer. We could take turns?"

"That's a good thought," Daphne said. "If no one comes soon, we should try it."

"Do you think your Best Sailor award will be revoked after this?" I joked.

Daphne stuck her lip out. "I hope not. What else have I done with my life?"

I rolled my eyes. More than most people could have done in three lifetimes.

"I am so excited Henry gets to come to Rock Springs soon," she said. I knew she was trying to keep our minds off the situation at hand.

"He is going to have the best time," Mary Stuart agreed.

"Do you ever think about what our lives would have been like if we hadn't all been in the Songbird Cabin together?" I asked.

"I loved you guys right away," Daphne said.

She smiled at me, and I knew then I had all but forgiven her. Daphne was always there for me, even from that first day we held hands and ran through the open field to feed the Holly Springs horses. I had no idea then that she and I would become family, that I would protect her in ways I couldn't even dream of. She would have—and had—done the same for me. It wasn't her fault her job prevented her from telling me everything about my fiancé.

"If we die out here tonight," I said, ninety-five percent joking, "I want you two to know that having you as my best friends has been the highlight of my life."

"I agree," Daphne said. "You two have gotten me through all the hard stuff."

"We always will." I looked out toward the riverbank, and, from the direction of Rock Springs, I could swear a boat was heading in our direction. "Is that a—"

"Ah! It's a boat!" Mary Stuart exclaimed.

We all started waving with both arms as it approached.

"Finally," Daphne said, sighing. I realized how worried she had been. "At least they can radio Sea Tow or something. How did that damn wind die down so quickly?"

"It's fine," Mary Stuart said. "It wasn't your fault."

"It was a memorable start to my bachelorette party," I said. "No harm, no foul." As the boat came into view, I blinked and then blinked again. It was like déjà vu. "I'm hallucinating," I said.

It was close enough that we could hear the engine of one of Rock Springs's twenty-five-horsepower Scouts. "You are not hallucinating," Mary Stuart said. "Unless we both are."

Daphne squinted and then burst out laughing.

"It can't be," I whispered.

"And yet it is," Mary Stuart said.

"Did you orchestrate this, you psycho?" I hissed.

Daphne laughed ironically. "Are you serious? Don't you think if I had orchestrated this, I would have had him arrive a long time ago?"

"This isn't exactly the boat stripper I had planned," Mary Stuart chimed in.

"Is this the sign of which you speak?" Daphne asked pointedly.

I wanted to say no. I wanted to tell her she was crazy. But as Rich

McNabb caught the mast line that Daphne threw, wrapped it around the Scout's cleat to tow us in, and said, "Ladies, we have got to stop meeting like this," I was completely speechless.

Rich was here. My heart was beating out of my chest. And, just like all those years ago when we were kids at camp, I couldn't deny that, at first glance, I was completely smitten.

• • •

Mary Stuart, Daphne, and I were the counselors for the youngest girls, the Songbirds we'd once been, the summer after our senior year of high school. We had been at Camp Holly Springs every summer for a dozen years, and we had earned our rightful place as counselors. We knew every staff member, every secret hiding spot. Our feet had traversed every square inch of these three hundred fifty acres so many times they could do it by muscle memory. And, what's more, what's better, was that we knew most of the counselors at the boys' camp. The ones we didn't know? Well, that was going to be fun too.

Secretly, I was as excited for Daphne to meet them as I was for myself. I couldn't put my finger on why it bugged me that she and Huff had been talking nonstop since our senior prom, that they had hung out together so much since. I should have been happy that my big brother and my best friend were both happy. But even in those few weeks between prom and our trek to camp, I felt like they had something real. And while my other friends would squeal, *Your brother and your best friend!* like I should be thrilled, I didn't feel thrilled. I hated the idea of the two of them having this whole relationship that I wasn't part of. Inside jokes. Secret glances. I was ready for Daphne to move on. And then Huff ruined everything by announcing he was going back to Rock Springs as a counselor. Which meant . . . He and Daphne would be together for the entire summer.

Still, Daphne was practically known for her inability to stay with the same guy. I didn't want my brother to be another boy she disposed of. But better now than later when he was super invested and she really broke his heart.

After an exciting first two sessions of camp where Mary Stuart, Daphne, and I helped each other deal with hard things—and hard campers—a zap of electricity ran through me as we boarded the small sailboat for a night off. We were heading to Rock Springs, just a half hour sail down the river, for a mixer with the male counselors. We deserved this after working so hard, and while everyone else was driving the few miles to the boys' camp, we decided to have a little adventure. I, for one, couldn't wait to see Rich McNabb again. Rich was my camp crush. Well, no, he was everyone's camp crush, the boy that all the girls—from Songbirds on up—absolutely swooned over. We'd had our usual flirtation the times our paths had already crossed that summer, but that had always been around the kids. I was hopeful there would be more now that the kids were gone. After several summers of dancing at the camp dance, trading swim bands, and then, as counselors-in-training, running sailing excursions together, I felt like maybe this would finally be our summer.

"Rich McNabb!" Daphne said in a singsong voice, wiggling her fingers at me as the wind caught the sail and the water rushed by.

I laughed. "Please. Rich could have any girl in this camp—or anywhere else, for that matter. It's not like he's going to be interested in me."

"He's always been interested in you!" Mary Stuart said.

I felt a blush rise to my cheeks. "And what about you?" I peered at the red elastic band hanging around her neck. "Is that Joe Carter's swim band from last summer you have on there?"

It was a tradition to trade swim bands with the boy you liked. It wasn't altogether safe, I was realizing now that I was a counselor, as the color of those swim bands dictated what activities you could do. But it was a tradition all the same, as far back as when June was a camper here.

Mary Stuart grinned. "It sure is. And, if he's telling me the truth, he still has mine too."

I was about to respond when I looked over at Daphne. She was squinting and her tanned skin seemed to have gone very, very pale. She sucked in her breath. "Is that?"

Mary Stuart and I followed her gaze. On a sunny, slightly breezy early evening, in the middle of the river, I saw what she was seeing. "A waterspout!"

As if I had summoned the storm, the sky went dark. Daphne lowered the sail as fast as she could, but there was no doubt about it: that waterspout was coming directly at us. I don't know why Mary Stuart and I looked to Daphne, except that she was our de facto leader. We did what she said. And, right now, she screamed, "Jump! As far out as you can!"

My heart racing out of my chest, I jumped, the brackish water burning my eyes and filling my nose in my panic. I wanted to stay under, to be protected by this river that had always beckoned me back to this place, summer after summer, that had always kept me safe. But I was too buoyant in my life jacket. I'd never heard a sound quite like what came next, a deep, low groan so loud I would have covered my ears if I'd had the presence of mind. I squeezed my eyes shut and had the overwhelming feeling that this was it for me. I was going to die.

The horrible noise subsided, and I felt like the waterspout had probably passed. Even still, I was terrified. For what must have been several minutes, I felt frozen in fear, bobbing in the water, too scared to even attempt to swim to shore. Finally, as the panic began to wane,

I remembered: Daphne and Mary Stuart! I looked around for my friends, was about to call to them with what I knew would be a shaky yell. But then I heard a voice I knew well say, "You're okay, Lanie. I've got you." Only one person in the world called me Lanie.

I opened my eyes to see Rich McNabb, rain clinging to his eyelashes, dripping down his nose and mouth, and streaming off his coat. "I saw the waterspout from the dock," he said. "I came as soon as it passed." He pulled me up by my life jacket as I struggled into his small powerboat, and then he got Mary Stuart and Daphne, who were bobbing a few feet away.

None of us said a word as the little Scout with the twenty-five-horsepower engine struggled against the wind and rain to get us to the dock. We helped Rich tie up as he pointed to the shoreline. There it was. Our sailboat. Crushed and battered against the rocks. I exchanged glances with Daphne and Mary Stuart. We didn't need words. All of our eyes said, *That could have been us.*

June was running down the dock. She wrapped her arms around Daphne and Mary Stuart. I wondered why she hadn't wrapped her arm around me. That was when I realized that Rich was leading me up the dock. "I'll get Lanie some dry clothes!" he called to June.

Dry clothes. Yes. The floral sundress with the tie straps I had picked out so painstakingly for seeing Rich was soaked, stained with river silt, and clinging to me awkwardly. I hoped Rich didn't notice as he led me up to his cabin and through the door. He threw his drenched raincoat out on the tiny front porch. I still hadn't said anything. He stood in front of me, unbuckling the snaps on my life jacket. "You're okay," he said. "You don't need this anymore." His fingers lingered on the bottom buckle, his face inches from mine. My mouth went dry. Was he going to kiss me? Did he like me the way I liked him?

But he only slipped the life jacket off my shoulders and set it on the porch. He grabbed a nearby towel and handed it to me, and then opened one of his drawers and handed me a Camp Rock Springs T-shirt and pair of cotton shorts. "They'll be a little big, but at least they're dry."

In his tiny bathroom, I closed the door and held the clean clothes to my face, inhaling the scent of Rich. Then I peeled my dress off, pulling on his shorts, cinching the rope on the waistband, and rolling the elastic at the top over a few times to make them shorter and tighter. When I walked out, Rich was in dry clothes too, and, as I caught a glimpse of myself in the mirror, we both laughed at how ridiculous I looked.

"Not exactly my planned mixer attire," I said, grinning at him, water droplets still running off my hair and onto his clean T-shirt.

He stepped closer. "You have never looked more beautiful."

That was when I noticed: He was wearing my swim band from the previous summer. I hadn't worn his because I didn't want to be presumptuous, to feel silly if he didn't reciprocate my feelings. But now I wished I had. My heart could have burst with happiness. I put my finger up to touch it, and he smiled sheepishly. "I just thought . . ."

"I brought yours," I admitted. "I put it on and took it off like five times before I decided not to wear it."

He laughed and took another step closer to me. "Do you think this could finally be our summer?" he whispered.

I nodded, feeling his strong, sure hand on the small of my back. I tilted my head up, smiling, as his lips met mine for the very first time, in a kiss that felt nothing short of inevitable. How many summers had we flirted and exchanged furtive glances, spent every free moment together? And now, finally, *I was kissing Rich McNabb*. I was aware of his hand on my neck as I felt the muscles of his back, made tight and strong from years of sports and outdoor activity.

I felt breathless and light-headed as he pulled away, resting his forehead on mine. He gently kissed my lips again. "I've wanted to do that for like, five summers."

Feeling overwhelmed, I said something that now, twelve years later, back in the sailing hut after Rich towed us to the dock, I heard myself saying again: "You saved me, Rich. You saved my life." The words meant more now than they had when I was eighteen. They meant more because they were laced with history, with meaning, with feeling. With regret.

Rich laughed, but I knew him well enough to know that it wasn't sincere. He had been a cute teenager, but he was an unutterably handsome man. The lines around his eyes and mouth from sun and salt made him more distinguished. But his blue eyes didn't twinkle when he laughed like they once had. And I knew instinctively it wasn't because they had changed. It was because they didn't twinkle for *me* anymore.

"I wouldn't say I saved your life, necessarily. You guys probably would have survived. You would have been cold, wet, and dehydrated, but you would have lived through the night."

I leaned back against the wooden counter of the Camp Holly Springs sailing hut. "I'm not as tough as I once was."

Mary Stuart and Daphne made themselves scarce as soon as we arrived, claiming they had to go find June. Boats were stacked and sails hung from the rafters, and Rich was returning our borrowed equipment to its rightful place. He secured the sail and then turned, leaning against the counter too. "So, you're getting married, huh?"

Suddenly I felt embarrassed, like maybe I didn't deserve to be married or to find happiness after what I did to him. I nodded, my throat constricting. Was I going to cry?

"He's a lucky man."

I searched his face for a hint of sarcasm that *must* be there. But I couldn't find any. Maybe only I knew there should be sarcasm there, as that lucky man—the one who had changed his entire life without mentioning it to me—hadn't so much as sent a text my way since I left. I was always the one to back down, always the one to apologize. Not this time.

Rich shifted to face me. I shifted to face him, and when I did, I saw it. Right there, carved in the twenty-foot-long counter amid hundreds of other names: RICH + LANIER = LOVE.

Just like that, I was thrust back to that summer, a month after Rich first saved me, the night when, tipsy off lukewarm beer and cheap champagne, we had snuck into the sailing hut while all our fellow counselors reveled in the mess hall. After weeks of sneaking off together whenever we could, of writing real, old-fashioned letters back and forth almost every day, we were inseparable. We had talked about what came after, how we would make this work when I was in school in North Carolina and he was in Georgia.

But that night in the sailing hut we didn't talk at all. The moment he locked the door behind us we both knew, without a word, what would happen next. My first time was right there on that hard countertop with a damp towel the only cushion. But it didn't matter. I didn't care. All I wanted was to be as close to Rich as I possibly could, to make that summer with him last forever. I knew even then I would never love anyone the way I loved him, that no matter what happened in my life, we would share something that superseded anything else I ever called love.

We talked and laughed for hours that night and, as we got dressed, Rich took his pocketknife out of his shorts and carved our names in that counter where they would stay forever, a testament to the summer love we shared when our lives were uncertain, when our futures stretched out before us long and languishing and full of possibility.

Now, all these years later, I watched as Rich traced our initials with his finger, his face full of something I couldn't quite name. Nostalgia? Regret? Oh, God, please not regret.

No matter how our story ended—and it had ended badly—I would never wish for it not to have happened. He looked into my eyes, and it was as if nothing had changed between us. I realized then that my virginity wasn't the only thing I gave Rich. I gave him my heart too. And, as was becoming clear to me, both of those were things I could only ever give once.

June

A PLACE TO BELONG

THIS WAS THE PART OF THE WEEKEND I'D BEEN DREADING, WHICH was ironic, because sitting around a campfire was the part of camp that felt the holiest to me. With the flames flickering, everything seemed ever-so-slightly shrouded in mystery. And, directly across the circle from me, the fire throwing shadows on her face, Daphne looked so much like my sister, Melanie, that it took my breath away. Daphne was animatedly saying, "No, but Lanier, what did Rich actually *say*?"

I always worried when I had to give Daphne bad news. She wasn't Melanie, no matter how much she looked like her. She'd had—and overcome—her own struggles with substance abuse. But Daphne was different from Melanie. She was very clear on who she was and what she wanted. Sometimes, Melanie was too. But she could fool herself into sliding back into addiction in a way that Daphne wasn't capable of.

I remember the first time Melanie relapsed. When we saw each other at Christmas, I had been shocked she was drinking, but I hadn't said anything. Alcohol had never been her problem, after all, and I wasn't well-versed enough in addiction to know that finding a new vice was a slippery slope. But I found out quickly when she called a few months later to say that things were bad, that she wanted me to help her quit drinking cold turkey and make sure she didn't die. Those were her literal words: *Make sure I don't die.* I'll never forget the shaking, the vomiting, the moaning, the way her fever spiked. I almost called 911 twice. But when she finally calmed, when her body started to adjust, she was so vulnerable with me. I lay in bed beside her and said, "Mel, you worked so hard to get clean the first time. Why did you go back to this?"

She lay her head on my shoulder, and I stroked her hair, matted from three days of not being brushed, much less washed. "Junie, it started out okay. I was on my first date with Danny, and he ordered a bottle of wine. And I didn't want to be rude so—"

"So you drank it," I said softly.

"Well, yeah. I drank it. I mean, I was addicted to Klonopin, not alcohol."

I think it's safe to say you were addicted to both, I added in my head.

"So then I'd drink a glass on our dates. And then we started going out more, so I drank more. And, nine months later, he's gone, and I'm having Smirnoff for breakfast."

I didn't realize it then. Not yet. It took me until her third relapse, when Daphne was six and Melanie had been clean for seven years, to understand that my sister's addictions weren't about the substance. It was that she lost herself in these relationships. She was an equal opportunity abuser. She never confronted the pain of a breakup, of a loss. She never got to know who she was. Maybe neither of us did. When our parents were killed, Melanie turned to drugs and alcohol; I hid at a summer camp.

But not Daphne. Daphne did the work. Every day. And that's how I knew she'd be okay; that was what pushed my infrequent worries about her sobriety away.

I forced my attention back to the conversation. "I don't know, Daphne," Lanier was saying. "Rich was really . . . quiet. We made weird small talk, I thanked him for saving us, and then I got the heck out of there and had dinner with the three of you."

"Did he mention the wedding?" I asked.

"He said Bryce was a lucky man," she whispered, looking down at her hands. I couldn't be sure, but I thought her voice cracked.

Legend had it that, around this giant rock firepit that had been by the water's edge for decades, you couldn't help but tell your truth—and it was the test of your Holly Springs's friendships to see if your friends could keep your campfire secrets. It was a sacred bond. I had to think that the power didn't lie in the rocks or the flames but instead in the many women who had spent a lifetime making that legend true, telling and keeping secrets for all these years. I wondered how many secrets these little girls who had become women before my very eyes had shared over this fire. I wondered how many more they would share tonight. For now, they all danced around them, whatever they were.

"Well, Bryce *is* lucky," Mary Stuart said. "We all are because we get you."

"And poor Rich doesn't," Daphne added.

Lanier shot her a look.

"I'm kidding, I'm kidding," Daphne said. "I know it can be weird to see an ex, and that it can bring up all these old feelings you weren't expecting. I was just wondering if that happened."

Lanier looked at each of us. "Campfire secret?"

"Campfire secret," we repeated in unison.

"I have always wondered what might have been if I hadn't screwed it up so royally. And his showing up tonight intensified that question." She paused. "What do you think, June?"

I shook my head. "No, ma'am. You are engaged, and it is not for me to say."

"Ju-une," Daphne said. "If you're going to be at the bachelorette party then you have to be in bridesmaid mode, not camp director mode."

I laughed. I couldn't think of much worse than being the fifty-year-old bridesmaid standing among the thirty-year-olds. "Okay. Fine. I think Rich McNabb is one of the finest men I have ever known. He is a role model for hundreds of boys, he is a top-notch businessman who helps Holly Springs and me every chance he gets, and I have always, deep down, believed that Lanier broke his heart so fully he was never able to move on." I took a deep breath. "There."

"Damn," Mary Stuart said.

"Damn," Daphne repeated.

Then Lanier shrugged as if the matter was settled. "Well, coulda, woulda, shoulda, I guess. I can't rewind. I can't go back. And I'm getting married, for heaven's sake."

I lifted my soda. "Well then, cheers to that."

I looked out to where the moon shone silver and bold on the water, the stars electric. As if reading my mind, Mary Stuart said, "I'd forgotten there were even stars like this." She was always the one stepping in and changing an awkward subject.

"So had I," Lanier agreed.

"I've spent so many years here I forgot places existed where the stars *didn't* shine like this," I said.

"I still remember my first night here at camp," Mary Stuart said as I stoked the flames with a poker. "With all of you," she added, taking a sip of her wine.

"Just three scared little six-year-old girls," Lanier said.

"Well, not Daphne," Mary Stuart revised.

"In fairness, June was the best mother I ever had," Daphne said. "So being with her for those months was the closest thing I ever had to being raised—well that, and living with Paula and John, of course."

Hearing her say that touched something so deep inside me that I felt like I might disappear into the atmosphere like this wood we were burning. Because I had failed Daphne in the ultimate way. In her time of greatest need, after her mother died, I couldn't muster the energy to fight for custody and care for her full-time. I had felt guilty about it every day since.

"You were so strong, Daphne," Mary Stuart continued, not noticing my discomfort. "And I was such a mess. I still can't believe you let me, a total stranger, crawl in bed with you that first night."

"I took you outside!" Daphne said, piecing that night together.

Mary Stuart nodded. "You pointed up at the sky and you said, 'If you miss your mom and dad while you're at camp, you can remember that they're looking at the same moon you are.'"

I laughed. "I never knew that. That's what I told you, Daph. Remember?"

She smiled into her hot cocoa. "Remember? Of course I remember." She fiddled with a string on her jacket. "At home, at least to my mom's husband at the time, I was a burden, an unwanted child. At camp, I had friends, I had grown-ups to look up to, and counselors who adored me. I learned how to sail and fish. I learned how far I could hit a golf ball and how fast I could run. I was free during those summers. I was alive. I had a place in the world."

"Girls, I can't tell you how vividly I remember those summers, watching the three of you grow up." I smiled at Daphne. "You were so tough and brave. You came into your own here."

The same thing happened to me when I took over Holly Springs, the only place I ever belonged. And for decades, I had provided that place for the thousands of little girls who ran through our ranks.

That was when the tears I'd held back since my favorite campers drove through the gate finally started pouring.

Mary Stuart was the first to notice. "What's wrong?"

"Girls, this isn't easy for me to say. But this is going to be our last summer here at camp." I said it quickly. No use dragging it out.

Mary Stuart gasped. Lanier's jaw dropped. Daphne was completely still. "So you're selling out to the developers?"

I didn't miss the accusatory chill in her voice.

"Honey, it isn't like I *want* to sell out to developers. We just can't get our feet back under us. We lost a whole summer because of the pandemic, only took half the campers last summer, and this summer just won't be enough to get us back in the black. I don't want to sell, but I don't have a choice. I've spent every penny I have trying to save this place. I honestly can't afford to get through this season, but we're about seventy percent full, and I can't tell all those little girls that they don't get to come to camp."

Daphne was tough. After the life she had had, she didn't have much choice. So it surprised me when she sobbed, "But this is my home."

I moved to put my arm around her. "Honey, it's mine, too."

"No, June, for real. When my mother was busier with her boyfriends than me, I always knew that in just a few more months, I would be back in my happy place. When school was hard, or life felt like it was closing in on me, I knew that camp was always waiting."

Lanier's sobs joined Daphne's as she said, "Do you remember how scared I was to do the zip line for the first time?"

"It took us twelve days and dozens of tries to finally get you to jump off the platform," Mary Stuart added, wiping her eyes.

"But when I did," she said, "I realized I could do anything. Anything at all. This place taught me that; the two of you taught me that."

I stood and motioned for them to do the same. We all held on to each other, crying, like we did at the end of every summer. I couldn't imagine saying goodbye to those summers, to those memories.

"It's the end of an era," I whispered, pulling away.

"How will little girls like me become brave?" Lanier asked, her tears choking her.

"How will girls like me make a friend so good they can climb in bed beside her?" Mary Stuart asked.

"Where will girls like me find their family?" Daphne chimed in.

I wondered how a woman like me, a woman used to spending three-quarters of her year alone and the other fourth surrounded by children, would make it in the real world. Was there a place for me out there? And, if so, how would I even begin to find it?

Daphne pulled back. "June, do you want to save the camp?" I noticed that the chill was gone now. She wasn't being accusatory. My niece was sincere.

I took a moment to think about it. A part of me *was* tired. Fielding calls from parents and attempting to fundraise, overseeing finances, and handling lists of necessary repairs could take its toll on anyone.

But that was the price I paid for the life I loved. And I would continue to pay it over and over if I could. If only I had that choice.

I nodded. "More than anything." Daphne stared intently at me for a split second, her eyes glinting.

She inserted herself back into the group hug and cried with the rest of us. But I had known Daphne since the minute she was born. Those wheels inside her brain, the ones that seemed to spin a little faster than anyone else's, were turning. And if the rest of us knew what was good for us, we'd better watch out.

Daphne

STRIKING OUT

THE SUN HAS YET TO RISE OVER THE RIVER, BUT, BETWEEN THE Bryce debacle and this camp news, I can't sleep. I am already pacing the green indoor-outdoor carpet in our room, watching my friends sleep in two of the four twin beds in our room in the doctor's quarters. June decided that, since we were all grown up now, we could sleep in here instead of one of the regular cabins. Also, it was pretty chilly, so she thought we needed the heat. But the intermittent whir of the unit that kept one side of the cabin infernally hot while the other remained freezing cold turning on and off made it impossible to sleep.

Mary Stuart and Lanier had wisely chosen the two beds in the center of the room. I started out in the bed closest to the heater, woke up in a full sweat, moved my sleeping bag to the bed on the other end, and was so freezing I couldn't possibly fall back asleep.

Instead, I lay thinking about my songbird summer. My mother had just married Vincent, who I barely knew, and we were leaving the only home I'd ever known in Cape Carolina to move to New York, where Vincent was from. I remember how excited my mom had seemed, how wild. I didn't know about drugs yet or what my mother was like when she was on them. How could I have? She had been clean for seven years. Maybe it was Vincent who yanked her off the wagon. Or the marriage. Or the move. But I know now the reason I spent the entire summer—almost three months—at camp when the rest of my friends only spent two weeks was because June had given my mother an ultimatum. She could clean herself up while I was gone or she would keep me. I know that's not how custody works, exactly. But the threat must have done the trick. And I guess my mother somehow convinced June that she was better by the time I had to go home.

I remember sitting in June's lap, crying, my tears falling into her camp T-shirt that smelled like whatever industrial detergent the laundry service used. "I don't want to go to New York. I don't like Vincent. I want to stay here with you."

"I know, baby. But you have to see your mom. And I have to stay here to see the staff off."

It probably took all the strength in her body to drive me to the airport, to drop me off with a gate attendant whose facial expression said *This is not in my job description* while I wailed.

June took me in her arms. "Remember how, when you came to camp, you'd never been on a sailboat?"

I nodded, sniffling.

"And how by the end of the summer you could take the boat out all on your own?"

I nodded, wiping my eyes. She kissed each of my cheeks. "That's how New York will be. It will be scary at first. But you'll learn something new every day, and in a few weeks, you'll be just as good at living in New York as you are at sailing."

I was dubious. "You're my brave girl," she whispered. Then she paused. "Do you remember my phone number?"

June had quizzed me on her number all summer long and implored me that I was to call her if Mommy seemed too sad or too happy or wasn't sleeping or if I was scared. I thought June sure did take good care of Mommy. Now I knew June was taking good care of me. Letting go of June felt like ripping out a part of my heart. But I somehow did it. And between the noise and confusion of the airport and the attention the flight attendants slathered on me aboard the plane—they were much more compassionate than the one in the terminal—I made it to New York without any more tears.

I held the flight attendant's hand as I rode down the escalator to baggage claim at LaGuardia Airport, where my mother was supposed to meet me. The excitement at how she would run to me and engulf me in a hug after being apart for an entire summer welled up in my chest. I knew how happy she was going to be to see me and began cataloging all the stories I had to tell her about camp. I started to feel like maybe I wouldn't have to be so brave in New York because my mommy would be there. We would make slice-and-bake cookies together and crank up Madonna and jump on the bed. And we would be okay.

Only, she wasn't waiting at the bottom of the escalator like she was supposed to be. I looked up at the flight attendant, who smiled at me. "It's okay. I'm sure we just got our signals crossed."

But after half an hour of walking around the baggage area, my legs were exhausted. The flight attendant had tried to get my mother on the phone to no avail and had just made an announcement over the loudspeaker. I thought my mom must be dead. I began to cry.

"It's okay, sweetheart," the flight attendant said. "Do you know anyone else we could call?"

That's when it hit me. I dialed the big phone in the security office myself and when June answered, I said, "Aunt June, I've been at the airport for a long time and Mommy isn't here."

"Stay right there," she said. "I'm getting on a plane."

My mother did come pick me up about an hour and a half later. I sprinted into her arms, resting my head on the feather necklace on her chest. She smelled like perfume and cigarette smoke. And she seemed sad, like she was faking being happy to see me. She didn't even sing with me in the car. As soon as we got to our new apartment, I asked where Vincent was, and it was her turn to burst into tears. She walked into her bedroom and closed the door, and I was left wondering what I had done wrong, and, maybe even more than that, who this woman was and what she had done with my mother. That was the first time she told me: *Never marry a man you love this much, Daphne. He will only break your heart.* Fortunately, June arrived a few hours later and, the next day, the two of us were on a plane back to North Carolina while my mommy went to a camp for mommies for a while.

It was the first time my mother ever agreed to go to rehab. Years later, I would realize that was a testament to how much she loved me. Before she'd had me, she had just picked herself up by her bootstraps and sobered up when she wanted to get clean. I consoled myself with the thought that she tried her best for me. Only, sometimes, our best isn't enough.

Now, almost twenty-five years later, the memory of being that little girl forgotten in the airport could still make me feel hollowed out to my core. But through my mother's ups and downs, her stints in rehab, her spells of being the most fun mom in the world and the saddest, I always had Camp Holly Springs to come home to. Each and every summer, no matter how bad the year had been, I could spend eight glorious weeks here in this place where I had a schedule, consistent meals, and life just wasn't so hard.

So, now, I take a warm shower in the blue-tiled box with the stained grout in the doctor's quarters that has probably been here for as long as the camp itself. The water and the steam soothe me, make me remember that I'm not that little girl anymore. And I will never be that mother. But it also makes me realize I cannot part with the one place in my young life where I was safe. How many other kids is this camp that safe place for?

By the time I get out of the shower, I am convinced I can save Holly Springs. No, that I *will* save Holly Springs. Because there is, for certain, at least one little girl out there—and probably a whole lot more—who needs this camp as much as I did. By the time I have spent twenty minutes pacing in my towel, my hair beginning to dry, I know exactly how we are going to do it. It is only five fifteen, and I know my friends are going to kill me. Even still, I move over to the nook in front of the large cutout with the rod that serves as our closet and fill the coffeepot on top of the dorm fridge with grounds. Maybe the smell of coffee will wake them so I won't have to.

A few minutes later Lanier calls sleepily, "What time is it? Why are you making coffee already?"

"It's five twenty-one!" I practically sing.

"Daphne," Mary Stuart groans. "Let us go back to sleep. If you're going to be crazy, go outside. Go for a sunrise sail or something."

"I'm not allowed to go without a buddy!"

"Raise your hand if you care whether Daphne drowns right now," Lanier creaks.

I raise my hand. I am the only one. I jump on her bed.

"I will kill you, Daphne," she says. "I mean that. I can't be held responsible for my actions before seven a.m."

"Girls, for real, you have to get up." I hear how annoyingly perky I am. I know they want to kill me. I don't blame them. But I can't help it. I'm just so *excited.* "We have to go find June," I say.

"We will find June at nine," Mary Stuart says. "She hates you at five thirty too."

"No, seriously." I am bouncing now. "I think I've figured out how to save the camp."

Lanier opens an eye. "For real?"

"Yup."

Mary Stuart actually sits up. "Do you think that's possible?"

I am prepared for them to be far more skeptical than this, so the impassioned speech I have been practicing seems a little superfluous now, but I launch into it anyway. "Ladies, every single week we tackle hard things together, don't we?"

"We do!" Mary Stuart says. She's waking up. She's feeling my speech.

Lanier seems less thrilled but has two eyes open now, which is progress. "We have fired sketchy employees and taken on that McDonald's that always swore their McFlurry machine was broken. We have raised thousands of dollars for causes that matter to us and written kick-ass résumés. We have planned weddings and baked cakes and even inadvertently caused a Twitter war between two of the Real Housewives. I think we can handle this."

Lanier leans on her elbow, which I feel is a sign of how totally fired up I've gotten her. Lanier lives for a good Twitter war. "Fine. We'll go talk to June."

I spring off the bed. "Yes!" I got her her McFlurrys back. She owes me.

Ten minutes later, we are all dressed in layered sweats. I am practically running across the dewy morning grass, coffee splashing out of the cup I'm holding in front of me. Mary Stuart and Lanier are doing something that resembles shuffling behind me and, every minute or so, I run a little circle around them to get them pumped up.

"Does it ever make you laugh that the wildest girl we knew in college has turned into *this*?" Lanier asks Mary Stuart.

"Yup, she's the greatest," Mary Stuart says.

Lanier's face reveals that perhaps she doesn't think I'm *the greatest*. But these comments give me a little boost.

I reach the small cabin that is June's private quarters and throw the door open. She pops up in the wood-framed double bed she sleeps in and, when she sees me, puts her hand over her heart, gasping. "Did anyone ever teach you girls to knock? You nearly gave me a heart attack!"

"There's an open-door policy at camp," Mary Stuart responds.

June rolls her eyes. "Not in the middle of the night!"

"But it's morning!" I say cheerily.

"Barely," Lanier grumbles.

I look around for a moment, remembering. This room is small and spartan and totally pristine. A cozy wood-framed leather chair with a matching footstool and reading lamp sits in a corner, a table overflowing with books beside it. How many nights did I sneak in here as a child so June could read stories to me while we cuddled in that chair?

The dresser across from her bed is only half-full, I know, because June doesn't need much stuff. Her daily uniform is shorts or jeans with a camp polo or T-shirt, depending on the day's activities. A few dresses hang in the tiny closet in case of a funeral or wedding. And I know if I open the door to her small bathroom, which is barely larger than a public stall, all I will see is her toothbrush hanging in the porcelain holder and her toothpaste atop a folded washcloth. She keeps some pressed powder inside the medicine cabinet for going out. A small kitchenette beside the bathroom holds a skinny fridge, two-burner stove, small oven, and microwave. The simplicity of her life awes me.

It drives me endlessly nuts that she lives in this tiny cabin, which is roughly the size of a studio apartment, year-round. She says nature is her friend and the solitude suits her, but I often wonder if she is simply hiding from the world. Four months a year, even six, I can see why she needs to be here. But all year seems ridiculous. June is my real-life family, and I wish more than anything that she was closer to Henry and me when she wasn't at Holly Springs.

"June, we're here to save the camp."

She flops back down dramatically. "Daph, it's too big. It's too much. We'd have to raise at least six hundred fifty thousand dollars to keep it going and—"

"No problem!" I say, undeterred. To be honest, I was hoping for more like $250,000. But that's okay. That is not insurmountable.

"Ladies," I say to Lanier and Mary Stuart, "we can handle that, can't we?"

"Yup," they say as unenthusiastically as possible.

"June, get up. Let's get to your office and get going. I have a plan."

"I'll meet you there in five," she says.

We walk past a couple of cabins, the mess hall, and the land sports hut before we arrive at the camp's main office. I am thrilled to find that Jillian, June's assistant, is already there, sitting at her computer. She throws me a lukewarm, almost sheepish smile as Mary Stuart and Lanier traipse in. "I'm sorry," she says. "I know this is your big weekend. I just—"

"We know," I say. "We know about camp."

She sighs. "Okay, good. I'm a terrible liar. I couldn't sleep, and I decided to come into work. I just keep thinking that if I go over the numbers enough, I can find a solution."

I snap my fingers. "Finally, a woman on my team. Ladies, get a pen and paper. We are all getting a hard things list—and it's going to be extensive."

"Hard things?" Jillian asks.

"We send a list of hard things every week that we do for each other," Mary Stuart explains.

"Which is seeming like a worse idea by the minute." Lanier glares at me but gets her phone out and opens her Notes app. At least Mary Stuart is starting to become more chipper.

"Jillian, I need a list of everyone in your database. Every person over the age of twenty-one who is a former camper or has a child here. We are going to launch a massive fundraising campaign."

"Great start," Mary Stuart says. She thinks for a second. "What if we run a sweepstakes of some kind? Maybe give away a free session? We could control the entries so that you get one for every hundred dollars you donate or something, and make entries unlimited to raise more money."

I point at her. "Yes. That. There's that brilliant publicity mind I know and love."

June walks in now and leans against the wall, surveying the scene. "Mary Stuart, we're going to need a kick-ass press release about our campaign to save this place."

"We'll call it a potential historic landmark. People eat that up," Mary Stuart says, scribbling. "We're saving it from the ravages of overdevelopment."

"Yes!" I say.

I turn to June. "Okay. Next part of the plan: Priority number one is to fill empty beds. Thirty percent vacancy means there are one hundred opportunities to change a little girl's life this summer."

"Oh, that's good," Mary Stuart says, typing furiously on her phone.

"I couldn't have written it better myself!" She pauses and looks from Lanier to me. "We're going to need publicity if we're going to fill those beds. Lanier, how are things with you and the future mother-in-law?"

She shrugs. "Fine. It's not really her fault Bryce quit his job with no warning to go work for her."

"Great!" Mary Stuart says. "I need you to see how many favors she can call in from McCann Media people to spread the word."

"She's a shark," I add. "She could be our golden ticket." We exchange guilty looks as Lanier nods. We need to get her away from these people. But, for now, we need them.

This gives me an idea. I pick up the huge phone from June's desk and dial Finn's number. My cell reception isn't good enough here to get through a whole conversation. He answers groggily. "Hello?"

"It's me!" I practically sing.

"Are you okay? What's going on?"

"Remember that grant writing class you took in college?"

"I knew I shouldn't have put that on my résumé," he says grumpily.

"We have a lot of empty beds to fill at camp this summer, and I was thinking maybe we could get a foundation or two to sponsor a session for maybe ten or fifteen girls?"

"Um, is it because it's so early, or does this seem a little out of left field?"

I am so amped up it hasn't occurred to me that Finn has no idea what's going on. "Holly Springs is in a little bit of financial trouble, so we were thinking grant money could help lighten the load this summer."

"Ah, then that is an exceptional idea. I'll get in touch with my old professor and get her to help me find the perfect foundations to write grants for. You know I'll help any way I can."

"Thanks, Finn. Any questions?"

"Just one: Can I go back to sleep now?"

"You may."

I hang up and clap my hands together. "Mary Stuart, about that huge database of influencers you have . . ."

She smiles. "I've already added contacting all of them to Lanier's list."

"Oh, yay," Lanier says, but only somewhat unenthusiastically. She's finally waking up.

"This is going to work!" Jillian says, already starting on a spreadsheet.

"June, I know that the time has passed on most of the Covid financial programs that could help, but maybe there's something we can still do on that end. I'll look into it."

June looks at me skeptically, and the energy balloon immediately deflates. "What if this doesn't work?"

"Well, if this doesn't work," I say, "then we have the Price Development offer in our back pocket and we bow out gracefully. But that is not a winner's attitude, June, as you well know."

June's doubt is the start of an epidemic. Eight unconvinced eyes are now on me. "Honey," June starts, "I love your enthusiasm, but I'm not sure—"

I clear my throat and stand up straight. "Ladies, what does the sign by the softball field say?" I melt as I say it, thinking of Huff, because that softball field is where we had our first kiss. *Focus, Daphne.*

They look at each other.

"Fine," I fill in. "The sign by the softball field says, 'Never let the fear of striking out keep you from playing the game.'"

The blank looks on their faces tell me they aren't following, and I want them to get there faster. "Six hundred fifty thousand dollars is a lot of money," I say. "But it isn't an impossible amount. How many families have come through this camp in the past seventy-six years?"

"Oh, gosh. Thousands," June says.

Mary Stuart jumps up from her seat. All eyes are now on her. "We bring them back to camp," she says in an almost ethereal voice.

"What?" June asks. "How?"

I bite my lip, my mind spinning faster than my mouth can keep up. "You're right. We need to get people to come back to camp."

June nods, and a smile slowly blooms on her face. "We need to remind them of their ten-year-old selves and how much this place changed their lives."

"Oh my God!" Lanier says. "Yes! We remind them and then we get them to write big, fat checks to save it." She gasps. "You guys. We should open Holly Springs for a weekend. Family camp!"

"Family camp," I repeat, nodding.

"Forget your mother-in-law," Mary Stuart says. "*This* is our golden ticket."

June has prided herself on this being her camp, her baby. But this place has changed the lives of so many girls, molded them into the women they are today with the friendships, values, and self-confidence they have now. It is so much more than just a camp. It is an institution.

It belongs to all of them. It belongs to all of us.

June finally smiles. "I'm going to get started drafting the email blast."

She is in. She is so in.

"We might lose," I say. They all nod. "But let's go play the game."

Lanier

BOSS MODE

AGES THIRTEEN TO EIGHTEEN MIGHT JUST BE, IN MY GROWN-UP opinion, the worst years to have absolutely no parental supervision. When I was that age, though? I thought they were the best. Sure, Daphne's dad was totally awful. But when we turned fifteen and our social lives were finally ramping up, we had a party house. And man did we ever use it.

Now, a dad who buys his fifteen-year-old and her friends liquor seems pathetic. At the time, though, Daphne's access to alcohol—combined with the amount of it she drank—elevated her social status from cool to queen.

Despite our party-house perks, as we neared our sixteenth birthdays it started to become pretty obvious that the situation was more than a little toxic for Daphne. I had noticed that she was partying more and more, but I wasn't worried. It just made her seem more grown-up. But when Mom and I went to pick her up to take her driver's test on the morning of her sixteenth birthday, I realized it had gotten a little out of hand.

Mom beeped the horn twice before I got out of the car. She never went inside Daphne's house. I don't know if it was because she wanted to pretend she didn't know how bad things were in there or because, even if she did, she couldn't fix them.

I pushed open the unlocked front door, cringing at the thought that anyone could have walked in, and headed for her bedroom, barely noticing the beer bottles, half-empty cereal bowls, and various detritus scattered about the dingy living room.

"Daph!" I called in a singsong voice when I saw her still in bed. Her room was shockingly tidy compared to the rest of the house. "Get up!"

She didn't move, so I rolled her over. Her hair was matted with sleep. "Do you have to be so loud?" she asked, her voice thick. She looked awful, but what was worse: she smelled like she'd just taken a shot.

"Daphne!" I scolded. "Are you drunk?" I was actually thinking, *You are going to ruin your surprise birthday party tonight if you're hungover!* But that wasn't as important as the task at hand.

She sat up and squinted at me. "Maybe a little. I wanted to celebrate my birthday early last night."

"What is wrong with you? You're supposed to get your license today!" I could just see the front page of the paper: SIXTEEN-YEAR-OLD CHARGED WITH DUI AT DRIVER'S TEST.

She sat up and gasped. "Shit! Let me brush my teeth. Maybe no one will notice!"

I crossed my arms. "That's your plan? Great start. The day you get your license you lose it for a year?"

She scrunched her nose. "Yeah. That wouldn't be good. What do we tell your mom?"

"I'll tell her you're sick," I said. "Hey, where's your dad?"

"I don't know," she said, yawning. "I haven't seen him in like three days." That really burned me up. As I walked out, I fumed that he couldn't even show up for his daughter's sweet sixteen. That was the final straw. I knew I had to find a way to get her out of there.

A few months later, when Daphne moved into our house—after, I must admit, some pretty top-notch scheming on my part—I truly believed I had fixed all her problems. No, I couldn't bring her mother back from the dead. I couldn't make her dad be . . . well, a dad. But my mom and I had done everything we could to make Daphne feel like a part of our family. We had family meetings while Daphne was at after-school activities to plan how we could make her feel more at home. Mom made all her favorite meals, Dad rented her favorite DVDs for family movie nights, and I arranged mani-pedi dates for us. Huff was away living it up in college, and having Daphne helped ease a little of my parents' partial empty nest brokenheartedness. And we were back to only being able to drink sneakily sometimes on the weekends while covering it up with mouthwash and perfume like normal teenagers, so that was probably a step in the right direction. Even still, despite our best efforts, I felt like Daphne was sad. In fairness, she had good reason to be. She didn't cry or complain, but I hadn't seen her super-excited Daphne energy in a while either.

The night before our first summer as Holly Springs counselors-in-training, Daphne and I were putting the finishing touches on our camp trunks.

I smiled at her as we filled them with camp shorts and T-shirts, shower shoes, candy (which wasn't allowed), about a million pairs of underwear, and, of course, stationery to write Mom, who would cry the entire drive to Holly Springs. With any luck, we'd write to the super-cute boys we'd meet at Rock Springs, too.

"What?" Daphne asked, noticing my smile as she shoved a pair of socks in her suitcase pocket.

"You're humming," I said. "I'm just so glad to see you happy."

"You know me and camp," she said.

I sure did. For the whole two months Daphne had been living with us, I'd been trying to fix her. It seemed like going back to camp was all it was going to take.

I sifted through the pile of random stuff on my bed. "Shoot! I can't find the glitter pens."

"Want me to help you look?" she asked.

"Nah. I bet Mom knows where they are."

"She probably hid them so we couldn't leave her," Daphne joked.

I walked to the den to find Mom. That's when I heard her whisper, "John, I just don't know if she's ever going to be happy again."

"I think she's okay," Dad said. I paused by the doorway, where I could hear the newspaper rustling in his hands. "The girl lost her mother, Paula. And, Lord knows, you did everything within human capacity to keep that from happening. Plus, three years with Ray would scar anyone. It isn't like she's acting out or getting into trouble. I think she just needs a little time to adjust to being in a stable family."

Huh. What had Mom done to keep Daphne from losing Melanie?

"Maybe I was wrong. Maybe I should have told June Melanie was using again. What if she could have helped her?"

My eyes went wide. "Honey," Dad said, "you did what you thought was best."

I was about to walk in and interrupt when I heard Mom say, "We should have fought harder for Daphne."

Fought harder for Daphne? I thought. What did that mean?

"Honey, we did everything we could. We filed for custody. We appealed the judge's decision. Ray is her biological father. We knew it was a long shot."

Mom sighed. "I know. I just wish we could have done more. Or at least talked June into trying to get custody. She would have won; I just know it."

Now my ears really perked up. I never thought about Daphne going to live with June.

"I don't know. That whole 'he deserves the chance to try to be a father' rigmarole from the judge seemed pretty firm."

"Deserves to try to be a father," Mom snorted. "He was gone for twelve years, but hey, let's do a science experiment with a kid's life. Maybe he'll father up now!" She sighed. "She would have been so much better off with June."

"No one can make a person want a child, sweetheart. Not even you. And she's here now, so all's well that ends well."

"Hey, John?"

"Yes, love?"

"I think it would really hurt Daphne if she found out about any of this. Let's let it be our little secret."

I shook my head. Mom's famous line. But I agreed. It *would* really hurt Daphne. And it was my job to protect her. Plus, even if I'd wanted to—even as much as I loved Daphne—I could never rat out my own mother.

"My lips are sealed." I heard Dad stand and took the opportunity to walk through the door as if I hadn't been eavesdropping.

"Hi, Mom!" I said with faux brightness. "Where are the glitter pens?"

"Glitter pens" was all it took to send her into tears. She stood and pulled me close. "I'm just going to miss you so much. Are you sure you have to go the whole summer?"

I heard footsteps behind me and turned to see Daphne holding a handful of pens. "Found them in the kitchen drawer!" When she walked in the room, Mom motioned for her to get in the hug too.

"Oh, Paula," she said. "We'll write you every day!"

"Oh, you will not," Dad said from the doorway.

We pulled away from Mom and giggled. "Okay, maybe not every day. But, like once a week?"

"Each," Mom said. "Once a week each."

We nodded agreeably.

The next morning, we were up at six, so ready to get to our first summers as counselors-in-training. One of our biggest duties this year? Being Make-Out Patrol at the Holly Springs/Rock Springs Dances. We'd even made T-shirts with puff paint to delineate our very important titles.

"I see," John said. "When I'm trying to get you two ready for school, I'm practically pulling you out of bed. When it's camp time, you're pulling me out."

"Yes!" we both shouted excitedly.

June had called my mom earlier in the spring to ask if Daphne and I should be separated, have some time apart now that we were roommates, and Mom agreed that would be good for us. I compromised. We would be CITs in adjoining cabins—with the caveat that Mary Stuart was in the same cabin as Daphne.

That summer felt like our best yet, filled with lots of adventures, crushes, and, of course, campfire secrets. But what struck me most that summer was that while other CITs and counselors would meet up at secret points around camp to smoke a cigarette or drink a beer, Daphne never did. By summer's end, I felt like the Daphne I knew before Melanie died was back. Camp did in one season what I had tried to do for months.

That time seemed so very long ago and yet, not long ago at all. I looked at my two best friends, who were now sitting on either end of a long plastic table we had set up in the back of Bookmasters. Mary Stuart and Daphne had switched roles today. She was now the one calling the shots and making the plans—starting with calling her personal media contacts, whom I was sure were just *thrilled* to chat with her on their Sunday.

We weren't supposed to leave camp until late this afternoon, but, honestly, who could bachelorette party when you had a camp to save?

"Yes, yes," Mary Stuart was saying on the phone. "We are just beginning to plan what is sure to be an epic family camp weekend six weeks from now. How can you write about it for *Sea and Sky* if you don't experience the wonder for yourself?"

She mouthed to us "*Sea and Sky*" with huge eyes. None of us had been able to believe it when McCann Media bought one of our favorite publications and relocated it right here to Cape Carolina. It was Southern-focused but had a huge readership across the country. Daphne and I both gave her a thumbs-up. I laughed as Mary Stuart hung up.

"What?" she asked.

"I'm just looking at our rickety folding table and our scrawled loose-leaf pages of ideas. This is the definition of a grassroots effort."

"Don't most really great things get off the ground in the back of a bookstore with a few passionate people?" Daphne asked.

"I'm going to say yes," Mary Stuart said. "Because we just landed *Sea and Sky*."

Daphne and I clapped and cheered, and Mary Stuart put her hand up. "Enough celebrating! We have work to do!"

As her phone rang, she answered and walked to the front of the store. Daphne and I pulled all our papers together to start making an actual list. I opened my laptop. "You talk, I'll type?"

Daphne laughed. “Just like high school.”

Daphne hated typing and I loved it, so she would write her papers freehand, and then read them out loud for me to type. We caught lots of mistakes that way, too.

As she grabbed the first paper, I said, “Hey, I was thinking about our Make-Out Patrol shirts this morning.”

She laughed. “We should print some of those and sell them.”

I shook my head. “Not quite the same effect as the puff paint.” I paused, remembering the summer we made those shirts, sidestepping into the question I wanted to ask—why it was that Daphne’s problems seemed to disappear at camp. “I remember how happy you were when we got to camp the summer after you moved in with us.”

Daphne nodded. “Camp was where I was normal. No one had families or parents around. It was just kids being kids. Plus, it was my one stable safe place. Not that your house wasn’t!” she added quickly. “I don’t mean that at all.”

“No, I know what you mean. My house was a couple of years. Camp was as long as your memory.”

A look passed over her face that I couldn’t quite read. “Camp and you,” she said.

I looked at her questioningly. “What do you mean?”

“You were my stable safe place, Lanier. You always have been.” She shook her head. “Honestly, until maybe Steven, you were the only person in my life who never left me.”

“And I never will. Not ever,” I said.

I was tearing up, so it was the perfect moment for Mary Stuart to huff to the back of the store, set her phone down a little too forcefully, and say, “Well, you can forget me giving those exclusive profiles to the *North Carolina Gazette* anymore.” She crossed her arms and pointed to us. “Less talking, more typing, please!”

“I love it so much when Mary Stuart gets in boss mode,” Daphne said.

“Oh, me too. This is my favorite Mary Stuart.”

“Our golden retriever turns into a Doberman!”

Her phone rang, and she pointed her pencil at us. “I’m serious. Get on it or you two are fired.”

We laughed, but Daphne started reading the “Family Camp Prep List” out loud. “Find Volunteer Counselors, Get Wine Donated.” She tapped on the table. “Lanier! This system only works if you’re typing.”

“Sorry.” I nodded.

She started reading again, and I started transcribing. The way her jaw clenched made me realize that, underneath her smiley exterior, she was doggedly determined to make this work.

Daphne wanted to save camp for little girls just like her. I wanted to save camp for Daphne.

Daphne

TGIF

EVERY TIME I'M WITH MY FRIENDS, I FEEL GUILTIER AND GUILTIER that I haven't told them about Huff. They've been working themselves to the bone to save a camp that we all love, and I'm keeping this huge secret from them. But, I reason, Huff and I haven't had a chance to decide where we are in our relationship, so it certainly isn't the time to bring my friends into the mix. And between our work schedules—and the fact that I've put every spare minute into saving camp—we've barely seen each other for more than a brief snippet of time.

But today is going to change all that. Today, I'm opening my great-aunt Gracie's house for the first time in . . . Well, it has to have been years since I've darkened the door of this old beachfront cottage, which is ridiculous since it is less than two miles from my house. Great-Aunt Gracie had no children and left the property to both June and me when she died. We decided to keep it because we thought it would only increase in value. And, today, it's a neutral spot where Huff and I can meet. There's almost zero chance Lanier will drive by, see our cars, and put two and two together before we're ready to tell her we've started seeing each other again.

What happened between Huff and me at the wedding was one thing. That was the culmination of memories and nostalgia, passion and intensity, and it was definitely unplanned. But this, today, isn't a random happenstance in a bathroom that was not ours for the taking. This is a plan. We will meet here at 10 a.m. and part ways at five. TGIF indeed.

I am surprised by how clean the house is when I walk through the door. The caretaker didn't quit coming when she realized June and I never did. Even still, I unload the vacuum cleaner and Swiffer duster and Seventh Generation sprays. I unpack the sparkling water and the PBR that Huff drank when we were younger. I don't know what he drinks now, but the thought of him sitting on this porch with me, a PBR in his hand, is the single sexiest thing I can conceive of.

I run the vacuum over the mattress in the tiny bedroom and fight with the fitted floral sheet that, worn soft and thin with time, has been here since Great-Aunt Gracie. The scent of Tide fills the air, and I have the most vivid memory of sitting here, squealing with delight as my mother snapped this very same sheet over this very same bed, the floral fabric billowing down around me and blanketing me from the world. Maybe it's the memory of my mother, maybe it's the house, but I find this bed so comforting that I want to curl up and take a nap. But I am too keyed up to sleep.

By the time I am finished vacuuming, dusting, mopping, and wiping every square inch, I feel a sense of accomplishment, even though it hasn't done much to soothe my nerves. I have been so busy with save-Camp-Holly-Springs items this week that in between work and Henry

I haven't had much time to obsess over this meetup. So, as ten o'clock approaches, I start to worry about what will happen when Huff gets here. Will it be awkward? I need something to calm my nerves, but if my mother taught me anything, it is that I have to face my feelings, not dull them.

As I wait, I imagine I am eighteen again, wearing my cutoff jean shorts and white tank top, my feet bare like the first time Huff ever picked me up in his truck. Only, maybe I was nervous then, too, when Paula asked me to go with Huff early to camp to make sure the tables were set up by the river for Lanier's surprise eighteenth birthday party. Huff was a sophomore in college then. Heartbreak Huff, they called him. And, yes, he could indeed break a heart. He was just growing into his looks then, his tall, once-gangly body filled out and strong from his position as starting pitcher on Yale's baseball team. Every time he was home from school, I knew my crush on him was intensifying.

My heart raced as I rode beside him on the way to Holly Springs, my long, tan legs balanced on the edge of the open window, pink toes wiggling in time to the Steve Miller Band blaring from the ancient sound system. The scent of jasmine enveloped everything, even this old truck that mostly smelled of that disgusting dip Huff and his baseball buddies always had stuffed in their cheeks.

It was early May, three weeks from high school graduation, three months until I set off to work to keep the college scholarship I knew I deserved. It wasn't just because I had qualified for the insensitively named "abandoned child program"—the main reason I had gotten it—but also because I had worked so hard to earn straight As all through high school. Admittedly, it had been a lot easier once I went to live with Lanier's family. It was amazing how much time I had to study once there was someone to cook me dinner and tell me to go to bed, to make sure I came in by curfew and spent my afternoons at sports practice, not working to make ends meet. For two years, Paula and John gave me the gift of an adolescence. And, instead of rebelling against their rules, I embraced them, craved them. Someone cared about me. Finally.

Once we pulled up by the river, Huff stopped at the softball field. "What are we doing?" I asked. "This isn't where Lanier's party is."

"I just need to loosen up my shoulder." He hopped out of the truck and turned. "You coming? I need a batter."

I laughed, my wavy hair flowing down my back. The grass on my bare feet was familiar and warm, and the sun on my face felt like heaven. Huff opened his tailgate, and, as he handed me the bat, our hands touched, and my heart started racing. That was how I knew, for sure, I liked Huff. The sporadic flirting of the last couple of years was real. In that moment, the rumor that Bobby Perkins, the guy I'd been talking to, was reportedly making out with Kyleigh Blackburn in his truck last weekend didn't faze me much. And, suddenly, I knew how I could explore my crush on Huff *and* get back at Bobby. So I hoisted myself up onto Huff's tailgate, legs swinging as he got out the equipment, and said, "What's in it for me?"

He laughed. "Um . . . the pleasure of my company."

This plan just might work. I smirked at him flirtatiously. "I was thinking more like I bat for you, you come to prom with me."

He laughed. "Daph, you're out of your mind. I'm a sophomore in college. Why in the world would I go to your high school prom?"

"The pleasure of my company."

"Touché." He slung his bag of balls over his shoulder.

"So is that a yes?"

He walked away and I jumped down, following him.

"It is definitely not a yes."

I sweetened the deal. "What if I hit a home run?"

He opened the chain-link gate to the field and laughed. "If you hit a home run, I'll come to prom with you dressed like a chicken."

I scrunched my nose. "I'd really rather you wear a tux."

"Have you actually ever hit a baseball?"

I shrugged. "I'm a fast learner."

Not exactly a lie. I was a fast learner. But what I didn't tell him was that the only thing my father ever did with me was take me to the batting cages. Could I hit a home run? Doubtful. But I was willing to try. Because the thought of seeing Bobby's face when I showed up at prom with Heartbreak Huff was too good to pass up.

"I get three strikes, right?"

Huff snorted. "Old pro, I see." He paused. "Come here. I'll let you try to hit my practice pitches."

I stood at home plate, choked up on the bat, my butt out, the wind blowing up the back of my jean shorts. When his first "practice pitch" barreled toward me, I screamed and ducked. This was not starting out well.

"Want to just call this off now?" Huff asked.

I laughed like I was supremely confident.

The second ball was much of the same. But by the third something strange happened. Huff barely even threw it. This was not a pitch; it was a toss to a toddler. And I had the most gloriously unexpected feeling that Heartbreak Huff wanted to go to prom with me.

I was so startled by the thought that I almost missed. But I didn't. I swung with all my might. The ball sailed way over Huff's head and into the outfield. I took off like a shot. I rounded first, then second. I was vaguely aware of the fact that Huff had the ball and was running toward me. I was also vaguely aware of the fact that Huff ran like a cheetah; I ran like a kitten. This likely would not end well for me.

As I was about to round third, I felt not a tap but both of Huff's arms wrap around my waist to lift me off the ground. I was basically still running in the air as Huff tripped over the base and, in slow motion, I landed on my side. Huff, who hadn't totally lost his balance, landed with his hands on either side of me. I was laughing as I rolled on my back. Huff wasn't laughing. He was studying me. He popped up and offered me his hand, pulling me up. I brushed myself off and stepped closer to him, wiping an invisible speck of sand from his face. "I didn't hit a home run," I said sadly. "And I scraped my hand."

He took the hand that was on his face and turned it over to kiss my palm, which felt like both the sweetest and the most illicit thing anyone had ever done. "Is that better?"

I grinned, trying to think of something clever to say, but found myself lost in his eyes, mesmerized by what I knew was about to happen. I rose onto my tiptoes and wrapped my arms around Huff's neck as his wrapped his around my back. And maybe it should have felt weird because this was Lanier's big brother, but as our lips met, I felt an electric jolt through my entire body that I'd never felt before. I was breathless as he pulled me toward him and kept kissing me. I don't know how long we kissed. Seconds? Minutes? But I knew when I pulled away that I was forever changed, that *this*, this thing right here, was what ruined my mother. Because I couldn't see a way out. I had no idea how I would possibly walk away.

"Damn," he said under his breath. And I thought it must have hit him too, how complicated this all was. But then he said, "Where did you learn to kiss like that?"

I didn't say anything, just smiled, although I could return the compliment. I had kissed my fair share of boys, and although Huff was a great kisser, there was more to it. We had a connection that, until this moment, we'd both been able to deny. There was no denying it now.

"You know we could do that a lot at prom."

He laughed. "That's a good point."

"So will you go with me?"

He leaned down and kissed me again. "Daphne Miller, I'll go anywhere you want."

It's a promise Huff is still keeping today, twelve years later, as Great-Aunt Gracie's house isn't a convenient place for him to meet me. When I hear the tires of his truck crackling over the gravel, I open the screen door and stand on the small stoop, waiting like I'm not nervous.

"Well, hi," I say as he gets out of the truck and grins at me, putting his hands over his heart. He walks to me, eyes glued to mine. And with one hand around my neck and the other around my waist, he pulls me in and kisses me long and slow. This is the kind of heat that I have dreamed of—that, I realize, I have missed. We have all day. We have nowhere to be. Before I can even realize it, he is pulling my shirt over my head, I have thrown his into the driveway, and we are skin on skin before we even open the door.

"This. You," he whispers as we stumble through the house toward the tiny bedroom.

I nod because I know what he means. I know what he feels. He is the only man who has ever truly known me. He knows all my secrets and scars and he loves me in spite of them. It is a feat that seems impossible in its undertaking, but here we are.

He is kissing my ankle and then my knee on Great-Aunt Gracie's floral sheets that I now hope she isn't somehow haunting. I sit up and tap him on the shoulder. He looks up at me. "I'm doing some of my best work over here."

I laugh. "You are. You totally are. But the purpose of this day was to, you know, figure out what the hell we're doing."

He sighs and makes his way up to the headboard and leans back on it, putting his arm around me and kissing my head. "So, lay it on me."

I'm so comfortable, so relaxed in his arms, that part of me wants to sink into the magic that is the two of us and forget the rest. I don't speak, so he does. "You're not that same girl anymore," he says, and I nod, thinking about the year in my twenties when I was frightfully like my mother. When I was drinking way too much to ease the pressure of getting into law school and making excuses to myself as to why the pills I was supposed to take for studying were now getting me through the entire day. The scary part was, it happened so slowly I hardly noticed it. Drinking a few nights a week as an undergrad while out with my friends turned into drinking too much every night, often alone, and hiding it from Huff. The Adderall I had gotten only for "study emergencies"—which I didn't actually need—became a many-times-a-day thing. Huff lived that with me. He wouldn't have let it break us. But I did.

"I haven't been that girl for a long time," I say. "I swear, Huff, after I got clean that first time, I haven't touched anything. I won't. Not ever again. I hated that version of myself. I hated feeling like I was destined to repeat my mother's mistakes." Even as I say it, a twinge of fear pings me. But I push it away.

"You are not your mother, Daph."

Huff used to remind me of that. When I went through my rough patch, I was at an age where reckless behavior was commonplace; it was easy to lie to myself about my vices. My *everyone is doing it* mentality pushed me over the edge. It kept me there longer than I'd like to admit.

"I know I'm not my mom. But I want you to know that I'm not."

He smiles and kisses me. "I know I wasn't there during your recovery, but Daph, I can't tell you how much I wanted to be. I've kept up with you through Mom and Lanier for all this time, and I'm so proud of you. I always was." He pauses and takes a breath, as if weighing something. "I don't want to scare you away, but I have to say this: I have never stopped loving you for one day. Not then. Not now. I know it might be too soon to say it, but I was all in then, Daphne. I still am."

I'm smiling so big I feel like my face might break in two. "I never stopped loving you either, Huff. Not for a millisecond. But—" I bite my lip. "What about Lanier?"

"She was worried about you back then," he says. "She was worried about us being together because of your . . ." He trails off. "Troubles." That was a very delicate way to put it.

"But what if it wasn't that? What if she just didn't want us together, plain and simple? What if she still feels the same way?"

"I think we just lay it out on the table. We're grown-ups. We want to be together for real." He raises his eyebrow. "Right?"

I don't answer. I say, "What about Henry?"

Huff gasps. "You have a child?"

We both laugh.

"What's Henry into these days?"

"Soccer, karate, and hammering stuff."

He snaps his fingers. "Me too!"

"Seriously, Huff. I need to be clear that I love Henry more than anyone or anything in this world. More than myself or Lanier or June. Even you. If I let you into his life, that's it."

For a moment, I wonder if this conversation is insane. But it doesn't feel it. Instead, it feels like we took a brief interlude, but our love hasn't aged. I have friends who have experienced this, who have said that when you get back together with someone after a breakup, you aren't starting over; the clock doesn't reset. You are just picking up where you left off. So maybe that's what we're doing. All I know is that the thought of being with Huff makes me feel whole.

He takes my hand and turns to look at me. "Daph, let me be clear. You are it for me. I will move in with you—or you can move in with me. I will face off with my sister no matter how mad she is at first. I could not possibly love a person more, and I will love your son just that much. Okay?"

I know this, but hearing him say it gives me that face-breaking smile again. I know he will be an incredible stepfather to Henry. Not only did Huff have an amazing example of a father but he is also a doctor, a caretaker. And I know how he's taken care of me. "This is a lot of talking," I whisper.

He nods enthusiastically, his mouth disappearing into mine. For a moment, a split second, I wonder how this is all going to play out. Can we make it work this time? Really make it stick without letting drama get in the way? Surely Lanier will see how in love we are, will understand that this is real—that this is healthy—and that we are meant to be together, after all. She will be excited because she knows that I have been completely clean for seven years and will continue to be for the rest of my life, so she won't worry. But, for a second, none of that matters. For now, it feels so magnificent to be lost in the moment that I can't worry about any of it.

Lanier

THROWBACK

Five Weeks Later

Subject: Hard Things

To: marystuart@harrispr.com; lanier@bookmasters.com

Dear Songbirds:

Lanier, you know we will help make your wedding favors. No problem at all.

MS, I truly cannot think of anything I'd rather do than be the plus one at your aunt's retirement party. (I can't believe Ted would go fishing and miss that!)

Now that that's out of the way . . . Are we ready for the big weekend? Can you believe it's finally here? Six weeks of campaigning, one hundred families. You two are dynamos. Lanier, the videos of local authors talking about their favorite camp experiences was nothing short of inspired. Mary Stuart, tapping into sorority and fraternity mailing lists to find interested families? Genius. I love you two more than words can say, and I cannot wait to party like it's 1999 with you this weekend!

Fair winds and following seas,
Daphne

I smiled as I closed out of my email, realizing that Daphne hadn't asked for any hard things. It made sense since Mary Stuart and I had devoted every free second to pulling together an epic family camp weekend on such short notice. There would be sailing, of course, and all the usual activities like horseback riding, archery, canoeing, riflery, basketball, softball, and arts and crafts. And it wouldn't be camp without a talent show—and a Holly Springs vs. Rock Springs softball game! One of the most amazing things was how hard Rich and the Rock Springs staff had worked to help make it happen, making phone calls, volunteering their cabins so we could have more families, getting their staff involved, and helping in every imaginable way, even though the event wouldn't benefit them. It warmed my heart. Everyone on staff for the summer was donating their time this weekend, so basically our only cost was food. When it was all said and done, we would net out close to $150,000 in this one weekend, not to mention the donations we hoped to rake in. This was, after all, more of a fundraiser than anything else. I honestly hadn't believed it would happen, but between the massive campaign Mary Stuart's PR firm had launched and Daphne and I begging everyone we had ever known to come, we had not only filled up camp for the weekend but were down to only twenty-six open slots for the actual summer camp—which Daphne thought Finn just might get a grant for. I was trying to get back to work when my email dinged again.

Re: Hard Things

To: daphne@millerlaw.com; lanier@bookmasters.com

Songbirds!!!

I completely forgot to tell you about the BEST idea I had a few weeks ago! Holly Springs Lemonade Stands! I already emailed our mailing list, and campers are having their own neighborhood lemonade stands and donating the profits to camp as we speak! (Type?) I've sent everyone who's participating cutesy lemonade recipes and donor information cards and cute logos and . . . we've already gotten a ton of interest! I don't know how much money it will raise—and I'm sorry I didn't tell you earlier—but as a PR stunt, it's perfect!

What do you think? (It's too late to say no!)

FWAFS,
Mary Stuart

Daphne and I must have typed back "Genius" at the same moment.

I didn't know how I was possibly supposed to concentrate on work with everything going on, but, well, duty called.

I needed to write a review for a new debut novel I just adored, but I couldn't quite figure out what I wanted to say. Before I could decide, the bell on the door tinkled and I looked up to see Harriet from the bakery walking in with about a dozen boxes precariously balanced between her outstretched arms and chin. I jumped off my stool to help her as she almost crashed into the front table, which was always filled with staff picks.

"What in the world is all this?" I asked as I took the boxes one by one and stacked them on the counter. Before she even answered, I was pretty sure I knew. Ever since I got back from my bachelorette party six weeks ago, Bryce had been super fiancé.

After our first camp strategy meeting, I had found him waiting in my condo, which is, conveniently, right above the store. It was the best commute I could think of. He jumped up off the couch, wrapped me in his arms, and said, "I am so sorry. You are absolutely right. Total honesty from here on out. I love you, and I don't want to have any secrets from you."

I was shocked, especially since I hadn't heard from him all weekend. Sure, the phone worked both ways, but I was being stubborn. I felt I deserved an apology. But, well, part of the reason I hadn't called was because I felt guilty. That spark I felt when I saw Rich was more than any engaged woman should feel. But it wasn't like anything had happened. So, I kissed Bryce and whispered, "Total honesty from here on out."

He handed me a long, thin box. I opened it and gasped when I saw a sapphire bracelet. "Bryce! This is too much!"

"Your something blue," he said, fastening it to my wrist. I ignored the little voice that told me he was still hiding something.

It was the first of many sweet and thoughtful gestures. Dinner dates, my favorite wine open when I came home from work, flowers at the bookstore. He had even spent every night at my condo, which he usually hated because it was so small. In fact, Bryce had scarcely gone back to his house in two weeks and hardly even complained about the aging bathroom, the barely functioning stove, and his usual laundry list of things wrong with the place I loved best. We would be living in the new house he was building for us after the wedding and I was savoring my space in the meantime. I ignored that not wanting to move in with him as soon as possible might be a red flag.

But red flag or not, it was the happiest I had been with him in some time. Things felt back on track. I knew I still needed to push him to tell me why he had quit his job so suddenly, but this bright, shiny Bryce and his bright, shiny gestures were great at distracting me. I decided I could live with what he told me—that it was a personal decision.

So, now, when Harriet from Cape Carolina Cakes walked in and announced, "Bryce told me to bring these cupcakes for your friends this weekend," I was bathed in love all over again. She handed me a sealed envelope, and I felt my stomach flip.

L,

Please forgive me. Please forgive me. Please forgive me. I've had something come up at work and I have to stay here to sort it out. I know this weekend is really important, and I was looking forward to visiting the place that has been so special to you. But I promise I will make it there someday soon. And I hope the articles helped in small part to save the place you love. I love you. Don't forget it.

Bryce

P.S. You don't even have to share the cupcakes if you don't want to!

I rolled my eyes and tossed the note on the counter, my excitement over yet another peace offering instantly deflated. This, *this* was why I didn't want him working for his mother. There was zero work-life balance, and there could be an emergency at a moment's notice. And now he had reminded me that his media connections had helped our cause greatly, so I couldn't even be properly mad. I lifted the top of one of the boxes. German chocolate cupcakes. My favorite. Well played, Bryce. Well played.

Even still, as Harriet walked out the door, I texted him:

Seriously?

No bubbles. I restacked some bookmarks, grabbed a cupcake, and went back to my desk. Halfway into my review writing, the bell tinkled again and in he walked. "Ah, the busy career man himself."

I could tell by his face that he was *not in the mood.* Well, guess what? Neither was I. I was already embarrassed that I had aired so much dirty laundry to my friends at my bachelorette. I was just venting, after all. So now I was trying to smooth things over so Daphne and Mary Stuart could see for themselves that all was well. Bryce not showing up for family camp was in direct opposition to that plan.

"I said I was sorry." Yeah . . . he was irritated. "I sent cupcakes. I wrote a note. I can't control my work schedule, and a little understanding from my fiancée would be nice. You're supposed to be on my team."

"I am on your team," I blurted out. "But you've barely even met Ted and Mary Stuart and they only live an hour away. I just wanted you to be there this weekend so everyone could get to know you and see for themselves how great you are."

Bryce leaned over the counter and massaged his temples. "Lanier, I have a lot going on right now. Impressing your friends isn't at the tip-top of my to-do list at the moment, believe it or not."

It was like Dr. Jekyll and Mr. Hyde. He had spent two weeks being a saint and now this. "It isn't about impressing my friends, Bryce." (Okay, it kind of was.) "But you know how important this weekend is to me. Holly Springs is one of the most important places in my life."

"And I could argue that no one has done more to try to help you save it than I have."

I exhaled deeply. I couldn't respond to that. Because he was right. His phone beeped, and he looked down. "Look, Lanier, I have to go. I just wanted to tell you good luck this weekend. I'm sorry I won't be there, but if we're going to get married, you're going to have to cut me some slack. I can't be perfect all the time."

That was it. No kiss. No goodbye hug. No "I love you." *I can't be perfect all the time*. I almost laughed as he walked out the door. What did that even mean? These past two weeks had been an act? He'd been pretending to be perfect and now the truth was out?

A trio of teenagers walked in, and I pinned on a smile. "Let me know if I can help you girls."

"Where's your romance?" the shortest one with a tight T-shirt and long cornflower-braided pigtails asked.

"I think it's gone," I said, under my breath.

"What?" one of her friends asked.

"It's in the back." I gestured toward the boxes. "Anyone want a cupcake?"

"I can't. I'm doing Keto," the third girl responded.

Bless her heart. Her two friends ate their cupcakes right in front of her.

"There are parts of your brain only fueled by carbs, you know," cornflower braids said.

"And there are types of cancer only fueled by sugar," Keto girl shot back.

I looked back at the computer screen, thinking that, for all the complications adulthood was handing me right now, I wouldn't be a teenager again for anything. Although, thinking about being a teenager made me think about Rich and that counter in the sailing hut and . . .

The bell on the door shook me out of my thoughts and I gasped. "Huff! What are you doing here?"

He shrugged as he strode over to the counter. I noticed the high school girls whispering and giggling. Oh my gosh. Was Huff hot? *Ew.* "I had the day off, so I thought I'd come see Mom and Dad."

An idea hit me. "You should go to camp! Bryce can't come at the last minute. You can be in my cabin! You could be my family!"

"I am your family."

"Well, you know what I mean. It's going to be great. June will be there, obviously, and Ted and Mary Stuart and Daphne, Henry, and Steven—"

"Steven's going to be there?"

I tried to ignore the way his face clouded over. "He's Henry's dad. It's family camp."

"So will he be in the cabin with Henry and Daphne?"

"Not this again, Huff. Yes. He'll be in their cabin. Where else would he be?"

"You know what, I think I will come. That might be fun."

It occurred to me then what I had just done. For years, I had made it my mission to keep Daphne and Huff apart, and here I was willingly thrusting them together. That said, Steven would be there, and between Henry and, you know, *saving an entire summer camp,* Huff would be the last thing on Daphne's mind. Plus, I didn't want to be the only one who wasn't bringing a family member this weekend. Mom and Dad were dying to come, but they had planned a weekend in the mountains with their friends ages ago, and I didn't want to take that away from them. I would risk a Huff and Daphne run-in to have my favorite big brother by my side any day.

So, I decided to embrace how thrilled I felt. I ran out from behind the counter and threw my arms around his neck. "You're the best brother in the whole world!" I turned toward the box. "You get a cupcake."

He eyed them and, because I knew him, I knew he was picking the one with the most frosting. "Don't mind if I do." He paused. "I'm going to get lunch with Mom and Dad. Then I'll run by the house, grab my high school bathing suits. That should be interesting . . ."

"It's perfect. A camp throwback." Dropping Huff off at Camp Rock Springs was perhaps one of my earliest memories. He was seven, I was five, and I cried every day for the entire two weeks he was gone. He was my best friend, and I wanted to do everything he did. I couldn't understand the next year why I had to go to Holly Springs while he was at Rock Springs.

He smiled. "This is a really great idea. I'll meet you there tonight?"

"I'll meet you there tonight."

I returned to my typing yet again. This time, I found the perfect words.

Daphne

A CARRIE

MY HEART NEARLY STOPS WHEN THE DOOR CHIMES AND I LOOK UP to see Huff walking through the front door of my office. At first, I'm nervous he's going to blow our secret, but then I realize there's no need to be. He could be anyone. Any client. "Huff," I say smoothly, even though my heart is beating like mad. The past eight weeks have been magic. Perfection. True love in every sense of the word. We have spent every free second together when he isn't at the hospital and I'm not at work, with Henry, or on Save Holly Springs patrol. When we aren't together, we're texting or talking on the phone. He has come over every night the last week to go over camp checklists and help me stuff and mail packets of fundraising information to campers past and present. And I have helped him study for a continuing education course he is taking and make a tough call about a grumpy nurse. Steven and I have discussed ad nauseam what this new phase might look like, and we are in agreement that letting Henry get to know Huff slowly is the right move, considering how serious my feelings are for him.

Even still, I was nervous the first time they met. But Henry, being four, didn't think much of it. Huff came by, and I simply asked, "Hey, Henry, want to come with my friend Huff and me to get ice cream?"

He replied with a very enthusiastic, "Yeah!" Obviously. Who turns down ice cream?

"So," I had continued, "Huff is Lanier's brother and Polly and J's son." Polly and J was what Henry called Paula and John. He looked up at Huff, studying him intently, and I was nervous about what he was going to say next.

"Are you sure?" Henry asked.

"Definitely," Huff said. "Why?"

"You're just so much taller than Lanier."

Well played, Henry. Ice broken.

They have hung out casually a few times since then, and it has felt so easy. Seeing Huff with Henry makes it feel like we are meant to be partners.

Finn looks up when he sees Huff, his eyes widening, then looks back at me, then at his computer. "Um. I'm sorry. I don't see an appointment on here."

"It's okay," I say confidently. "This one wasn't in my calendar. Huff, come on in."

"Um, Daph," Finn says as Huff walks in my office.

"I'll be just a second," I say. I turn to Finn.

He whispers, "Oh my gosh. That's him, isn't it? Your secret lover?"

I glare at him. I have told Finn zero details, only that I am seeing someone—which is driving him insane. "Do not call him that. This is a very sensitive situation."

Finn perks up. "But it's him, isn't it?"

I half smile, and he says, "Oh my gosh. This is the most *Sex and the City* thing that's ever happened to me. I'll hold your calls."

"There will be none of that at work," I say. But as soon as I shut the door behind me, Huff picks me up and I wrap my legs around his waist, kissing him urgently. We are in that glorious beginning where being separated for two days feels like an eternity, a cruel joke from an evil god that is testing our sheer will to live. Because how can we breathe if we aren't together?

He sets me down on my desk and says into my ear, between kisses, "How's the checklist?"

I pull away, remembering. "It's terrible!" I moan. "The mom who volunteered to be camp doctor this weekend is sick, ironically, and the chef cut off the tip of his finger slicing garlic bread. He'll be fine by tomorrow, but what in the world am I going to feed hundreds of people tonight?"

To my surprise, Huff smiles. "Well, for one, I can be camp doctor. And two, have you forgotten who the king of church dinners was?"

I shake my head.

"Why are you shaking your head? Do you not remember the massive vats of spaghetti you and I used to make? Or the millions of pancakes?"

I have not forgotten. "You can't just swoop in and save the day, Huff."

He pulls back, looking puzzled, then kisses me. "I'm not saving you, Daphne. I'm helping you. That's what couples do."

I have taken care of myself and Henry for so long that I have forgotten that. "That aside," I say, "you aren't coming to family camp."

"Oh, I'm coming to family camp."

I pull back from him, stunned. "Um, no you are not. You absolutely cannot come."

His lips make their way down my neck to my collarbone. "Lanier insisted that I come, so how can I not?"

"If you come, she will know," I say, somewhat breathlessly.

"We can be discreet," he says, pulling away, with a wink.

"I think we both know that isn't true."

"No one knows yet."

"Finn knew the moment you walked in the door."

He's on the other side of my neck now. "Just think how fun it will be. We can sneak out at night and meet by the river, make out behind the activities hut while everyone else is at archery . . ."

I can't help but laugh. I don't know if it's how cute he is or how woozy these kisses are making me, but I give in. "Okay. Fine. You can come. And I find you totally irresistible. Is that what you'd like to hear?"

He nods in the most adorable way. "Yes. That's exactly what I want to hear. Always."

"Okay. But this begs the question—"

"When do we tell Lanier?"

I nod. It has been weighing on me perhaps even more heavily than usual because of this other huge thing I've been keeping from her, the thing Mary Stuart and I thought we could resolve. But, alas, six weeks have passed, and Lanier's wedding is still very much on.

"I was thinking we get married and *then* we tell her," he says. "Then she can be as mad as she wants but she can't do anything about it."

I tilt my head. "We get married without my best friend—your sister—there?"

He flops down in one of the chairs across from my desk. "I will admit, the plan could use some work. You just have to promise me, Daph—"

I sit on his lap. My turn to kiss his neck and whisper in his ear. "No matter what she says, no matter how upset she gets, it's you and me. We weather the storm."

He kisses me, inhaling like maybe he can breathe me in. "I love you, Daph."

"I love you too," I say, and I marvel that it is true. These past few weeks have felt realer than any other in my life. More vibrant. Truer. What I can't figure out is how I lived this long without Huff, how I missed him for this many years without breaking down, begging him to take me back, to run away with me. Okay. Maybe run away is dramatic. We probably wouldn't run anywhere.

"Oh," he says. "I've decided. I'm selling my house. I'm moving here."

My eyes widen. He lives an hour and a half away, in the same town as Mary Stuart and Ted, but still. This is big for a lot of reasons. "Did you get a job here?"

"No. Not yet. But everyone needs doctors, right?"

"But will you have to take a pay cut? Work part-time? Aren't you still paying off your student loans?"

He smiles at me. "Literally the only thing I care about is you and me and Henry and the family we could start. The rest will work itself out."

I sink into him, smelling that part between his neck and his shoulder where all his pheromones must collect. I do not need anything in the world but my two boys. Huff and Henry. We will be the happiest family in the world. Well, with Steven thrown in, too, of course. And even if I have to tell Lanier about Bryce and I get disbarred and—

My phone alarm goes off, startling me straight off Huff's lap. I smooth my skirt. "If you are sure you want to come to family camp, I will slot you in as camp doctor and, to add insult to injury, I will put you on KP with me. Spaghetti for four hundred fifty here we come?"

He gets up and kisses me again. "I can't think of anything I'd rather do than kitchen patrol."

"Daph," Finn calls through the door. "Do you want me to move your eleven o'clock?"

"You can open the door," I say, rolling my eyes.

"Are you sure?"

"As much as you want it to be, this isn't the *Sex and the City* package delivery scene."

Finn flings the door open. "I wish it were. I was born to be a part of Samantha Jones's office staff."

Huff starts to walk toward the door. "Oh, please. I think we both know Daphne is a Carrie." He doesn't so much as crack a smile as he walks out the door, leaving Finn and me standing in momentary shock before we double over in laughter.

"Oh, Daph. That tall drink of water is a keeper."

I smile because I know. I really do. He is a keeper, he is all mine, and, this time, I'm not going to let him get away.

June

PERFECT TIMING

I DIDN'T INHERIT MY MOTHER'S ANGELIC VOICE. NEITHER DID DAPHNE. But Melanie? Melanie had a voice that could bring spirits up, houses down, and grown men to tears. Even though it sometimes felt like she was slipping away from me—her scent, the feel of her hand when it squeezed mine, even her face—I remembered her voice perfectly. Just the thought of it immediately sent me back to the pew at Christ Church listening to one of her melodic solos, or to the front row of the Holly Springs talent show knowing that no one could possibly beat her.

After she died, during those long cruel months, I would dream of her voice. I would hear her and feel her so close to me that I would wake feeling like if I could just stay in that other world for a moment longer, I could bring her back. Even all these years later, when I was particularly stressed or especially tired, I'd dream of Melanie singing to me in the choir loft. If only I could reach her.

I awoke the morning of family camp weekend covered in sweat, another night of Melanie slipping through my fingers. The sweat was appropriate because I felt like I had been sprinting on a treadmill for six solid weeks.

As I got up and got ready for the day, I worried I hadn't fully thought through the details of what it would take to feed, house, and entertain four hundred thirty-seven men, women, and children. I certainly hadn't thought about how much more work it would be to not only fill up Holly Springs but also Rock Springs. Rich had very kindly offered to let us use it. He was a good kid. A star camper. I fretted for years that we had been too hard on him the summer he was head sailing instructor—the summer we had to let him go. Fortunately, he hadn't let one misstep define him.

I grabbed a stepladder and climbed onto it to hang a fresh shower curtain in Cabin 14. To get through this, I told myself that all I was doing was hosting a camp weekend. How hard could that be? I could do it with my eyes closed. But these weren't children who were ready to accept a new experience. These were adults quick to find fault. These were adults that I needed to have the time of their lives because their fun, quite literally, would define Holly Springs's future.

As I fastened the last clip, I looked around and wondered: Were the parents going to be totally underwhelmed and unimpressed with the spartan wood cabins, each with six sets of bunk beds, that the kids enjoyed so much? Would they turn their noses up at the rings of rust around the sink drains that, no matter how thoroughly they were scrubbed, were impossible to keep at bay? Would the fresh air coming through the windows and the lack of AC be too rustic for them? Would the puppy chow Chex Mix the kids loved as an afternoon snack seem messy and unhealthy? The dining hall food too basic? If so, this would be a failed experiment. If so, our dreams might be dashed and we might have to accept, once and for all, that Holly Springs would be gone for good.

But today was not a day for such thoughts. Today was a day for positivity, for possibility. It was a day to see, as I told our little songbirds during their first summers, how high we could fly. As I walked out of Cabin 14 and past the canteen and the camp store, the morning dew on the grass soaking through my shoes, I checked the slender watch that had been on my arm every day for the past twenty-six years. It was a fancy Swiss watch, one of the only nice things I owned. Every time I looked at it, it reminded me that time was a gift.

I could use a little more of it now. A wave of panic washed over me as I realized that our guests would begin arriving in five short hours. It was the same feeling I had the first time I walked these grounds as the official owner of Camp Holly Springs.

I had quit my teaching job with health insurance and a 403(b), had sunk every dime my parents had left me into camp. Was it an emotionally charged, potentially catastrophic decision? Absolutely. I had a half-full camp for the summer that would not meet expenses and zero safety net. And I knew that the major changes those previous few months hadn't exactly fostered my clearest decisions: My parents dying. Planning their funeral. Cleaning out their house and putting it on the market. Want to be gutted? Try selling your childhood home and trashing everything inside it, every memory you have ever had, knowing that it's all you have left when you are just barely past childhood yourself.

I remember sitting alone on this very grass, the day after I closed on Holly Springs, wondering what in the world I had done. Just as I was about to enter a full-on panic spiral, I heard a noise in the distance. Tires on gravel. When I squinted, I could just make out the aged black Cadillac that had belonged to my grandmother and now belonged to Melanie.

The night before I had called my sister, needing to hear her voice. I had tried to act happy, upbeat, and totally certain about my decision. When she stepped out of the car, I ran and threw my arms around her. "You're here," I whispered into her hair.

She pulled back and smiled at me. "You're totally *fine.* Fine, fine, fine," she said in a high-pitched voice.

I laughed, realizing she was mimicking me from the night before, as I walked to the back seat to get my precious niece. "Junie!" she squealed, reaching her arms out to me. I unbuckled her booster and she jumped into my arms. "You bought a camp?"

"I did." Then I turned to Melanie, who was standing right behind me. "What in the world have I done?"

Melanie turned and started to walk toward the river, and I followed her, Daphne on my hip. When we reached the river, she dug in her pocket and pulled out a watch. I just looked at her. "For you," she said. Then she turned it over and I saw the inscription: *Perfect timing.*

I couldn't help but smile. "That is so nice," I said. "So I'm guessing you knew this panic attack was coming?"

"Maybe a little."

As I slid the watch on, Daphne said, "Ooooh. Pretty."

Melanie smoothed my hair and tucked it behind my ears. "Junie, Mom would be so proud."

That was all it took for the flood gates to burst. "Do you think?"

"Do I think? Oh my gosh, I know! No one loved this camp more than Mom. No one. We knew the camp cheer before we knew nursery rhymes. I think this is the perfect way to honor her memory."

And that was the way I had been living my life for twenty-six years. Honoring my mother's memory with this camp. For twenty-six years, I had been all but alone in that. Now, as I opened the door to my office and saw Daphne, Lanier, and Mary Stuart leaning over Jillian's computer monitor, I realized I wasn't alone anymore.

"My songbirds are here!" I exclaimed.

Daphne was wild-eyed. "Henry and Steven are unpacking," she said. "But, June, we did it. The grants for the scholarships came through. We officially have a full, sold-out summer at Camp Holly Springs!"

"And four girls on the waiting list with more adding every day!" Jillian noted.

They all hooted and hollered as I felt a kind of bliss wash over me that I experienced fairly often here. It wasn't only that we were one step closer to saving this place; it was that they had done this. They had used their bright, creative minds to come up with a plan, to work as a team, to engage the other alums that had been a part of their summers here.

For seventy-six years that was what Camp Holly Springs had been doing. It had been turning scared little girls into self-sufficient women. We weren't saved. Far from it, in fact. But we were closer; we were trying. Twenty-six years ago, I had left behind my life and my friends for an existence that no one had understood.

As I pulled my clipboard out to review the checklist for the day with these three who had grown from girls to women right in front of me, I thought that maybe no one else needed to understand my choices. Only I did. And I was more confident than ever that I had done the right thing after all.

Lanier

A BLANKET OF STARS

AS I LOOKED AROUND THE FULL DINING HALL, MARVELING THAT WE had managed to get all these families here for the first dinner of this camp weekend, I remembered something I had forgotten: Few things in life were as joyful as a full dining hall at Camp Holly Springs. Sure, it was a little strange that instead of just girls, it was also crowded with moms and dads, little brothers, and a spare grandparent or twenty. But the sounds of voices rising and falling, laughter breaking out in clumps, songs emerging from corners where camp friends were reunited, were all the same.

Even so, I was barely aware of anything that was going on around me. All I could think about was that Rich was so close his shoulder was nearly touching mine as we stood at the end of the room and wrapped utilitarian forks and knives—still hot from the sanitizer—in paper napkins for breakfast in the morning. I hadn't seen or talked to him since my bachelorette party. But that night had thawed whatever chill was between us. I wouldn't say it was like old times necessarily, but Rich seemed relaxed, which made me relaxed. And, what's more, he had to have sought me out. Because no one really wants to wrap silverware.

Henry tore down the center aisle of the room as Steven looked on from the picnic table they were sitting at a few feet away. "Aunt Lanier! Guess what!"

I scooped him up onto my hip. "What?"

"Mommy taught me the camp song in the car on the way here!"

"She did?"

He nodded. Then he looked at Rich inquisitively. They had met earlier in the day. "Do you think you could teach me the Rock Springs camp song? So when I go to camp I'll know it?"

Rich put his hand up. "Oh yeah, man. For sure!" Henry high-fived him. "Do you think I could come to camp this summer? I asked Mom to call you. I am very tall, you know."

Rich looked at him seriously as Henry wriggled out of my arms.

"Your mom and I will discuss it." Henry stood up as straight as possible. "You *are* very tall."

Huff, wearing an apron covered in spaghetti sauce, came out just as Henry was saying, "Now, I'm bored. What should we do?"

Before I could tell Henry to go back to his table, Huff jumped in. "How about I teach you some of my killer baseball moves?"

Henry's eyes widened, and he nodded. Then he looked from Huff to me. He had met Huff a long time ago, but he didn't know him that well. "Huff, can we practice that spin pitch again?"

I looked at Huff. "Again?"

Huff shrugged, but he looked a little red. He squeezed Henry's shoulder. "Vivid imagination. Smart kid."

"I did get all Es and Ss on my report cards this year," Henry said seriously, leaving us doubled over in laughter.

As Huff and Henry walked away, June and Daphne came in from where they'd been standing outside. They were arguing behind us in hushed tones about who was going to do most of the talk onstage to welcome everyone to family camp.

"You did most of the work to organize this," June was saying. "You should talk."

"June, are you kidding me? This is your camp. You've done all the work, and, besides, everyone wants to see you."

June sighed. "Fine. I'll welcome them, lead them in a camp song or two, and then let you take over."

This was old hat for June, but I could still feel her nerves. The place she loved was on the line. And I understood how she might have felt like it was on the line because of her, so she wanted someone new to step into the spotlight.

Rich raised his eyebrow as they passed us. "Since when does Daphne argue about doing most of the talking? Seems to me she has always loved to hear herself talk."

"You don't say."

Rich looked around. "Man, this was a great idea. We should have thought of family camp a long time ago."

"I had no idea how many people would want to do this—and in such a short amount of time."

Rich shrugged. "I guess we should have. I mean, who wouldn't want to go back to a simpler time in their life? To feel young again? I'm pretty sure flying through the air on a piece of wire and splashing into the lake can make you forget all about your problems—at least for a little while."

I smiled. "Is that how you feel about owning Rock Springs now? Is it like being at camp all the time?"

"Well, I mean, yes and no. These past couple years have put us through the wringer, but not like June. But, no, it isn't quite like being ten, when my biggest worry was whether I was going to get Reese's Cups or M&M's at the canteen before rest hour."

I remembered those days, when the sweetness of a Reese's Cup combined with the electric acidity of a Coca-Cola was life-giving, an antidote to the summer sun. Life was so simple.

"I'm glad you've been able to power through the last few years. Not that I'm surprised. That's always been you, Rich. Making the best out of a bad situation. Finding the good in the bad. I wish I could be more like that."

As he reached across me to put a bunch of wrapped cutlery in the gray tub housing finished sets, his arm grazed mine, and I tried to ignore the shot of electricity that ran through me.

"So," I said casually, "are you dating anyone?"

"Well, I know this might come as a shock, but dating in my line of work is a little tricky. I'd never date anyone on staff and it's kind of hard to be like, 'Hey, I know this is going great, but for the next ten weeks, I'm basically going to disappear. In fact, not only will I not see you, but you likely won't hear from me for days at a time.' "

We both laughed. "Yes, but you can make up for it the other seasons."

"Maybe. But so far, that hasn't been a compelling argument. At least, not compelling enough to make anyone stay."

I ventured a glance at him, wondering how that could possibly be true. "I don't know how June does it, staying here all year long, alone for months at a time."

Rich shook his head. "Me neither. I always come visit her when I'm down, but besides a few work weekends and a weekly check-in, I'm not here if it isn't April to September. It gets cold on this river. And dark. And terribly lonely. And she's by herself in that tiny cabin . . ."

A chill ran up my spine. I often thought of June here, alone, and wondered why she stayed year-round. After all the loss and heartache she had endured, maybe the solitude soothed her soul. Or, maybe, after months of being on every minute of the day, she needed to recharge her batteries and get ready to be everything to everyone again. Although, I had to admit, being here alone in the winter with only Rich checking on you didn't sound so bad . . .

Stop it, I scolded myself. I was only feeling this way because I was mad at Bryce—again. Should one be this mad at her fiancé before they were even married? I mean, I knew every couple had their ups and downs, but lately it felt like more than that. It almost felt like for all these months he had been playing a part and now, finally, he had taken off the mask. But was this who he really was? Or was the sweet, doting Bryce his true self, and the stress of a big life transition was just getting in the way of that? Or maybe he was a little bit of both. I had always been willing to take the good with the bad, but this bad felt different. The voice in the back of my mind told me he was hiding something. And that was a feeling I didn't like at all.

As if reading my thoughts, Rich asked, "Where is your fiancé this weekend?"

"Oh, um, he was going to come with me, but then—" June took the stage, interrupting me. "Testing, testing," she said, tapping the microphone. I was about to add that Bryce had to work, that he would have been here otherwise, but it was too late. My eyes locked with Rich's, and it washed over me that he could think I didn't bring Bryce because of him. There wasn't time to correct myself. Did I even want to?

"Ladies and gentlemen," June began. "Welcome to the first ever Holly Springs and Rock Springs Family Camp!" The room filled with hoots and hollers, bangs on the wooden picnic tables, and as was camp tradition, kids and adults standing on the benches at their tables. Someone from the back started chanting, "Holly one!" A few more people chimed in, "Holly two! Holly me, holly you! Holly who?" And before I knew what was happening the entire room practically shouted: "Holly Springs!" Then everyone who knew our camp cheer was singing: "From sunup to sundown, any city, any town, there's nothing better in the whole wide world, than a sweet and spunky Holly Springs girl!"

It was awful. Off-key, pitchy, nothing beautiful about it. Even still, it brought tears to my eyes. And I knew when June handed Daphne the mic it was because she was too emotional to continue. This camp meant just as much to all these people as it did to us. It was a place that had affected them deep down in their hearts and souls in a way that was worth way more than a $5,000,000 development deal. And, well, that was saying a lot.

June came over and put her arm around my shoulders, squeezing me to her side. "Thank you," she whispered.

Unable to control my tears, I said, "No, June, thank *you*."

She hugged me just as Daphne said into the mic, "Wow! That was the ugliest, most hauntingly beautiful rendition of the camp song I've ever heard!"

More cheers and table banging.

"Let's see who we have here. This year's Songbirds, raise your hands!" Cheers erupted again as they stood on their benches. They were so cute! This continued for Chickadees, Nightingales, Finches, Canaries, Starlings, Cardinals, Doves, Sparrows, and, finally, Blue Jays, the oldest group. If Daphne had intended for this little exercise to get all the girls in the room pumped and on their feet, she had succeeded.

"Seriously, friends, I think you all know this has been a hard couple of years for Camp Holly Springs. Our fearless leader, June, has held it together with prayers and Scotch tape, but your being here tonight is a real, tangible way to help save this place. Please thank everyone you see working around here the next couple of days. They have all volunteered their time so your fees for the weekend go directly to camp. I'm going to let you get back to the party, but I just have to say that Holly Springs taught me everything I needed to know and gave me the innocence of childhood that I didn't get at home. Let's keep that going for another seventy-six years so that more kids can grow up with a safe place, happy memories, and a song in their heart." She paused. "And, judging from what I heard earlier, maybe we keep the songs in our hearts?"

Everyone laughed and the singing commenced again.

Huff, Henry in tow, made his way over to me. "I feel so inspired now." His tone was light, but I could tell he meant it. Whether he was inspired by the speech or by Daphne I couldn't be sure.

"No big ask?" Rich asked as Daphne joined us, picking Henry up.

"No way," Daphne said, seeming slightly out of breath. "We save the big ask for tomorrow night, when everyone has had the best day of their adult life and is ever-so-slightly tipsy on the wine Mary Stuart got donated."

"Booze at camp?" Huff asked with awe in his voice.

"Desperate times, desperate measures," Daphne said. Everyone laughed except me. The idea of drinking at camp and Rich being right there made me squirm.

Steven appeared at Daphne's side and, arm around her, kissed her temple. "Brilliant, as always."

I couldn't have been the only one who noticed Huff staring daggers at him. Why, why, did I bring him here?

Everyone began to file out of the dining hall, and Rich said, "Well, duty calls. Back to the Rock. We'll bus our families over in the morning and give them a day so good they'll throw their checkbooks at us!"

We all laughed, and I touched Rich's arm. I felt like I couldn't breathe, which was absurd. It was just an arm. "Hey," I said, "thank you for doing this. The fact that you would go to all this trouble and get nothing in return . . . June and Daphne are my family, and—"

He stopped me. "June is my family, too, Lanie. If I was in trouble, she would do anything in her power to help me. In fact, she has. On quite a few occasions." He squeezed my wrist, which made me feel all melty inside. "I know Holly Springs means a lot to you. But it means a lot to me, too."

I smiled.

"Best of luck manning sailing tomorrow," he said. "Fair winds and following seas."

He saluted as he walked out. He was such a dork, and what was better than a hot dork? Best of all possible worlds.

Huff took Rich's place beside me, rolling the last few silverware bundles as Daphne kissed my cheek and headed out with Henry on her hip, his head on her shoulder, Steven saying something that made her laugh.

When we were alone, Huff said, with a slightly accusatory chill, "Why did you tell me Daphne and Steven were still together?"

Alarm bells jangled in my head. "What do you mean? When did I tell you that?"

I remembered, of course. I had told him at the wedding. The little white lie had felt wrong even as I told it, and the memory made me ashamed. I pointed to the door. "I'm sorry. But you can't look at those two humans and tell me nothing is going on between them." Then something hit me. "When did she tell you they weren't together?"

He flushed ever so slightly. "Oh, Mom and I were talking about it."

Well, that made sense. Mom couldn't ever see the bad in Daphne. She only saw her beautiful, sparkly side. My dad was like that, too, and I envied it a little when Daphne lived with us. Huff and I both had a lot of pressure on us to succeed, to live up to our parents' sterling educations and reputations. When Huff got into Yale, that feeling only intensified in me until I got into Duke. Yale might have been harder to get into, technically, but Dad's heart never left Durham. He was so proud. And I felt worthy.

They had no expectations for Daphne. She wasn't their child, obviously. But even though my parents thought she could do no wrong, I saw the damaged side of her, the side of her that, sure, deserved to be loved, but that also made her hurt the people who cared about her most. It wouldn't happen to my brother again. Not on my watch.

"I'm just saying," Huff continued, "that it's a little weird you would say they were together when, as her best friend, you would know that they weren't."

I slammed the silverware in my hand on the table. "What's your deal lately? Are you thinking about going after her again? Because you seem awfully interested. And I think we both know what happened last time."

"You!" he practically spat at me. "You are what happened last time. I never would have let her walk away if you hadn't talked me into it."

I crossed my arms. "Fine. That's fine. You can blame me all you want. You can tell yourself that your evil witch of a little sister stood between you and her fairy princess best friend. But when you look way deep down inside yourself, I think you know that isn't true. I think you know as well as I do that I gave you an excuse. She was unraveling. Your relationship wasn't good for either of you. Forgive me for trying to protect the people I love most."

With that, I stormed out of the dining hall, my heart pounding. I had clung to my moral superiority for years. But was I right to? If I hadn't interfered, would Huff and Daphne be together now? Would they be happily married with a kid or two? I pushed the thought away.

Yes, she had stayed on the straight and narrow for all these years, but Daphne could have gone down a different path—and she could have taken my brother with her.

As I practically stomped across the grass, beneath a blanket of stars, I saw Mary Stuart. "Hey," I said. "Where have you been?"

"Ted and I lay down to take a nap and slept through dinner!" she lamented.

"It's over," I said snappily.

She looked taken aback. "Geez. Sorry, Lanier. I've been working twenty-four-seven taking on Holly Springs as my biggest new client—for free—while continuing to do my job for my actual paying clients. I'm exhausted."

"Sorry." I softened. "I know you're overwhelmed. It's not you. Huff and I had a fight."

She rolled her eyes. "I probably need only one guess as to what that was about."

I ignored what she was implying. "Sorry about dinner. But I have wine and granola bars in my room." Mary Stuart and Ted, Huff and I, and Daphne, Henry, and Steven each had one of the three separate rooms in the doctor's quarters, which shared one long screened-in porch overlooking the swim lake.

"Let me grab Ted and we'll be right over. When Daphne gets Henry to sleep, can she come too?"

I laughed. "Of course she can come. I'm not mad at *her*."

And I wasn't, which was weird. I didn't blame her. I knew what she had sacrificed for me. For all these years, no matter the ups and downs, I was content in the knowledge that she had, in essence, faced the decision of choosing between Huff and me, and she chose me. It was only now, all these years later, that it hit me what a terrible friend I was to ask her to choose in the first place.

Daphne

THE RIVER

"WERE LANIER AND RICH TALKING AT DINNER?" MARY STUART WHISpers. Henry is in the shower, washing up after playing baseball with Huff, and Steven has gone out to the porch to get the fishing rods organized for the morning.

I nod, hope flooding me. "But, I mean, they were just talking." I pause. "But I haven't seen her laugh like that in a long time."

Mary Stuart grins. "That seems like a good sign, right?"

Oh, how I hope she is right. Rich is, at this point, my only hope. Because if I tell Lanier about Bryce, how will I support my son? We will have to change our entire lives—and I will have such a huge black mark on my record. Who will hire me then, even for something completely different? I have worked so hard, overcome so many obstacles to get where I am today, that giving it all up feels impossible. And being with Huff makes me feel even guiltier. Not only am I deceiving my best friend in multiple ways; I am betraying the man I love's sister and, by extension, him. So I mean it even more than Mary Stuart could comprehend when I say, "I just hope she realizes she never fell out of love with him and that Bryce was just a filler."

"Mommy!" Henry calls from the shower. I practically jump. "Oops. I left him for too long."

I walk into the tiny bathroom, where the mirror is fogged up despite the roar of the industrial exhaust fan. I open the glass door and peek in to find a little soapy head. "Did you shampoo your hair all by yourself?" I ask with glee.

Henry, eyelids creased from squeezing them shut so tightly, nods. "But now I'm afraid it will get in my eyes when I wash it out."

"I've got your back, buddy. Don't worry."

Twenty minutes later, Henry is clean, in fresh pajamas, and snuggled inside his sleeping bag on a mattress that is perhaps five percent more comfortable than the dock. And that is being generous. I am snuggling him while Steven sits on the end of the bed finishing Henry's bedtime story. He is the best at making them up, and tonight's is no exception. Steven is saying, "And then, the epic wave came and Henry, at the perfect moment, jumped on his board and rode it all the way to shore."

"And his mom was there taking pictures the whole time!" I add.

Henry giggles as I nuzzle his neck.

"And his dad was there telling his mom to be cool."

Henry yawns. I kiss him one more time and stand up. "Good night, little dude," Steven says, getting up too. "We'll catch some big fish tomorrow. But now I'm going to get some sleep with you while Mommy goes and plays with her friends."

I turn and smile at him. "Really? I can stay."

Steven shakes his head. "Nah. You work so hard. You're super mom. I've got this one. Have fun."

"Thank you." I look back at Henry, who is almost asleep, one more time. "Love you, buddy."

"Love you, Mommy," he barely gets out.

I remember those days. Camp is exhausting. I bolt out the door and straight into—"Huff!" I shout-whisper. I look around to make sure Lanier isn't out here, which is stupid because we're staying in side-by-side rooms. We could easily bump into each other.

I take his hand and pull him out the screen door, into the dark. Silently, I lead him to the back side of the swim lake, where no one will be this time of night, and, as soon as I feel like we are far enough away, I throw my arms around him and kiss him. I notice immediately that something feels . . . off. I lean back. "I've been wanting to do that all day."

Huff nods.

"Hey, I saw you out there playing with Henry earlier. That was so cute."

"I hope it was okay," he says.

I smile. "I love that he's getting to know you. You're the greatest."

"That kid is the greatest. He is so funny, Daphne. I don't know how you get anything done because I'd just want to hang out with him all the time."

He's trying to be normal, but I can tell something is bothering him. I put my hand on his cheek. "Hey, what's up?"

He sighs and sits on the patch of sand with paltry grass running through it. I sit beside him, feeling my pulse race uncomfortably. I peer over at him. "Huff?"

"It's nothing. It's just, you and Steven—"

"Huff!" I cut him off. "There is nothing between Steven and me. I swear."

"You can't see it. But you're a family. I mean, I want you to be a family, obviously. But you, Henry, and Steven . . . *Steven.* He casually touches you or kisses you goodbye. He tells cute stories sitting in bed with you."

I bite my lip. He must have seen us from outside the door. "I get that," I say, softening. "And I'm sure that must be hard. But we have had Henry together for almost five years. We have our dynamic. What matters is the person I love. That's you, Huff."

He smiles a little and picks a piece of grass, twisting it in his fingers. "I'm sorry. I guess I'm just jealous. But more than that . . ."

He trails off, looking out over the lake, and I get that nervous feeling again. "More than that, what?"

"I'm quitting my job, Daph. I'm selling my house. I'm moving to be with you and what does that even look like? You, Henry, Steven, and I, one big happy family? Is there room for me in your life? Your real life when we aren't just sneaking around?"

I see his point. "Well, I mean, would that bother you? If Steven still stayed at our house every other weekend?"

He laughs. "Oh my God, Daphne, yes. Yes, it would bother me to have your former lover under our roof. It would indeed. Would you like to spend every other weekend with my ex? Maybe she and I could make breakfast in our jammies before you get up?"

Well, now he was just being snarky. "Fine," I say, an edge to my voice. "I see your point. But give me a little grace here, Huff. Steven and I have been doing this for years. Forgive me for not having everything figured out."

He shakes his head. "I'm sorry. I know I'm being dumb. Part of this is that I'm feeling insecure and letting Lanier get into my head—"

"Wait. What?"

"Oh, she's always going on about how you three are this unbreakable unit, and there's this spark between you and Steven."

I want to say that that's ridiculous, but I know it isn't, at least not completely. There's chemistry between us. But chemistry isn't love. Regardless, I have a sickening feeling that Lanier is not going to be okay when Huff and I tell her about us.

"I was lying in bed last night," Huff continues, "picturing our future kids thinking they have two daddies because Steven still spends weekends with us."

I laugh before I realize he isn't kidding. "But, honey, a lot of this will work itself out. I mean, obviously Steven will always be a huge part of our life."

"Of course he will," Huff says. "I want Henry's dad to be there for him as much as he can. It's just, the whole all-living-under-one-roof thing . . . You two are so . . . connected."

"But that will pass. Steven will find someone, have another family."

"You're joking, right?"

"Joking about what?"

"Steven will never find another family. He has the perfect situation. Most of the time, he does his surfer/pilot thing and sleeps with anyone he wants and then he gets to come to you and play house."

I am taken aback. "So that's the perfect situation? Is that what you want? To sleep with anyone you want and play house with me occasionally?"

Huff tosses the piece of grass in his fingers. "No, Daphne. That's not what I want. I want all of you. I just don't want to share you with *him*."

I shouldn't be shocked by this. Huff has always wanted me all to himself. But it makes me nervous. I get not wanting to share me with Steven. And, when I really think about it, we do have a flirty dynamic that, roles reversed, would drive me crazy. But it isn't so much lust as it is a deep comfort level, a love that has grown out of a life-changing experience we shared. I can see why that bothers Huff. But he also can't be this possessive over me. Not now.

I take his hand. "Look, I'm glad you brought this up because it's super important. But what I need you to hear me say is that, for seven years, whatever I was doing, whoever I was with, I was thinking about you. In the quiet moments of the day, when my mind wandered, it wandered to you. When I thought about feeling really happy and safe and fulfilled, it was you who made me feel that way. When Lanier scolded me for breaking up with a really good guy, it wasn't because I couldn't see a future with him; it was because I could only see a future with you. So Steven and I might have a bedtime routine with Henry, but what you and I have is a real, true love story. It's a connection I've never felt with anyone else, and I know I never will. If you want to throw that away because the logistics are hard, then that's fine. I hear you. We're grown-ups and we have our own lives, and logistics *are* hard."

I sound confident, but this still gives me butterflies. What if Huff takes my offer and walks away? "This new situation is something Steven and I have been talking about and will continue to talk about. But I need you to know that no matter what we decide about our living situation, I will never, ever stop loving you."

Huff lies down, his hands under his neck. "For real?" he asks.

"For real," I say, lying down beside him.

"Then I guess I'm the luckiest guy in the world." He kisses me, running his fingers through my hair. He pulls me closer. "I mean, I guess I could get used to having Steven as a roommate if it means getting to do this all the time."

But as I kiss him, a wave of panic washes over me. This hiccup reminds me how much I don't like change. Steven and I have made magic of our coparenting, of being there for our son in a way that feels healthy and honest. How would adding Huff to that dynamic affect that? Could I let Steven solo parent on his weekends without feeling totally bereft? Will Henry be able to accept two dads in his life? I know Huff will be an incredible stepfather. But I can't quite reconcile how we will get there just yet.

"I love you," Huff whispers. "You're right. It will all work out. I am willing to do whatever it takes."

I nod and smile as we get up and he walks back toward the room he is sharing with his sister, my best friend, the one I am betraying with every breath.

Instead of going into my room, I walk down to the river's edge, the stars seemingly not just in the sky but all around me, glittering and twinkling, as alive and vibrant as children's laughter. I sit on the bank of the river, watching the ripples the wind makes on the flowing water. I remember the summer when Huff and I were counselors, the last time we were here together, in fact. What possessed him, I don't know, but my father had shown up, totally unannounced. I hadn't seen him in four years. In that time, he had sobered up, gotten married. He was having a baby and he wanted me to know my sister. He wanted us to be a family. I told him I had a family. I wasn't interested in another one. I had spent most of my life feeling scattered, forgotten, tossed about. I had learned that just because you shared blood with someone didn't mean you were family.

It was Huff who sat with me on the riverbank that night, as I, in my shell-shocked state, tried to process what it meant to see my father again, even if it was only for a few minutes. As I worked through the fact that he had never been there for me when I needed him, but now he was going to be a new man for this new daughter, Huff didn't tell me how I should feel or what I should do or that the sun would come up tomorrow. And I think that was how I knew, truly and for sure, that he was the love of my life.

Something Huff said that night has always stuck with me: "There's something about the river that washes everything away. All the bad stuff. All the pain. All the fear." He'd turned to me. "Want to take a dip?"

I shrugged. "Can't hurt."

We left our clothes on the riverbank, jumped in the chilly water with nothing but the moon and the stars to light our path. Huff took my hands, and we went all the way under until we totally ran out of breath. When we came back up, laughing, I realized he was right. I felt better. I felt free. I felt *cleansed.*

Now, silently, as I muse about the past and ponder my future, June sits down beside me on the grass and takes my hand as a realization floods me. A truth. All those years ago, what had made me feel better that night hadn't been these ripples, the cleansing movement of one of earth's finest creations. I look at June and say the truest thing I can think of. "It's Huff," I say. "Huff is the river."

June doesn't ask any questions. She just nods, and I know that, somehow, she understands. "Maybe you're the river, Daphne."

Maybe we all are.

Lanier

SUMMER SHAPE

I WOKE UP FEELING THE BEST I HAD IN SOME TIME, READY TO TAKE on the day despite the pure discomfort of the bed I'd slept in, the whir of the old AC unit, and the musty scent of the cabin that had been closed for months save the one weekend we were here for my bachelorette. Huff was snoring, and I realized I hadn't even heard him. That was how well I had slept. Because that's how good it felt to be back at camp. I picked up my phone and realized, with irritation, that my fiancé had neither called nor responded to my many, many texts.

Fine. That was fine. He wasn't going to ruin my weekend. If he didn't care about me, I didn't care about him. It was very mature. As quietly as possible, I went into the bathroom to get ready for the day. I pulled on the one-piece practical-yet-sexy swimsuit with the deep V and little ruffles on the shoulders that, I will admit, I had bought specifically for camp. Usually, I would have worn an old Speedo suit for sailing and getting dirty in the river or lake. But the idea that Rich might see me was on my mind.

I walked outside to find Henry drawing with sidewalk chalk on the concrete floor of the porch that connected our three rooms. The door to Daphne's room was open. "Henry!" I exclaimed. "My main man! What's up?"

"Daddy is taking me fishing on the pier!" He jumped up in excitement. Then, very seriously, he said, "We are having a dude's day because Mommy has a lot to do, and we can help her by having fun."

I nodded back seriously. "That is a very responsible plan, I think." I looked around. "Hey, where is your mom?"

She stepped out, smelling of perfume and sliding an earring into her ear. "Only you would be wearing perfume at camp."

She laughed, but she seemed uncomfortable. She kissed Henry. "You be good for Daddy, and I'll come find you soon." Then she looked down at his chalk dog and gasped. "It's fabulous! Practically a Picasso!"

Henry scrunched his face, and I thought he was going to ask who Picasso was. Instead, he said, "Mommy, Picasso's dog is black and white."

We both laughed as Steven came out and they waved goodbye to us. "Hey," I said. "How you feeling?"

She brightened—maybe artificially so—as we walked off the porch, the screened door swinging behind us. "Oh, I'm great. For sure. I guess I'm just worried that, despite our efforts, Holly Springs won't make it."

"Are you sure that's all?" I asked, lengthening my stride to match hers.

"Absolutely! We're at camp! What could be better? You'll man sailing all day, I'll be overseeing the blob—we're living the dream, my friend."

I laughed. "Oh, the blob. I've always had a bit of a love-hate relationship with that one, as you might remember from the time that *someone* insisted I go on it."

The blob was like a giant pillow in the lake. One person jumped off the platform, landed on it, and scurried to the end. Then the next person would jump off the platform as hard as they could to "blob" the other person. The first jumper would fly into the air and land in the lake. Well, ideally. Sometimes, if you were really, really small, you'd just fly into the air and land back on the blob. Ask me how I know.

Daphne winced. "Sorry about that. You had a pretty good bruise for like two weeks."

I bumped my hip against hers. "I'd do *anything* for you, including the blob. You know that, right?"

"Absolutely." Daphne squeezed my hand as she waved bye to me.

As she walked off, I wondered: Would I do anything for her? She would do anything for me. She always tried to help, never judged me. I always thought I was doing the same, but I was still, seven years after a run-in with drugs and alcohol, watching her a little too closely, was a little too protective when it came to what she should or shouldn't do. She was grown-up, stable, and an amazing mother. Maybe I wasn't giving her the trust she had earned. I vowed to let go of my fear, to be as good a friend to her as she was to me.

Before I could decide exactly how to do that, the sun broke through the clouds and, hand to God, a ray of light shone on Rich as he effortlessly made his way out of the river, up the bank, water beading off his perfectly toned abs. He was a work of art and, as he grinned, I was speechless. He grabbed a towel off the bench and rubbed his hair.

"What are you doing here?"

He pointed toward the pier as he walked up to meet me. "I wasn't going to let you man the docks all day by yourself. Do you have any idea how many idiots are going to be out here trying to sail, not to mention run the powerboats?"

"That is really kind of you." I stared at him again, this time not entranced by his handsomeness but his kindness. "Rich, honestly. I don't know if I'd even talk to me."

"Lanie, I don't hold grudges, especially for years on end. You know that."

I nodded, my mind flashing to that fateful night off during camp, when we'd sat on the edge of a crowded sidewalk in a charming town just a short ferry ride inland. He was stone-cold sober. I was more than a little tipsy. And oh so very in love, a chemical that was more potent and intoxicating than any alcohol.

"Our first customers!" Rich practically shouted, breaking me out of my memories. A dad in water shoes and a life jacket was padding down the dock, his small daughter, zinc on her nose, a life jacket *and* water wings on, following behind him.

"They look like real pros," I whispered.

"Good morning!" Rich said. "Lanier here is going to help you learn how to sail today."

They headed toward the sailboat Rich was pointing to as I shot him a look. He shrugged. "What can I say? You owe me."

I did indeed.

The morning flew by, a series of campers, families, and, most notably, little exchanges and jokes with Rich that reminded me of our history. Mary Stuart came down to bring us sandwiches and pulled me under the shaded overhang on the dock while Rich helped a camper. She nodded toward him. "When you didn't make it up for lunch, I figured things were going well."

I laughed. "There's no going well, Mary Stuart." I held my hand up, but then realized I wasn't wearing my engagement ring. I was a terrible person. "I'm engaged."

"But are you really sure?" she asked. "The invitations haven't even gone out yet. You have time if you want to change your mind."

I should have been annoyed, but she was so cute and so sincere. "The invitations go out next week. And, I mean, seeing Rich has been fun, but . . ." I looked down at my hands.

"What?"

"But it's time to get back to reality. I guess it just makes me sad to think this is the last real time I'll ever spend with Rich. Like it's the end of an era or something."

"Only if you want it to be, honey." Then she stood and brightened, noticing Rich walking toward us. "Rich! I brought our fearless sailing leader a little sustenance."

"Nut-free spread and jelly! Yay!" I couldn't tell if he was being sarcastic or not.

"Why is he the leader? Why not me?"

Mary Stuart acted as if she was seriously considering that. "Well, I hate to bring this up, but I feel like once you get rescued, the rescuer becomes the leader, no?"

"Twice," Rich said, his mouth full. "I rescued her twice."

She gestured his way. "The man has a point."

I faked a laugh, thinking that he had actually rescued me three times. That night we had off from camp, ten years ago, I was sitting on the crowded sidewalk, beer in my hand, and underage. We never even saw the police coming, but when a flashlight shone in my face, I sat up—and sobered up—quickly. Rich took my beer so fast I wasn't sure he had even done it.

"It's illegal to have an open container on the sidewalk," the officer said.

I pointed to the bar, which was only steps behind us. "Isn't this sort of an extension of the bar?" That was a moot point considering we were twenty and couldn't have alcohol anyway.

"You kids have ID on you?"

I was debating, running fuzzy facts through my mind. Was it worse to have a fake ID or no ID at all? That was when my heart began to pound. I was at Duke on a full scholarship, which I would lose if I was accused of any crime or misdemeanor. There was no way my parents could afford private school tuition, and my English degree likely wasn't going to help me pay off a ton of student loans. That scholarship to Duke was the thing that made my parents the proudest. I couldn't even imagine facing their disappointment. That's when Rich said, "She hasn't been drinking. It's my beer."

My face got hot. Even though I knew he was trying to help, I needed to pipe up. Rich would also face serious consequences from this. But it's like my lips wouldn't move. I couldn't bear to look at him.

The officer looked skeptical, but then Rich added, "No reason to bring her into this."

The cop sighed like he knew we were lying but didn't really care. "Since I'm assuming you're underage, throw that away and follow me to the car."

I'd like to think it was because I had too much to drink. I'd like to think it was because I was so terrified I couldn't think straight. Either way, I didn't say one single word about how Rich was completely, totally sober, that he had taken the blame for something that wasn't his fault.

The cop took mercy on Rich and only gave him a drinking ticket when he could easily have given him an open container ticket as well. And Rich and I got a free ride back to our respective camps. I didn't say one word in the back of that cop car, didn't catch Rich's eye, didn't apologize. I was afraid if I so much as moved wrong, I would get a ticket too. But the thought of what I had done to Rich hurt maybe even worse than losing my scholarship would have. I knew I had made the wrong choice.

The next session of camp started the next morning. When I went to take a long letter of apology to drop in the inter-camp mailbox, June said, "Oh, honey, didn't you hear? Rich got fired." Her face looked stern and sad. "He got a drinking ticket. We have a strict no-alcohol policy. We didn't have a choice."

That was a make-or-break moment for me, a time when I could have come clean about it all. June and I were close. Almost family. I could have told her the truth, that I was the one who should have gotten the ticket, that Rich was only taking the blame for me, that I should be the one fired, and he should have the job. But I stood silent.

"I know, honey." She took my silence for sadness. "I'm upset, too, but rules are rules."

"Can he come back?"

"Maybe next year," June said, continuing to sort the mail. "You know Rich is beloved around here."

I walked away with my letter, couldn't bring myself to send it. Was he furious with me? Of course he was. I had used his love, caused him to lose his job. I couldn't even look at myself in the mirror, and I certainly couldn't respond to the three letters he sent me over the next week. I didn't even open them. I couldn't. He quit sending them. And I never saw Rich McNabb, my first great love, again.

Until now. I looked up into his face, bathing in shame all over again, as Mary Stuart said, "Okay, I'm off to the basketball courts. I let Ted pick our activity, obviously."

As she walked away, I said the truest thing I could think of. "Mary

Stuart is still a Songbird. Even though it's been decades, she's exactly the same."

"I think that's what I like about her," Rich said.

"Me too."

Rich loved my friends. And, really, they were his friends too. They had known Rich as long as I had, and Daphne in particular saw him frequently on her visits to see June. Rich's phone lit up with a notification. He looked at it. "Great," he said under his breath.

"What?"

"That storm that I thought was going to pass over looks like it isn't. We have about another hour, but that's it."

That would put us at four o'clock. "I don't think anyone will mind an afternoon rest."

"Least of all me," he said. "I'm out of summer shape!"

His abs seemed to twinkle of their own accord, defying him. He was definitely, definitely not out of summer shape.

"Do you think you'll always do this?" I asked. "Work at camp, I mean?"

He sat down on the bench beside me, finishing his sandwich. "I don't know. I'm enjoying it for now. But I've thought about getting my master's. Teaching. Or taking over Dad's furniture store." He paused. "But, on the other hand, I can't imagine my life without camp. Even though I work so hard all year long, with planning and fundraising and general camp communications, I also have a ton of flexibility during the off-season. I get to travel a lot. Take long stretches of days off."

"Sounds pretty great," I said.

He nodded. "But more than that, when you're here with these kids . . ."

"You're changing their lives," I filled in for him.

"Yeah, I mean, they become resilient and strong and independent. They see what they can do without their mom there to pour their milk. It makes the stress of the summer worth it."

I laughed. "I wouldn't be the person I am without camp." I held his gaze for a long moment. "And, Rich, I wouldn't be the person I am without you. My future, my standing in my family, my education . . . Well, you saved all of that. I've never thanked you for it. So thank you."

He looked down at his feet. "It all worked out, you know? I mean, I ended up where I wanted to be."

That was true. But he was giving me an awful lot of grace. "For years I've wanted to apologize. I thought about it often, but I was never brave enough to reach out, and I'm embarrassed about that too." I felt my cheeks burning red, my body reacting to my words. "I truly am, from the bottom of my heart, so sorry. I don't deserve your forgiveness, but I think it's really big of you not to hold a grudge."

Before he could respond, a family walked down the dock. "Back to the salt mines!" he said so cheerfully that I wasn't sure what he was thinking.

I didn't know how to feel. I was grateful I'd finally had the chance to say what I wanted to say, to apologize. It had weighed on me for years. But he hadn't exactly accepted my apology, and that made my stomach turn. Roles reversed, would I have forgiven him? And had I truly forgiven myself?

As I watched Rich help a little boy behind the wheel of a Scout, I wondered if I had been punishing myself all this time by not reaching out to him sooner. But most of all, I wondered if, by not doing so, I had walked away from the only person I had ever really loved.

June

FRIENDSHIP BRACELET

THE DAY MY SISTER DIED WAS THE WORST DAY OF MY LIFE. THAT sounds obvious, maybe, but for someone who had lost both her parents less than ten years earlier it was a bit of a toss-up. What made both losses so much worse was the element of surprise.

After seven years of sobriety in Daphne's early childhood, Melanie hadn't been able to get and stay clean for more than a few months. There were years where I woke up in the middle of the night in a cold sweat, wondering if that was the night I would get the call from the authorities that my sister had overdosed. But the night she died wasn't one of those nights. My sister had been happy, stable, and clean for more than a year. Paula and John definitely had something to do with it. After my parents died, my sister had used part of her inheritance to buy a cute house in Cape Carolina, near the Bradley family's. Fortunately, it hadn't sold during her short stint in New York, so she and

Daphne had it to come home to. John had given her a job she loved at his commercial real estate firm. Paula had been there for her, always, but she and Melanie seemed even closer than ever lately, too. Melanie was on the right track.

So when my phone rang early that evening, I picked it up expecting a parent with a camp question or a telemarketer. Suffice it to say, my phone didn't have caller ID. But I recognized the voice on the other end right away.

"She's gone," Paula sobbed.

Despite her sobs, I didn't register the true severity of the situation. Paula hadn't known Melanie as long as I had. "It's okay," I said, my heart racing. "Sometimes she does this, but we'll find her, get her cleaned up, and back home."

"No, June, you don't understand," she said, her voice breaking. "She's dead. Melanie is dead. I found her an hour ago, and the paramedics pronounced her dead at the scene."

It felt like all the blood had drained from my body. "No. She isn't. She can't be." I dropped the phone. I felt so weak I couldn't even hold the receiver. The weight of it was too much to bear. She was gone. Not only had I not had the chance to tell her goodbye; I hadn't even had the chance to try to help her.

My sister had left no will and no plans, which wasn't a shock to anyone. By default, Daphne would have to go to Ray, her biological father, unless a better option materialized. I tried to tell myself it would be okay, to convince myself he would be a better father now than when he ran off and left my sister and my niece when she wasn't even two. When I talked about it with John at the funeral, he said, "Don't worry. I've talked to a great lawyer, and Paula and I are happy to help you in any way. You shouldn't have any trouble getting custody—"

"I can't raise her," I'd said, cutting him off. I didn't know where that came from, but it was already out of my mouth and out in the world. It was in direct opposition to everything I'd been taught, every value my parents had instilled. *Family first.* John looked taken aback. "June, you're our only hope. Paula and I can try, but no court in the world is going to grant custody to family friends over a biological relative."

Of course not. Even in my state I knew that. I felt like my throat was closing. I loved Daphne more than life, but if I had custody, how could I justify going back to camp alone, spending six cold, dark months barely getting out of bed? It was the only future I could see for myself. I couldn't take care of my sister. I hadn't saved her. How could I take care of a child?

I shook my head. "Melanie's dead, John. I'm dead too. Daphne would be better off alone." I turned to walk away, and John grabbed my wrist, catching my mother's pearl bracelet. It was old and fragile, and when John pulled his hand away, the clasp snapped and the pearls bounced across the stone floor of the church.

Now, a tsunami of beads cascading onto the floor of the arts and crafts hut broke me out of my memory, the past merging with the present. Little Alee's face scrunched at the sight of the pieces of her necklace scattering. "It's okay!" I said, jumping up to help her. "We'll fix it together!"

These kids had saved me. That summer after my sister died, after those long months alone bathing in my shame and loneliness and grief, the sun came out, and the children—including my niece—came back. They laughed and sang and danced and loved me back to life. They put me back together like this necklace I was restringing for a six-year-old, like the pearl bracelet Paula had later fixed for me. She had each of the pearls hand-knotted. That way, if the bracelet ever broke again, only one pearl would fall, not all of them. But it didn't matter. I never wore that bracelet again. It was a reminder of losing my sister; it was a reminder of failing my niece. I had never forgiven myself for that.

I did, at least, attempt to get custody two years later when I got my head out from under water and felt like I could be a responsible caregiver. Daphne was fifteen. There was no evidence Ray had done anything to warrant losing custody of her and, by that time, I got the feeling that Daphne didn't care all that much anymore anyway. She spent so much time with Lanier and her family, was so involved with her school and friends and boys that, when Ray maintained custody, I think Daphne almost felt relieved. And her moving in with Lanier's family felt like a natural transition, gave her a stable end of her childhood that I didn't want to disrupt.

Daphne and I were so close as adults, and I hoped we would talk about this really big thing between us one day. But right now, I had to focus on the families around me—the siblings, parents, and grandparents making sand art and tying friendship bracelets, stringing beads and knotting macramé. The sea of their voices swimming together was practically a melody, the sweetest song I had heard in quite some time. It was the sound of joy. The sound of hope. The sound of finally believing I wasn't the only person who cared about saving this camp, that, if all these families came to help, we had to be onto something really good. Right?

I had read once that you had to believe in something in order to make it happen. No one ever ran less than a four-minute mile until the first person did and then, suddenly, many other famous athletes did too. It wasn't that their bodies couldn't do it. Their minds simply couldn't conceive of it. So maybe that had been my problem all along: I couldn't conceive of a way to overcome the camp's latest hurdle. But

Daphne? Daphne could. She understood and saw and felt that this was a place worth saving. And then she made it so.

"June!" An eight-year-old girl with sandy blond hair and a smattering of freckles on her nose bounded over to me. She held her friendship bracelet up.

I gasped as if it was the first and only friendship bracelet I had ever seen. "Katelyn, it is a work of art!"

"It's for you," she said.

I put my hand to my heart. "For me?"

She nodded. "Because you're my friend. And you make it so that every summer I get to come to camp and see my other friends. It's my favorite two weeks of the whole year."

Katelyn's mom came up behind her, stroking her hair. "We have a calendar in our kitchen where Katelyn marks off the days until she gets to come to camp. We try not to be offended."

We laughed as Katelyn skipped away, back to her table. "She's shy at home," her mother said, looking over her shoulder. "She has trouble with the girls at school, and some days are really hard. So thank you for giving her something to look forward to."

I willed them not to, but tears sprang to my eyes. "Well, thank you. Stories like that are what keep us going. They remind us that Holly Springs is necessary."

I could tell she was about to say something else, but, before she could, the door flew open and Henry, my little bundle of great-nephew, flew over to me at breakneck speed, flinging himself into my arms. I smiled as Daphne came up behind him.

"Ah, to be that openhearted and unafraid of the world," I said, looking down at Henry. "Daphne, you are the most spectacular mother. I see a lot of kids and only one that feels very safe in his surroundings can pull off joy like that."

She smiled, but something in her face told me my compliment didn't quite hit the mark. Before I could figure out why, Henry said, "June! Mary Stuart and I have a surprise for you. A big one!"

He jumped out of my lap and pulled my hand. I looked at Daphne, but she only shrugged. Henry pulled me outside into the warm afternoon where storm clouds were, much to my chagrin, forming to the east.

A group of girls was flipping and cartwheeling all over the grass, and hysteria ensued when their mothers tried to copy their movements. A group of kids was throwing a Frisbee in the grass. No one was on a cell phone or a tablet. And everyone was happy, smiling. This was the life. This was bliss.

I walked toward Mary Stuart, who was smiling like her face might break in two. I was expecting another friendship bracelet, Henry's target paper from archery. Instead, Mary Stuart handed me this month's *Sea & Sky*. I looked down and gasped. The teaser said, "SAVING SUMMER CAMP WITH LEMONADE & LOVE." And on the cover was a picture of Melanie and me, in our starched Holly Springs uniforms, arms around each other, grinning. I put my finger to it, as if I could touch her again, as if this story could bring her back to life. My eyes filled with tears. "I hope it's okay that I sent them that picture," Daphne said. "Mom kept it in her nightstand, and it seemed appropriate."

She kept it in her drawer. She had saved our picture. Sometimes I worried that Melanie hadn't loved me as much as I had loved her, that my love hadn't been enough to save her. But this was proof that she cherished our sisterhood just like I did.

I nodded, overcome with emotion, and flipped to the article. I started reading aloud. "Two hundred forty-three Holly Springs campers from North Carolina to California, Maine to Texas, and everywhere in between hosted fundraising lemonade stands in their hometowns to help save their ailing all-girls summer camp that has been a staple in North Carolina for more than seventy-six years."

"What? How?"

Mary Stuart smiled. "Well, to be honest, I didn't think it was going to happen. But Amelia Saxton, the editor of *Sea and Sky*, switched out a monthly home feature for this spread literally the day the magazine went to press."

"She was always one of my favorite campers." I smiled. "I need to write her a note." As if that would be thank-you enough. I held the magazine to my chest for a moment. I pulled it away and flipped to the next page, which featured a photo of a letter from Daphne to Melanie that began, *Mom, this is the best summer of my life*. As I continued to skim, my eyes zeroed in on a number. I gasped. "What? They raised $56,842? From lemonade stands?"

"That's a *lot* of lemonade, Aunt June," Henry said.

There was even a little blurb at the bottom of the article instructing people on how they could donate. I threw my arms around Mary Stuart with about as much force as Henry had just thrown his arms around me. "There are no words to adequately thank you for this." This article might not save our camp and the lemonade money might not get us to our goal, but it reminded me that what I had done all those years ago meant something to all these people supporting us, and for now, for today, that was enough.

I hugged Daphne too. Just then, thunder boomed through the sky. "Oh, gosh," I said. "I have to make sure everyone is out of the water!"

I ran through the pouring rain, down to the river, barely even noticing how drenched I was because I was floating on air. I thought of the message Jillian had left on my desk earlier from David Price of Price Development asking if I'd made a decision. I couldn't tell him to take his deal and shove it quite yet; I needed him as a safety net. But the idea I might be able to do that now felt so close I could practically taste it.

I spotted Rich and Lanier running through the downpour, noting that no campers were in the water or on the dock. And with the rain pouring around me, I felt revitalized. We still had a long way to go, but I was more determined than ever to save Holly Springs. Not because, like all those years ago, it was all I had left. But because, now more than ever, it was all I had ever wanted.

Lanier

YOU, ME, AND THE POURING RAIN

RICH HAD BEEN RIGHT TO GET EVERYONE OUT OF THE WATER AND back to their respective cabins as soon as the dark clouds started rolling in. I was reluctant to ruin their fun, but he certainly knew more about water safety than I did. Hence the rescues. We were frantically getting sails and life jackets together so they wouldn't get wet, but when the thunder boomed the first time, I jumped so far I actually landed, conveniently, in Rich's arms. All at once, the rain seemed to break free.

Rich grabbed my hand. "Leave the rest. Run!" It was kind of funny because we were already damp, but by the time we made it up the dock and the small grassy incline to the sailing hut, our feet were muddy and we were absolutely drenched, rain pouring off us. As we practically dove inside the hut, Rich pulled a towel out of his canvas bag on the floor and wrapped it around me, the closeness intensifying the heat between us.

"Is this our thing?" I joked. "You, me, and the pouring rain?" Why did I say that? I was *engaged*, for heaven's sake.

He smiled. "I think it must be. The rain is good luck. I get to rescue you in the rain."

We were standing inside the hut, too close for a woman who was engaged, too near for someone whose feelings were rushing back. But, worst of all, I realized the intense, throbbing guilt I felt had more to do with how I had betrayed Rich all those years ago than what I was now doing to Bryce. I tried to keep the tears from coming down my cheeks but found it impossible.

"Lanie, what's wrong?"

I shook my head. "I do not deserve your kindness. I don't now and I didn't then." He hadn't said anything about my apology after we were interrupted and, while part of me wanted to let it lie, another part just had to know what he was feeling. "You lost your job!" I said, sniffling.

He rubbed the stubble on his chin, as if he was thinking. "Yeah. But you would have lost your scholarship. I took the blame willingly. That was on me."

Hearing him say that made me smile just the tiniest bit, and I thought that maybe we were okay. But, as the rain pounded on the tin roof of the sailing hut, Rich's face clouded, and he turned away from me.

"See," I said softly. "I knew you were still mad."

"It wasn't the drinking ticket that pissed me off," he started. He turned back to me. "It was how you handled the aftermath. I mean, what the hell, Lanier?"

I hated when he called me Lanier. I felt like a child being scolded, which, let's face it: I kind of deserved.

"I got not talking to me in the cop car. But not responding to my letters? I felt like I had done the most chivalrous thing in the world, had proven my love for you in a big way, and you just ghosted me!"

Shame washed over me anew. "I know," I whispered. I moved closer to him, feeling like I was stepping into dangerous territory but unable to resist. "I was so ashamed I couldn't bring myself to open your letters."

"You didn't make Daphne do it? It could have been your 'hard thing.'"

He was attempting a joke, but it didn't feel like one. I took a deep breath. "I couldn't bear to open the letters. I was too afraid of what they might say. I imagined how, after camp, I would just show up at your fraternity house, unannounced. I would apologize. I would beg for your forgiveness. I would tell you how broken up I was inside and ashamed that I didn't take responsibility for my actions, that I let you take the blame for something that wasn't your fault. And, as a result, ironically, I didn't take responsibility for my actions again."

"So what stopped you?"

"The same thing that stopped me from opening your letters. I thought you hated me," I said. "But if I didn't see you, if you didn't tell me, then I'd never know for sure."

"Lanier, do you know what those letters said?" I shook my head. "They said I loved you, that I forgave you, that I would wait for you forever." Rich was so close now that I could feel his breath, his steady inhale and exhale. "They said I would always protect you, always keep you safe, and if getting a stupid drinking ticket was a way I could prove that, then I would do it a million times over."

I didn't even mean to open my mouth, but somehow, it happened and out it slipped. "I loved you, too, Rich. More than I've ever loved anyone."

It felt like I'd just said, *More than I've ever loved Bryce.* It was so wrong. I needed to walk out. But then, my heart beating fast, he stepped closer to me.

With the rain thudding on the roof and the wind whipping outside, our eyes locked.

"You're engaged," Rich said, stepping even closer.

"We're not in a good place," I said honestly. "It isn't working between us."

"Even still, we shouldn't," Rich murmured, inching so close the water from his hair dripped on my shoulders. For a second, it seemed like time had stopped.

"Screw it." I took that final step and threw my arms around Rich's neck, our mouths melting together like they had never been apart. I pulled Rich's soaking-wet shirt off his body, and we both laughed as he hoisted me up onto the counter, his lips never leaving mine. His skin was so warm, I felt like I might dissolve into him as he pulled me even closer. I was so lost in the feeling of him that I couldn't imagine ever being apart again.

Our hearts beat in time, our bodies were a melody, our breath the lyrics. And I knew that nothing had changed. Just like we had carved all those years ago: RICH + LANIER = LOVE.

Daphne

CHAOS AND DESTRUCTION

LIGHTING A FIRE IS STILL ONE OF MY FAVORITE THINGS TO DO. There's such power in the feeling of adding light and heat to the world. It must have been a marvelous—and truly terrifying—experience for whoever first rubbed two sticks or rocks together and made a flame.

The storm had passed, leaving a lovely crispness in the air, and I decided to build a fire in the cobblestone campfire circle by the river for my friends and anyone else who wanted to come. As I set it up, I feel the paper in my pocket rustle and smile. There is something terribly romantic about being somewhere with horrible cell service and having the man you can't get enough of send you love notes instead of texts.

Sure, I had some concerns yesterday about my future with Huff. But I woke up this morning realizing that Huff is right: My routine with Steven has to change. I've been clinging so hard to a past that has worked that I haven't been able to envision a future. And even though Henry is well-adjusted, he is four; he can adjust again. He already loves Huff, and we will take both quality time with him and weekends at his dad's house at the same slow pace. Steven isn't that twenty-three-year-old kid I first met, and I've been holding on to control of my son a little too tight.

As the circle bursts into flames—the dry wood from the shed had done the trick despite the humidity—I notice Lanier coming toward me. I pin on my happiest, least suspicious face as I thrust my arms toward the firepit and shout "Campfire!" This has always been our favorite camp activity, where truths are told and fates melded. Which reminds me that I have a lot of truth I'm not telling . . .

Lanier walks over to me looking nothing short of dazed. "Hey," I say. "What's up? You look like you've seen a ghost."

"I think I have," she says. She plops down in one of the Adirondack chairs and I sit on the edge of the firepit, facing her. "What is it about thunderstorms and that sailing hut?" she asks wearily.

I gasp and put my hand to my mouth, feeling as though I have just lost a thousand pounds of worry. "Does that mean what I think it means?" *Oh, please God, please.*

She nods, biting her lip. She looks around and whispers, "I slept with Rich."

"On top of the Rich plus Lanier carving?" *I am saved,* I think.

She rolls her eyes. "Daphne!"

"What? It's romantic. It's a fair question."

"It's not really romantic. It's kind of weird and gross for all the other people who have to use the sailing hut."

She isn't wrong. For years after I knew Lanier lost her virginity there I wouldn't come close to that countertop. And I have to think

Rich and Lanier aren't the only two people in the history of Camp Holly Springs to have used that counter for that exact purpose. "So, what does this mean?"

She leans over, head in her hands. "It means I am the most immature person in the world. I literally was like, 'Well, Bryce hasn't responded to my texts or called me in two days. Might as well sleep with Rich.'"

"Or . . ." I say.

She looks back up at me, tears in her eyes. "Or I'm actually in love with Rich, have always been in love with Rich, and was kidding myself all this time to think otherwise?"

I snap my fingers. "That one. I think it's that one."

I spot Mary Stuart walking toward the firepit. "Is this a secret?" I whisper.

Lanier shakes her head. "Not from Mary Stuart."

Mary Stuart sits down beside me on the rim of the fire circle. "What's up?"

"Our Lanier has re-consummated her love with Rich."

Mary Stuart's mouth gapes. "Seriously? Was it great?"

Lanier leans her head against her legs and says, muffled, "Of course it was great, which makes it even worse and makes me even more of a terrible person."

I rub her back. "You aren't a terrible person."

Her still-subdued voice says, "And now I have to go back over there and help him put up the sailboats in a few minutes. I don't know what to say or how to act."

"Put up the sailboats," Mary Stuart repeats. "Is that what the kids are calling it these days?"

Lanier sits back up so Mary Stuart can see her eye roll. "I hate to say this because I might feel differently later. It's just that, I know I told y'all how things with Bryce and me have been off lately. It's like, he swept me off my feet, spent months on perfect behavior, and now his true colors are showing. And I tell myself that it's the wedding stress that's making him act like this, and maybe it is that. But these past few weeks have been harder than they should be at this stage in a relationship. And I have to think that maybe . . ."

"Maybe he isn't who you thought he was," Mary Stuart fills in quietly.

I feel like anything I add to this conversation implicates me, so I am trying to stay quiet, but I am nodding in a way that borders on furious. "I think that's very well said."

Lanier peers at me. "What do *you* think?"

What to say? What to say?

"Are you thinking about calling off the wedding?" I hold my breath.

She shakes her head. "No. I mean, maybe? I don't know. I'm so confused. I never should have done this with Rich. But, also, is it fair to marry Bryce when I'm feeling this way?"

I let her spiral.

"But I can't call off my *wedding*. Oh my gosh. Can you imagine? I mean, can I call off my wedding?"

"Of course you can, sweetie," Mary Stuart says brightly.

I nod. "Lanier, calling off your wedding would be nothing compared to living a life with the wrong person."

"I mean, marriage is supposed to be the hard part, right? Isn't the dating supposed to be easier?" Lanier asks.

It makes me think of Huff and the note folded neatly in my pocket. I get up and grab a long stick to stoke the fire, bending and twisting to get it just right. And I have to think that maybe the dating part isn't really that easy when you already have a kid and a coparent and a friend who doesn't want you dating. But if we are going to give this a real go, we have to tell Lanier. Tonight.

I lean way into the pit, trying to get one of the logs to fall onto the embers. I vaguely register Lanier saying, "Hey, what's this?" but I'm concentrating too hard on this fire to really notice. But then she says, louder, "Daphne, what the hell is this?" And I look up, slightly sweaty, and recognize the fairly damning piece of evidence she is holding. As if its contents don't already implicate me, the top of the paper is embossed in navy blue with Huff's initials.

I try to snatch the paper from Lanier, but before I can, she opens it and starts reading out loud: " 'Daph, I think you are the most amazing mother I've ever known, and if we need to keep the Steven thing status quo for a while, I can handle it. I *will* handle it. All I know is that I love you, and I can't be apart from you again. Whatever that looks like. Whatever it takes. I'm all in.' "

My face is blazing, and Mary Stuart is frozen on the ledge of the firepit, like if she just doesn't move maybe none of this will be real.

"Lanier, I—"

She wads the paper up and throws it in the fire, which sort of riles me. That's *my* note. "One thing, Daphne. I have only ever asked you for one thing."

This is so categorically untrue that I want to laugh in her face. She asks me for things *all the time*. And I do them willingly with a smile on my face because that's what friends do.

"Why is it that you can't just stay away from my brother?"

I start to chime in, but Mary Stuart comes to my defense. "Because she loves him, Lanier. Because he loves her. Because they broke up and neither of them has been happy since."

"You knew?" she asks Mary Stuart.

"I didn't know they were together, but good Lord, Lanier, everyone knows they're in love. And when things were rocky with Daphne, I kind of got where you were coming from. But we're older now. We're all in a different place. You can't really play the card that Daphne will drag Huff down with her. She hasn't so much as looked at a drink in years. We practically had to shove a *Tylenol* in her after Henry was born and she was hurting all over, for heaven's sake. She will never go there again because of him. And because of us. And because she has yoga and journaling and therapy and whatever the hell else she does constantly, every day, to keep herself on track. She was twenty-three. You've punished her enough."

I'm floored by Mary Stuart standing up for me this way. And I'm also grateful. Because yes, yes to all those things. I try to be compassionate. "Lanier, I understand your concern, but—"

"No! You do not understand my concern because you don't have a brother."

That is technically true. But it burns through me, breaks my heart. "What is so wrong with me, Lanier? What is so bad about your best friend, the person who knows all your secrets, who you always run to first? What is so wrong with me that I'm not good enough for Huff?"

Lanier looks as if she's going to burst open. "We're back here again, the two of you keeping secrets from me. Do you know how it feels for the two people you love the most to just leave you totally out in the cold?"

I feel as if the wind has been knocked out of me. "No, that's great, Daphne, let's just go right back there. Call me in six months when he's dying to get married and you're on the verge of falling apart. Can't wait to clean that up. Again."

I am expecting her to be upset, so I'm trying to maintain my composure despite my heart beating out of my chest. "I seriously don't know how you could even say that. You, of all people, know how much I've changed."

"You've changed? Is that why you didn't tell us about Huff? Is that why you aren't telling me whatever you know about Bryce?" She pauses, and I'm flooded with shock. "I know you know something, Daphne."

I want to respond, but my mind is a total blank. So I give Lanier the perfect window to add, "It isn't fair to pretend with Huff that you're going to settle down and then break his heart when you can't handle a change in your routine. It isn't fair." She takes a breath. "And I know you need that routine. If this disrupts that, I hope and pray to God that you never relapse because I have never—not ever—seen an enabler as bad as Huff."

"He was not an enabler!" My calm facade has shattered.

Lanier takes a deep breath, and I feel myself start to relax. "I'm sorry. I'm overreacting. But, damn, Daphne. You and Huff together was the literal definition of chaos and destruction. Please don't bring my brother into that again."

I rush off toward the cabin. I have to because she doesn't deserve to see me cry.

I hear Mary Stuart calling behind me, but I can't turn around. I can't stop. I spend the first few minutes of my walk in cold shock, listing all the reasons in my head why Lanier is wrong. She is *wrong*. I love Huff, and he loves me. My past never has and never will have a bearing on my future because I will never go back to where I was.

I can't believe that I have spent all this time stressing and worrying about possibly losing my career for a person who doesn't even think I'm good enough to be with her brother. I have always thought of Lanier as my family. So it breaks my heart in a million ways to realize that she could never really see me as a part of hers.

Lanier

TRUE BLUE

IT'S HARD TO TELL WHO'S AN ADDICT IN COLLEGE. BECAUSE AT MIXers and cocktail parties, Tuesday DJ nights and football game days, Thursday nights—a sacred going-out night—and weekends, there is always an excuse for drinking, drugs, and general debauchery.

Daphne and I went to different colleges, so the first time I was with Daphne on her new turf in Wilmington, I wasn't worried when she and her three suitemates snorted lines off the counter in their bathroom before we went out. I didn't partake, but I wasn't there to be Officer Bradley either. Drugs were a part of college, right?

That night, dancing in a crowded, smoky bar, I was happy about the adorable boy dancing with Daphne, watching her like she made the earth turn on its axis. We drank and danced and laughed and drank and danced and laughed. Daphne seemed wild and free and, best of all, happy. When I asked her about the boy, as she continued sipping vodka sodas as the sun came up back at her house, she said, "Oh, he's precious, but I can't hang out with him anymore."

"Why not?"

"He wants me to be his, like, actual girlfriend. And what's the point?" she answered, shrugging. "I'm never going to get married anyway."

The only consistent in Daphne's dating life was Huff. They were at different colleges, so they only saw each other on breaks and random weekends. When they were apart, they were apart. But when they were together, they were . . . together.

I didn't love that they were always casually dating, but I knew it would pass. Sometimes I wondered how I would fit in if they got serious. But when Huff got accepted to Johns Hopkins for medical school, I figured any relationship they had would end. He would be studying all the time. Daphne loved Wilmington, and she was never going to leave the beach, even though, by that time, I honestly wished she would. There was always drinking, always drugs. I felt like the very uncool friend among her very cool ones, but I still worried. I'm not saying it was her friends' faults, but I knew that sometimes it was harder to change a behavior when you were in the same place with the same group and the same habits.

When I walked through the back door of my childhood home spring break of our senior year, Huff and Daphne didn't see me at first. They were sitting at the dining room table like they had a million times before. Daphne was saying something, Huff was laughing, and, in the split second before he saw me, he looked at her in a way I had never seen him look at anyone. It washed over me that he was in love with her.

But I didn't feel *panicked*. Yet.

"Hi, guys!" I said as cheerily as I could muster.

Daphne jumped up to hug me. We hadn't seen each other in a few weeks, since I had road-tripped from Durham to Wilmington to visit her. The first thing she said was, "Guess who's moving to Baltimore?"

Huff was grinning bigger than the day he got accepted to med school. He got up to hug me too. "Hi, sis. Pretty great, huh?"

"I'm sorry," I said. "Who's moving to Baltimore?"

"I am, silly!" Daphne said. I had wanted to talk to Daphne about possibly moving. But I hadn't wanted her to move *with my brother*. "I need to take some prerequisite classes I need to apply to law school, so why not do that in Baltimore? After camp, of course."

In what seemed like slow motion, Huff let me go and took Daphne's hand. "We're finally doing this for real."

I think my heart stopped beating. I knew Daphne. I had known her almost my entire life. She would only, could only, break his heart. How many times had she said she didn't want to get married? How many days had I laughed on the phone while she regaled me with tales of drunken nights out and random hookups? I really let my fear sink in: Was Daphne just a college party girl? Or was she destined to repeat the mistakes she'd seen growing up? Either way, I couldn't let her go down. I couldn't let my brother go down with her.

They lived in Baltimore for months before I went to visit them for the first time. It was like if I didn't have to see them all shacked up and cuddly in Huff's shitty apartment, it wouldn't be real. Still, I was used to the fact that they were together, and I had even started to come around. Until that visit.

The first thing I noticed when I hugged Daphne in front of the Baltimore building whose beautiful brick facade belied its musty, dark interior is that she seemed a little bit jittery. She was jumping up and down, and that in and of itself wasn't strange because I was *so* excited to see her too. But something about the way she greeted me seemed almost manic. And she was so, so painfully thin.

"You're here! You're here!" she squealed.

"I'm so excited!" I squealed back.

She took my hand and led me inside and up the stairs to a spartan, perfectly clean, and totally organized apartment. "I got up super early to do my LSAT studying and get all my work done for my classes so I wouldn't have anything to do tonight but hang out with you. And I don't have to be at work until noon tomorrow, so you and Huff can spend the afternoon together."

Had she taken a breath? I hugged her again, thinking she was anxious. "Oh, and I'll drive tonight so you and Huff can have fun. I have to get up early to study anyway."

I pulled away from our hug, examining her. Never once had Daphne been the DD. But that meant she was in a good place, right?

We did this fun downtown bar crawl with a bunch of Huff's friends, and I noticed Daphne sipping a beer at one or two stops. But she could certainly drive after a beer or two, so I didn't think much of it. About midnight, we headed to one of Huff's friend's houses. Sitting beside Daphne on a couch with loud music playing, kind of wishing we could just go home and go to bed, I said, "Hey, Daph, I've met a lot of Huff's friends. But when do I get to meet yours?"

She tried to maintain that upbeat persona, but I could see how her face changed. "Well, I mean, Huff's friends *are* my friends. And I'm going to be off at law school soon anyway, so I guess I haven't worried about it."

I looked around a room full of future doctors, many of whom were broken off into clumps discussing classes or professors or things that only they really had in common. They were certainly not Daphne's friends, but I reasoned that she probably hadn't had time to make any between school and work and studying and Huff. Maybe she just hadn't connected with anyone yet.

She shrugged, even though she looked a little sad.

"I'm going to grab a water. Want one?"

"Sure." As she walked off, I wondered if she was happy. Friends had always been so important to Daphne.

An hour and three more drinks later, the party had swelled to a loud, drunken mass of college and grad students. I was walking around the yard of this stranger's house, trying to find my best friend. She had never come back from her water run, and I had to make all this weird small talk with random people and fend off a few creepy advances from guys I didn't know while waiting for her. I finally found Huff in a crowd of friends, laughing. I grabbed his arm and pulled him away. "Hey, not to be a buzzkill, but I'm ready to go."

He nodded, seeming more than a little buzzed himself. "Okay. I'm more than ready." He looked around. "Where's Daph?"

I shrugged. "I don't know. I can't find her."

As if she'd heard us, Daphne appeared by the front door. "Daph!" I shouted, waving my arms, feeling a little drunker than I had meant to get. But, well, I had nowhere to be tomorrow, and I wasn't driving. Daphne stumbled down the steps toward us and I said, "Whoa! Are you okay?"

She shook her head. "No, I'm fine. I just tripped." I peered at her. Huff slung his arm around her shoulders and kissed her sloppily. "I love you so much," he said.

Gag.

Then he put his other arm around me. "I love you too, sis."

It had been a weird night, but this made up for it. This was a nice moment. A normal one. "Aw, I love both you guys. I can't wait until we all grow up and move back to Cape Carolina and are together all the time."

Huff laughed. "The chances of that seem slim, but okay, Lanier. Whatever you say."

"Oh, that would be *amazing*," Daphne said. Was her *z* a little too long? Was her mouth drunk or were my ears? I was too sleepy and too buzzed to care. We walked to the car and I slid in the back seat while Huff got in front. "Put your seat belts on," he mumbled.

"I'm in the back seat, Huff."

"Yeah, but your body would be like a missile coming at me if we got in a wreck, and I've worked too hard in med school to die now."

We all laughed. The idea of dying was impossible. The party had kind of been in the middle of nowhere, outside Baltimore, so we had a bit of a drive. As soon as Daphne pulled out onto the dark two-lane road—which felt twistier than it had on the way here—my eyes started to close. The car was warm and the music nice and the night pitch black; Daphne's and Huff's voices were so familiar, so comforting. And I realized that maybe I liked them being together, that maybe this life was right.

I was about to drift off when I heard Daphne scream and Huff scream and my entire body hurled forward, smashing into the hard seat in front of me. There was a loud thud, then a crack, then a crashing on the hood. The front airbags deployed and, finally, I screamed, too, my eyes adjusting to the dark, my delayed senses trying to unpack what had just happened. "Huff!" I practically screamed as he moaned in the dark. "Are you okay?"

"I'm okay," he said, breathlessly. "But my shoulder . . ." He inhaled sharply.

"Daph!" I screamed.

"I'm okay," she whispered. But when she turned to me, even in the dark, I could tell the right side of her face was swollen. I pulled my phone out. "We need an ambulance," I said, about to call 911.

"No!" they shouted simultaneously.

"What? We were in a wreck. We need help."

"No," Huff said again. He opened the door and peeked his head out. "I can get out, but there's a tree on the car. Can you guys get out?"

I nodded that I could.

Huff got his phone out, his left arm dangling in a way that turned my stomach. "Hey, Siri," he said. "Call Kenny Lyle." He gave me a once-over and then, turning, winced when he saw Daphne's face. "Are you okay?"

We both nodded. "But you're not!" It was only then that I realized I was sobbing.

He held his finger up to me. "Hey, man," he said into the phone. "We got in an accident. I think I dislocated my shoulder. Can you come get us?"

Over the next horrifying hour, three of my brother's friends—one of them sober, thank God—arrived. One of them, the orthopedic resident he'd called first, popped his shoulder back into place on the side of the road. Huff screamed, I started to sober up, and I started to piece together that my friend—who had not uttered one stark word of explanation—was so drunk or high or *something* that she had totaled her car. And my brother must have known it. Otherwise, why wouldn't he have let me call the police?

One of Huff's friends drove us home. "I'll come get you in a few hours," he said to Huff in a hushed tone, "and we can deal with the car, call a tow truck."

"What if someone calls the police in the meantime?" Huff asked, voicing the concern in my head.

Daphne, still resting her forehead on the back window, finally spoke. "There was a squirrel. I swerved to miss a squirrel."

"Oh, you did not!" I practically spat at her. The more I sobered up, the more furious I became. *She had put our lives in danger.* My best friend could have killed us. “Is this how it is now?” I asked Huff. “She’s gone from party girl to depressed addict and you just watch her do it? Cover for her? Let us nearly all get killed so as not to face the truth?”

“Lanier, calm down,” Huff said from the front seat. “It was one bad night.”

I looked at Daphne. She did not look back at me. It was not one bad night. It was hundreds of bad nights. Hundreds of bad nights where I reasoned Daphne was just having fun when in reality she was going down the same slippery path as her mom. We finally got back to Huff and Daphne’s downtown apartment. Instead of going inside, I cried as I paced the sidewalk.

“I need to get some ice on Daphne’s face,” Huff said. “Please come inside. It’s the middle of the night.”

I didn’t want to go in. But I couldn’t stay out here. And what was I supposed to say to Huff and Daphne? I didn’t know what to do.

Now, seven years later, I was in the exact same boat. I didn’t know what to do. And I felt like the biggest bitch on the planet. Even if I still worried about it sometimes, I should never, *ever* have said what I said to Daphne. She had worked so hard to not be like her mother.

But she also didn’t know how much that night haunted me. I’d realized the girl I loved most was spiraling into addiction, and I’d seen my own brother enable that behavior. I could have lost her. I could have lost him. The thought still terrified me to my core. My reaction to their being together stemmed from that deeply rooted fear that had never gone away. Unfair? Absolutely. Warranted? Yes.

Even still, I knew I was in the wrong. I needed to apologize, to fix it, but I didn’t know what to say. So instead of dealing with it, I decided to leave. You know, like a grown-up.

When I took a long, hard look at myself, as I crammed my clothes into my duffel bag in our dimly lit cabin, I realized Daphne wasn't being like her mother; I was being like mine. Not that I didn't love my mother. I did. I admired her, respected her, trusted her. But she was overprotective to a fault.

Daphne was right. She had changed so much. At twenty-three, yes, Daphne needed my input. At thirty, we all needed to be free to form our own families as we saw fit.

As I folded the last sundress and slipped it into my duffel, about to scribble a note to Huff that I had an emergency at the store and had to get home, the door flew open. Before I could even turn, I heard, "There's my girl!" I looked up to see Bryce practically running toward me. He wrapped me in his arms and kissed me passionately, like when we first met. And then I saw Rich standing in the doorway.

I remembered suddenly: I was supposed to go help Rich at the sailing hut. His mouth was hanging open. I mean, sure, he knew I was engaged. But I had intimated that my relationship was on life support, which, in the moment I had said it, had been true. Before I could stop the speeding train, though, Bryce was saying, "I kept calling and texting you, but nothing was going through, and I knew how important this weekend was to you, so I wrapped up work early and came down to surprise you."

"Surprise!" Rich said sarcastically from the doorway.

I tried to laugh, but I'm sure it gave away how incredibly uncomfortable I was. "Um, Bryce, this is Rich. He's the owner of Camp Rock Springs."

Bryce turned, walked confidently toward Rich, and took his hand. "Bryce Jenkins. Nice to meet you. Are you as good a sailor as my girl here?"

"Better," I interjected, laughing uncomfortably again.

Rich pointed behind him. "I was just going to tell you that I can finish putting everything away myself."

Rich's face told me that that wasn't what he was coming here for at all. And I got the feeling that I had broken his heart all over again. I tried to give him a look that said I was sorry, that I had meant everything I said, that I didn't know Bryce was coming, that I would never have put him in this situation, but I'm not sure I adequately conveyed all of that. He looked positively sick as he turned and walked out the door.

I wanted to run after him. But Bryce was here, and he acted like Rich had never even walked in. "Babe, I'm sorry I wasn't here for you. I should have just cleared my schedule." He took a deep breath. "But what I really wanted to say is that I'm sorry for how awful I've been lately. I've been really stressed about work, about making this huge career decision, and, honestly, I know it was wrong not to tell you. I have felt so guilty, but I just couldn't admit it." He took a step toward me, took my hands in his. "I love you, Lanier. And I know I haven't been my best self. But I promise you I'm going to be the best husband in the world. I'm going to prove to you that marrying me is the best decision you could ever make."

Well, shit. I replied, dumbly, "You tried to call and text me?"

He showed me his phone, which held fourteen undeliverable text messages and eleven failed calls. But what was even sadder is that I had somehow deluded myself into thinking that his lack of communication somehow made it okay for me to have sex with my ex. Wow. Bryce had been in a bad place? *I* was in a bad place.

"Look, I know family camp is almost over, but I was thinking maybe you could show me a couple things. I can stay for dinner, spend the night with you and Huff—I'll take the third bed, so he doesn't feel weird. I know this place is special to you. And now it's special to me, too." He kissed me again, and I felt like an absolute heel.

Before I could respond, Mary Stuart blew in. "Lanier, look—" She stopped abruptly. "Bryce! You're here!"

He walked over to hug her, and she made the biggest eyes I've ever seen at me. I made them back at her.

"Here to do all the fun camp stuff!" he exclaimed.

I pointed to my full duffel bag. "Yeah, but the irony is that I missed you so much I was heading home."

"Yeah," Mary Stuart said. "She's missed you so much. She's hardly been thinking rationally." She shot me a look.

Bryce kissed my forehead. "Well, I think we know our girl isn't the most rational. Maybe it's all those books."

I wanted to say, *What the hell is that supposed to mean?* But considering I had just cheated on him two hundred yards away from where we were currently standing, I felt like maybe his comment wasn't the *worst* thing.

"No, babe, seriously," Bryce said. "I want to be here for you. Introduce me around. Let me meet some of your camp friends that have been so important to you."

The thought of having Bryce here with Rich, Daphne, and Huff made my stomach turn. I had just been intolerably cruel to my best friend. Who's to say she wouldn't even the score? I was trying to formulate some plausible excuse as to why we had to leave when Mary Stuart blurted out, "Lice!"

"What?" Bryce asked.

"There's been a lice outbreak in Cabin Nine. That's what I came here to tell you. I was going to get Lanier to help me get that under control, but if she has to go . . ."

"Oh, man. Yeah. I don't think we want to stick around for that," Bryce said.

I smiled gratefully at Mary Stuart. "Can you just tell June I had to leave, and I love her?"

She nodded.

I slung my bag over my shoulder, noticing that Bryce didn't even offer to help me when he saw it weighing me down. But, then again, that wasn't quite as bad as the whole sex-with-Rich situation, so I let it go. Bryce walked out in front of me.

Mary Stuart grabbed my wrist. "Thank you so much," I said. But her face darkened.

"I saved your ass because that's what friends do, but seriously, Lanier? You just destroy Daphne like that and then walk away? Did you hear what you said to her? That was truly, literally the single worst thing you could have said to that particular friend of ours. Or friend of mine, anyway."

I felt indignant at being scolded, but also ashamed. I turned to the vanity counter, which was actually in the bedroom, to scoop my toiletries into my duffel bag so I wouldn't have to see how disappointed she was. "Mary Stuart, you don't understand."

She crossed her arms. "No, Lanier. You don't understand. Look, you have no trouble dealing out the hardest, worst truths, so let me enlighten you on one of your own. Daphne is the most responsible person we know. You aren't afraid she's going to hurt Huff. You're just jealous. I don't know if it's because they are so good together or if it makes you insecure about your relationship or if it's because you're afraid they love each other more than they love you, but you were jealous back then and you're jealous now."

"That is not—" I stuttered. But I couldn't finish because I knew it was true. I had been jealous of them the first time they dated, afraid there wasn't room for me in the equation. Now? Well, now I hadn't even had time to form an opinion. "Mary Stuart, you weren't there. You didn't see how bad things were. She needed help."

"And Huff wouldn't have helped her?"

I couldn't answer because *of course* he would have. If he'd only opened his eyes a little, faced the truth that she needed his help.

"Look," she said, "tell yourself whatever you want, but you should know: You and I, Daphne and I, we're friends. Really great, true blue, in-the-trenches friends. But you two? You're sisters. I would kill to have what you have. If you want to ruin it, fine. But you should think really hard about what you're giving up."

The car horn blared outside the cabin. I pointed. "I have to go."

"I assumed as much." I made it as far as the porch when she added, "Oh, and Lanier, Ted would never blow the horn at me as I schlepped out with my own luggage. You might want to factor that into whatever decision-making you're doing."

I didn't respond, didn't acknowledge her comment, but my face was on fire. Did I think Mary Stuart thought Bryce was a bad guy because he beeped the horn at me and didn't offer to carry my bag? No. But she was right. They were little nothings that added up to the fact that he factored his comfort and needs in before mine.

But we both had flaws, I argued with myself. And, in many instances, our weaknesses and strengths complemented each other so well. That's what made us work. That's what would make our marriage work. I had committed to Bryce; I had committed to that future. I couldn't walk away from that because of an old crush in a weak moment.

I put my finger up toward Bryce and walked back to Mary Stuart, guilt overwhelming me. What had I been thinking? I was *engaged*. I was acting insane. I couldn't call off my wedding, get back together with a boyfriend from a million years ago. I was mortified by everything I had done and said this weekend and wished I could erase it all. "I should never have told you or Daphne that I was having cold feet, because that's all it was. Cold feet. I'm marrying Bryce whether you're on board or not."

"What about Rich?"

"Rich was an idiotic mistake, a last panic screw before I walk down the aisle. Nothing more."

She rolled her eyes. "Lanier, come on. Take a few days. Think about you. You need to be really, really sure."

"I've never been so sure about anything in my life," I lied.

As I walked toward the car, I steeled my jaw, my heart, my nerve. Bryce and I were getting married. In the real world, outside of this ancient camp that made me forget I was a grown-up, Bryce and I were perfect for each other. Everyone thought so. Bryce was smart and good-looking, confident and successful. And he loved me. I knew he did. And maybe that was good enough.

Daphne

AN IMPOSSIBLY LONG TIME

I HAD HEARD THE PHRASE "ROCK BOTTOM" PLENTY OF TIMES IN MY life. But, that night after the wreck, it was the only thought I was capable of having. *Rock bottom*. I was there. And, honest to goodness, I hadn't even realized I was that bad off.

That night, I was so consumed with the panic that I had almost killed the two people I loved most in the world that I couldn't think about anything else. I couldn't speak. The intense pain in my face didn't even really register. I didn't sleep that night, but I knew I had to get up. I had to face Lanier.

The morning after the accident was the first time in a long time I realized, as I dry-swallowed an Adderall to wake myself up, that it was not appropriate to drink every night or smoke pot every afternoon or sneak a line in the bathroom between classes. I certainly shouldn't have to pop Adderall all day to stay awake, especially when that meant

I couldn't possibly ever sleep without an Ambien—or three—to bring me back down.

I splashed water on my face, cringing as it hit my bruised, swollen eye, looking at my sunken cheeks. I knew, somewhere deep down, that I was constantly looking for something to dull the fear of what was next for me—the pressure of school, the anxiety I wouldn't make it, and, yes, the terror that, just like my mother, I would screw things up with the only man I'd ever loved. I'd lost tons of weight from the Adderall, and it was only now occurring to me how it had flattened my face.

I had been unhappy in Baltimore, and maybe that's where it had started. I was taking two prerequisite classes I needed to get into law school and working at a local restaurant as much as humanly possible to pay for my classes and save up for future ones. And in between, I had to study for the LSAT and work on applications. My top choice was UNC—I figured Huff and I could handle long-distance—but I had to make sure I applied for backups too. No matter where I got in, though, law school would be a pipe dream without some scholarship money and financial aid. I was working all the time and never sleeping. And between my schedule and his, I never saw Huff. I loved him, and I loved our relationship. But I wasn't happy here; I hadn't found my place. And it wasn't fair for Huff to have to be everything to me. Coming here had been a huge mistake.

As I looked at myself in the mirror, I finally faced the truth: I was out of control. I was twenty-three, and while yes, some of what I did was normal, I had also figured out how to get Adderall prescriptions from three different doctors and three different small pharmacies, all of which would never be the wiser. I was paying a kid $200 a month for his Adderall, too, because, let's face it, that was a lot cheaper than buying them on the street. That was not normal behavior. That was addict behavior.

I walked out of the bathroom, vowing to be better. I'd quit the Adderall. Tomorrow. Or, maybe instead of twelve a day, I'd take six. That would be a good start. And no more drinking. Ever. When I walked into the kitchen, I pinned on a happy face for Huff, who was also pinning on a happy face for me. I pulled out a pan to start scrambling eggs. "I need to check you for a concussion," he said in a tone that seemed as casual as he could muster.

Before he could, Lanier walked in, fuming. "I need to talk to you, Daphne. Alone."

I knew what she was going to say. I knew it, and I wasn't ready to hear it. Huff looked at me as if asking my permission. I didn't want him to leave. But he didn't know the full extent of what was going on with me. He didn't know how many pills I was taking or how much I was drinking or how often I was getting high. I was afraid if he knew, he'd leave me. So he had to go.

I nodded at him. "Okay," he said. "I'll work on getting your car towed."

Thank you, I mouthed, unspeakably grateful for him. As he walked out our apartment door, I sat beside Lanier on the bloated leather couch Huff and I had bought at a thrift store. It was hideous but comfortable.

"Lanier . . ." I started.

She put her hand up. "Nope. I get to talk."

I crossed my arms.

"Daphne, I want you to know that I'm saying this because I love you. I love you and I want what's best for you. I worry about you because I knew your mother. I lived that with you. And, like it or not, you have her genes."

"I'm not an addict like her," I protested. But even as it came out of my mouth, I felt beads of sweat form on my forehead.

"Fine. Maybe you aren't. And maybe today you can quit, walk away, wash your hands of all of it. But how long until you can't? Six months? A year? How long until you wake up and realize that you can't stop?"

It infuriated me that she could even say that. "I'm not like her!" I protested again.

"Daphne, you could have killed us all last night!" she said. "I've been ignoring my concerns for a long time, but if you are in a place where you are not only wasted but also think it's fine to drive . . ." She put her head in her hands, and my stomach rolled, the three tequila shots I'd done with a stranger at Huff's friend's house sitting hard. Combined with a few beers at the crawl and a completely empty stomach—no one could possibly eat while taking as much Adderall as I did—I knew it was bad. But I hadn't felt bad. I had felt on top of the world. I'd felt like I could fly. I could *certainly* drive. Lanier sat up. "Daph, how many pills are you taking?"

I could have confided in Lanier. I could have broken down. "The pills I take are prescription." *Mostly,* I added in my head.

She nodded. "Good. That's great. I'll give you my copy of *Valley of the Dolls*. Those pills were prescription too."

I'd never actually read the book, but I was pretty sure everyone died, so that probably wasn't ideal. My face was on fire. It was the most embarrassing, awful thing in the world to realize that your best friend sees the behaviors you are trying to hide, recognizes the truths that you have buried so deep that even you don't see them. But I couldn't face her. I couldn't face my choices. So I just stood up. "Get out."

She didn't move. "Daphne, I'm not leaving. I love you, and I'm the only one who will say this to you since my brother has clearly decided to enable you to your grave."

I leaned in close to her and, with my coldest voice, said, "You, of all people in the world, should know that the worst thing you could possibly do is compare me to my mother."

"Fine, Daphne. Tell me I'm wrong. Show me I'm wrong!"

But I knew I couldn't. So I leaned on my anger again. "If you won't leave, I will. You'd better be gone when I get back."

"Daphne!" she called behind me. "Daphne!" I finally turned around, and the look in her eyes was so pleading, so pained, that I almost forgave her. But then she said, "If you are going to keep going down this road, fine. But please, I beg of you, don't take my brother down with you. He deserves so much better than this." We stared at each other a long moment. "It's up to you. But I can't stick around and watch you hurt him." I knew what she was saying: It's Huff or me. Addiction or sobriety.

Now, seven years later, I pace back and forth in my office with a pen in my mouth, ruminating over the fact that we are back here again. Huff or Lanier.

After Lanier absconded into the night with Bryce, who was still, much to my chagrin, her fiancé, I felt relieved at first. When Huff asked where she was, I only said she had gone home with Bryce, which was technically true, even if it wasn't the whole story. I felt like I was sleepwalking through our final dinner and our last breakfast and the moment that should have been the highlight of the weekend: the announcement that we had raised $200,000 between donations and fees for family camp. Combined with the nearly $300,000 we'd raised between the camp sweepstakes and filling up the rest of the camp sessions—including the grants—and the $57,000 from the precious lemonade stands, we were so close to saving the place that had brought my best friend and me together. But now that we were apart, that victory didn't feel as big.

Through all of this, I fumed every time I thought of Lanier. Only, now that I am back home, now that the Lanier-shaped hole in my life has had time to form, I realize I can't lose her. She is, after all, the only person in my life who has never left me—Huff included. She knows how it kills me when she is mad at me, and she hurled that lit torch and watched it burn me to the ground. But I shouldn't be surprised. Fire is Lanier's preferred method of destruction.

That fear that Lanier is right has had time to sink in, and now I'm worried I can't actually give Huff the life he wants, that I'm too set in my ways with Henry and Steven. I know what I have to do. But every time I think about it, I can't breathe.

Finn opens the door and peeks his head in, thank goodness. I need a distraction. I fill him in on the gory details of the Lanier drama while we are supposed to be setting up an LLC for one of my favorite clients—assuming I can get my head in the game. "Do you need some Finn-therapy?" I nod. "And a smoothie?" He hands me a glass, and I smile gratefully.

My phone beeps and I walk to my desk to pick it up, figuring it is something beautiful and romantic from the man I love, the man whose heart I might shatter into a million pieces all over again. But it isn't from Huff. It is from his mother. Lanier's mother. *Hi, Daph! The invitations go out tomorrow! I thought we could make a big production of it. Have a little toast and send one out in the mailbox, the three of us?*

I groan.

"What now?" Finn asks.

I text Mary Stuart:

Invitations go out tomorrow, and I have to make some hard choices here. You think Lanier and Bryce are still a go?

She texts back immediately:

I tried. I swear I did. But she says she's marrying him.

I bite my lip and toss my phone aside, sitting in my chair and propping my feet up on my desk. "I have to tell her," I say. "She's going to marry him."

"Well, she deserves it after what she did to you," Finn huffs. I don't actually disagree. Now he is pacing. "Who wouldn't want my beautiful, perfect boss with their brother? If I had a brother, I'd be bribing you to go out with him."

He is sweet. "Be that as it may . . . Here we are."

"Daphne, you can't tell her," Finn says. "You just can't. You could get disbarred. Or suspended. And you owe more to Henry than you do to Lanier."

Yes. Of course I owe more to my Henry, whom I have sworn to love and protect no matter what. And that is why, knowing there is some truth to what Lanier said, I know I should end it with Huff. Because what if this change isn't just big for Henry but is big for me too? What if I relapse like my mother—whose relationships were always her biggest trigger—because it's all too much? That feels unlikely, but the idea that I could break Huff's heart again isn't impossible. I've never been able to commit before. Why now?

Despite all that, I ache to the point of nausea over the idea of letting Huff go, of feeling safe and happy and, dare I say, *whole*, and then kissing that goodbye.

"And what if she's mad?" Finn continues. "I know you think she's going to see you as her savior, but what if she thinks you're making it up? What if she thinks you're telling her a lie about Bryce in retaliation for her not wanting you to be with Huff?"

This is something I haven't considered, which is surprising because I consider myself excellent at looking at things from all points of view. But, also, if I get disbarred, Finn loses his job, which must be weighing heavily on him. He has a stake in this, too.

"You know you'll get a job if I tell her," I say, changing the subject. "A great one. One better than here."

He sits down. "There is no job better than here, with you. And if you think I'm saying that because I'm worried about my job, you don't really know me at all."

Before I can express my gratitude, Wendy Carlson walks through the open door. I smile at her tentatively. "Hi, Wendy. You know I was serious that I couldn't represent you against Bryce, right? I would love to but—"

"Don't worry. I have new representation," she says. "I'm just here to take Finn to lunch."

They both grin at me. This seems fishy. I want to ask who her new lawyer is. In truth, I want to make sure she won't love her new one more than me. As someone whose practice is founded on about a dozen main clients, her business is paramount to my firm. But that seems insecure and self-serving, so I let it go.

"Wendy and I have some business to discuss, so I might be a little late," Finn says. I look warily at him. "Oh—and you'll do the right thing." He walks out the door. I groan because who even knows what that is anymore?

Still, this statement bolsters me as I leave the office and drive the excruciating ninety minutes to see Huff. Steven is coming to pick Henry up at school for me. Usually, I would ask Lanier, who's one of Henry's favorite people. "Assisting" Lanier at the bookshop is one of his favorite things to do. The thought of him never being able to do that again breaks my heart in a million pieces. And that thought reminds me of why I'm doing this. It's not just for me, not just for Huff—it's for Henry too.

I pull into the driveway of Huff's beautiful two-story house on a tree-lined street in the oldest part of town. It is at least twice the size of mine, extremely impressive, and sits right on the same river that flows by Holly Springs—and yet, he is willing to give it up for me. His Sub-Zero glass door fridge and wide front porch, the basketball court he had built in the backyard and the outdoor kitchen that is worthy of *House Beautiful*. And it occurs to me, briefly, that I am playing this all wrong. Not only do I love Huff, but he can—and will—take care of me. Henry too. Breaking up with him, losing the security he could give me at the same time I might do something that could cost me my job, is the absolute worst decision I could make. But isn't that what my mother would have done? Stayed with the man who could take care of her?

He pulls into his driveway, and I step out of the car. His face lights up so much when he sees me that I almost lose my nerve. Huff's face changes, falls slightly, and I wonder if he senses what is coming, much in the way that animals can anticipate a storm. This might very well be the biggest storm of my life. And I ask myself, as he wraps me in his arms, smelling like Huff mixed with the chlorhexidine he uses to sterilize his hands and forearms before he enters surgery, why I'm doing this again. But then I remember Lanier's rage by that campfire, the silent ultimatum she laid down all those years ago when Huff and I broke up the first time: I could choose her or Huff, but not both. And her anger somehow juxtaposes the good memories we have together: the surprise party she arranged the day I opened my office, the nights she helped when Henry wouldn't sleep, the way her tears fell the day my mother died. Her voice telling me we were sisters; we would always be sisters. I wanted my great love. But you don't choose anyone—not even your great love—over your sister.

"Aren't you a sight for sore eyes?" Huff says, pulling away, kissing me.

I shouldn't let him kiss me because I know it's going to make what I'm about to say even worse. "I missed you," he says.

"I missed you too," I say, truthfully. I missed him today. I missed him for years and years, in every moment.

"Can I take you to coffee?" Huff asks. "Let me shower really quick and we can—"

He points to the upstairs of the house, and I touch his raised arm gently.

"Daphne?"

I look down at my feet. "Huff, I can't," I whisper.

I have practiced this perfect speech that has now completely left my mind because it is taking everything inside me not to vomit all over Huff.

"Well, we don't have to go to coffee," he whispers back, a questioning look in his eye, and I know then he knows what I'm saying. He takes my hands. "Daphne, I love you. And we are going to disagree sometimes in our life together. But I already told you if the Steven staying at your house thing is a nonnegotiable, I will concede that point." He tries to laugh as he says, "If you want our future kids to call him Daddy Number Two then fine."

I lean into him and wrap him up so tight I think I must be cutting off his circulation. "I love you, Huff. I swear I do. But my life is too complicated now. I can't complicate yours, too."

He pushes me back, gently, and looks me in the eyes. "Where is this coming from? Why would you do this to me? To you? To us? Things have been going so well." He pauses, searching my eyes for answers. "Is this about Henry? Because I will coach his basketball team and throw the baseball in the yard with him. I will take him camping and fishing. I will be the best stepdad in the world. No one else could love him like I will because no one else could love you like I do."

Tears are streaming down my face because I know this. And I want to scream, *Because your stupid sister doesn't think I'm good enough for you, and if she doesn't believe it, how can I?*

It was the exact same thought that ran through my mind that day seven years ago when I came back to the apartment and Huff was waiting for me. It had taken me an hour of walking around downtown Baltimore to come to terms with the fact that Lanier was right. And I had known she was right for a long time. I had felt myself sinking. But I'd been too afraid to face it.

"Where have you been?" Huff had asked. He tried to come to me, to comfort me, but I walked by him, straight into the bathroom. I opened my Adderall and dumped it in the toilet.

"You actually shouldn't flush prescriptions," Huff said. "They stay in the water system."

I turned to him as I flushed. "Seriously?"

"Well, I mean, I'm just saying." He paused. "What's going on with you?"

I flushed the Ambien and a few hydrocodone left over from a sprained ankle prescription that I kept refilling. Then I went to the kitchen and opened the freezer, removed the vodka, and poured it down the sink.

As I truly digested the scope of what I had been doing to myself, I realized I had to leave. And who would miss me? Huff was the only friend I had here. And I could finish the two prerequisite classes I was taking online. Right now, none of that mattered.

Lanier was right. I was hurting her brother by staying with him; I was being selfish. I was drowning. If I didn't let him go, Huff would drown too. The idea that I could ruin his life was the only thing that gave me the courage to say, "Huff, I love you, but I can't do this anymore. I'm leaving to go to law school. You have another year of medical school and then internship and residency and on and on . . ."

Huff was very calm. He took me by the shoulders. "Daphne, it's going to be fine. We will get through this together."

"But why? For what? You want to get married. You want kids and a family. I will never have any of those things." It shocked me how, for the first time in my life, I couldn't say, *I don't want any of those things.* Because maybe, I was realizing, I did want them. Maybe it was my fear I would ruin other people's lives, just like my mother, that had made me think I didn't. And now here I was. History repeating.

"Daph, I didn't realize what a hard time you were having, and I blame myself. I've been working so hard and studying so much that I haven't been paying enough attention—"

I looked up, catching his eye in the mirror. "That's just it though, Huff. I shouldn't need you to be responsible for me. I shouldn't have to count on you to keep me from channeling my stress and anxiety into the wrong things."

"Maybe. But you haven't been happy here, and I've been too busy to make you happy."

I shook my head. "It's not you, Huff. It's me." I realized once I'd said it, it was a classic breakup line. Really, though, it was the truth.

Huff nodded. "I understand." His eyes filled with tears, but he said, "Give me a few days to find a new place."

I felt like I couldn't breathe. He was letting me break up with him? He was letting me walk away? I was shocked. I didn't think he was wrong, necessarily. But I was devastated all the same.

"No. You stay. It's your apartment. I need to go home. I have to get myself in order."

That night, June picked me up. I didn't say anything as I got in the car. I was sick and shaking and dehydrated already, my body in total panic about subsisting without amphetamines. Finally, I cried, "I don't know what to do!"

June squeezed my shoulder. "I do, sweetheart. Don't worry."

It was off-season, fortunately, so June hid me away at camp and lived through detox with me. She didn't scold or judge me, but she did say, many times, "Please, Daphne, please. Remember how awful this is." I felt so guilty that I made her live through this again. I never felt like I was able to truly thank her for coming to get me, for wading through the dark and desolate days of the hell of withdrawal and heartbreak.

And now, today—when Huff and I are at this same crossroads—I find myself choking on the realization that I'd let him go the first time because I didn't believe I was good enough for him. And I still don't believe, deep down, that I deserve any of this—the love he can offer me, the good life I have. And that is why people like me, people who live lives filled with trauma, find it so impossible to break the cycle. Because we can get the fancy degree and wear the power suits, but deep down, we still believe we are our damaged, dangerous parents. And the one person who is supposed to love me more than anyone, my *sister*, believes that I can never be better. That I cannot change. That I am destined to repeat the sins of my mother, the sins of my past, at the expense of her brother.

Huff comes closer. "Seven years ago I let you walk away because Lanier said that was what you wanted, what you needed, to get clean. I respected that, but I'm not going to let you walk away this time so easily. Are you seriously doing this to me again?"

"Huff, I don't—" I am so stunned that I can't finish my sentence. I knew Lanier had played a role in the breakup on my end, but I had no idea she had done the same on Huff's. He looks at me, a question in his eyes. But then he shakes his head and hits the hood of his car with his palm.

"Damn it, Daphne! I believed with every ounce of myself, truly, that you wouldn't do this to me again. That you wouldn't give up on us, that you would believe in me—that you would *trust* me to be there for you, to be the person you could lean on, in good times and bad. But here we are. And nothing has changed."

And I can't say anything. I can only cry because he's right and Lanier's right. I haven't changed. Maybe I can't. Maybe no one can. And if I have only one shred of decency to give to another person, it's going to be to my son. That's it.

He takes a step toward me and looks me dead in the eye. "Daph, you can change your mind right now. This is your get-out-of-jail-free card. You can tell me you had cold feet and I can pretend this never happened. But this is it. If you walk away now, we are finished. Forever. No coming back. So whatever you decide, you better be damn sure because if you walk away, you have lost me, Daphne. I can't go through this again; my heart can't take it. This is the end of the road."

He wipes his nose, and I have never seen him so distraught. And I am so distraught I can hardly eke out, "I love you, Huff. I love you so much. And that's why I'm leaving you. You deserve better than me."

"There is no one better than you, Daph," he says softly. "How can you not see that? I have been out there. I've looked. I've searched high and low for someone to take your place and there isn't anyone like you."

I wish his words could soak into my skin like a thick cream, so that they could stay with me, so that I could believe them. Instead, they wash right off. "I will miss you every day, Huff. But I have to go."

I get into my car, and it occurs to me that forever without Huff seems unlivable. Forever is an impossibly long time.

Lanier

THE SAME CHRISTMAS TABLE

I WAS A BUNDLE OF NERVES OVER POSITIVELY EVERYTHING. THE wedding invitations were going out today, and I hadn't seen Daphne in five days, which felt like an eternity. But it wasn't the longest I had ever gone without talking to her. The longest, I knew well, was exactly thirty-one days. After Daphne walked out of her apartment in Baltimore seven years ago, I panicked. I called and called her. She never responded.

The next week, Huff was furious because, even though I was only trying to help, he thought I'd pushed her away. I had had a long talk with Huff about Daphne, about how he couldn't understand how damaged she was or what she had been through. When that tactic hadn't worked, I switched. "Huff," I remember saying, "Daphne can't get clean and sober if she has you here enabling her. Can't you see that? By staying, you'll only hurt her."

"I take care of her, Lanier. I will help her get better. She knows that."

That's when I lied. *My little secret.* "But, Huff, that's what's good for *you*. She seemed very clear on the fact that she needed to be alone to focus on her sobriety."

"Wait. What?"

I just shrugged. It didn't matter if he wasn't convinced breaking up was the right thing to do. I had already convinced her. And I knew my assertion—that he was protecting Daphne, helping her get better—would keep him from fighting harder for her.

Huff hated me, blamed me, for the breakup, for Daphne disappearing. And, well, I started to blame myself too. It was the loneliest time in my life. And I couldn't help but wonder if I had done the wrong thing. I hadn't meant to push her away. I almost hadn't said anything. But the idea that her behavior had become so reckless that it could have killed us all wasn't something I could push aside. It occurred to me that my mom must have known that Melanie relapsed. They were too close for her to hide it; that must have been what my dad meant all those years ago when he said that no one had tried harder than she had to save Melanie.

I couldn't repeat my mother's mistakes, so that's what I was doing; I was saving Daphne. In fact, I'd pictured being the one to help her get clean. But my approach might have been all wrong.

But then, after thirty-one days, Daphne showed up at my apartment in Raleigh. She knocked, I opened the door, and I froze, my heart pounding. Was she here for the showdown we'd never had? Was she mad at me? Was she clean? Before I could ask any of those things, I threw my arms around her. Whatever she was, she was here. And we would get through it.

She laughed and walked in behind me like nothing was out of the ordinary. "Want to live together while I'm in law school?" she asked.

I gasped. “The scholarship money came through?”

She nodded. “I’m going to UNC!”

The University of North Carolina had a top-tier law school that was Daphne’s first choice.

“I’m so proud of you,” I enthused. I weighed my options, but I knew I couldn’t just let the elephant in the room go. “Can you handle that right now, though? Is it too much stress? Are you . . . okay?”

“You were right,” she said. “I wanted to be one hundred percent clean and sober for thirty days before I came here and told you that you were right. I’m okay now. And I will never, ever go back to that place again. I’m sorry I put you through that. If it gets to be too much, I’ll pull back. If I’m scared or anxious or worried or tired, I’ll tell someone. I’ll get help. I promise.”

It was the most relieved I’d ever been.

“And, just so you know, I would never, ever push you away when you needed me,” I said. “That wasn’t my intention, and I’m sorry. If it gets hard or scary, I’m here for you. Always.”

Daphne nodded. “I know. Soooo . . . Do you want to live together?”

“Well, you’ll have to take the small bedroom,” I said, winking at her. I had to joke to keep from crying with pure joy. UNC was only thirty minutes away, and, incidentally, Duke’s biggest rival. So I scrunched my nose. “Although I can’t believe you could go to that inferior institution.” We would have a great time with this rivalry, especially during basketball season. “That lapse in judgment aside, of course I want to live with you,” I said.

She bit her lip.

“What?” I asked.

“Do you think I should call Huff?”

Huff, as I knew, was a miserable, wretched wreck of a human. He missed Daphne. Now *he* wasn’t sleeping. And he was trying to get through medical school while nursing his broken heart. But his moans in the car that night haunted me. And I had to make a command decision. "You know, Daph, this has all been a lot for him. I think it might be better to let him move on, because otherwise—"

"Enough said."

I saw the devastation in her face. I almost relented, told her to call him. But I reasoned that this was always going to suck. Whenever they broke up would be hard, and they already had a month of healing behind them. It was best for both of them to keep a clean break.

Now I realized that plan had totally backfired. They were back together despite my meddling. And I had hurt them both. Again.

I knew I needed to apologize to Daphne, but I still didn't know what to say. I was so caught off guard—and hurt they hadn't told me—that I jumped to the worst version of myself, said things I didn't mean, and reverted to a fear that I should no longer have. Daphne and Huff were the two people I loved most in the world. No one was a better friend or better mother than Daphne, and no one was kinder or more supportive than Huff. They had always been right for each other. I was actually glad they were together. So why, then, hadn't I told her that yet?

Maybe it was because seeing what Daphne and Huff had shone a light on everything I didn't. Because there was no doubt about it: Bryce might love me, but he did not look at me the way Huff looked at Daphne. And that was on me, not her. If I had misgivings about my relationship, it was up to me to fix that. I needed to apologize to her; I needed to make things right. But, like all those years ago with Rich, I was afraid she wouldn't forgive me.

I sighed, the stool behind my desk feeling mighty uncomfortable as I thumbed through a Scholastic catalog. Today was the day the invitations were supposed to go out. Today was, in many ways, the point of no return. And despite Bryce's showing up at camp and apologizing, I still felt torn. I missed Rich. He looked at me in the way I wanted, the way Bryce didn't.

But I was thirty years old. Did you base a life on a look? Maybe that was childish. And the idea of calling the wedding off—especially without my two best friends to help me wade through the heartache and fallout—made me feel nauseous.

As I circled The Baby-Sitters Club graphic novels in the Scholastic catalog (okay, they were for me. But they totally held up!) the door to the store burst open and I pinned on a smile. "Welcome to Bookmasters!" My brother strode in, wearing his full-on scrubs and white doctor's coat, his face deathly stern. He literally looked like he might have left a patient open on the table. My mind flooded with worst-case scenarios: Mom was dead. The invitations had killed her! Dad had a heart attack. Daphne! Oh my God. Was Daphne okay?

"You!" he yelled, storming toward the desk.

Uh-oh . . . So maybe, just maybe, Daphne had told him what I had said. Traitor. Although I knew I deserved it.

"All night and all morning I've been running over it in my head: Why would Daphne break up with me?"

I was stunned. "She broke up with you?"

It was like he didn't even hear me. "Why would she suddenly change her mind about the life we had planned together, about the family we were going to make, about how we were finally going to get married—"

"Wait," I interrupted him. "You were going to get *married*?"

"Um, yes. Married. Bride and groom, rings, vows. You should know since your wedding is the only thing you've been capable of talking about the past six months."

"And Daphne knew about this? I mean, like, she was on board with the plan? She was actually thinking about marrying you?"

"I was quitting my job to move here to be with her!"

Damn. He was worked up. But, also, whoa. I didn't know it was actually this serious. And I had no idea Daphne would break up with him because of me. Again.

I bit my lip as shame washed over me for what felt like the millionth time. And I really saw my brother. He wasn't a kid anymore. He was a grown-ass man, a renowned surgeon. And I didn't trust him to pick his own girlfriend? Or, well, future wife, as it were.

I still wasn't ready to admit to my part in this, though. And I wasn't sure what, exactly, Daphne had told him. "Well, I'm sorry," I said. "But I don't control Daphne. I don't see what this has to do with me."

He leaned over the counter and peered at me. "Oh, you don't? You don't see what it has to do with you? Because see, Lanier, as I was going over and over this in my mind, I realized something. I'm not that insecure kid I was the last time she dumped me. I know now that she loves me. Like *really* loves me. The only person she loves more than me, in fact, is Henry—or so I thought. But when I was in surgery this morning, it hit me: you. She loves you more than me. So the only explanation as to why she would pull the plug on our life together is because you told her to. And I swear to God, Lanier . . . You are my sister, and I love you, but I'm not doing this shit with you again."

I put my hand up. "I'm sorry, just to be clear. You didn't like leave some poor person on the table, did you?"

"What?"

"Well, you said you were in surgery . . ."

"It was an emergency appendectomy, Lanier. For God's sake. My nurse could do it herself with her eyes closed. But no. I didn't leave my patient on the table. He was in outpatient when I left. He'll be home watching Netflix in like an hour."

"Okay, well, I mean, I think that's a fair question."

He crossed his arms. He didn't think I was cute. He glared at me. "Lanier!"

"I might, *maybe* have said something to her."

He started pacing, and I was grateful that the store was empty. "What did you say?"

"I just suggested . . ."

"Lanier!"

He was going to kill me.

Superfast, like I was ripping off a Band-Aid, even hardly breathing between the words, I said, "I-might-have-told-her-that-the-two-of-you-together-is-chaos-and-destruction-and-she-would-only-ever-hurt-you."

He stopped pacing, his mouth hanging open. "Well, I hope she never forgives you because you don't deserve her forgiveness. I hope that you feel awful and awkward for the rest of our lives when we're at the same Christmas table, and that Mom always gives her the good, most burnt corner of the dressing that you like."

"She doesn't even like the burnt part," I said quietly. He was being kind of mean, yeah. But he was my brother. Our entire lives we'd said the most terrible things to each other and then been fine two seconds later because we were siblings and that's what siblings do. But no matter what I said about Daphne, she and I were not siblings, and we could not talk to each other that way. And I really didn't deserve her forgiveness. "So the Christmas table? You think you're getting back together?"

"I am one hundred percent sure we're getting back together because you are going to fix this." He pointed at me. "You'd better. I'm not kidding."

He started toward the door. "Where are you going?" I called. "Can't we at least get lunch or something?"

He turned. "I have a hernia operation at three." He sounded

calmer now, almost back to normal. Then he walked back over to me. “All those years ago, when you told me that Daphne said she wanted to be alone to focus on her sobriety—was that true? Did she really say that? Because that seemed like new information to her.”

I bit my lip. “Well, Huff, you know you aren’t supposed to date anyone for a full year after you get sober and—”

He put his hand up. “Lanier. Did she or did she not say that?”

I looked down, color spreading up my cheeks. “She didn’t actually say that. But I was trying to protect you, Huff. Maybe it was wrong, but I was trying to protect you both.”

He studied me for a moment. Then he nodded. “I know. Somewhere deep down—even though it was twisted, and *very* wrong of you—I know. But Lanier, we are not at that place anymore. We’re good. Things are good . . . well, they were good. So I mean it: You fix this or I will tell Mom.”

I gasped. The only person who loved Daphne more than Huff and me was Mom.

The door tinkled as if she had been summoned, and Mom walked in, looking pristine in her black pants and white blouse. “You’ll tell Mom what?”

I glared at Huff, and he glared back.

It was like Mom suddenly realized Huff wasn’t always here and this wasn’t a fight in my childhood bedroom. “I knew that was your car! Honey, what are you doing here?” Then she noticed his attire. “You didn’t leave a patient on the table, did you?”

He rolled his eyes. “You are both impossible. Lanier, I’ll let you tell Mom what you did. And best of luck sending out the invitations. It seems like a Herculean task.”

He was being sarcastic. And then he was gone. And even though he was mad at me, my heart hurt with how much I loved him.

Mom set her purse on the counter and sat in the chair in front of it. I was much higher than her on my stool, which gave me a little bit of the upper hand. But then she gave me that *what aren't you telling me?* look that they must teach in that top secret Mom school I'm pretty sure they all go to, and the laws of nature were restored. She once again trumped me.

"So I maybe might have sort of broken up Daphne and Huff."

Mom gasped. "Daphne and Huff were back together?"

I nodded.

"Honey, why does this matter to you so much? Are you jealous?"

"Why does everyone keep saying that?" I shook my head, then grimaced. "Well . . . you might not be totally wrong. But really, I was just shocked and hurt they hadn't told me. I didn't mean to break them up, though."

Mom pointed toward the door. "Did you see that full-grown, board-certified, Phi Beta Kappa Yale and Johns Hopkins graduate that just walked out the door?"

"Yes, ma'am," I huffed.

"He doesn't need you to run his love life."

"Doesn't it worry you, though, Mom, at least a little bit? I mean, you weren't there to see the full extent of it, but Daphne has had some rough spots."

Mom was exasperated. "Sure. But haven't we all? I don't think our behavior in our early twenties should define the rest of our lives. Do you? Because I could lay out some examples of yours that might not make you so proud."

"Fine. Okay. I guess I just always worry about Daphne's past and how she grew up. I mean, we both love her, but she spent her young life with a mother who was an addict, who told her love would ruin her life. That was something Daphne saw firsthand with all Melanie's breakups and heartbreaks. That affected her; I've lived those effects with her for decades. I just don't want those demons she carries to hurt Huff."

Mom laughed. "Well, Lanier, your grandfather always told you to get your nose out of that book, that the real world was happening around you." She gestured. "So I guess I've just always believed that people come into their own in their own time." She stood up and grabbed her purse. "Maybe Huff and Daphne won't make it long-term. It's possible. Half the time marriages don't work. But I've watched him be unhappy for a long time, and I have to think that it has something to do with letting her go. So if my baby boy wants Daphne, if she makes him happy, then that's a-okay with me."

"But—" I wanted to protest, but I was out of things to say.

"Sweetie, I couldn't save Melanie. I couldn't control her. Maybe I shouldn't have kept her relapse a secret from June all those years ago, but, really, it wasn't my secret to tell. And it took me a long time to realize that what happened to her wasn't my fault. It wasn't my fault because we can't control other people. Not really. We have to love them as best we can and help them when they need us. That's it." She patted my hand. "Darling, I will see you at three."

Mom was right. I didn't need to keep secrets and tell lies to protect the people I loved. I didn't need to try to control them because they could handle their own lives. Daphne could handle her own sobriety. I would always be there to help her because that's what best friends do. But if she and Huff wanted to be together, I needed to butt out, once and for all.

I looked out the door and could see the blue USPS box where our invitation send-off would take place, picturing how sad it would be without my best friend. We would have champagne inside. Prior experience had taught me that drinking on the sidewalk was a bad idea. I thought of Rich. My heart ached for him and all I had lost. And I realized that I had caused that same ache for Huff.

"Oh," Mom said. "And I'm assuming we shouldn't expect Daphne?"

"You know, Mom, Daphne is a better friend than I will ever hope to be, so I don't know what to expect." It was my responsibility to apologize. And I'd better figure out how fast or Huff would never forgive me.

She blew me a kiss. "Going to have lunch next door with Daddy. Come by if you feel like it."

The man walking in—finally! A customer!—held the door for her.

"May I help you find anything?"

"Just wanted to surprise my wife with a little something."

How nice, I thought, when a book was a surprise your husband got you, not the news that he had quit his job without telling you—or that honesty wasn't all that important to him, actually. Although I didn't have a leg to stand on there. I cringed at the thought of what I had done with Rich in that sailing hut. Again. And I figured that, whatever Bryce had done, it couldn't be worse than that. Maybe we were just two liars. Maybe we deserved each other.

The sailing hut made me think of camp, which made me think of Daphne . . . and Huff . . . And, all of a sudden, I knew exactly how—in the words of Huff—to fix it.

I rang up my customer and then texted Huff:

I have a plan.

It better be a damn good one.

I smiled. It was a good plan. It totally was. Maybe I was the only person in the world who knew how to break up my brother and my best friend. But, then again, maybe I was also the only one who knew precisely how to put them back together.

June

THE ENDS OF THE EARTH

THE SOUNDS OF LAWN MOWERS OUTSIDE MY DOOR MADE ME PRACtically leap out of bed. Family camp had given me a renewed sense of energy. And, with that extra money in our coffers, it made me believe that maybe we could save it after all. We needed more. Ninety-three thousand more, to be exact. But I could see it now. It was possible.

I brushed my teeth, threw on my clothes, and opened the door. The air was ever-so-slightly chilly, the grass damp. Everything smelled like earth and water and a quickly approaching summer. I practically skipped over to Dudley, Holly Springs's lead landscape technician. He stopped the lawn mower, its roar dulling to a gentle hum, and removed his large headphones.

"Sounds like family camp was a great success!" he said.

I nodded enthusiastically. Dudley hadn't had any idea about the dire straits we were in before we announced the plans for family camp. Part of my hesitation in telling the larger staff earlier than we absolutely had to was because I didn't want to worry them or make them feel like they had to look for new jobs. On the contrary, everyone on our wonderful, dedicated team volunteered to pitch in for family camp. Everyone had really leaned in to their positions, supporting us more than ever before. It was a good feeling. We really were a family.

"The guys and I were talking and, you know, June, we could probably all pick up some outside work over the next few weeks. You don't need to pay us if that'll help you out."

I was somewhere between bursting with pride and bursting into tears. "You are so kind, but no. You all have families and responsibilities. This isn't a volunteer position."

"Okay, well, just know the offer stands."

"Thanks for all you do!" I called as the lawn mower roared back to life.

Birds were erupting into song, and the entire camp felt alive, teeming. We were only a few weeks out from our first session. Then it would *really* feel alive. Instead of turning right to walk to my office, I turned left, taking the long route so I could circle by the river. I stopped for just a moment to take a deep breath.

This morning I'd decided that I was going to focus on the beauty of the sunlight on the river. I would worry about money later. Only, when I got to my office, it seemed the day had other plans.

Jillian was at her desk and across from her was a man in a navy Price Development polo. I smiled tightly as he stood up. "June. What a pleasure to see you again."

It was not a pleasure. It was not a pleasure *at all.* I didn't want this man sniffing around my camp. But I knew why he was here. I'd never followed up with him after his last offer. And men like David Price don't just slink off into the darkness and take your silence as a no.

"I was just telling Jillian here how great the camp is looking."

I tried not to smile at the compliment, but I couldn't help myself. "There's nothing better than this place when it's all shined up for summer."

He nodded. "And I was just thinking as I drove in this morning how beautiful and secluded your house would be if we built it on top of the bluff. You could have two acres to yourself. Your own little piece of paradise. You've certainly earned that after all the years you've invested in this place."

In an instant, I became irrationally angry. And it was irrational. Because here was this man offering me a way out of a potentially dreadful situation—a situation that, without him, could end in bankruptcy, having to ask my niece if I could live with her for a while, and trying to reenter the workforce after an entire career as a camp director. I knew as well as my own last name that I still had to come up with almost $100,000, and I didn't have a way to do that yet. David's offer, although a last resort, was my safety net. I needed more time.

I pinned on a fake smile. "David, could we maybe revisit your proposal at the end of the summer? I have a full camp of girls, and I'm just not sure how I could muddle my way through knowing I'd sold the place they love most."

He crossed his arms and leaned against Jillian's desk. "See, June, I'm already putting my guys out quite a bit by giving you this one last summer. We've found another piece of land that we could start developing now—with a seller eager to unload it. So I'm sorry to say that, if you want to sell to Price Development, time is of the essence. We're willing to give you this last summer, but as far as getting those papers signed, I'm afraid to say it's now or never."

Now or never. *Now or never . . .* I wanted to feel supremely confident that we would raise the money, that we would close the gap. But, well, I didn't. And knowing I had David's money to fall back on was a huge relief.

I opened my mouth. My answer only registered after I heard Jillian's gasp.

Daphne

A PLAN

Subject: Hard Things

To: marystuart@capecarolinapr.com

My Dearest Songbird,

First, I'm sorry. I know I've made your life weird, and I didn't know if I should even send this email—and it feels so strange without Lanier included on it—but . . . well, you were there for family camp. So you can probably imagine why I'm only sending my hard things to you this week. Thanks for coming to town last night. I'd like to say I feel better about the Huff stuff, but I just miss him, you know?

Anyway, on to my hard things: Want to get together with June tomorrow and do some hard-core save-camp strategizing? I know you're busy, so if you can't, it's okay. But I'm still worried about Holly Springs. Like really worried. I know we've all been Pollyanna, but we have a lot of money left to raise. The thing that keeps me sleeping at night, though, is knowing that Price Development wants the property. At least June will be okay, even if Holly Springs isn't.

Whatever shakes out, we'll get through this together. Thanks for being there for me, always.

Fair winds and following seas,
Daphne

Even though I don't put it in my email, what I really want to ask Mary Stuart is: Do I go to Lanier's stupid invitation send-off party or not? Especially after all the work Mary Stuart has missed to help Holly Springs, she certainly can't leave in the middle of the day and drive an hour to be there. Do I, in these final hours before this wedding is truly signed, sealed, and delivered to the rest of the world, tell Lanier the truth about the man she's marrying?

Honestly, I do not feel, after how she has treated me, like I am any longer the one to bear the brunt of Bryce's—and Lanier's—mistakes. But I also know that, as hurt as I am right now, Lanier and I will eventually make up, and when we do, I will spend the rest of my life knowing that I didn't tell her the truth.

I'm at a stop sign when I see Mary Stuart's email notification come through.

Subject: Re: Hard Things

To: daphne@millerlaw.com

Daph, I'm thinking about you constantly. I know how much your heart must hurt. And I know I've said this already, but this is Lanier's problem, not yours. As her friend, I should try to get to the bottom of it, but even though she said those things to you and not me, I can't quite forgive her yet. I've got your back. I'll see you tomorrow. Hang in there. And, Daph, most of all, I know you're scared sometimes. Don't let her words get in there. You are literally the strongest, most stable adult I know. Don't forget it. Love you the MOST.

FWAFS,
MS

Well, at least someone still loves me. I sigh as I pull into my driveway. I just need *a minute*.

But I won't be getting that minute because June's car is in the driveway.

"June, why are you here?" I say out loud. She would be able to help me through this, if only I could tell her. If only I could tell Huff. He'd know what to do. *Huff*. I feel nauseous again. How many days until this stops hurting? Will it ever?

Steven will be here in an hour to get Henry from school with me, and I'm excited. Henry is my whole reason for being, but single parenting can get lonely—especially now.

I get out of the car and June does too. I felt certain she was here with some really great news, but one look at her face tells me that is not the case. I hug her. "What's the matter?"

"I think I just did something really stupid," she whispers.

We walk up the steps, and I pull her inside the unlocked front door. "Do you want some tea?" I ask. "Lemonade?"

She sits down on the couch, discarding her flip-flops and tucking her legs underneath her. It's like watching my mother. It takes my breath away. "What's going on?"

"So, David from Price Development stopped by this morning."

"Ew. Oh no." Maybe that wasn't fair. From our professional conversations—I was June's lawyer, after all—David seemed like a nice enough guy. And, well, he was giving my aunt a way out should we not be able to prevent the worst from happening. "What did David say?"

"He said I could have one more summer at camp, but that I needed to make the decision to sell or not. He said it was now or never."

I brace myself for the news that she has sold, that that part of my life is over. So it stuns me when she says, "So I told him it was never."

I practically melt into the club chair I've been standing in front of. "June!" I know I shouldn't scold her. She is here because she is panicking, and my job is to soothe her. But between Huff and Bryce and Lanier and now this, I am at my wits' end. "I am your attorney! This is why you have me!" Granted, she doesn't actually pay me. But we are family, so that is fine. "When David Price says now or never, you say, 'Thank you, David. I will contact my attorney and get back to you as soon as possible.'"

"I know," she says, her head in her hands. "I know. I messed up big-time."

I feel awful for her, but, even still, I can't help but say, "June, how in the world are we going to come up with almost one hundred thousand dollars? That money from David was our backup plan."

She looks up at me and, in a shocking role reversal, says, "Well, we just have to figure out how to get that money."

She says it casually, like I haven't devoted every spare minute to that very cause. Finn and I have spent hours and hours trying to get bank loans, secure any Covid funding that might be left. Not to mention that Mary Stuart is working herself to the bone trying to bring in more donors, more press. I feel out of options, out of time. And June has just sunk her lifeboat.

"What if I call David," I say. "Tell him you were having a bad morning and that if they could just give us thirty days—"

"No."

"No?"

"You know, Daphne, I realized something on the drive over: I'm a hider. I don't trust myself enough to take risks, so I stay at camp all year instead of interacting with friends in town. I don't date because I've had so many losses I can't move forward. I'm going to save this damn camp. And if I don't, I'm the one who will pay the price."

My eyes widen. June is usually so calm and reserved. And now here she is just letting it all fly.

"June, may I ask you something?"

"No," she says, and we both laugh.

"Do you think that there is any chance—even just a tiny one—that losing your parents and your sister in tragic accidents could potentially have caused you to hide away at camp for so long?" She doesn't respond, so I add: "Look, June, we both loved my mother dearly, but I think we have to face the fact that while she loved us, she also hurt us. And I think we've both spent enough time holding back because of the scars we carry."

June sniffs. "I know I've used her as a crutch to keep from moving forward, and, Daph, I really am considering getting back out in the world, having a life outside camp. But, well, aren't we the pot and the kettle?"

I laugh. "We are. We totally are. And I know I can't keep living a life where I'm terrified to do anything because I'm so afraid I can't be anyone but her . . ."

June shakes her head. "Honey, you have Melanie's eyes. And her lips. And that gorgeous hair. But otherwise, you are all you. The way you are with your son and your friends—and, hell, even perfect strangers who need you. The way you stepped up to save my camp, the way you encouraged everyone to rally around this cause . . . really, Daph, they rallied around you. *You.* Not some paper-doll version of my sister."

I bite my lip, and I'm surprised to feel tears come to my eyes. "I guess I'm just scared. Mom was sober for seven years and then she met Vincent and got married and—"

Her eyes widen and she whispers, "And you've been sober for seven years. Are you feeling . . ."

I know what she's trying to ask but that she can't find the words—or she's too scared to. "No. I feel great. It was sort of, like, this superstition I was pushing to the back of my mind, but then when Lanier said I was like Mom . . ." I trail off, trying to compose myself.

"She called out your biggest, deepest fear. That must have been scary." June sighs. "But the thing that makes you different from Melanie is the way you dug deep and did the work—continue to do the work—to stay sober. You figured out who you were and why you turned to drugs and alcohol so you wouldn't do it again. She never really did that." June grasps my hand. "You know, Daph, I can't promise you that you'll always be this solid in your sobriety. But I can tell you that you have all of us, no matter what."

That is a relief.

She pauses. "I know we're dancing around it, but if Lanier won't support you and Huff, that's her choice."

I smile sadly. "I know it doesn't make sense to other people, but Lanier is the person I just can't bear to let down. After Henry, of course."

"I know why you can't bear to let down Henry. But Lanier?"

I know it will hurt her when I say this, but it's the truth. "Lanier is the only person in the world who has always been there for me. No matter what." Lanier has stepped up for me in ways that even June doesn't know about.

She nods, and I see the pain on her face. I didn't mean to cause it, but there is no way to sugarcoat the truth. I'm not emotionally equipped to have *that* conversation today, though, so I change the subject. "Mary Stuart is coming tomorrow. Want to spend the night?"

June smiles gratefully. "I would love it."

I feel fragile, and I need my aunt June. "Me too."

Steven opens the door and calls, "Weekend wife!" He sees me and smiles. I smile back. And it hits me like a pile of bricks what Huff was saying back at family camp. He is intimidated by Steven, my weekend husband, by how my loyalties might be torn. Roles reversed, I would feel the same way. Not that it matters now. I stand and hug him.

"Ready to go get Henry?" he asks.

I look at my watch. I have to decide now about Lanier. I sigh. I feel this pit in my stomach that means the hard thing to do is also the right thing. I can't keep this secret about Bryce from Lanier. It would be the ultimate way to let her down. Whatever she has said to me, whatever she has done, she is still my family. She has saved me. And I must save her too.

"Maybe you and June could go? I hate missing school pickup, but there's somewhere I need to be."

He nods and I walk down the porch steps, turning back to him. "You have your key, right?"

He nods and smiles again. “How about I make dinner?”

“You can do that?”

He laughs, but I’m kind of serious. I’ve underestimated him. But maybe I’ve underestimated myself too.

As I begin walking down the sidewalk, I realize that no matter what Lanier said, she deserves to know the truth. Even though she broke my heart, I couldn’t live with myself if I willingly broke hers. It feels impossible to face her. But hard things are something we know. Hard things are what best friends do. Some friends swear that they will walk through fire for each other. Lanier actually has.

Lanier

ACCORDING TO EMILY POST

I HAD PICTURED THE DAY MY WEDDING INVITATIONS WOULD GO out about a thousand times. I know. So lame. But I had always imagined that Daphne and I would make some big to-do about the whole thing because no one could make even the most mundane things feel as fun as Daphne. But Daphne wasn't here. Because I had ruined her life. Again.

Mom, Bryce, and I were standing at the front of the store. Customers were milling in and out, and I was enthusiastically, heartily, waiting on them because it bought us some time, a few more minutes where I could at least pretend that Daphne was going to come. I don't know why I hoped she'd show up. I still hadn't apologized.

After the last customer was checked out, Mom turned to us. "Well, kids, I think it's time to pop the champagne!"

She was trying to be cheery, but it felt forced. "Okay, Mom, fine.

Just say it. The afternoon is ruined because Daphne isn't here and it's all my fault."

She looked taken aback. "Um, I'm just standing here popping champagne thinking about this big moment, not Daphne."

I rolled my eyes and leaned against the counter. "Fine. I don't know if I can do this without her."

"Honey," Bryce chimed in, rubbing my shoulder. "Our wedding is about us, you and me. We are taking the first step toward our happy ending today, and whether Daphne is here or not, it's going to be extraordinary."

He was being so sweet. Guilt welled up in me again. I had texted Rich to say I was sorry. No response. That kind of irked me, because he knew I was engaged. I mean, yes, I was perhaps a little more affirmative about the unraveling of the engagement than I should have been. But still, it's not like I'd been pretending I was single. And I'd meant what I said in the sailing hut: I'd never loved anyone like I loved him. But then Bryce apologized and he was so great when we got back home, and . . . This was just cold feet, right? Wasn't that what was really behind this whole freak-out about Daphne not being here?

"We can wait," Mom said. "But according to Emily Post—"

"Oh, God, Mom. Okay. If the queen of wedding etiquette says the invitations go out today, let's just get them out."

She smiled self-assuredly as she poured champagne into three flutes. I tried to ignore the fourth—and the bottle of Pellegrino—sticking out of the top of her bag. She wanted Daphne here too. On the bright side, I had a plan to earn Daphne's forgiveness. I was going to fix it, just like Huff said. Although it was hard, I hadn't tried to talk to her yet because I knew whatever I said now would fall on deaf ears. I needed a grand gesture. But my grand gesture was going to take days and, according to Emily Post, we didn't have days. So, right now,

I was going to have to smile at my mom and my fiancé and suck it up. So I lifted my glass. "Cheers to this wedding becoming real!"

"Woo-hoo!" Mom said.

Mom had the invitations in a cute wicker basket with a pink bow tied on the side. She was so good at this stuff and thank goodness. We both knew I could never plan a wedding on my own. I wanted a wedding, and I wanted it to be amazing; I just didn't have the vision she did.

I put on my bravest face as I marched out the open door to the sidewalk and took the few steps toward the blue USPS mailbox. Mom handed me an invitation with my own name on it in perfect, scrawling calligraphy.

"This one is just symbolic," she said.

"You paid for a wedding invitation for me? Pretty sure I'm going to show up." I laughed uneasily because . . . Was I going to? I had to be very, very sure.

"Symbolic?" Bryce asked.

"Yes. I'd never run all these through the mail sorter." Mom laughed like we were dense. "I'll take them down to the post office to have them hand-stamped in a minute so they don't get any of those icky lines on them from the machine."

"Oh, Mom. That is so sweet, but you don't have to do that."

She looked at me sternly, and I realized this matter was very important and had now been put to rest. Bryce opened the mailbox, and, as I slid the invitation inside, just as my fingers let it go, I heard a wild, loud "Nooooo! Stop!" from the other end of the sidewalk.

It was too late. The first symbolic wedding invitation was gone. Even still, I smiled. She had come. She had forgiven me. But, when Daphne reached us, panting and unusually disheveled, she didn't look happy. "I know we aren't friends right now," she said. "And, honestly, after hearing what you really think of me, I can't believe I'm doing this."

Bryce took Daphne's arm. "Why don't we go inside before you do something you regret?"

Mom and I shared a glance. Something weird was going on. Daphne yanked her arm away. Despite the weirdness, I waved at Officer Mitchell and Officer Weed, who were walking down the sidewalk toward us. They were both customers. As teenagers, I couldn't count the number of times we had doubled over with laughter over the idea that a police officer's name could be *Weed.*

"Daphne?" Mom said gently. "Are you okay?"

She pointed. "Bryce—"

She stopped when she saw the police officers heading straight toward us. I thought they were coming to say hi until I heard a woman's voice from behind me. "Did you seriously think I was going to sign that NDA, Bryce? Take that paltry bribe from your mom? Buy into that little 'I'm no good to anyone if I'm in jail' song and dance?"

I turned to see Wendy Carlson, a girl I had gone to high school with. She and I had played on the basketball team together, and I had thought she was the most annoying person on the planet. But, in a twist of fate, she was now one of Daphne's best clients. She owned the flooring and lighting gallery in town, and she and Bryce worked together all the time. I could barely respond before one of the officers handcuffed Bryce.

I looked from Bryce to Wendy to Mom to Daphne and managed to eke out, "What the hell is going on?"

Wendy patted my shoulder. "Oh, honey. You really didn't know?"

"Know what?" I turned to Bryce and Daphne. "What is going on here?"

"They are arresting him for writing eighty thousand dollars in bad checks to me," Wendy filled in. "Because I'm the only one brave enough to actually have him charged." Wendy stepped close to Bryce. "I spent fifteen years saving up to buy that shop. I'm not losing everything I have because I'm scared of your mother."

"But she was going to pay you back!" Bryce yelled.

"Over three years? I don't think so. I need that money now."

Of all the possible things I had imagined for the day my wedding invitations went out, seeing my fiancé stuffed into the back of a police car was definitely not one of them. "Lanier, don't believe anything they say! This isn't what it looks like!" he yelled as they shut the door.

Tears ran down my cheeks. "Daphne! You're his lawyer. Do something!"

She looked stricken. "Actually, I'm not. It's a conflict of interest because Wendy is one of the people pressing charges against him."

I was furious. "So, you did this to him?" I spat at Daphne.

Wendy took my arm. "No. She wouldn't take any of our cases."

"Cases for what?"

That was when I realized we were all standing on the street, putting on a show for anyone who walked by. Mom took my arm to lead me back into the bookstore, and Wendy and Daphne followed. "Paula, maybe you should go call Bryce's mom," Daphne said. "She'll know what she needs to do."

I sat down in one of the chairs and watched my mom go outside. She pulled out her phone, pacing the sidewalk.

Wendy cleared her throat. "I'm sorry," she said. "I know this is terrible. But you should know that your fiancé was writing bad checks all over town. He wasn't paying his subcontractors, and there are people whose projects he was working on that are in danger of losing everything because they are on the hook for hundreds of thousands of dollars to subs and suppliers—money they have already paid to Bryce—for houses and buildings that aren't finished."

My head was pounding. On the one hand, this was *Bryce.* I loved him. I couldn't just let him rot in jail. On the other hand, how could I have been so stupid? Or, more to the point: Why had I repeatedly ignored the gut feeling that told me something was wrong? "That's why he went to work for his mom," I said, everything suddenly clicking into place.

"It's the only way she would clean up his mess," Daphne chimed in. "And make sure everyone got paid. On her terms."

I looked up at her, tears filling my eyes. "And you were going to tell me. You were going to disbar yourself for me even after what a nightmare I've been."

She shrugged.

Mom walked in. "Honey, why don't you come home tonight? I feel very unsettled. And, Wendy, I am so sorry that we are even remotely connected with this."

"Oh, old Mrs. Moneybags won't let him rot in jail. I'll get my cash. But I feel bad for all those people who may not."

I was reeling. Part of me wanted to get in my pink bathtub in my condo upstairs, but the other part didn't want to be alone. I still couldn't believe this was true. I needed to talk to Bryce. I needed to see him.

"So," Daphne said in a low voice to Wendy, "that secret business lunch with Finn was more like a planning session?"

"I can't fathom what you're insinuating," Wendy replied with a wink.

The look on Daphne's face told me Wendy was no longer annoying high school Wendy. She was boss-bitch Wendy.

"Well, ladies," Wendy said, "apologies all around, but this is business. And good luck, Lanier. Seems like you're going to need it."

Okay, so, maybe high school Wendy was still in there somewhere.

Daphne got up to leave too.

"Daph!" I called after her. She didn't turn around, and I realized that even though she was going to tell me about Bryce, that didn't mean she'd forgiven me. I got up and ran out onto the sidewalk. "Daphne!" I called again. "I'm sorry! I'm so sorry."

She stopped long enough to say, "You're only sorry when I save you."

Maybe she was right; maybe that was true. But I had saved Daphne too.

• • •

The beginning of our junior year of high school, Daphne's dad's house had officially become our hangout spot. He was, after all, never there, and we could do pretty much anything we wanted.

One afternoon after school, while we were watching reruns of *Keeping Up with the Kardashians*—which Mom wouldn't let us watch—and downing Cheetos—which Mom wouldn't let us eat—Ray burst through the back door. He had been gone for like three days, which wasn't unusual. I could tell by the sideways way he was walking that he was really drunk. His shirttail was hanging out, his eyes bloodshot, his hair messy. And he definitely hadn't shaved in a while.

He startled when he saw the two of us, as if he had forgotten he had a daughter at all. "You!" he said, pointing at Daphne. "This is all your fault. If I didn't have to see your face, which is just like *her* face, I could forget about your damn mother once and for all!"

He was barreling toward her, and I started to panic. But then he flopped down on the couch. One foot, curiously, was missing a shoe. He whimpered for a few minutes, saying, "Melanie, why?" over and over. Daphne and I looked at each other, in shock, and stayed very, very still.

"It's my mom's birthday," Daphne whispered when the moaning stopped, when Ray's eyes were shut, his breathing heavy. "I'm actually kind of impressed he remembers."

It wasn't long before Ray was snoring, his right arm flung off the side of the couch near a pile of *Cosmopolitan*s Daphne and I had been reading. (Mom didn't allow those either.)

"We need a plan," I'd said, looking into her beautiful face that, yes, I was sometimes jealous of. Who wouldn't have been? Every boy loved Daphne. But those boys were disposable to her. Maybe this was why. Maybe when you are disposable to your own father you don't know how to make anything stick.

"A plan for what?" she whispered.

"A plan of how you're going to come live at my house."

She raised her eyebrows, but, for the first time, she didn't argue. That she needed to get out of here was as plain as day, even to a couple of teenagers who liked to have a place to watch E! in peace.

Before we could discuss further, I noticed the open liquor bottle on the coffee table, the gas station book of matches beside the ashtray, the pile of magazines, the Newports peeking out of Ray's shirt pocket. When I got up and slipped the pack out of Ray's pocket, he stirred. That was a good sign. It meant he would wake up.

He wasn't a bad guy. Just a shitty dad. I got the most intense burst of love in my heart for my own doting father, who made his special famous Chex Mix when I had friends over and took me to play golf and tried to talk to Daphne and me about boys even though we laughed at him. I swore in that moment to appreciate him more.

I took a cigarette out of Ray's pack and held it between my lips, menthol coating my tongue. I leaned over to grab the matches.

"Lanier, what are you doing?" Daphne hissed. "You don't smoke."

I didn't answer. Instead, I slid the arm of my oversize T-shirt over my hand and grasped the handle of the open liquor bottle, tipping it and dousing the magazines and cigarettes on the floor by Ray's arm.

"Lanier!" she hissed again. "What the hell are you doing?"

"I'm getting you out of here," I said. I remember how cold I felt as I struck that match, as I held it to the end of the cigarette and inhaled. I'd only smoked a few times, mostly to look cool, but this time I didn't sputter or cough.

"Call nine-one-one," I said. "And then call my mom."

The cigarette slid perfectly into Ray's fingers. His hand was relaxed with dreaming but cupped to have just enough tension to hold the cigarette. I held the gleaming match above the liquor-soaked pile and said, "I mean it, Daphne. Now."

She was wide-eyed, mystified, probably because in our relationship Daphne was the doer. She was the one who enacted the plans. She scrambled to her feet, ran toward the kitchen where the phone was, and as I dropped that match, I realized I was calling the shots now.

I saved Daphne then, just like she had tried to save me now. I knew I had a long way to go toward earning her forgiveness. But I also had hope. And, just like that day when we were sixteen, I had a plan. We were experts at getting through hard things together. As she didn't turn around, didn't look back, I hoped against hope that we could make it through just one more.

Daphne

A HAPPY FAMILY

EXHAUSTION SEEPS INTO MY BONES AS I WALK UP THE STAIRS TO MY office. I nearly jump out of my skin when I see Finn sitting behind his desk in the reception area. When he sees my face, he says, "Oh, Daphne, you didn't."

I shake my head as I sit in the chair across from his desk. I feel like I've narrowly avoided a car crash: rattled and shaken but so, so grateful. "I didn't have to. Wendy had Bryce arrested. At a super-convenient time, as you well know."

Finn smiled conspiratorially. "I mean, I might have happened to mention the date, time, and place of the wedding invitation send-off. I do have access to your calendar, you know. But I kind of can't believe she followed through. Damn, Wendy. Good for you, girl!"

"You saved my ass, Finn. For real. I can't ever thank you enough."

He shakes his head. "Nah. It would have worked itself out. Things have a way of doing that. I just helped it along a little." He gasps. "I did your hard thing! Am I an honorary Songbird now?"

As if with a magic wand, I tap each shoulder. "I anoint you!"

We both laugh. "Is it weird that I kind of hate to think Bryce is sitting in jail right now?" I ask. "I mean, Paula called his mom, so I'm sure she'll pay his bail, and he'll be out by morning. But I still like Bryce, you know? Despite all of it. I think he just got in over his head."

Finn nods. "I like him too. He's funny. But he messed up pretty bad, and he didn't even need to. You know?"

"I know. Why do you blow up your whole life for no reason?"

"Huh. There's someone in this room I could ask the same thing."

"I didn't have to blow my whole life up, thanks to you."

"Not your nine-to-five. *Huff.*"

Just hearing his name sends a shot through my heart. "I thought I was breaking up with Huff for Lanier. Or maybe for Huff, because there is this teeny part of me that is afraid of what happens next. But, honestly, Finn, at the end of the day, I am so afraid that I will make a bad decision that will screw up Henry's life. We're so happy now. He's so content. He has Steven and me and June and Lanier and Mary Stuart and now you . . ."

"And you're afraid that he'll get attached to Huff and things won't work out and he'll be heartbroken."

I nod.

"Damn Lanier for putting this in your head. Daphne, I know you love them, but I think this family might be kind of toxic for you."

I see where Finn is coming from, but he doesn't understand just how much that family means to me. I think of my dad on that couch, the afternoon I was afraid of him. For the previous three years, I had been alone and terrified and devastated and exhausted all at once. That afternoon, it all came to a head.

I was sixteen again, watching a match, dropped—on purpose—by my usually very level-headed best friend, fall into a pile of alcohol-doused magazines. The pile erupted, and I caught Lanier's eye across the flames. I was terrified, but her eyes danced. And, for a second, we were at camp, around the firepit, red, yellow, and orange doing a burning, beautiful, cleansing dance. My father, cigarette in hand, stirred. As the smoke detectors squealed to life, I did as Lanier said. In the old kitchen that still had a harvest-gold phone on the wall, I called 911. "My house is on fire!" I yelled. Lanier and I hadn't discussed this at all. No words had passed between us. But, even still, I said, "My dad passed out drunk with a cigarette in his hand!" I gave them the address and told them to hurry.

Then I dialed Paula. I was crying for real as I told her to come, as the smoke started to burn my throat. I saw my dad jump off the couch and throw what was left of the liquor on the fire, which made it explode. He was attempting to beat the small fire with a cushion as I ran out the front door, and I met Lanier on the porch. We said nothing as the fire truck roared into the driveway. My father stumbled out as the firemen ran past us into the house.

Time must have passed between the time Dad walked out and Paula arrived, but memory is tricky, and I don't remember what, if anything, transpired between us during those minutes.

All I remember is Paula running to us, holding us to her, whispering that we were okay. The firemen walked out then. "It's under control," the chief said to my dad. "No major damage. Just some cleanup there by the couch. But, son, I suggest you get yourself in order. Next time you pass out with a cigarette in your hand, the whole house could go down. These girls saved your life."

Lanier and I shared a look. Only we knew we didn't save his life. Only we knew we set him up. And only we will ever know.

Paula waited until the firemen were gone. She looked at my father, who was sitting on the top step with his head in his hands, in a stupor. I felt sorry for him, pity for his innate weakness. Even at sixteen years old I knew he didn't mean to be this spineless and unfeeling. Even at sixteen, I knew he was both the villain and the victim in his own life story.

"This is how it's going to go," Paula said to him. "Daphne is coming to live with us. No custody battle, no court, no fighting. I won't say why, and neither will you."

He looked up at her, his bloodshot eyes overflowing. He looked at me with such love and regret that my heart broke a little. "I could have killed my girl. I'm sorry, Daphne. I'm so sorry."

"You could have killed her," Paula said. Then I detected a small smile. "But you didn't. And if you agree to my terms, that can be our little secret."

And it has. Even now, years later, we've never talked about it. Every now and then, I wonder what it would be like if I saw my father again—if he would apologize, if I would tell him the truth. Since that night at camp, he's never reached out to me again. But, for now, I'm content with the family I have.

And that family includes Lanier, who fought for me. She always has. Finn doesn't know what Lanier has done for me, what Paula has done for me, how John went along with the plan and became a damn good surrogate dad at that. Yes, they might sometimes be bad for me. But they are good for me too.

"Can I ask you something, for real?" Finn asks.

"Always."

"You've known Huff for like, most of your life, right?"

I nod.

"So, let's just say that you date, maybe you get married, and, like, ten years from now, it all goes up in a blaze of glory."

I laugh at his choice of words. "I'd rather not say that, but okay."

"Is Huff the kind of guy who would just walk out of Henry's life? Is he the kind of man who would say, 'Well, I've lived with this kid and been in his life for a decade, but now I'm out'?"

The mere idea of it almost makes me laugh. "No. Huff is not even in the same zip code as that kind of man." It strikes me that he's nothing like my father. And isn't that what I'm afraid of? Being abandoned again? Or Henry feeling abandoned the way I did?

Finn nods. "What if you went through a tough time? Is he the kind of guy who would walk out on you?"

"No way," I say. I know that now.

"Okay. So, opposite scenario. Let's just say that you and Huff get married, and you're radiantly happy. I mean, you argue. You aren't automatons. But you have more kids, brothers and sisters for Henry. And you sit around the dinner table every night and laugh about your day. And when Henry gets strep throat, you don't even have to go to the doctor because your husband can just call in the prescription."

I laugh. "Seriously? That's what you think of?"

"It's not a bad perk."

He's right. It's not a bad perk. And of the two scenarios, I know that number two is more likely.

"So . . ."

"So, I think I screwed it up permanently this time. He said if I walked away, that was it." Before I let myself get too lost in the dream of what if, I remember: Lanier.

Finn waves his hand at me. "There's no walking away from a love like that. Not really. And you don't know if you don't try."

If only it were that simple. "I should pay you overtime for this."

Finn laughs. "Are you joking? I was up here trying to figure out what the hell we were both going to do when you got disbarred!

This is a welcome surprise. Free love advice is part of the services I offer you."

I stand up and he does too. I hug him. "You are the greatest thing that has happened to me in a long time. Friend and paralegal all in one."

"And don't forget excellent smoothie maker."

I nod. "Yes. And you know how picky I am about those."

"I'm going home," Finn says.

"I want to get ahead on the Lentz-Craig merger for next week." Two of our local pest control companies were joining forces, and I was at the helm. It was a pretty simple merger, but you never knew what crazy requests would come down the pike at the eleventh hour.

"I can stay," Finn says.

I shake my head. "We both know I'm using this excuse to avoid thinking about the mess I've made of my personal life."

He pauses and then says, "You're a good person, Daphne. It will all work out."

So why hasn't it yet? I want to ask. But I don't.

After work, I walk down the tree-lined sidewalk slowly, savoring my favorite time of day, when the heat dissipates and the shadows play, when lights from inside happy homes shine on families filled with love. I pin on a smiling face as I walk through my front door.

Henry races through the hallway in clean but ever-so-slightly too-tight pajamas that accentuate his tummy and jumps into my arms. I bury my face in his warm neck, kissing his wet hair that smells of baby shampoo. The panic of how I almost risked his future today overwhelms me. The day he was born I promised I would protect him no matter what, that I would choose him over everyone and everything else. Today I almost broke that promise. But, in the end, I didn't have to. We're okay. It's all okay.

"Where's Daddy?" I ask as I put him down.

"Making dinner."

"Is that what I smell?" I walk into the kitchen, where music is softly playing on the Bluetooth speaker and Steven, as if he is in *Top Chef*, sprinkles salt on something in a pan. "I'm sorry. Who are you and what have you done with my baby daddy? Clean kid? Dinner on the stove?"

He turns and smiles that glittering Steven smile. I have to admit, this picture of domesticity is pretty appealing. He pops the cork on a bottle of champagne and pours himself a glass and me a glass of sparkling water. "What are we celebrating?" I ask.

"Being alive."

And I remember what I adore about him. Today I had been consumed with the idea that I have ruined everything, that I have done nothing productive and that I am making everything worse for everyone around me, while Steven is celebrating because he has oxygen in his lungs. And so I decide that I will be like Steven. I will celebrate tonight because I am still youngish and upright and healthy, and I have a beautiful child.

"Henry," Steven says, as he raises his glass, "to your wonderful mommy."

"My *beautiful* mommy!" Henry chimes in, hugging my leg. He looks up at me. "Mommy, Aunt Lanier came over when you were gone."

"Oh, yeah," Steven says. "She said . . . I don't know. Something, something, something, she's sorry. Something, something, something, can you meet her at camp at five tomorrow?"

"Um, no. No, I cannot."

June walks in, and I squeal and hug her. It's the first time I have seen June wearing something other than a camp shirt in years, and I like it. My heart aches a little that Lanier won't be here with June,

Mary Stuart, and me for our hard-core, save-camp strategizing tomorrow. "See how fun this is, June? Regular life. Outside of camp?"

She laughs and squeezes my arm. "What can I help with?" she asks as Steven carries a bowl of salad to the table.

"Nothing," he says, handing me my water and pouring June a glass too.

As we all sit down around the dining room table that I found on the side of the road then sanded and painted almost five years ago, I see Steven for who he really is. When Henry was born, yes, I had concerns about his being able to single-parent on his weekends. But if he's shown me anything these past few weeks, it's that he has grown up. Just like I have. He is different. I am too. I love our weekends together. I love laughing around this table together. And maybe that doesn't have to end. But it also doesn't mean we can't move forward. There's always room for more at this table.

As Henry does a "magic trick" that involves "disappearing" his vegetables under his napkin, I look at June's happy face. And Steven's. And I feel how much being with these three people soothes my soul. It is unconventional. But we are a family. We made it through the day. Henry and Steven and I made it through the last five years. June and I made it through the last thirty. And so I raise my glass. "To us," I say simply. "To the family we have made, the love we have found, and the futures we will create."

"To us!" Henry repeats. "And to never eating vegetables again!"

Maybe it makes me a bad mother. But he's so cute when he says it that I can't help but drink to that.

• • •

It weighs on me all day whether I should meet Lanier at camp at five. It weighs on me through pancakes at the waterfront Coffee Cove with June and Mary Stuart where we devise what I think are some very interesting leads on how to close the fundraising gap, namely a mother-daughter camp weekend. It weighs on me through Henry's soccer game, which, let's be honest, does give me some thinking time. Four-year-olds playing soccer is not exactly exciting.

It's an hour drive, so I have to plan a little. But, then again, Steven and June are here with Henry, so that requires less planning.

After the game, when we get back to my house, June says, "Well, my girl, I'm heading back to the salt mines. Just a few weeks until opening day!"

She is truly, genuinely thrilled. I can see it in her face. "Do I meet Lanier at five?" I ask.

She shrugs. "You know, sweetie, you and Lanier have been together longer than a lot of married couples. So, it's up to you to decide: Is this a rough patch you work through? Or do you get a divorce?" She squeezes my arm. "I will support any decision you make. But I think today is a crossroads. If you don't go, you've sort of served her the papers."

I wince. I am still upset with her, sure. Her words cut me to my core, made me doubt the life I had spent years rebuilding, the sobriety that felt like the centerpiece of my existence. But, also, Lanier had been the one to live those hard years with me. Especially in those early months, when I had a stressful day and felt like I couldn't cope without drugs or alcohol, it was Lanier who would spend hours walking with me. When my body was learning to sleep again totally on its own, it was Lanier who stayed up and watched movies with me. Even years after I felt like my sobriety had really "taken," if I was ever having a weak moment, it was always Lanier I called. And she always answered. Every time.

I decide to get in the car, to drive in the direction of camp and see how I feel. That seems reasonable, right?

Steven and Henry are already embroiled in a video game, making a lot of loud noises. I smile, laughing at the two of them.

"Hey, boys," I say.

Steven elbows Henry. "Pause it."

"I'm going to go see Aunt Lanier. I'll be gone for a few hours."

"Okay!" they say.

"Good job on the field today, buddy. I vote we have a big celebration breakfast if I'm not back in time for a big celebration dinner." I lean over and kiss his doughy cheek.

"Dad! If Mom isn't going to be here for dinner . . ."

"Pizza Hut!" they yell simultaneously.

"You know what a gift it is to be the fun parent, right?" I ask.

"I will not squander it," Steven says wistfully.

I laugh and walk down the steps to the car, thinking this is dumb. I have all I need in my life. I don't need Lanier. But my throat grips.

Lanier isn't just my best friend; she's my family. Her family is my family. The fact that we would fight about anything is just dumb. In fact, I start feeling afraid if I don't show up on time that she might think I'm not coming, so I drive a little more aggressively than usual. Part of me feels insane for going. But I can't end our friendship. I just can't. Maybe I shouldn't have to rely on memories to help me decide, but I can't forget.

I was the one to find my mother the night she died. And it's almost annoying how nondramatic the moment was. No blood. Nothing gruesome. In fact, I thought she was sleeping. I came home from tennis to find her, dressed in a pair of very grown-up, fancy mom-looking black pants with a pale pink blouse tucked in at the waist, still wearing a pair of ballet flats that matched the blouse perfectly. Her hair was blown out, and she had on fresh lip gloss. This version of Mom was the boyfriend-free one, who loved working for John, spending time with me, and keeping our cute little house pristine. She was so happy. So responsible. Or so I'd thought.

Mom was lying on the couch, her face serene. I didn't even walk to her at first, just said, "Mom, you'd better watch out. I'm going to be better than you at tennis soon."

Mom was pretty competitive, so when she didn't answer I knew she must be sleeping soundly. "Mo-om," I called. She didn't budge. I had seen her passed out before, but she usually looked . . . sloppy. She wasn't sloppy now. She was perfect. The previous week I had seen her with a man in her bedroom. Well, coming out of her bedroom. He was not perfect. He was rough. And, somewhere deep inside, I knew he was her dealer. Somewhere deep inside I knew he wasn't hanging her new curtains. And somewhere very much on the surface, I knew she was back on drugs. I knew I should have told Paula or John or June or someone. But I couldn't. I just couldn't. This was the most stable my life had been since before she met Vincent. I couldn't bear the thought of letting it go. So every night I prayed that she would stop. Every night I prayed that we would get to stay just as we were. She was always good at pretending, my mother. I didn't want to be like her. But I was good at pretending too.

That night, I pretended I didn't know she was dead. I pretended I thought she was napping in her PTA outfit. When I walked over to her, I didn't shake her, didn't scream. I put my shaking hand to her face. She was so still. I whispered, "Paula and Lanier are pulling in to take us to dinner." I cleared my throat and leaned down to kiss her. "Fair winds and following seas, Mom." My voice caught in my throat.

I walked out onto the porch. I felt preternaturally calm, but my face must have been stricken because Paula ran out of the car, past me. I didn't follow her. I sat on the steps, and Lanier sat beside me. I left my mother so that I could have that last peaceful moment, so I could remember her flawless face with her slender nose and perfect contouring. I let Paula be the one to call 911 so that my last moments with my mother as I knew her were quiet and calm. If I had stayed even a millisecond longer, I would have had to acknowledge that she wasn't napping. That that man wasn't hanging curtains. That he had very likely killed my mother with whatever he had given her, with whatever she had willingly taken.

I made Paula be the one to tell me that my mother was dead. But it wasn't Paula who held me as I cried, who told me it was going to be okay. It was Lanier. Lanier was the one who got me through those long, sad months when I had to face the fact that I didn't have a mother. It was Lanier who lied to Paula and told her she was spending the night with another friend when, instead, she was spending her nights with me at my dad's so I didn't have to be alone. And when Henry was born—when I was racked with fear that I could only be a parent like my parents—it was Lanier who reassured me, who came over every single day to help me, even on days when Henry and I were grumpy and she could have made other plans. That is why I choose her. Because she has always chosen me.

But even though I love her, I realize on the way to Holly Springs that I love Huff too. And June's confidence in me and remembering my mother on the couch that night have reminded me that I am not my mom, that I never will be. Seven years isn't a curse. It isn't an omen. Each year is another 365 days of strength. Another 365 days further away from that one really bad year that could have gone the other way. But it didn't. Because then, just like now, I had people who loved me enough to stand beside me every step of the way. And, I have to admit, maybe I am simply afraid of what comes next, of the unknown.

Because Huff is not only my love; he could also be my family, Henry's family. We could have something really special. And I think that, no matter what transpires with Lanier tonight, I will go to Huff's house when I leave. Maybe he has really given up on us. Maybe I have broken his trust one too many times. But maybe he will feel the same way. Maybe he will understand. I am going to be very honest with Lanier about my plans. What she chooses is up to her.

As I approach the open gate at Camp Holly Springs, despite all the worries that have gnawed at me for the past few days, the camp magic prevails. I roll the windows down and inhale the earthy scent of dirt and grass and, in the distance, water. And, instantly I relax.

As I approach the raw wood gazebo by the softball field, I park. My stomach fills with butterflies as I get out of the car. I realize I won't have to drive to Huff's house tonight. Because I don't see Lanier. I see Huff. I don't know if he knew I was going to be here or if Lanier summoned him. But when he sees me, I take off toward him. Not in a romantic-movie, slow-motion kind of way. In an I'm-in-the-Olympics-and-I'm-going-for-the-gold kind of way.

He jogs down the steps toward me, and I know that I don't have to convince him to change his mind. I leap into his arms and he kisses me, hard, and it is only then that I realize I am crying. "Hey," he whispers, putting me down and wiping my eyes. "It's okay. You don't have to cry. I'm here and I'm not letting you walk away from me again."

He takes my hand, and as I turn, Lanier appears out of nowhere and sits on a nearby bench. She waves tentatively and pats the spot on the seat beside her. I turn to Huff and raise my eyebrows. He nods with a soft smile and hangs back as I walk over to her and sit down. I don't know what to say. But fortunately, she seems like she knows just where to start.

"I want you to know, first and foremost, that what I'm about to say has nothing to do with what you tried to do for me yesterday."

I venture a small smile. "I think I finally like Wendy now."

I look out over the softball field where a game seems to be starting—with, like, a *lot* of players. Has June organized some sort of fundraiser? Did she tell me about it and I forgot? Or is this Lanier's surprise? *She* organized a fundraiser?

"You are the best friend in the world to me," she says, bringing my attention back to her, "and the fact that you didn't even tell Huff you were breaking his heart because of me was pretty big. You could have blamed me. I would have understood."

I shrug. "Well, I think it would have hurt him less. But I felt like pitting the two of you against each other would have hurt you both in the long run."

Lanier nods. "I know." She takes my hand, and I let her. I'm not sure I want to, but I am so filled with relief knowing that Huff and I are at least breathing the same air again that anything and everything feels okay. "But what I want to say to you," Lanier continues, "is that I am sorry. I am so, so sorry. I never, ever should have said what I did, and I didn't mean it."

"Yes, you did," I say. "You did mean it."

She pauses. "Well, maybe in the heat of the moment I did. But I was wrong. You are nothing like your mother. I have lived so much of your sobriety with you, and I'm so proud of you. And I know better than anyone on the planet that, when you love someone, when you decide to pledge your loyalty to something, you give it everything you have. No one has been a recipient of that unconditional love more than I have. I don't deserve you, Daph." She pauses. "But Huff does."

I smile then, feeling all teary again. I look over my shoulder, but Huff is gone. Lanier stands up, still holding my hand, and says, "Could you come with me for a second?"

I don't want to. I want to go wherever Huff has gone. But I don't see him, and that feels a little immature to say. So I follow Lanier to the softball field. The last thing I want to do is go to a softball game, but I smile remembering that my first kiss with Huff was in the middle of this field. "I never expected you to break up with Huff because of me, Daph." She grimaces. "Well, I mean, not this time."

She looks down at her hands. "I'm sorry about that, by the way. Huff told me you found out about my little white lie. All those years ago, I was just trying to help you both. Instead, I was . . . well, I was being like my mom. Being overprotective. I should have learned my lesson a *long* time ago."

I can't help but laugh.

"I never wanted you to feel like you had to leave Huff," she says, "and I'm sorry for the pain I caused."

I stop walking and look at her. "I was having a bad moment and hearing you say my worst fears out loud panicked me."

Lanier flinches. "Seven years."

"Seven years," I echo.

She shakes her head. "I'm sorry. It didn't occur to me until later. But, Daph, you are the strongest person I know. Stronger than your mom—than anyone, really. Seven years is just the beginning for you."

I smile because I know. I really do.

As Lanier puts her hand on the gate, I realize that the "players" in this game, the people poorly batting and awkwardly running and calling out phrases that aren't really softball related, are all people I know. Friends. June. Paula and John. As Lanier leads me to the center of the field, she says, "Remember how, when we were little, we used to say that we wished we could be sisters, that we wished there was a way to make it official?"

I nod at Lanier, but my eyes notice Huff, who is standing in the middle of the field. I would walk to him, even if Lanier wasn't leading me there.

"Well," Lanier says once we reach him, "I think I've figured out a way to make it legal."

With that, Huff gets down on his knee, and a hush comes over the crowd. I stop breathing. But then I look down at him, and the most profound sense of calm washes over me.

"Daph, I had a big speech prepared, but there are all these people here, and all I want to say is that I love you. I have only ever loved you, and I want to love you for all eternity." He reaches into his pocket as I smile so big, I think my face might break in two. He opens a box that contains the most beautiful, simple solitaire I have ever seen. It is exactly what I would want to wear for the rest of my life—not that it really matters right now. "So, will you let me do that? Will you marry me?"

Those pesky tears again. "I will love you for all eternity too, Huff. And I can't wait to marry you."

Huff slips the ring on my finger, scoops me up, and kisses me as the crowd cheers. Second to when I first held Henry, this is the happiest moment of my life. I inhale it, breathe it in, try to make time stop so I can remember the way the lights come on as the sun begins to descend and Huff kisses me, his lips tasting a little salty from sweat and tears.

Paula is the second person to hug me, after Lanier. "You get to really be my daughter now!" she says.

"You've never treated me like I was anything less, and I can never repay you for that." I look around and, as it seems like no one is listening, I whisper, "Paula, are you worried?"

"About what?" she whispers back.

"About me. Does, you know, my past worry you?" I don't say my upbringing or my parents or my demons because I think I mean all of it.

She puts her hands to my cheeks. "Oh, honey, no." She smiles. "Do you know what I can promise you?"

"What?"

"You and Huff will have hurdles. You will have struggles and hard days and rough patches. That's universal. It's just the human experience."

"Okay," I say, pretty sure I feel worse not better.

"But you know what else I know?"

I shake my head. "You two are about as well-equipped to handle whatever comes your way as any two people I've ever known. So, no, Daphne, I'm not worried. I'm ecstatic."

I feel lighter somehow. Paula could always do that for me. My future mother-in-law. The idea of that thrills me. Simultaneously, it breaks my heart in a million pieces that my actual mother isn't here. She had her faults and her flaws, but on her good days, no one would have been happier for me than she would have been. Mary Stuart flings herself onto me at that exact moment, screaming and jumping up and down.

I take that back. Maybe Mary Stuart is more excited than my mother would have been.

"You're a good friend," I say to her.

"I sure am! I've basically planned your whole wedding already. You are welcome!"

I laugh. "That's going to save me so many hard things emails."

"I know!"

Lanier comes over, and I finally ask, "Are you okay with this?" Because I know this must be hard for her, given the state of her relationship.

"I'm great. I'm better than great." She points around her. "Who do you think organized all this?" This is something Lanier would usually hate organizing.

"You didn't make Mary Stuart do it?"

She shook her head. "I deserved to have to do all my own hard things this week."

I shrugged. "I don't know, Lanier. You had a pretty rough week, too."

She nodded. "Yeah. But I was having major reservations about Bryce. This was just a lesson, a reminder to trust my gut."

"Have you talked to him?" I whisper. "Is he out of jail?"

"Not now. Now we celebrate. We can worry about him later."

June squeezes my shoulder. "I am so happy for you!"

I raise my eyebrow at her. "You know there will probably be more children in my future. I sure could use some Aunt June help with them. You know, maybe in the off-season?" I know I can't make June do anything, and maybe it isn't my place anyway. But I love her, and I want her to be happy.

She laughs. "I think that sounds absolutely divine."

Huff clears his throat behind me. I put my finger up. "Hold that thought. I have a brand-new fiancé I need to kiss." I pause and turn to Huff. I have so much to say to him, but before I can open my mouth, Henry tears across the field, Steven on his heels. Henry's arms are spread wide like he's flying, and he yells, "Surprise, Mommy! Dad and I are here, not at Pizza Hut!" I kiss him and look at Lanier, whose tiny head shake is enough for me to know that my son does not actually know why he is here. Even before I said yes to Huff, I was worrying about how to introduce the idea of this marriage to my son.

"Hey," I say to Henry. "You remember Huff?"

He rolls his eyes. "Of course, Mom. He helps me with my baseball moves." Henry gets a very serious look on his face and mimics the most dramatic swing I've ever seen.

We all laugh. "Hey," Lanier says, "what if you and Huff and I play a little baseball here?" She looks at me and I smile gratefully. Because there is a very obvious thing I have to do.

I look at Steven. He smiles at me, but his smile is dimmer than usual. I wrap my hand in the crook of his arm and say, “Let’s go have a little chat, you and I.”

He nods. “I think that might be a good idea.”

I look back over my shoulder at Huff, who winks at me. Maybe there are no perfect words in a situation like this. But there are people who are perfect for each other. Huff and I just might be two of them.

Lanier

THE BEST PART

HUFF, HENRY, AND I LAID ON OUR BACKS IN THE MIDDLE OF THE SOFTball field, gazing up at the clouds floating in the perfectly blue sky above us. Every few minutes, one of us would sit up to eat a slice of pizza or a brownie or a breadstick. Henry got his Pizza Hut after all. After fifteen minutes of "baseball practice," he was kind of worn out.

Our friends and family had dispersed, and I was very glad I wasn't the one having to talk to Steven right now. I knew Daphne loved him. He was her family. But I'd always gotten the feeling that Steven still carried a torch for Daphne. So that was going to be hard.

"Huff," Henry said.

Huff turned his head. "Yeah, buddy."

"Who do you think would be a better swimmer, a Transformer or Catboy from *PJ Masks*?"

He was deadly serious as he said it, and I knew Huff was going to be an amazing stepfather because this was the kind of thing he could take very seriously in return.

Huff leaned up on his elbow. "Even though I bet he hates the water, I've got to go with Catboy on this one."

"No way!" Henry said, giggling. "The Transformer could just turn into a boat and zoom through the water."

Huff laughed. "Oh, man. You're right. You're totally right." He paused. "Who do you think would win a race, Shaggy from *Scooby-Doo* or Egon from *Ghostbusters*?"

Henry was quiet for a second. "I think Shaggy. He has his own running sound effects."

Huff sat up to take a bite of pizza. Henry sat up and took the piece out of Huff's hand and bit the crust.

"You're killing me, man," Huff said. "The stuffed crust is the best part."

"Don't I know it," Henry said.

That kid cracked me up. I squeezed him and kissed his head. I was going to be his real aunt now. That was cool. I had been there when Henry was born and held Daphne's sweaty leg while she was giving birth and looking less than perfect for once. I had cut his umbilical cord when Steven fainted at the sight of all that gunk his baby was covered in. Nothing will bond you to a child quite like holding him before he's had his first bath. I loved him instantly. I always will. So I guess maybe I've always been his aunt. Even still, this engagement made it more official.

I looked into Henry's face. Henry would never go through what Daphne had. He had a million people who would make sure he was taken care of. I was at the top of that list. And I'd like to think that I took care of Daphne, too. I hoped she could forgive me now; I hoped that she remembered that I would walk through fire for her. That I already had.

"Huff?" Henry said, loudly enough to make me jump.

"Henry?"

Henry peered up into Huff's face. "Do you love my mommy?"

Huff looked at me questioningly. I shrugged. I didn't know what to say.

"I do, buddy. I really, really love your mommy."

Henry turned to me. "Aunt Lanier, do you love my mommy?" I thought of that night, of that Newport, of that match.

"I love your mommy almost as much as I love you."

"I love her too," he said.

"She's easy to love," Huff chimed in.

I got up and dusted the dirt off my pants. "Speaking of your mommy, I'm going to go find her and then how about you and I watch a movie, huh?"

Henry nodded. As I got ready to leave, Henry said to Huff, "She always wants to watch baby movies like *The Little Rascals*."

"Oh yeah? Well, how about if you and I watch *The Sandlot* together next time I see you?"

"What's that?"

"Oh, you're going to love it. It's about baseball."

As I walked across the field and out into the open expanse of grass, I thought about how I almost prevented all of this. I almost kept my brother from being the stepfather to my favorite kid. I almost stood in the way of my best friend's happiness and my brother's fully realized life. I was glad I wouldn't have to look back one day and regret all of it. I was grateful that it wasn't too late.

As happy as I was, though, it did sting a little that my best friend and brother were getting their happily ever after as my world was going up in flames. People would talk about me; there was no way around it. Some would think I knew about Bryce. Some would think

I was an idiot for not knowing. And the reality was probably somewhere in between. I knew something weird was going on, but I never could have predicted *this.* And starting over again seemed too hard, too scary.

I was better off alone, I decided. But even so, my mind couldn't help but wander a few minutes up the road, to the man who had stolen my heart first. I had made too many mistakes with him. I knew I had. But, then again, if Daphne could forgive me, maybe Rich could, too.

Daphne

ON BRAND

AS STEVEN AND I WALK ACROSS THE CAMP THAT HAS BEEN MY HOME for so long, I feel something I never, ever am around him: nervous. I squeeze his arm tighter as I say, "Do you know that I told Lanier I was pregnant before I told you?"

He looks down at me. "I want to be offended, but I guess I kind of get why the twenty-three-year-old surfer you'd been hanging out with wasn't your first call."

I laugh. "I was terrified. Steven, I thought you were going to bail. Not just bail. Move to Mexico. Change your name."

His turn to laugh. "Again, I want to be offended, but that seems on brand. I mean, I thought about it."

I stop, looking out over the river. The sun is just beginning to set, and it looks like fire spreading across the deep navy of this overflowing, ever-changing spot that has always been my safe place. I lead

Steven to a bench and sit down. He angles himself to face me, crossing his ankle over his knee.

"I guess what I want to say is that you showed up for me in every sense of the word. You have been the most incredible father, the most amazing coparent. And I know that I am overbearing and too protective, and that I don't give you enough leeway—"

Steven interrupts me. "But see, that's not true. If I'm a great dad, it's because you taught me how to be, Daphne." He puts his hand on my knee. "But I get that you are moving into a new phase of your life. And I'm happy for you. I really am. But I wanted to tell you that I'm moving forward, too. As much as I love you, it's time for me to stop being so dependent on you."

I must look shocked because he doesn't wait for me to respond. "I've been wanting to tell you that wherever you and Huff settle down, I'll be there. I've started working on my commercial pilot's license so that I have something a little steadier than the private piloting I've been doing. The lease is up on the beach shack I've been renting, and it's time to buy something. Near you, preferably."

I shake my head. "Steven, I don't want you to have to change your life just because I'm changing mine. That's not fair to you. And how will you surf if you move to us?"

"There's surfing in Cape Carolina."

I squeeze his hand. "This is great news. I can't thank you enough."

He nods. "You don't have to thank me. I want to be there for Henry. For you. You guys are my family. It's time to do this for real." He pauses. "And, Daphne. I can take care of him. I promise I can."

I lean in and hug him, and tears well up in my eyes. I'm filled with a mixture of pride over this hot, sweet surfer boy that I half raised and the devastation that his growing up means I won't be with my little boy every other weekend. My heart might cave in on itself. But it isn't fair to keep treating Steven like a child. If the last few weeks have shown me anything, it's that he's ready for this.

"Steven," I say, "I want you to know that I couldn't have done this without you."

"Of course you could have!"

I shake my head. "No, I mean it. I can't express to you how panic-stricken I was when I found out I was pregnant. I didn't think I could be different from my parents, and I didn't think I could do it alone. And I didn't have to because you were so great from the jump."

"We were both great. And I'm happy for you, Daph," he says. "I'm even happier for the man who finally pinned you down. I never thought I'd see the day."

I laugh and pull away. "Me neither."

"We've got this," Steven says.

"You know that's what you said when I told you I was pregnant?"

He shakes his head. "Nope. Don't remember that conversation at all. In my head I was just saying, *Don't throw up. Don't throw up.*"

I grimace. "But you did throw up."

We both laugh again, and I realize how far we've come. We've grown up together. We've been through things I will never go through with anyone else.

Before I can say anything more, Henry jumps up from behind the bench. "I've got you now, Mega Mort!"

And Steven, in a truly creepy voice, says, "Never. I will shrink you!"

Henry squeals as Steven slings him over his shoulder. "Don't shrink me, Daddy. Don't shrink me!"

There's another squeal coming from the direction of the campfire that I recognize as Mary Stuart's. I head in her direction, seeing June, Lanier, Huff, Paula, and John all gathered around the flames. "You're here!" I exclaim.

"Oh, we're spending the night," Paula says.

"Yeah. We packed sleeping bags just in case you said no and Huff was too shattered to drive home," John adds. I think he's joking, but I can't tell.

"We have a wedding to plan!" Mary Stuart says.

"I can't believe it!" June enthuses.

"Me neither," Mary Stuart says. "Oh, if you guys could figure out when you're having a kid, that would be great. I want us to have them at the same time so they can be best friends."

I laugh as I sit down on the arm of the Adirondack chair that Huff is in. I love her so much. "We'll discuss it very first thing," Huff says.

I roll my eyes.

Steven and Henry appear, and I grab my own chair next to Huff and gesture for Henry, who curls up in my lap. Steven sits in the chair on the other side, and I catch Lanier's eye over the firepit and can't help but laugh. She laughs, too, and I know we're thinking the same thing. This is my family now. Steven, Henry, Huff, and me. It's going to take some getting used to, but it already feels kind of right.

"Okay," I say. "Now that that's done, can we talk about how we're going to finish saving our favorite place?"

June laughs. "No! Tonight we celebrate."

"And tomorrow we plan?"

"Tomorrow we plan," Mary Stuart and Lanier repeat in unison.

I pull Henry to me and kiss his head. And I look at all the people I love the most around this campfire. There are still problems to solve and wounds to heal, just like there always have been. But I'm reminded of another of my favorite signs at camp: It's true that we can't control the wind. But this group is better than any that I know at adjusting our sails.

Together, there is no hard thing we can't do.

June

A HUGE GLASS OF MILK

I HOPED I SEEMED JOYFUL AT DAPHNE'S ENGAGEMENT, I THOUGHT AS I lay in my double bed, looking at the raw wood ceiling I'd looked at for almost three decades. I was, of course, so happy for her. But through the night of celebration, all I could think about was how her engagement could potentially be our last celebration at Holly Springs. And not only could it be our last celebration, but now that I told David no, it might be my last summer of having an actual income, which absolutely terrified me. It was the same feeling I had just weeks after buying the camp. That tight-chest, I-have-gambled-it-all-and-might-lose feeling. But I won that time. I would win again—with the help of my songbirds. I took a deep breath. Nothing could be sweeter than if we managed to pull this off together.

A light rap on the door broke me from my thoughts. I sat up. "Come in." There were no door locks at camp. Who was coming out here? And to get what? My toothbrush? Some Holly Springs T-shirts?

I should have known. It was that little girl I should have saved all those years ago. Only, now, she was all grown-up. She was barefoot in a pair of pink long-sleeved pajamas. I patted the end of my bed just like I had when she was little and scared during the night.

"Are you okay?" she asked.

"Daphne!" I scolded. "You just got engaged! Let's take a minute to be happy here."

"I know, but I've been thinking about camp. I know you have been too. I just don't want you to worry," she said. "If we can't come up with the rest of the money, you can stay with Henry and me until you get back on your feet."

"And Huff?" I asked, thinking how great it would be for them to start their newlywed life with a broke spinster aunt under their roof.

"Well, I mean, once we're married, yes. But it's going to be a little bit. I want Henry to really get to know Huff first. I want to take this slowly."

I nodded, guilt engulfing me again. "Daphne, I'm not your responsibility." I sighed. "You were *my* responsibility. And I failed you a long time ago. What you said about Lanier being the only one who was always there for you was true. It should have been me. I should have done more."

She smiled. "June, I wasn't your responsibility. I was my mother's responsibility. And my father's. And that didn't go so well. So then I became my own. Even when I lived with Paula and John, even when everyone rallied around me to help with my sobriety, I knew that I had to be the one to worry about me. And, for at least the past few years, that's gone pretty well."

"All the same, I owe you an apology."

She laughed. "Of all the people in the world, you owe me an apology least of all."

"I owe you the biggest one. Daph, when your mother died, I should have fought your father for custody. I should have been the one to raise you. And I am so deeply sorry. I was in such a dark place."

Just the mention of that terrible time filled me with dread.

"I'll be honest: For a few years, I carried some resentment that you didn't try to win custody. But when I found out I was pregnant with Henry, I was so terrified that I couldn't be a good parent because of all the loss I had experienced. And I realized that you must have felt that way too. I always knew on some level, even at thirteen, that you would have taken care of me full-time if you could. But you couldn't. And that's okay."

I squeezed her hand. "That is precisely, exactly how I felt. I was afraid I would hurt you worse by being in your life, especially when I was at such a low point myself."

"I know," she whispered. "And, really, even then, I didn't want anything between us to change. Even during the worst times, I always knew that I had you and summer to look forward to. I always knew that in a few more months I would be at camp. If you had gotten custody of me, all that would have changed. I would have had to switch schools. You probably would have sold this place." She paused. "Paula and John took care of me. Their house was happy, even when I was sad. I needed that to survive."

I leaned over to hug her. I wanted to say more. To fight for my absolution. But it seemed it had already been granted. Just like that. "You are so generous with your forgiveness, Daphne. I am so grateful for you."

"I'm grateful for you too. I'm grateful that you were always my safe place, my getaway." She smiled. "And I am always ready and willing to be yours."

It brought tears to my eyes.

"Speaking of getaways," Daphne said. "I came here to tell you that I think we should sell Great-Aunt Gracie's house. We could use the money to save Holly Springs."

I surprised myself at how vehemently and quickly my "No!" burst out. I hadn't wanted to tell Daphne my plan yet because I wanted to be really sure. But this seemed like the right time. "I know I sort of mentioned this, but I've been thinking that maybe you are right."

"I so often am," she joked. "But what am I right about?"

"I think it's high time I got away in the off-season; it's high time I spent more time with you and Henry and hopefully a new baby or two. If it's okay with you, I'd like to move to Aunt Gracie's from September through late March or so."

Daphne squealed and clapped her hands. "Nothing could make me happier, June."

"Well, that makes me happy." I smiled. "Facing the possibility of losing camp has made me consider what a different life could look like. I can have hope. But I also need a plan B."

Daphne sighed. "June, I love you, but honest to God, if you had just told me your Paycheck Protection application was denied . . ."

I cringed just thinking about all the money I left on the table. "You were just so busy, and it was a pandemic. You had Henry at home and were trying to work, and I didn't want to bother you."

What a misstep that had been. And while there was no use crying over spilt milk, that was a huge, life-altering glass of milk that I should have fought harder for.

Daphne shook her head. "Well, it's too late now. We move forward," she said.

"We move forward," I repeated, resolutely.

I truly didn't know what moving forward would look like. But right then and there I vowed that, no matter what happened with Holly Springs, whether plan A materialized or I had to face plan B, I wouldn't waste another moment ruminating over what might have been.

Lanier

TWO TYPES OF PEOPLE IN THE WORLD

Hard Things

To: daphne@millerlaw.com; lanier@bookmasters.com

Dear Songbirds:

Do you remember the fight we had on the archery field when we were fourteen? (A very dangerous place to have a fight, by the way . . .) I don't remember what it was about, but I do remember running to June, crying that my two best friends and I weren't best friends anymore. She sat me down and said, "No, no, no, Mary Stuart. You, Lanier, and Daphne have an unbreakable bond. When you're best friends, you're a little broken after every argument. But you grow back even stronger." She was right then; she's right now. I just want to remind both of you how much I love you. And I'm mostly just saying this to butter you up because I need you this week.

Daphne: I need to change my last name! Help! That paperwork gives me nightmares.

Lanier: It's my mother-in-law's birthday next week. Could you put together an awesome gift basket for her? Your favorite new reads, a cookbook, candle, notebook—whatever. You know the drill.

Love you both.

FWAFS,
Mary Stuart

This morning, I had plenty of time to make a gift basket for Mary Stuart, and it wasn't hard at all. In fact, I was very grateful because her purchases were only my fourth sale of the day, and it was already noon. I needed to send my own hard things email, but I didn't feel like I'd made up for my bad behavior yet, so it seemed too soon to ask for anything.

While slow days at the store usually made me uneasy, today I was grateful that I could slouch down in one of the comfy chairs near the front and lose myself in *Anne of Green Gables*. It was times like these that made me especially grateful for books. No matter what was going on in my life, I was always able to lose myself—and find myself again—in the pages of a favorite novel.

When the door opened, I nearly jumped. I never wanted to seem unprofessional. Although a bookstore owner curled up reading shouldn't be off-putting to a true reader. But the person walking through my door wasn't a true reader. It was Bryce.

They say that it's good to switch up the exercises you do because, at some point, muscle memory takes over and your body just goes through the motions. That must be the same with relationships because when I saw Bryce, I swear, for just a minute, I almost ran into his arms. I wasn't happy about what he had done, but you aren't engaged to someone you don't love.

Fortunately, I didn't do that. Instead, I said, "Oh, um, hi," super awkwardly. I should have been grilling him. Maybe yelling at him? But really, I just didn't have the energy.

"Hi," he said. He looked terribly contrite. "I know the other day was crazy, so I wanted some time to talk, just the two of us."

"Well, I'm pretty busy."

"Reading *Anne of Green Gables*?" he said. "I hear that's a new one."

I rolled my eyes. He knew it was one of my favorites. He looked around at the empty store. "Seems like there's a lot going on with all the new books and customers."

Okay, so I couldn't pretend I was busy. "Coming in hot with the sarcasm. Bold move."

"I just wanted to tell you that I'm sorry," he said. "I didn't mean to hurt anyone. Not my clients, not my vendors, and certainly not you. I was trying to prove to everyone that I could make it on my own, and I ruined everything in the process."

"Uh-huh. Well, see, here's the thing. Maybe you didn't mean to hurt your clients or your vendors or your family. But you did mean to hurt Daphne. You put her in an impossible position where she could have lost everything. And you should know by now: If you hurt her, you hurt me."

"No, you're right. But, Lanier, I want another chance. My mom is helping me dig my way out of the hole to pay everyone back, and it will be like it never happened. You'll see."

I snapped my fingers. "That," I said. "That's the problem."

He looked truly dumbfounded. "What's the problem?"

"I'm not going to be with someone like that. I'm not going to raise children who never experience consequences because their parents are still cleaning up their messes for them in their thirties."

He seemed stunned. Was he not even aware that was what his mother was doing?

"I don't really think that's fair," he said.

"Which part? Because it seems to me that your entire life, whenever you have done anything wrong, your mom has made it go away. And now, you're a grown man, you've committed real crimes, and she's still doing it."

"I just spent the night in jail. I lost my entire career. I'm beholden to my mother and will be working for a company I don't even like for the rest of my natural life. I'm paying the consequences."

Any inkling I might have had of hearing him out, of seeing this in a different way, of realizing that maybe I could forgive his mistakes and move forward, was gone. Repeating our parents' mistakes was part of growing up. But we didn't have to keep making them.

"You lost your job? If the consequence that doesn't come to mind first is all the people whose livelihoods you put in jeopardy—or how your actions could affect me—then I don't know what we're doing here."

"I don't want to lose you," he said, stepping forward tentatively. "Lanier, I behaved badly because I didn't know what to do. And I was wrong. But I think there are two types of people in the world: the ones who move on from their mistakes and the ones who let their mistakes define them. I will never let my mistakes define me or keep me from asking for forgiveness."

It was a compelling argument, but probably not in the way he thought it was going to be. I walked back to the counter and hastily scribbled a "*Closed Temporarily! Be Right Back!*" sign to hang on the door and grabbed my small brown purse.

"What are you doing?" Bryce asked as I began taping the sign to the door.

"You're right," I said. "You're absolutely right. I have let a mistake from a long time ago define me, and I can't do that anymore."

I opened the door and, when he didn't leave, I gestured for him to walk through it.

"So what does that even mean? What about us?"

"Oh, gosh. I respect what you're saying, but I can't marry you, Bryce." I paused. "We aren't right for each other. We never really were."

He couldn't even argue with me because he knew it too.

"Now," I said, "there's somewhere I really need to be."

As I got in my car, I didn't give him another look. I didn't need to. Bryce and I were brought together for a reason. We were torn apart for a reason, too. And now I had to get busy on the business of moving on with the rest of my life—and not letting mistakes from ten years ago define me for one more minute.

Daphne

A SIGN

Hard Things

To: marystuart@harrispr.com; lanier@bookmasters.com

Good morning, Songbirds:

I can't bring myself to say this to June yet, but I've done all the paperwork filing and phone call making and begging government entities that I can possibly do. And I have the feeling that no miracles are coming through for Holly Springs. I know June is going to be stressed enough over making what might be her last summer at camp perfect. (Even typing that makes my stomach hurt.) So maybe we could get together and work out the particulars of mother-daughter camp to take that off her plate? Even if it doesn't bring in enough to save camp, it will be a wonderful goodbye for all of us. (I'm not crying, you're crying.)

Fair winds and following seas—always and forever,
Daphne

The next week, Finn and I are antsy and on edge. As soon as we learned about Camp Holly Springs's situation back in March, we started looking back over June's records. Her PPP loan paperwork was a moot point because all those funds had already been distributed. But she had also applied for an Economic Injury Disaster Loan—which had also been denied. But the minute we looked at it, we knew it was likely because the application was a total mess.

So Finn and I redid her paperwork and submitted a request for reconsideration. We applied for $400,000, which was only a portion of what we could prove she lost due to Covid, in hopes that she would walk away with *something.* She would have to pay the money back over time, but, at a low interest rate, we had figured out how she could make it work. Plus, a family camp or two over the next couple of years could pay the whole thing off. (Selfishly, I wanted to go back!)

I hadn't even mentioned the reapplication to June because if we didn't hear back by tomorrow, we were out of luck. I didn't want to let her down if I didn't have to. It was still possible we could raise the remaining $93,000 on our own—and we'd try no matter what. But the loan would give us some much-needed breathing room.

Finn is trying to be especially upbeat for me, which makes me love him more. "I got us some new hibiscus tea," he says, handing me a steaming cup as I sit down in one of the chairs flanking his desk. "And, if that doesn't help, maybe this will: I heard this morning from a colleague that Bryce's mom has worked out payment plans with everyone. It will take a long time to make it right, but no one will lose their houses or businesses."

I let out a huge sigh of relief. I look up at the clock. It's almost two. Steven is going to pick me up, and then, after we get Henry from school, we're going house hunting for him. It hits me: I'm engaged. And I'm about to spend my afternoon with another man.

"Finn, do I have to tell Huff I'm doing stuff like house hunting with Steven now?"

"Hmm . . . I mean, I think it's probably a good idea."

I nod and sigh. "I'm so set in my ways. This is going to take some getting used to."

"True story."

So I text Huff:

Going house hunting with Steven. Finn and I are debating: Is this something I tell you about now? I'm not sure.

He doesn't text back right away, but I don't expect him to because, you know, most of his day is spent digging around inside someone else's body.

"How are you feeling about Steven moving here?" Finn asks.

"I'm thrilled. The idea of Henry being two hours away every other weekend was torture. But this way, Steven can have his time, Huff can have his space, and I don't have to miss any soccer games."

"Thank goodness. Henry is a real soccer prodigy." We both laugh. "You think surfer god is up for the challenge of solo parenthood?"

"Steven's showed me another side of himself. He can take care of Henry on his own." I scrunch my nose. "I still don't want Henry to leave me every other weekend, though."

Finn nods as my eyes fill with tears. "I know, honey. But it might be good. It will give you and Huff some time to settle into married life."

I raise my eyebrows, the phrase shocking me.

Finn laughs. "You are getting married, right? Because I've already ordered a new tux."

"I am definitely getting married." And I'm beside myself. I cannot wait. But I'm also worried about how it's going to be, factoring in another person when it's just been me and Henry for so long.

My phone beeps at the same time the front door chimes, and Finn pops up to meet the mailman. Maybe there's nothing in the mail. But maybe there is.

Huff has texted me back:

Don't spend too long checking out any of the bedrooms.

I send him back an eye-roll emoji.

"Thanks," Finn says. I can tell just from the tone in his voice that there's something from the Small Business Administration.

He walks in slowly, the letter clutched between his thumb and forefinger as if it's a dirty sock. I shake my head. "I can't open it. You do it."

He looks aghast. "You would make me do this?"

"I thought you were an honorary, hard-thing-doing Songbird now."

He nods enthusiastically. "Oh, if this helps cement my Songbird status then I'm ripping off the Band-Aid." He slides his finger along the flap. The noise seems louder than it should, and I realize I'm holding my breath. Finn's eyes scan the letter, and I can't read his face. He gasps and looks at me, then back at the letter, then back at me.

"We didn't get approved for four hundred thousand," he says, and I feel like my heart stops. I'm about to launch into a full, exhausted meltdown when he screams, "But we did get two hundred and fifty thousand!"

"What? Are you serious?"

He nods and jumps up and down.

I jump up and down, too, and throw my arms around his neck, and then we are both jumping up and down. I am overwhelmed with relief.

The door chimes as it opens and Steven says, "What? What is happening?"

"We got the money to save June's camp!"

"You have to go tell her," he says. "Right now."

"But what about house hunting?" I ask, breathless.

"I'll go chaperone," Finn says. "You know how much HGTV I watch."

That makes me feel so much better.

As I walk out the door, I'm grateful to have so much to celebrate. I think about Steven and June, Huff and Henry, Lanier and Mary Stuart, Paula and John, and now, Finn. In some ways, I think I've always felt like that six-year-old girl whose mother forgot her at the airport. But now I'm starting to realize I don't have to go through it alone. I have people. I have a family. And, no matter what happens with Holly Springs, that's all I've ever really wanted.

• • •

A few hours later, June, Jillian, and I are sitting in her office at Holly Springs, which feels ridiculous since it's such a gorgeous day outside. I am staring at a stack of actual books that contain facts and figures from the last several summers. June practically threw them at me when I walked in the door, which prevented me from sharing my news right off the bat. Plus, it's kind of fun sitting on this secret. I finally set the ledger down, cross-eyed from trying to make sense of all those little numbers. "June, have you ever heard of a spreadsheet?" I ask, exasperated.

"I'm trying, Daphne," Jillian says. "But this one isn't big on change."

"Maybe you should come down here for the summers and run my numbers for me," June says. "Bring your husband and son."

"Don't tempt me." I shake my head. "What would Huff do? Just say, 'Please, no one have a ruptured spleen or hernia' for three months?"

This makes Jillian laugh. I like her. "June, Jillian has a business degree. Perhaps you should let her digitize your bookkeeping. Then your accountant and I can have access to records whenever we need them without you having to mail things to us. Just think of all the time that would free up for when you're away from camp property during the off-season."

June's forehead crinkles in despair as she drops one of the ledgers to the desk with a thud. "Oh, Daphne, we might not even have a camp next year."

"Funny you should bring that up," I say. "Because I didn't drive an hour to say hi and go through your books—as fun as that has been. I came to give you a piece of news."

She raises her eyebrows.

I pull the letter out of my back pocket, coolly. "Guess who got a loan."

June stands and grabs the paper from my hand, and Jillian screams. Like, really screams. I have to resist the urge to cover my ears.

I stand now, too, and they both throw their arms around me. "You didn't think to lead with that?" June asks, through her tears. "We're saved! We're saved! I'll let Jillian do the books from now on, and we'll never, ever get in a mess like this again. I promise. Oh, I am so thrilled!"

I'm smiling so big my face hurts.

"How did you do it?" she asks.

I pretend to wave a wand. "My lawyer magic. And some cleaned-up paperwork."

The door to June's office opens, and we all look surprised to see Lanier. She stops in her tracks when she sees me. Then she rushes over to give me a hug. “You have such a knack for being at the right place at the right time, Daph.”

“Do I?”

This strikes me as funny because, well, my life has not exactly been one of being in the right place at the right time. But okay.

Lanier’s face changes, and I see her processing how odd it is that I’m here. “What are you doing at camp?”

These are the gray areas I’ve always been bad at. Do I tell her? Or should I tell Huff first? I sigh and sit back down. “Lanier, I don’t know how to navigate all of this. If I tell you things I haven’t told Huff yet, does it make you think I’m going to be a bad wife?”

She laughs. “Part of the thing that made me crazy when you were together the first time is when he knew stuff before me. So, no. Best friends first.”

June blurts out, “Camp is saved! Daphne got our EIDL!”

Lanier claps. But then her face falls. “Wait. Does that mean we don’t get to do mother-daughter camp?”

None of us has a daughter, of course. But it would be kind of cute if Lanier and I brought Paula. “Of course we’re doing mother-daughter camp,” I say. “We have to pay the loan off somehow.”

That’s when it occurs to me: “Wait. What are *you* doing here?”

She grits her teeth. “I’m going to apologize to Rich.”

That’s a brave woman right there. I’m pretty sure I wouldn’t have the guts to do that. But, obviously, I don’t say so. “If it goes well, the sailing hut is available.”

She swats me, and June laughs. Lanier gasps. “You told June!”

“There are sanitary protocols for sex in the sailing hut. It’s like when someone vomits,” June jokes. Or at least, I think she’s joking.

“Want me to come with you?” I ask Lanier. “Sit in the car? Be your wingwoman?”

She shakes her head. "Daph, you rock at taking on my hard things. But unfortunately, I think this is something I'm going to have to do myself."

That's the thing about hard things. Sometimes no one can do them for you. But, even still, it's nice to have best friends to help you carry the burden.

Lanier

GUARDHOUSE

IT WAS LIKE RICH KNEW I WAS COMING. I BRIEFLY CONSIDERED THAT maybe he did, but then again, I didn't think June or Daphne would have betrayed me by giving him a heads-up. When I pulled up at the gate at Camp Rock Springs, Rich was sitting in the guardhouse. He looked surprised to see me and then, moments later, not surprised at all, like my showing up was ordinary. Instead of coming out of the booth, he opened the little window, which I found both funny and sad.

"May I help you, ma'am?" His guard was way, way up.

I had this whole perfect speech planned about trust and love and our past and what our future could be and how I knew he might not ever be able to forgive me. But sitting in my car with the window rolled down, him looking so adorable, it all flew out of my mind. What was that speech again? *I know things between us haven't always been smooth, but I'd love to take it slow, earn your trust back, show you I'm worthy.*

That's what I wanted to say. Instead, I blurted out, "I love you. I don't know if you can ever forgive me, but I love you, and I called off my wedding."

Smooth. The exact calm, clear, calculated speech I had planned . . .

"You called off your wedding?"

I held up my now-ringless left hand.

"For me?"

Well . . . I heard my mother in my head, *our little secret.* I had made a pact with myself that I would only be honest with Rich from now on, but the whole Bryce debacle was way too much to launch into now. I wanted to begin with the simple truth, "Yes. For you. Always you."

So, sure, it had been ever so slightly more complicated than my just wanting to be with Rich, but it was still true that he played a large role in my decision. And if we got back together, I would tell him the whole sob story.

"So how do you see this going?" he asked. That was when I started to worry.

"Um . . . honestly? I thought you'd take me in your arms and say that you loved me too and you'd dreamed about this moment." I smiled coquettishly because I was still half expecting him to do that. I just thought he was punishing me a little in the meantime.

"Lanier . . ."

Oh, God. *Lanier.*

"I walk in and see you with your fiancé and then you don't so much as text me. Not to tell me what's going on, not to let me know what I should be expecting. Nothing. So, it seems to me that things have changed but you haven't."

My jaw dropped, and now I was kind of mad. "First, I *did* text you.

You guys have got to get a cell tower out here. And second, you knew I was engaged when you slept with me. It wasn't like I hid it from you."

He nodded. "Uh-huh. Yes. But the happy-go-lucky man waltzing in to see you at camp wasn't exactly how you described things. I was anticipating that you were, like, halfway broken up, putting a final nail in the coffin. And I can only assume . . ."

"You can only assume what?"

"I can only assume that you lied to me about the state of your relationship."

I realized how ridiculous it was that he was sitting in the guardhouse while I was in my car having this life-altering conversation. "Rich, why don't we go somewhere more suitable to talk this out?"

He shook his head. "There's nothing to talk out, Lanier."

Was he serious? "Fine. Okay. I see your point. But Bryce and I were engaged, for heaven's sake. I couldn't just, like, break up with him in Cabin Nine and sail off into the sunset with you. These things take time. They take finesse."

"They take your fiancé getting arrested for check fraud?" He crossed his arms.

These damn small towns. Bryce's arrest hadn't hit the paper, surprise, surprise—but Rich knew anyway.

And, well, yes, Bryce being arrested was exactly what it took. "You really aren't being fair here."

"I'm not being fair? No. Lanier, I'm not your plan B. He got in trouble, things fell apart, and now I'm good enough for you. Now you love me. Now you want me. I'm tired of being your backup guy. Find someone else."

I felt something close to desperate. Why couldn't I make him understand? "No, no, no. You could never, ever be my plan B. That's what I'm saying. You've always been the one for me, Rich."

He crossed his arms but said nothing.

He couldn't even respond? Couldn't do me the courtesy of a real conversation? "I called off my *wedding* for you, *Rich*."

"I never asked you to do that, *Lanier*."

He made a big show of pressing down on the button in the gatehouse. The arm lifted, and he gestured for me to leave.

I was fuming as I backed out. Furious. How could he do this to me? As I made my way back to the highway, I knew already that fuming was good. Furious was perfect. Because the heartbreak that came next would be a million times worse.

• • •

I yelled into the car's Bluetooth as Daphne sat patiently on the other line. "He didn't ask me to call off my wedding? Can you believe he said that? Do you have sex with people in sailing huts when you don't want them to call off their wedding? Do you, Daphne!?"

I had been ranting like this for a full fifteen minutes, and she hadn't said a single word.

"Daphne!"

"I'm sorry. I assumed that was a rhetorical question. But no. No, Lanier, I personally do not have sex with people in sailing huts and then not want them to call off their weddings. I have never once done that."

"Okay, smarty-pants."

She laughed. "I'm teasing. But, for real, I'm so super sorry. I would have bet anything that this would have gone a different way." She paused. "I always thought you two would end up together."

"Right? *Right?*" I obviously thought we were going to end up together too. I really, truly believed that history would fix itself. I made a mistake, but this time I'd owned up to it. This time I'd made amends. And this time, he was supposed to forgive me, and we would ride off into the sunset. I was riding off into the sunset, all right. Down the highway. In my Prius. Alone.

"Babe, how can I help?"

"Well, for starters, you can have wine waiting for me when I get home." I never asked Daphne to have drinks waiting for me. It felt like a slippery slope. But this was DEFCON 1.

"Wine? Or tequila?"

"Anything with alcohol will do." I paused. "Does this warrant Mary Stuart driving an hour?"

"I think so. I will call her. Okay. Well, I'm actually pulling into Huff's, but I will see you soon."

"Ah, pulling into Huff's. Yes. What real, eternal love is supposed to look like. Remind me tonight to tell you about how my mother is having a conniption over our outfits for the rehearsal dinner."

"Lanier, we haven't even set a date."

"Exactly."

"Wait! Wait!" I yelled into the phone before she hung up. My stupid brother could wait. "Did Steven find a house?"

"Yes!" she exclaimed. "It's literally a block away. He made an offer so cross all your fingers and toes."

"That is the best news!" I said. We hung up and I mused that that was going to be awfully cozy. Daphne, Huff, and Steven all on the same block. The things we do for love. Still, I was happy for her. I was happy for Huff. I was happy for Henry. But I had to admit that there was a small part of me that ached for the happy ending I had almost gotten, not once but twice this year.

Maybe that wasn't in the cards for me. Maybe it wasn't meant to be. Maybe I would find someone else or no one at all. I parked my car on the street and unlocked the bookstore, the happy little bell tinkling as I entered. I took a deep breath, smelling those millions and millions of fresh pages. I wanted my own romance. I wanted my happy ending. But maybe for now, for today, being surrounded by love stories was enough.

Daphne

FULL HOUSE

TODAY IS A BIG DAY. HENRY IS IN THE BACK SEAT SINGING ALONG TO Raffi as we drive the ninety minutes to Huff's house. Henry and Huff have been getting to know each other better these past couple of weeks. Steven has been a huge team player in facilitating this, too, going on "dude dates" with Henry and Huff. Not that I don't trust Huff alone with Henry. I one hundred percent do. But I want this transition to feel seamless for my child—and, in truth, for my fiancé too.

"Mom," Henry pipes up from the back.

"Yeah, buddy."

"Why does Huff have to live so far away?"

That is the absolute best question he could possibly ask. Because I want him to love Huff, obviously. I want him to want Huff to live super close. So close, in fact, that he's under our roof.

"Well, Huff is a doctor, and his patients are here." *Not for long,* I add in my head. Huff has scored a job at Cape Carolina Regional Medical Center. It's a smaller hospital, but it's a pay raise and likely fewer headaches, so all's well that ends well, I think. He starts his job in six weeks, and so, bless his heart, he is going to live with his parents until it feels like the right time for him to move in. Today, I am going to help him start packing up his house so that he doesn't have to do it all at once. We have a meeting with a listing agent this afternoon. And I start to think that maybe I shouldn't be asking him to leave this riverfront beauty. Have I been so adamant about keeping Henry's world stable that I've disregarded Huff's?

"Mom! Did you know that one time Huff sewed a guy's thumb back on?"

Lovely.

We pull into Huff's driveway, and he is waiting on the front steps for us, waving. His hair is askew, he's wearing the same Patagonia shorts that have been his staple since high school, and I love him so much I want to squeal with delight. Henry has been to Huff's once before, so he jumps out of the car and runs up the steps. "I'm going to play with the train!"

Paula gave Huff all his childhood trains back, and he and Henry spent almost two hours setting them up last weekend. Henry's attention span astounds me.

I smile after him and, when he is gone, Huff kisses me. "I need to talk to you."

His face goes ashen.

"No! No, no! Not talk to you like that. Just, I have something to run by you."

He walks in the front door and into his spacious kitchen, and I follow him. It's very, very clean, the marble countertops practically gleaming and the brass range hood spotless. Having a child is probably going to throw a wrench in Huff's polished life. I hope we're worth it. He opens the fridge and hands me a sparkling water then pops the top on a beer, leaning over the counter.

"What's up?"

"Do you want to stay here?" I ask. "At your house? Henry and I can move. Then you don't have to quit your job. I mean, your house is bigger, it's a million times nicer . . . And Steven hasn't closed on his house yet, so there's still time to work that out."

"I love your house," Huff says. "I love that crooked front porch and the mismatched floor planks in your kitchen and how the upstairs doorways are barely taller than I am."

I try to read his face. Is he serious?

"I love that you are happy and comfortable there and that Henry has known that house as home his whole life." He pulls me to him. "I love that my parents are two blocks away and that we can walk to Lanier's bookstore and your office. I even love that Steven will be a few houses down so that Henry can see his dad whenever he wants."

I lean into him, my head on his chest. He leans down and kisses me when he sees my eyes fill. I want to tell him he's right, but I don't want to cry. Henry tears into the pristine kitchen and eyes us curiously. "Mommy, are you sad?"

I shake my head and pick him up. "No, baby. I'm happy. I'm so, so happy." I look at Huff, and I realize we haven't planned to tell Henry yet. It hasn't been as long as I assumed we needed, and I haven't thought about what I want to say. But I'm standing here with this man who sees my messy little life as superior to his fancy, shiny one, and I feel like there's no better time than right now. "Sweet boy, there's something that Mommy wants to tell you."

He nods.

"Mommy and Huff are going to get married. It won't be for a few months, which is a long, long time. But Huff is going to come live at our house with us one day."

Henry looks from me to Huff and back to me. "Is he going to bring the trains?"

This is not the question I'm expecting, but he's four, so I guess this seems fitting.

"Oh, yeah, man," Huff says. "I'm bringing the trains."

Henry nods. "So, are you and me and Huff going to all live in one room together?"

I am puzzled by this. "No, sweetie. You'll still have your room and Huff will live in Mommy's room with her."

"Oh, okay."

"Why would you think we'd all live in one room?" Huff asks.

"Well, because Aunt Becky and Uncle Jesse and Alex and Nicky all live in the attic on *Full House*."

I want to burst out laughing. *Full House* is one of the only shows Henry and I both like. It was my go-to rerun as a kid. Henry and I have just made it to season six, and Henry loves the twins.

Huff looks at me questioningly. "You haven't seen *Full House*?"

He shakes his head and Henry says, "Huff, you have to see it! Uncle Joey has a woodchuck and Uncle Jesse rides a motorcycle and Danny has a little vacuum to clean his big vacuum."

Huff laughs. "Sounds like quality TV to me."

"Do you have any other questions?" I make the mistake of asking.

"Yes. Is Daddy going to marry us too? And then he will live at our house all the time?"

I grimace. "Well, no. Daddy is going to be staying at our house a little less because he is going to have his own house down the street so that you can go visit him anytime. Remember?"

He nods. "So I can see him on a Tuesday."

"Right." This is the example I used when I explained this last week. It must be a lot for a child's mind to take in. But Henry scurries down from my hip and says, "Okay. Huff, let's pack up the trains!"

Huff shrugs, and I watch as he follows Henry up the steps. I hear him say, "What if you're living at our house and a guy needs his thumb sewed back on?"

"Oh, I'll be sewing thumbs on in Cape Carolina."

"So, if I cut off my thumb you can sew it back on?"

I cringe at the thought. He skinned his knee last week and I could barely sleep.

"Oh, yeah, man. For sure. I could probably do it right in the kitchen."

I can't help but laugh because, clearly, my child has been worried about what would happen if his thumb fell off.

I walk out onto the front porch, gazing out over the river, the same river that just a handful of miles up the road flows through Camp Holly Springs, Camp Rock Springs, and holds all my favorite memories. I remember that even though my mom is gone, even though I don't remember my grandmother, even though June isn't with me today, they are all here. They are all part of this river. This river is a part of them, a piece of their souls, and just a little bit of the blood running through their veins. I've always known that bodies are about two-thirds water, but I have to think that, for me, for the women in my family, maybe memories are too. For two months a year, this river ran over us, through us, washed us clean. And now, all these years later, it still carries our secrets, our scars, our greatest joys, and our biggest hopes.

Through the open door I hear my child laughing. It is a happy sound, a coveted one, the only one that, these days, matters to me. I am moving forward. Am I doing the right thing?

Standing out here, I feel like the river, with all its twists and turns, knows the answer. And I have to think it's telling me yes.

Lanier

SUMMER LOVE

"I STILL CAN'T BELIEVE IT'S OPENING DAY OF CAMP," I SAID TO MARY Stuart as we walked around with clipboards, helping June with the final inspection. It had been a month since we'd both been here, during Huff and Daphne's engagement. Campers would begin arriving at noon. I had butterflies in my stomach like I was the one coming to camp for the first time.

"I kind of can," she said. "I mean, between the Bryce debacle and Daphne's love affair and all your fighting in between, you two have put me through a lot. I'm ready for summer. I need camp."

I laughed. "If only we were the ones who got to come back."

Mary Stuart nodded. "I'll tell you one thing—my mom and I will be at that mother-daughter camp Labor Day weekend come hell or high water. And you and Paula will be, too, right?"

I nodded.

"And I know Daphne will. Who loves camp more than Daphne?"

I wiped a rag down the end of a bunk bed. I used to think that Daphne would be running this camp one day. Maybe she still would. Life was long. I wasn't sure if I could see Huff at camp, but, then again, I think Huff wanted to be anywhere Daphne was, plain and simple.

"How do you feel about the wedding?" Mary Stuart asked.

I shrugged. "I mean, good. I'm excited for them. I just can't believe they're doing it in December."

Mary Stuart held open the screen door for me and we walked to the next cabin. "That's almost six whole months. You know I'll get her all squared away between now and then."

"She's just going to be so busy this summer with the move and getting Henry acclimated to all the changes."

"And she has us to help, just like we have her. Just like it has always been."

Daphne strode across the lawn toward us and called, "Have I told you lately that I love you? That you would do this for Aunt June is just the greatest."

The three of us stood together on this expansive, beautiful property overlooking the most exquisite stretch of river. *Just like it has always been.* My heart felt so full it could burst.

"Do you think we'll have daughters one day, that they can go to camp together just like we did?" Mary Stuart asked.

I groaned. "It isn't looking good for me. I think you two are going to be far ahead of me on the baby train, considering I'm not even dating anyone."

Mary Stuart squinted, shading her eyes from the sun, which was burning bright across the river. "Actually," she said, "I wouldn't be so sure about that."

My heart fluttered as I realized the man in the daysailer coming toward us was none other than the one who had saved me more than once, who had stolen my heart and never let it go. "He's just here to wish June a good opening day. He doesn't even know I'm here." I sighed. "He made it pretty clear that I'd burned my bridges with him."

Daphne scrunched her nose. "Well, I'd better go down there. Want to come be the bigger person?"

I rolled my eyes. "I hate being the bigger person. I don't want to be the bigger person."

Mary Stuart looped her arm around mine. "I can stay up here with you and pretend we didn't see him."

That would be easier, but even though it would hurt to see him, I knew it was the right thing to do. We walked down the dock, my heart thumping, and Mary Stuart squeezed me tighter.

As Rich tied up the boat, he looked back and saw us. "Here comes trouble," he called.

I couldn't help but laugh. We heard that a lot growing up. He casually walked up the dock to us and said, "Well, I just wanted to make sure June was okay and ready for opening day. But I see she has you three here, so I can answer that question for myself. No one's better at camp than you."

Daphne pointed at us. "My two best trusty sidekicks and I have Aunt June all set I think. The dozens of counselors helped just a smidge too."

I noticed Rich looking at me, but I turned away quickly. Seeing him was harder than I thought it was going to be. I felt embarrassed and ashamed that the tears I had shed these last few weeks, the moping I had done, had little to do with Bryce or the dissolution of our engagement. It was Rich I was mourning.

"Well," Rich said, "I do want to prepare you that the Rock Springs counselors are going to demolish the Holly Springs ones in the opening night softball game."

I laughed. Despite my heartache, he was still so cute.

Daphne, who always loved to have the last word, shocked me by not even responding. Instead, she looked from Rich to me and said, "Mary Stuart and I have to go make sure the new tennis balls arrived. Lanier, can you see Rich off?"

I glared at her. How could she do this to me? I was down here to be the bigger person; they couldn't just leave me like this. But I couldn't very well run after them. "I'm sorry," I said to Rich as I watched them walk away. "I didn't mean for them to thrust us together like this. That isn't fair to you."

He nodded and looked at me long enough that it bordered on staring.

"I wanted to stop loving you," he said.

"Okay, Rich. I've got it. I already said this wasn't my plan—"

"No," he said, stepping closer to me. "I wanted to stop loving you, but ever since our last conversation I've been totally miserable. And I don't know if you've changed your mind, but—"

"I haven't changed my mind!"

He laughed and took my hand. "I admit that I was hurt by the Bryce thing. But I get it. I know you were still figuring things out. And I've loved you for so many years; I've always wondered what might have been between us. I mean, I know real life isn't summer camp but—"

"It is for you." I paused then said quietly, "It's the best life ever got for me."

He raised his eyebrows. "It's ridiculously too soon to say this, but it's the overarching issue: Do you think you could do this life? Not now, obviously, but one day?"

I looked around me at the gorgeous setting, my heart welling up with memories and pride. "I think whatever life you're doing is the life I want to do."

He pulled me close. "What about your store?"

"It's just logistics. Huff and Daphne figured out how to make their lives work, and his job as a surgeon is almost as complicated and stressful as mine as a bookstore owner." We both laughed. "Let's just see who we are. Take it from there."

Rich nodded. Maybe it took us a long time to get here, but I truly believed it was all for the best. And I knew that, no matter what it took, I'd never let him go again. I inhaled the scent of him—salt water and Irish Spring—that I knew so well, and completely relaxed into him. As he leaned down to kiss me, every cell in my body reverberated with relief.

"Ah! Get away from the sailing hut!" I heard from somewhere behind me. But I didn't even turn around. I laughed and kissed Rich again.

"I'm sorry for all the ways I've hurt you," I said. "I want to start over. I want to build back that trust we once had. I want to prove I can be the person you deserve."

He smiled down at me. "That sounds really nice. But I will never, have never, needed you to prove anything to me. I just need you to be honest with me. I need you to be you."

I nodded. "I think I can do that."

"Hey, Lanie?"

Lanie. I was back in his good graces.

"Want to wear my swim band?"

I put my hand over my heart and gasped. "Oh, Rich, I thought you'd never ask."

As he removed the red piece of elastic from his neck and stretched it to go over my head, time and space merged, my past and my future converging into one seamless present. You never knew where life might lead, how the universe was conspiring to set you on your path. I certainly never would have imagined that, after all these years, I'd find myself on the bank of the same river, kissing that same boy I'd loved a lifetime ago. But sometimes life is like that. Sometimes your summer love becomes something more.

Maybe it was that the first day of camp was here, but in this moment, I felt like anything could happen. In Rich's arms, by the river I loved, I felt like maybe we would get it right this time. Rich smiled down at me. I smiled up at him. And I realized it wasn't just a season; it was a feeling. Maybe when you finally find where you're meant to be, summer never ends.

June

PART OF THE MAGIC

WE CALLED IT THE SUMMER OF SONGBIRDS, THAT FIRST YEAR MY Daphne was at Holly Springs with her best friends, Lanier and Mary Stuart. And now, as they sat around the "staff" table on the opening night of camp—all my campers tucked safe and sound in their beds—I couldn't help but think that maybe the summer of songbirds never really ended. I loved knowing that this camp played a role in their forever friendship.

Daphne raised her paper cup. "To you, Aunt June. You saved Holly Springs again, and we are so grateful you did."

I shook my head. "The three of you did that."

"Nope. The four of us," Lanier said.

Mary Stuart raised her cup. "To the four of us!"

I wasn't one of the songbirds, not really. But when I was with them, when I was a part of the magic that the three of them could make, I felt like maybe I was. I looked around the mess hall of this camp where I had spent every summer since I was six, and I felt how deeply it was ingrained in my heart, in my mind, in my history.

I was as shocked as anyone that at the end of the summer I would pack up my meager belongings and move to my aunt Gracie's house, in the town where I grew up. It was a place that, much like this camp, held both joy and sadness for me. But that was the balance of life, I believed now. Joy and sadness. You could not have one without the other.

I used to wonder what my life would have been like if my parents hadn't died young, if my sister was still here. Maybe I would have been happier. Maybe not. Either way, what I had learned in the past fifty years was that we don't get do-overs. This was our one life—as far as I could tell, anyway—and while coming back to camp was a step along life's journey for the hundreds of little girls who came here every summer, it was a hideout for me for far too long. Now I could keep Henry after school during the off-season and, fingers crossed, a new little baby of Daphne and Huff's. I wanted to, as my mom had always preached, put family first.

"I have an idea!" I suddenly said. All the faces around the table quieted and turned to me. "Midnight zip line!"

Daphne was the first one up, scrambling outside and running through the grass like she was a kid at camp herself, handing out harnesses that Mary Stuart checked for safety.

"June, you lead the way," Daphne said. "You always have."

It filled me with pride; I hoped it was true. I hoped that she felt I had led her in the right direction. Her forgiveness was like salve on a wound that had been throbbing for years. It wasn't until we finally talked about it that I realized forgiving myself for not fighting for custody of her was the last step toward starting the next chapter of my life.

I climbed the tower first, Daphne right behind me, and we stood on a pair of platforms, clamping our carabiners to the parallel zip lines. I looked out at the shallow water at the other end of the line, where we would make our landing. I closed my eyes as Daphne counted, "One! Two! Three!" I didn't step off the platform—I jumped, full force. I was not afraid anymore. And, as I flew through the air, I realized I was free now. Anything could happen, and, for the first time in decades, I was ready to find out what anything might be.

For most of my life I had lived for summer, pined for it, longed for the seasons to change and the girls to come back to camp so I could be happy again. But I was starting to learn—at far too old an age—that there was more to life than summer. Just like each year, every phase of our life had its seasons. Cold ones, windy ones, sunny ones, warm ones. We could not choose which part we were living; we could not predict how our future would play out.

As I hit the water, I looked beside me at my niece, who I admired more than words could say. She had taken her hurt and her pain and overcome so much. She had embraced every stage and phase in all its complexity, much like she gripped the zipline rope right now. I smiled at her, feeling the sandy bottom of the lake beneath my feet. "Thank you, Daphne."

"For what?"

I did not answer as I waded through the chilly water to the shore. The answer would be too long. The little girl I wanted desperately to save had, in so many ways, been my greatest teacher.

No, it could not be summer all the time. There were oh so many seasons. And, for the first time, I was excited by that prospect. Finally, at long last, I was ready to experience them all.

EPILOGUE

Daphne

SOUND OF SUMMER

Seven Years Later

I WAKE TO GIGGLES. NOT LIGHT, QUIET GIGGLES, BUT A FIT OF BELLY laughter that my six-year-old daughter Melly has broken into with Smith, Mary Stuart's daughter, and my little niece, Nina, named for Rich's mother. *The sound of summer,* I think.

They are gathered in the corner of Cabin One, the Songbird Cabin, whispering secrets. I want to be annoyed that they are waking me before seven in the morning, but they are so happy. June has let us all come to camp a night early, and I am so overwhelmed by how quickly time passes that, for a moment, I find it hard to breathe. They giggle again and, in that instant, they aren't themselves. They are Lanier, Mary Stuart, and I thirty-one years ago. Any pretense of my still being asleep ends when the three of them crawl into my bottom bunk, peering into my face.

"Mama, are you *awake*?" Melly asks. I lie still, pretending to be asleep, and then, in one smooth motion, grab her and tickle her. All the girls scream, and Lanier calls down from the top bunk, "Still not responsible for my actions before seven a.m."

"There is no way Johnny doesn't wake you up before seven. He's two years old, for heaven's sake," Mary Stuart chimes in.

"Nope," she says. "Rich is a morning person, so he does that shift. I'm the middle-of-the-night-and-can't-fall-asleep shifts."

That's the only thing I'm not looking forward to doing all over again. The middle-of-the-night stuff. I pat my twenty-week pregnant belly, savoring it, as I know this will be my last pregnancy, my last baby.

Huff and Steven, who have become nothing short of total best friends—such best friends that I'm kind of jealous sometimes—will be bringing Henry and our four-year-old, George, here so we can drop Henry off at Camp Rock Springs later this afternoon.

I have worried a little about how George will survive four weeks without Henry. I just love the bond they have, and I can't help but wonder about the sex of this new baby, which we are going to let be a surprise. It seems fitting since this baby was a surprise in all ways. Huff had a vasectomy, and I found out I was pregnant while he was still using frozen peas as ice packs.

"Mommy!" Melly says, about three inches from my face. She definitely has not brushed her teeth.

"Yes, baby?"

"We are Songbirds today, Aunt Daphne!" Nina chimes in. "Aren't we?"

"Please say yes! Please say yes!" Smith practically sings.

I look up at Mary Stuart, who is in the top bunk across from me. Her chin is resting on her hands as she looks down at this little world we created. "Were we really this young once?" she asks.

"Did our mothers really send us off to camp when we were this age?" Lanier asks. "Because I'm having second thoughts about leaving."

"M-om!" Nina protests.

I take in Melly's electric smile, the blond hair that I think is even more beautiful when it's messy like this, framing her face. She has my mother's, her namesake's, blue eyes. Huff and I struggled with the decision to name Melly after my mom. But, in the end, I decided that while I do have some bad memories of her, I'd so much rather hang on to the good ones. And this child is, hands down, a reminder of everything good and right with the world.

"Girls," I say, "it is official: Today, you are Songbirds!"

"Yay!" they all scream.

The screen door to our cabin slams shut. It is a noise that evokes such nostalgia I might as well be six again myself. I peek up to see June. "Anyone want to take a sail before breakfast?"

Three little girls say "Me, me, me!" and scurry out of my bunk.

"Don't say I never did anything for you," June says, winking.

I lie back in my bunk, the mattress creaking. I could never say that. Six months a year, Aunt June is a staple in our lives. She takes care of George in the afternoons after preschool and helps Huff and me navigate the world of pickup and drop-off, ballet lessons, baseball practice, tennis clinic, and piano for Henry and Melly. We couldn't make it without her. And I would be a lot more panicked about this fourth baby if I didn't have her there to help.

"I don't want to leave," Mary Stuart whines, jumping down from the top bunk as spryly as if she is still six.

"It isn't fair that the kids get two weeks of camp and we only get two days," Lanier whines with her, covering her face with her sleeping bag.

I don't know if it's the pregnancy hormones or the fact that I'm leaving my little girl for two whole weeks, but I am overcome with emotion. "We did it," I say. "We saved it for them." It has been years, but I feel like this is the first time I've really stopped to consider the enormity of what we pulled off, the legacy we helped maintain.

"Hard things," Mary Stuart says, pulling on a pair of shorts and smiling at me.

"Speaking of," Lanier says sleepily, "I have a doozy of a list for y'all this week."

"You would give a big list to a pregnant lady?" I ask in faux shock.

"Didn't faze you when I was pregnant," Lanier says.

Truth. When Lanier was pregnant with Johnny, and Huff and I added on to our old house—which we'd been rapidly outgrowing—poor Lanier, with her much more flexible schedule, had done quite a bit of meeting with plumbers and painters, electricians and roofers.

But that chaos was nothing compared to this. Because three hours later, the camp is that same soda bottle it has always been. Little girls are running wild with excitement and parents are various degrees of thrilled and devastated. I am somewhere in the middle. Thrilled that Melly has this opportunity. Sad to be apart from her. But we will drop Henry off for a month at Camp Rock Springs right after this, and there will be something special about having two weeks with just George. He's never experienced only childhood, and, once this new baby comes, he likely never will again.

Huff, Steven, Henry, and George have arrived to tell Melly goodbye and pick me up for Rock Springs. "Melly, I'm not going to be here to watch out for you," Henry is saying. "You have to wear your life jacket. You have to be careful."

His hair is straight now; it's lost that baby curl it had when he was George's age. He is so grown up it takes my breath away. I reminded him recently that Huff and I were the ones who had to be in charge of Melly and George, not him. I never want him to feel burdened. He looked at me with shock. "Mom," he'd said, "I'm the big brother. It's my job to take care of them." How could I argue with that?

"I'll come see you on Saturday, okay?" he says.

Siblings can visit each other on the weekends, something I never got to experience, something I am so happy my children will get to. Melly's chin quivers, and it hits me that she is sadder to be away from Henry than me. It's too adorable.

George flings himself at Melly. "Bye, Melly Moo."

"Bye, Georgie. I'll miss you." The day before we left for camp, they spent the better part of the afternoon pinching each other, crying, and then telling on each other, so this is a nice moment.

"I'm going to go on ahead and meet you at Rock Springs, okay?" Steven says. "I'll get Henry's bunk made up."

I smile and nod at him as Huff picks his little girl up, kisses her, and then hands her to me so I can do the same. I want to tell her to be safe, to be careful, to watch out for ticks, and wear her bug spray and sunscreen. But she has counselors for that. So, instead, I look into her blue eyes and, as I put her down, say, "Have the time of your life, baby girl."

She grins and then, as a gaggle of girls runs by, she is off.

She stops for a moment and turns around. "Fair winds and following seas!" she calls.

All the little girls reply. "Fair winds and following seas!"

I tear up just hearing those beloved words from those sweet, sweet voices. At the beginning of each summer, at the end of each camp session, and when I kissed my mother's serene face for the very last time on this earth, that phrase didn't mean goodbye. It meant the hope of moving forward, the promise of good to come. Huff reaches over and squeezes my hand, and I smile at him as we make our way to the car. I climb in the front seat. "Rock Springs here we come!" Henry cheers.

George kicks the back of my seat. "Mommy! I need a snaaacckkkk."

George literally always needs a snack. Twenty-four hours a day that child needs a snack.

I hand George a granola bar and look down at my stomach as Huff puts the car in drive. I whisper, "What have we done?"

He laughs. "We have done what I, for one, always dreamed we would do. As long as it's me and you, Daph, I'm all good." He kisses my hand.

I love him, just like I love the little voices arguing in the back seat. Against all odds, I love this life that I never, ever dared dream I would have. For thirty years, I thought it was a myth, a fantasy. But I have never felt so happy.

And this week I begin something new. My darling Finn was so good at his job that he decided to go back to law school. He is now in his second year of practice with me and, with the new baby coming, I decided I'm only going to work three days a week. One of those days, I'll spend with my children. The other I will spend with other people's children, devoting my time to pro bono custody cases so that kids like me will have someone to be their voice. My first client comes tomorrow, and I am filled with something I can only describe as joy.

As the car winds through the dirt path, past the cabins, past the stables, we reach the Holly Springs softball field that has played such an important role in the story of us, this growing family. Huff puts the car in park and says, "Everyone stay in your car seats and seat belts." He jogs around to my side and opens the door for me.

Henry protests. "Huff, we're going to be late!"

But Huff ignores him and helps me out of the car, and we make our way through the gate to the softball field where we had our first kiss, where we got engaged, where this summer our first baby together will play my husband's favorite sport. I take a deep breath, and I hear Huff do the same. "Do you hear that?" he whispers.

I shake my head. "No. What?"

"That's the sound of silence." He puts his hand on my stomach. "And in seven more years, when the four of them are all at camp, we'll experience this sound again."

We both laugh. Huff kisses me. Not a quick husband-and-wife hello kiss, but a long and lingering, I-still-choose-you kiss. And I spot the sign that inspired me all those years ago: NEVER LET THE FEAR OF STRIKING OUT KEEP YOU FROM PLAYING THE GAME. I haven't, I didn't. And that makes me proud. We walk out and close the gate behind us. Huff squeezes my shoulder and walks back to the car.

I turn toward the river, feeling the breeze on my face, hearing the wind rustle through the trees. I smile, feeling grateful for the years of joy Camp Holly Springs has brought me, has brought generations of women in my family and so many more like us.

Then I see them. Three little girls, tiny versions of my best friends and me. They are holding hands, running toward the stables, a sliver of light peeking through the trees, bathing them in a sepia tone that makes them feel timeless. This new generation is here to live something that my mother and my grandmother and I did. That my best friends did. We have all been bathed in this light, washed in this river, changed by weeks of fresh air and sunshine.

In the blink of an eye, the three little girls Mary Stuart, Lanier, and I had once been grew up and became mothers, passing down the best parts of ourselves to a new generation experiencing that ecstatic first taste of freedom. I know already that these next two weeks will change them in ways they won't understand until they are much, much older, that they will find things inside themselves they didn't know were there. It is a gift, a miracle, really, how time marches on, how things change, but also stay so very much the same. How the river ebbs and flows. How this camp, our camp—my home—lives on.

Melly stops at a huge oak tree growing wild and strong toward the light. I smile as Nina and Smith help her up to the lowest branch. As I watch them, I whisper an oath, a promise, into the breeze: *Fair winds and following seas.*

And just like that, a new summer of songbirds has begun.

ACKNOWLEDGMENTS

SUMMER OF 2020 WOULD HAVE BEEN MY SON'S SECOND SUMMER AT Camp Seagull, a rustically charming sailing camp in North Carolina that has garnered acclaim and gathered campers from all over the world. For obvious reasons, the camp couldn't open for campers but, instead, was able to figure out how to have a safe and fun family camp at its sister camp, Camp Seafarer. My friend Millie Warren, who was a lifelong Seafarer camper, suggested that we all go. I savored my summers at Camp Hollymont in the beautiful North Carolina mountains and was thrilled by the prospect of going back to camp. I think we were all anxious to do something—anything—where we could cut loose and let down our hair after the previous few months of being cooped up. Plus, how often in your adult life do you get to do the zipline with your kid?!

While at Seafarer, I remember texting my Friends & Fiction group—Mary Kay Andrews, Kristin Harmel, Patti Callahan Henry, and Meg Walker—and saying, "If these walls could talk, the stories they could tell . . ." I had already been toying with the idea of writing a book about three best friends from summer camp who reconvene to save the place they once loved, and this trip became almost a fact-finding mission. (Ladies, consider this my big, huge thank-you to all of you for all you do all the time. You are my dear friends, my treasured family, and I am so grateful for you every day!)

But the story really came alive for me when Millie (one of the camp's star sailors!) and our friend Garland Graham and I set out in a sailboat together with no radio and no cell phones, much like our ladies in the book, and, with no warning at all, the wind died. We were stuck. Very stuck. We weren't panicked because we knew that at least our children would eventually realize we were missing! To pass the time, we told camp stories, reminisced about dances and favorite activities, afternoons at the canteen and infirmary stays, talent show mishaps, and, of course, camp crushes.

Some of my readers might know that I seldom write my books chronologically. So when I got home, the first chapter I wrote of this book was the one where Lanier, Mary Stuart, and Daphne are stuck in the sailboat. "Is this the sign of which you speak?" was my first favorite line in this novel. (Although now I have many!) And it set the stage for this entire book, which, to me, is a testament to female friendship, especially the lifelong kind that loves unconditionally, that fights and forgives and knows the nitty-gritty, real, dirty truth about the people we are and chooses to show up alongside us anyway. It is also, as the back of the book says, a love letter to the places who make us who we are, the ones that burrow down deep in our hearts and souls and show us what we're made of. Camp did that for me. And, even if you didn't have a camp in your life, I know you know what I'm talking about. I know some place—whether it was your grandparents' house or your favorite park, that waterfall you visited once or the spot where you first saw the ocean—must have shaped your life, too, and I hope that, when you think of Camp Holly Springs, you think of that place that made you feel happy and loved.

Speaking of places I feel happy and loved, I have had the best publishing experience at Gallery Books and can't sing the praises of my team loudly enough! Thanks to Molly Gregory for being by my side every step of the way to make this the very best book it could be and for all your support and encouragement, always. Lauren Carr and Bianca Salvant, you are the PR and marketing dream team! I always love working with the two of you and can't thank you enough. Jennifer Bergstrom, Aimee Bell, Jennifer Long, Sally Marvin, and Eliza Hanson, endless gratitude to each of you for your tireless efforts in bringing my books into the world. Gabrielle Audet and Sarah Lieberman from Simon & Schuster audio: I am always in awe of the magic you create!

Ron Block is another magic creator in my life who is a dear friend and brilliant Friends & Fiction Writer's Block podcast host. Lisa Harrison, Brenda Gardner, Annissa Armstrong, and Shaun Hettinger, thank you for all the love and light you bring to this world—more than 100,000 members strong!—we've all created together. To our newly minted Friends & Fiction Ambassadors, where would we be without you? Amber Prater, Anne Floccari, Barbara Wojcik, Bubba Wilson, Clare Plaxton, Dallas Strawn, Dawne McCurry, Debby Stone, Francene Katzen, Irene Wenner, Jill Mallia, Jodena Pysher, Kathy Saccamano, Laurie Brown, Lesley Bodemann, Linda Burrell, Maria Lew, Marilyn Rumph, Marlene Waters, Mary Vasquez, Meredith D'Agostino, Michelle Marcus, Mindy Ehrlich, Molly Neville, Nicole Fincher, Rhonda Perrett, Robin Klein, Sharon Person, Susan Seligman, Susie Baldwin, and Taylor Lintz, thank you so much! Many of you have been friends and supporters long before now, and I couldn't do this without you!

Elisabeth Weed, I have to thank you for so many things I can't even think of them all! I don't know what in the world made you drag yourself to the Hotel Elysee all those years ago to meet me for breakfast on a Sunday, but I sure am grateful you did! Kathie and Roy Bennett, Susan Zurenda, and the Magic Time team, thank you for all you have done for me over the past years. Nine books together and you still outdo yourself every time!

Ashley Edmondson, you hold the entire world together, and I have no idea what we would do without you! Tamara Welch, I am inordinately thankful for our years together and your friendship. Ashley Hayes, what a joy it has been to work with you this year—and with you and Meagan Briggs with Uplit Reads for the past four books.

I would not be here after nine novels were it not for the selfless support of the Bookstagram and blogging communities. To all of you who share my work: Thank you. Thank you. Thank you. There's no way I could name all of you in this limited space, so I'll be giving you lots more love online! But Kristy Barrett, Stephanie Gray, Andrea Katz, Cristina Frost, Susan Roberts, Susan Peterson, Ashley Bellman, Susan McBeth, Zibby Owens, Judy Collins, Courtney Marzilli, Jennifer Clayton, Chase Waskey, Kristin Thorvaldsen, Randi Burton, Melissa Steele-Matovu, and Jess Williams, big hugs for always being there and going above and beyond for me!

Authors have long been my rockstars and, ten books in, asking for endorsements still gives me nervous butterflies. I don't even have the right words to thank Susan Wiggs, Susan Mallery, Sonali Dev, and Nancy Thayer for their gorgeous blurbs. To have authors I admire so much lend their kindness is something I will never get over! Thank you so much for your time and support. It means more than you know.

Independent bookstores and libraries everywhere have long been my heroes, so a huge thank-you to all of you. But a special thanks to those who made this launch so very special! *The* Elin Hilderbrand and Tim Ehrenberg, I can't think of anything more exciting than launching this summer novel in Nantucket with Nantucket Books and both of you. The Ocean House, especially Deborah Royce, and RJ Julia, Thunder Road, South Main Book Co, Litchfield Books, Cherokee County Library, Hub City Bookshop, M. Judson, Henderson County Public Library, Pelican Bookstore, and Oxford Exchange, thank you so much for hosting me! (There are so many others, but the tour wasn't confirmed when this book went to print, so please know how grateful I am to each of you!) And Booktowne, thank you for organizing our Friends & Fiction First Editions Subscription this year. What a task!

I often thank my family and friends last when they should be first because no one does more than they do. Thank you to my husband and son, both Will, since, evidently, I was out of names, for being with me through every step of this journey, every time. I love you both so much! And thanks to my parents, Beth and Paul Woodson, who are so involved, helpful, and supportive in my career and my life and who raised me to believe that I could do anything I set my mind to. I foolishly believed them and here we are! Book ten!

Thank you to you, my reader, for choosing this book out of all the others, for turning the pages and going on this journey back to camp with me. Sometimes, when I'm finished writing a book (and especially as I write these acknowledgments in the depths of winter) I can feel a little bit homesick for the world I'm leaving. But it helps me to remember, as I say goodbye to Camp Holly Springs, that it's always summer somewhere. Even if it's just in the pages of a favorite book.

The Summer of Songbirds

KRISTY WOODSON HARVEY

This reading group guide for The Summer of Songbirds *includes an introduction, discussion questions, and ideas for enhancing your book club. The suggested questions are intended to help your reading group find new and interesting angles and topics for your discussion. We hope that these ideas will enrich your conversation and increase your enjoyment of the book.*

INTRODUCTION

Nearly thirty years ago, in the wake of a personal tragedy, June Moore bought Camp Holly Springs and turned it into a thriving summer haven for girls. But now, June is in danger of losing the place she has sacrificed everything for and begins to realize how much she has used the camp to avoid facing difficulties in her life.

June's niece, Daphne, met her two best friends, Lanier and Mary Stuart, during a fateful summer at camp. They've all helped each other through hard things, from heartbreak and loss to substance abuse and unplanned pregnancy, and the three are inseparable even in their thirties. But when attorney Daphne is confronted with a relationship from her past—and a confidential issue at work becomes personal—she is faced with an impossible choice.

Lanier, meanwhile, is struggling with tough decisions of her own. After a run-in with an old flame, she is torn between the commitment she made to her fiancé and the one she made to her first love. And when a big secret comes to light, she finds herself at odds with her best friend . . . and risks losing the person she loves most.

But in spite of their personal problems, nothing is more important to these songbirds than Camp Holly Springs. When the women learn their childhood oasis is in danger of closing, they band together to save it, sending them on a journey that promises to open the next chapters in their lives.

TOPICS & QUESTIONS FOR DISCUSSION

1. What can we learn about Daphne, Lanier, and Mary Stuart through the "hard things" they ask of each other?
2. The novel is told from three points of view: Daphne, June, and Lanier. Why do you think the author chose these three characters? How would the story have changed if different characters' perspectives were included?
3. Discuss June's choice not to seek custody of Daphne when Daphne was younger. Do you agree with this choice? Why, or why not?
4. Daphne goes back and forth in her opinion on whether people can change. On page 242 she says, "I haven't changed. Maybe I can't. Maybe no one can." Do you think people can change? Do you agree with Daphne that she doesn't change throughout the novel?
5. If you were in Daphne's situation, would you have shown up to Lanier's wedding invitation sendoff after what happened at family camp? Do you think Daphne's decision to tell Lanier about Bryce was the right one?
6. On page 250, Lanier tells Huff that she lied and facilitated his breakup with Daphne seven years ago because she was trying to protect him. What do you think of this decision: was it justified, or was Lanier out of line? Take a few minutes to discuss both sides of the argument.
7. The power of friendship is an important theme throughout the novel. What can we learn from the songbirds' friendships and how loyal they are to each other through every stage of their lives?

8. Daphne is open about how her mother's addiction and her father's aloof behavior have informed her personality and how she approaches relationships. What examples of these effects can we see throughout the novel? In what ways can we see Daphne's growth by the end?

9. Many of the characters keep secrets from each other. Paula and John kept Melanie's relapse a secret, Lanier kept secrets from both Huff and Daphne about why their relationship ended the first time, Daphne and Lanier share a secret about the accident at Daphne's father's house, and more. How do these secrets inform the characters' relationships and how they handle the events of the novel?

10. On page 263, June says to Daphne, "I don't trust myself enough to take risks, so I stay at camp all year instead of interacting with friends in town." Why do you think June is afraid of taking risks? What risks does she end up taking in the novel?

11. On page 184, Daphne says to Huff, "There's something about the river that washes everything away. All the bad stuff. All the pain. All the fear." Later, on page 335, she walks onto Huff's porch and says that she believes the river "carries our secrets, our scars, our greatest joys, and our biggest hopes." Discuss the significance of the river at Camp Holly Springs and throughout the novel. What does it mean to each character?

12. Lanier struggles to reconcile Daphne and Huff's adult relationship with Daphne's history of substance abuse. When is it important to keep a friend's past in mind, and in what situations should you put it behind you?

13. Discuss the idea that summer is a time of renewal, a time when "anything could happen" (page 342). Why do the songbirds feel this way? Do you agree?

ENHANCE YOUR BOOK CLUB

1. In the acknowledgments on page 356, author Kristy Woodson Harvey shares that the inspiration for Camp Holly Springs came from the time she spent at Camp Seafarer's family camp in North Carolina; she reminisces about how special a place like sleepaway camp can be for the many generations of people that pass through it. Does anyone in your book club have a place that feels as significant to them as Camp Holly Springs is to the songbirds? Try to host your book club meeting there! Go around and share what makes these places special to each of you.

2. The songbirds and June each go out of their comfort zones at some point while working to save camp. What is one way that you can step out of your comfort zone? Discuss with the group and strategize the next steps for making it happen.

3. Daphne, Lanier, and Mary Stuart look forward to sending their daughters to Camp Holly Springs. Daphne's mother (and aunt, of course) went before her as well. What are some of your traditions that have passed through generations of your family, and how do they strengthen the relationships of the people that share them?

4. Take your group to do a camp-inspired activity: sailing, swimming, archery, land sports, camping, or anything else reminiscent of summer and camp!

Don't miss the next novel from

New York Times bestselling author

Kristy Woodson Harvey

A Happier Life

Coming soon from Gallery Books!

Keep reading for a sneak peek . . .

Keaton

All (Are Not) Welcome

"I will get this promotion *or something better*," I whisper as I walk down the gleaming, glass-walled hall of All Welcome, the lifestyle brand I have been working for since I was a college intern twelve years ago. Allison, our CEO—and, well, my hero—is big on the phrase. She claims she has used it to manifest her massive success over the last thirteen years, when she started this brand as a recent college grad. Who am I to doubt her? If I'm going to manifest something, now seems like a good time to start.

Casey, one of our interns, winks at me as she passes me in the hallway and crosses her fingers. Her encouragement boosts me as my stomach rolls with the reminder that Jonathan, the head of HR and my ex, is going to be in this meeting about my "future with All Welcome" too. We broke up about a month ago, after eighteen months of dating, but I still haven't told my family. I can almost hear my mother's voice in my head: *I don't like to interfere, but, darling, the man still works for his ex-wife's company. And you work for him. It is unsavory at best, a recipe for disaster at worst.*

Despite my mother's concerns, I had always felt proud that Jonathan—who was *not* my superior when we started dating, I might add—Allison, and I have always been able to work together so seamlessly. Allison and Jonathan used to say it was because their relationship was ancient history. And now, so was ours. Because after we moved in together six months ago, Jonathan and I realized that the single thing we had in common was work. Now the three of us are back to being just coworkers. Coworkers with weird personal histories, to be sure, but just coworkers all the same.

I walk to the end of the hall to the smallest conference room. It is the only one that has solid, soundproof walls instead of glass, so it's the most private. And it's where most promotion meetings take place.

Allison is already there, as I assumed she would be. Punctuality is one of her core values. The others, as I well know, are transparency, honesty, innovation, and excellence. She is a motivational speaker who gets paid in the high five digits each time she flies off to inspire companies and their employees to reach their full potential. She has a huge conference—All-Fest—each year that literally fills an arena, a line of journals and goal-setting notebooks, and has penned four *New York Times* bestsellers. We even decided to publish her last book in-house. We were nervous, but it went so well that we're publishing a handful of other meaningful titles this year by other authors in the space.

It's very exciting. It is also very on-brand for Allison, someone who many, many women aspire to be like. As I open the door, I see that right now—aspirationally—she is walking on the quiet, non-motorized treadmill in the corner of the room. She has exercise equipment in every conference room and her office because she doesn't have time for regular workouts, but this ensures she can still honor her body and spirit each day—her words, not mine. She is *such* a badass. I feel the tiniest twinge of guilt that I can't remember the last time I actually exercised myself.

"Oh, hi!" I say as I spot Jonathan shifting a stack of papers at the head of the table. I thought the breakup would be harder, but since we have had to work together every day since, it already sort of feels like we're back to just coworkers. Even at thirty-seven, he still has ashy blond hair and big puppy-dog brown eyes. He's a good guy. Not *my* guy anymore. But a good guy all the same. He has been letting me stay in the town house we shared while I frantically look for another apartment. Something decent in my price range in New York City is, evidently, hard to come by. And our breakup made me realize I don't have so much as a friend's couch to crash on. My parents' place is a last resort that I hope I don't need.

A glass of water is in front of the seat next to him, so I figure it is mine. I take my seat and am shocked when Allison quits walking. She usually keeps working out, getting progressively more breathless as a meeting goes on. Usually, by the end of an hour, I'm translating because I'm the only one who can understand her. Curiously, though, the woman never sweats.

"Keaton, Keaton, Keaton," she says as she sits down. "Our girl wonder."

I sit on the edge of my seat, keeping my fingers crossed under the table.

"I brought you here today to tell you that I'm pregnant."

That's not what I'm expecting to hear, but, still, I gasp and clap my hands. I would know if she was seriously dating someone, so I wonder if she has done in vitro or, knowing Allison, has engineered some new pregnancy procedure that doesn't involve sperm at all. A woman-only pregnancy. She'd be really into that. It would also be great for our brand. I briefly wonder how on earth she's going to take care of a child when she works absolutely nonstop. All that aside, she's obviously telling me I'm promoted because she can't take on anything else in her state.

"That is great news, Allison," I chime in. "And I'd like you to know I'm here for anything you need."

She smiles with an ethereal glow and reaches across the table to take my hand. "I am so glad to hear you say that because there *is* something I need from you."

I feel a grin spread across my face, and I glance briefly at Jonathan. He looks kind of . . . constipated. Which I know he never is because we shared a bathroom in his two-bedroom town house. Maybe he's worried about what Allison's pregnancy is going to mean for his job, which I totally get. But now he'll have me—with my corner office and big, fat salary—to lighten his workload. I try to convey that with my glance, but he doesn't seem to notice.

Then Allison says, with a light squeeze of my palm, "I'm going to need you to move out of the town house."

I look at Jonathan again, not quite comprehending. "Well, I'm looking for a new place, but . . ." I trail off. Some fuzzy atoms are connecting in my brain.

I remove my clammy hand and take a sip of water just as Allison lets out a breathy little laugh. "Oh my gosh. Pregnancy brain. The baby is Jonathan's, and I am going to move back into the house y'all have been living in. My apartment is too small."

I honestly don't mean to, but I choke and spit the water out, spraying it all over Jonathan. He barely moves to wipe himself off—he only looks really apologetic. And kind of sick.

"*My* Jonathan?" I squeak.

Allison smiles in a way that feels very condescending. "Well, mine," she says as she rubs her impossibly flat stomach.

Jonathan barely pipes up. "Well, actually, Allison, I'm not sure I would say I *belong* to you."

She smiles at him in a way that conveys, *Oh, but don't you?*

"I. What? No. You can't. It doesn't . . ." I'm obviously having some trouble with my words.

"Don't worry," Allison says. "We'll have someone pack up all your things and get them moved wherever you go next."

"That is literally the last thing I am worried about." I turn to Jonathan, doing the math in my head. We've only been broken up for four weeks. "How long has this been going on?"

"Well, I'm twelve weeks along," Allison says, batting her eyes at Jonathan.

"What?" I practically scream, realizing *this* is why I'm in the soundproof conference room. I turn to Jonathan. "Are you insane? We only moved in together like six months ago! You're the one who talked me into getting rid of my apartment!"

"I'm really sorry," Jonathan says. "It was so obvious things weren't going to work out with us that I just . . . moved on before it was official. It didn't mean anything at first."

"But then we realized we were still in love," Allison says. "That we wanted to start a family. I truly hope this doesn't hurt you, Keaton, but Jonathan and I think consciously recoupling is the right thing for us."

Consciously recoupling. This can't be real. Anger, which I am usually good at controlling, rises in me. The hypocrisy is too much for me to take. "Do you believe your own psychobabble bullshit?" I ask her, my face turning red. "I mean, do you hear yourself? Oh, *honesty and transparency are my core values*," I say in a singsong voice.

"I'm sorry you feel that way," she says, "because we were here to offer you a promotion to director of marketing. But if you aren't committed to the brand then—"

"You were going to offer me a promotion?" I practically spit. "A *promotion*? So we can work more closely while you and your ex remarry and start a family?"

"Oh, we won't remarry," Allison says. "Marriage feels so archaic and confining now. But we assumed if the two of us could work so well together after a divorce that surely you could manage . . ."

That's when I know I'm going to cry, and that's the last thing in the world I want to do. I *want* to be archaic and confined. I want to be *married.* I don't want to be married to Jonathan. But the fact that he cheated on me really stings. And, well, explains why he's been so nice about letting me stay in the town house. Guilt is powerful.

"Jonathan, how could you do this to me? All that time we were planning our future together, and you were screwing your ex-wife?" *And I had no idea?*

"I'm sorry, Keaton. I really am."

"You should never be sorry about living your authentic path, Jonathan," Allison interjects.

I take a long look at Allison, and I can't believe that I was so enamored with her for so long. Yes, she's beautiful in this bird-boned, hippie-at-Woodstock kind of way. And she has this soft voice that you have to lean forward to hear, that makes you want to listen. But she's also selfish. It's always about her. I know this, and yet I've always forgiven her for it because I believed she was a good person deep down.

When I got my internship the summer after my junior year at our shared alma mater, UNC–Chapel Hill, I felt like I had won the lottery. Allison and I together felt like kismet. It was clear I would come work for her after graduation. I knew she was going to change the world. And, well, she has. And so that's why it's so hard for me to say, "Why did I buy into this for so long? I did your program to the letter for years, and it's just now occurring to me that I'm not any better, any more enlightened, than I was when I started."

"What do you mean *did*?" Allison asks.

I squint at her. "*Did*. Now, a lot of mornings, I don't even make my bed." *I don't have time since I'm basically running your company*, I add, only in my head.

Allison gasps. "Making your bed is a Vision One, Track One foundation habit. Are you even drinking your eight glasses of water? Moving your thirty minutes?"

"Nope!" I say, crossing my arms, feeling childish. I know she is going to be offended by this admission.

"The foundation habits aren't really that difficult if you're committed," she says. "Keaton, maybe you and I should dive into why you're letting yourself stay stuck."

"Because your entire company is crap, Allison, based on making women feel like they aren't good enough if they aren't as perfect and motivated and successful as you." I know I've gone too far. All Welcome's whole premise is that everyone can find their happiness if they make the time to do what inspires them. And Allison has helped people do that. Even still, I can't help but hit her where it hurts most.

She smiles sadly at me, and I'm torn between regret and hatred. "Keaton, I'm sorry to say, but I think your journey here at All Welcome is coming to an end. I can overlook a spiritually unenlightened reaction in a moment of turmoil, but I can't have people who don't believe in the process be a part of this company."

Jonathan finally speaks up. "Well, maybe it isn't fair to fire her . . ."

I know he's thinking it isn't fair to fire me because in what world am I *not* going to sue the hell out of this company for wrongful termination? "Nope!" I say. "I'm fired."

"Maybe we can discuss a severance package that feels right?" Jonathan says, hesitantly, still trying to smooth over something that has already gotten out of hand.

"Well," Allison says, still with that slick calm voice of hers, "I feel that giving Keaton severance is offensive; it's like saying we don't believe in her or her ability to begin anew. And that simply isn't true. I do believe in Keaton and the power and beauty of her dreams."

I am too nauseated to respond.

"Okay," Jonathan says, standing up. "Allison, we might be making some hasty decisions here."

No severance, bigger lawsuit. For all her preaching, Allison isn't a very good businesswoman. Which is why she needed me. Well, that, and the fact that my role as marketing coordinator had morphed really far from my job description. In addition to handling marketing strategies—like advertising, paid editorial placement, and merchandise—I also oversaw all of All Welcome's social media (which is technically a different department), scheduled all of Allison's podcast guests, the launches for the four books a year (and growing!) the company is now publishing through its publishing arm, sat in on practically every meeting, and on and on and on.

Allison and I worked together nonstop. We laughed together. We dreamed together. I couldn't imagine that it could come to this. And I had no idea what she would do without me. It looks like she's about to find out.

I stand up. "You heard her. I'm fired. No severance. I want all my stuff returned to my parents' place right away. And you damn well better bring my dog."

I'm not moving there, I tell myself. Just staying until I find a new apartment. I have some money saved, and besides, I can always go live with my brother for a while instead.

Only, as I storm out of the building and call said brother to tell him what happened and ask him if I can stay, he flat-out says, "No, Keaton. You cannot come live with me."

I am aghast. "Harris! Are you kidding me? Why can't I live with you for just a little bit? I'm looking really hard for an apartment." I pause, putting the pieces together. My brother is my best friend. There is only one reason he wouldn't want me to live with him. "You have some rando woman living with you, don't you? And you haven't even told Mom and Dad. Or me. What is wrong with you?"

"Well, you won't approve," he says.

"She's like twenty-three, isn't she?"

"Thereabouts."

"Harris! Get your shit together. Break up with her and choose your sister for once in your freaking life."

"I'm not not choosing you, Keat. I love you. But just think about it. How cool would it be to use your severance to get away for a while?"

"I didn't get severance," I say. "Allison feels that would send the message that she doesn't believe in my ability to begin anew."

"O-kay," Harris says. "Well, you still can't live here, but I am hiring you a lawyer."

I enter the code in the keypad to Mom and Dad's building, which is an easy couple blocks walk from my office—well, it *was* anyway—and swing open the door. "Mom told me not to move in with him," I say out loud as I step into the elevator, more to myself than to Harris. "If I had listened to her, maybe I wouldn't be in this mess."

"Oh, Keat. I'm sorry. But, look, I'll help you find a place to live. We'll figure it out."

"Okay," I whisper. "Can you help find me a job, too? *Oh my gosh I don't have a job!*" I am filled with dread. "I have to go." Tears puddle in my eyes, and I literally have to sit on the elevator floor since my legs won't hold me up any longer. I realize that I have given every single part of myself to this job that I just walked away from. I don't have hobbies. I don't volunteer. All my meals are either from a frozen meal delivery service or DoorDash because who has time to cook? I barely have friends because when would I see them? My social life consisted of Jonathan and Allison and my colleagues and now it's all just . . . gone.

The elevator opens, and a woman pushes her walker through. "Hi, Mrs. Ellis," I say with zero enthusiasm.

She starts. "Oh dear. What are you doing on the floor?"

"Bad day," I say.

"Well, a bad day is always a good time to visit one's parents."

I nod, but then another sick feeling washes over me: Worse than getting dumped, worse than getting fired, I'm going to have to tell my mother she was right.